Rufus's heart fluttered. It was like old times, good old times. Why did life have to be so damn complicated? He had spent the last six months trying to forget her. Twenty-four hours after she came back, all the wanting, the hunger, the love hit him in the face and down south, too. When they split this time, it'd be for good. He knew he'd miss her, not because she was a sensational lover or a talented bassist, but because he loved her. Her lusty spirit and sexy sizzle ignited his senses. When they were high, they made love like wild tigers. When they were mellow, they made love like purring kittens. They savored passion's sensuous delights. They tasted its succulent juices, smelled its intoxicating scents, and stroked those hidden pleasure points and secret hollows unique to them.

THE LAST TRAIN TO MEMPHIS

ELSA COOK

Genesis Press Inc.

Black Coral Fiction

An imprint of Genesis Press Inc.
Publishing Company

Genesis Press, Inc.
P.O. Box 101
Columbus, MS 39703

ISBN: 1-58571-146-2
Manufactured in the United States of America

First Edition

Visit us at www.genesis-press.com
or call at 1-888-Indigo-1

DEDICATION

To my staunch friend and fellow writer
Boni Heck

ACKNOWLEDGMENTS

Special thanks to my husband and computer guru, Frank, and my friend, Pat Selby, who loved the characters in *The Last Train to Memphis* as much as I did. Thanks, also, to the members of my critique group, Debra Burns, J. Steve Fulbright, and Karen Kalinevitch, and to my daughters, Patricia Grant and Barbara Larson, for recognizing the fact that I had to write.

Thanks to Niani Colom, Angelique Justin, Deatri King Bey, and Heather Smith, the dedicated editors at Genesis Press, Inc., whose initial vision, editorial talents, and enthusiasm for the book are greatly appreciated.

I want to acknowledge the encouragement and support given to me and many other writers and artists by the following artist colonies:

Mantalvo Center for the Arts, Saratoga, CA

Ragdale Foundation, Lake Forest, IL

Virginia Center for the Creative Arts, Amherst VA

Many, many thanks to the members of the Designers Writers' Club in Calumet City, IL. They are hard-working group of dedicated readers and writers who support and inspire published and unpublished writers. They also write and publish a monthly magazine, *Rendezvous*, in which they critique the latest fiction.

CHAPTER ONE

…'Round midnight on a cold, blustery Tuesday, a spotlight snared Rufus Johnson and stenciled his muscular frame on the dance floor at Ella's Lounge. Sweat glistening on his nut-brown skin, he tongued his tenor sax and growled out the melody of the ballad, "My Ideal."

Staying a fraction ahead of the beat, he unleashed his own version of the song by shifting from a low growling tone to a flurry of metallic notes. When he finished, he flicked a smile and waited until the last sounds drifted away on a waft of smoke-filled air before he bowed to a room filled with empty tables.

A hand nudged his arm. He looked up. Ella, the boss, the sophisticated lady with the bullhorn voice, stood nose-to-nose in front of him, her jowls wiggling like jellied pigs-feet, her eyelashes fluttering like black spider legs.

"If I think you got the sense of a Missouri mule, I'd kick your ass from here to hell's door, but I ain't gonna waste my juices on a simple fool. You got five minutes to heave that white ho outta here, or I do it myself." She placed her hands on the sequined belt that girdled her huge waist and closed the small gap separating her from Rufus.

"What's the matter with you, woman? You been sipping Bojay's rat poison? A white chick would be crazy to come in here at this hour." He pointed to two mahogany chicks and three slick-haired dudes sitting at the bar. "They're all that's left, and they've been here since we opened, sipping beers and sucking Camels."

"Set your eyeballs on table three over in the corner." Ella rolled her shoulders and let out an indignant snort. Her mammoth breasts rose from a sea of shimmering purple lame. "I damn near lost my license last time she come here. I ain't putting up with her shit no more."

"Don't sweat me with your problems. I'm a musician, not a bouncer." He was a breath away from telling her he was too tired to listen to a bad-tempered woman, but a unsettling image flashed in his mind. He licked the caustic rebuttal off his lips. He didn't have to see who was sitting at table three, he already knew. He pulled a handkerchief from his pocket and dabbed his forehead. Was it his imagination, or did his sweat smell like embalming fluid?

He set his sax on its stand and tugged the neck of his sweater. "Tell Bojay to bring a scotch on the rocks and a gin and tonic to the table." Brushing past Ella, he headed to the back of the room, his expression tight with strain. When he reached table three, he paused and stared at the woman looking up at him. His heart did a fast two-step. Claire Burton! Where did she come from? He bit his lip. In the months since she had been gone, he had almost forgotten how beautiful she was, how brown her eyes, how red her lips. Her long, brunet hair was short now, clipped like a puppy's. The two-step slowed to a dirge.

He sat down and drummed his fingers on the table, scatting notes on an imaginary scale.

"What are you doing here? he asked.

"It's been a long time." She smiled.

Bojay shuffled to the table, set down two glasses, nodded a greeting, then took off at a fast clip.

Claire eyed the gin and tonic with a critical squint. "I haven't had a drink in six months. Guess one won't hurt." She raised her glass in a toast. "You're looking fine, Rufus. I see you're still wearing your jazzy outfit." She shrugged. "Why not? That black tweed jacket and turtle neck sweater are so cool, so sexy. They're as much you as that dazzling white smile of yours. It drove the chicks crazy. Me too. What a feeling that was."

"How can you remember how you felt? You were so high you could barely walk most of the time." He downed half his drink in one swallow. "Ella wants you out of here. She doesn't want trouble."

"I'm not here to make trouble. I'm clean. I just got off the bus. I thought you'd like to know I'm out."

A loud clang from the bar reverberated around the room. Rufus spun around. Bojay waved. "Snow coming down real hard. Ella say we gotta close in fifteen minutes."

Rufus nodded and returned his gaze to the woman sitting across from him. It couldn't be Claire. She walked out on him six months ago. Maybe if he didn't say her name or show any emotions, he could convince himself she wasn't there and this wasn't happening. He finished his drink, stood up, and stuck his hands in his pockets.

"I got to pack up and get home 'fore the roads get too bad." He flashed a tight smile. "I'm glad you're out. You're looking great. Take care of yourself. Tell Bojay to call you a cab. We'll say our good-byes at the front door."

She grabbed his hand. "I don't have any money. Somebody

grabbed my wallet when I went to the restroom at a bus stop. Luckily, I had enough change in my pocket to get here."

A chain-mail shirt tightened around Rufus's chest, imprisoning him in a past he didn't want to resurrect.

"I'll loan you a ten-spot. You can pay me later. Your dad'll be good for it."

"I'm not going home." She sucked in her cheeks and assumed a defiant air. "My counselor told me to stay away from my parents until I was stronger. She said if I went back to the same old crap, I'd start again." Her bottom lip quivered and tears streamed down her cheeks, as if the dam she had built to harness her emotions had burst. "Let me spend the night at your place," she pleaded. "I swear, I won't be any trouble. I'll sleep on the floor. Whatever you say." Her hand was trembling as she tightened her grip on his hand. "Please."

The chain mail grew tighter. He took a deep breath and exhaled loudly.

"I'd prefer a quicker death," he said. "A knife in the back. A bullet in the head."

"Well, fine. If that's the way you feel, I sure as hell don't want to put you out."

"It's not a matter of putting me out, and you know it."

"Whatever." She flipped her hand in the air. "On your way home, I'd appreciate it if you'd drop me off at a shelter, if it isn't too much trouble."

"Don't be stupid. You know what those shelters'll be like on the coldest night of the year. Every druggy in the city'll be crawling in, looking for a warm hole," he said, then added in a husky whisper, "yours for starters."

4

Her eyes snapped open. "Not at the Christian Citadel. I'll be safe there."

Rufus shook his head, showing his amazement at her lack of street smarts. "The boozers and druggies'll be there, too. You want to sleep on a hard floor surrounded by smelly bodies? The staff'll try to keep 'em in line, but they can't watch everybody. You wouldn't last the night."

"A hard floor'd be better than a pile of snow."

Rufus let out a low growl. What choice did he have? She had him by his balls. He had to take her with him. Too bad he couldn't return the favor, assuming, of course, she had balls.

He rapped the rhythm to the "Chain Gang Blues" on the back of a chair. "You can stay the night, but you're out first thing in the morning. I'll hog tie you if I have to. It's time you grew up and faced the fact that life is hard and shitty, and running away doesn't make it any less so. But if you're going to run, don't count on me to help. I'm barely walking." He paused and took a deep breath. He wanted to yell at her, to shake some sense into her, but the exhaustion and fear he saw in her eyes made him realize he'd said enough.

"I'll get the car and meet you out front." He glanced around. "You got a suitcase? I'll take it to the front door."

"Just my bass." She leaned down and pulled her instrument case from under the table.

"They let you keep it the whole time you were in rehab?" He cocked a brow. "I'd 've thought they'd take it. Some folks, particularly rehabbers, think musicians and druggies are joined at the hip."

"They tried, but I told 'em they'd have to put me in a padded cell like they did Billie Holiday if I couldn't play my bass."

Rufus slammed his fist into the palm of his hand. He knew that expression. She was hurting and trying not to show it. When they were together, it had made his hands tremble and turned his mind into mush but not anymore. He was free of her. She could hurt. She could bleed. He didn't care.

"Where's your suitcase?"

"Outside. I figured Ella would throw a fit if she saw me carrying my bass and my suitcase." A glint of humor sparked in her eyes. "Tell you the truth, I was afraid she'd get a gun and shoot me dead. Ella doesn't hold a grudge, but when she gets mad, watch out." With a shrug, Claire stood up, thrust out her chin, and left the lounge, holding her bass in one hand and her parka in the other.

Rufus watched her go, her head erect, her eyes focused straight ahead like an eagle, proud and free. He rolled his eyes. He knew she could be a real pain, but all the same, he was thankful her caretakers hadn't lobotomized her spirit. Months of eating institutional food hadn't fattened her up either. Her butt was still high and taut, her waist pinched. He hadn't noticed her breasts, but they had never been overly large. That had suited him. He preferred grapefruits to watermelons, just enough for a mouthful.

He returned to the bandstand, opened a leather case, and placed his sax on its velvet bed. He closed the lid and ran his hand over the smooth, brown leather. Mesmerized by its luster, he rubbed harder. The friction generated a honey-brown mist that swirled around him. His eyes widened, and his heart jumped to his throat as the image of a stunningly beautiful African-American woman appeared. She drifted toward him, her smile broad, her expression leery.

"Salinas," he whispered.

Tears streaked her face.

"Don't cry," he said. "I won't let you down. I swear I'll be on that train to Memphis next Wednesday. Meet me at the station. Bring our little man with you." He reached out to touch her, but she disappeared in a puff of smoke.

He pulled on his overcoat, grabbed his sax, and headed out the rear door. After several attempts to start the engine on his temperamental bucket, he eased out of the parking lot and drove down an alley ankle-deep with wet snow. He gripped the wheel to keep from fishtailing into a row of trash cans lining a weathered wooden fence. When he reached the front door, he gunned the engine and waited while Claire tossed her bass and suitcase in the back. Once she was seated, he eased his foot on the accelerator and took off down the icy street.

"I'm cold," she said. "Mind if I turn on the heater?"

He nodded.

"Thanks." She flipped the switch on high and held her hands in front of the vents.

It was several seconds before Rufus caught the heady scent of gardenias perfuming the warm air. He groaned. It would be a long, sleepless night.

CHAPTER TWO

Claire followed Rufus into the foyer of his apartment building and glanced around. She had been gone for six months, yet nothing had changed. The terra-cotta reliefs on the ceiling were still crumbling, and the carvings on the walnut staircase were barely visible, but the structure of what had once been an elegant home in the heart of the city was still in tact. She tightened her hold on her bass and headed up the stairs, worn smooth by a century of footsteps.

Rufus pushed ahead when they reached the second floor. She trailed behind him down the rank-smelling hallway, waited while he unlocked his door, and stepped inside.

He flipped on the overhead light. "You know the layout. Make yourself at home. I'll put your suitcase in the bedroom."

She nodded, then took a frank and admiring look at him as he walked away. She was tantalized by the broad sweep of his shoulders and the slight sway of his tight buns. Her breath caught in her throat. He hadn't changed either. Rufus Johnson was still the most gorgeous, the most sexy hunk of manhood she had ever seen. She couldn't believe they were finally together again. She had imagined a warmer homecoming, but she was content to know he was still here and their nightmarish separation was over.

During her long months at the rehab center, isolated, frightened, and alone, only her memories of Rufus, her bass, and her fantasies had kept her going. When she couldn't sleep, which was most of the time, she lay in bed and conjured up fairy tales filled with heroes and villains, lovers and lechers. In one of her fantasies, she created an idyllic scene of her and Rufus meeting on the banks of the Mississippi. They were alone. With no one to bother them, they played music by day and made love by night. She thought their paradise would last forever, but soon, other people arrived, black and brown, red and white. All of them strangers, they resented, perhaps envied, their Edenic life. In their anger, they dragged Claire and Rufus before a magistrate who accused them of sloth and promiscuity, of contaminating the races, and breaking society's rules.

The magistrate imprisoned them. Their jailers brainwashed them. Happiness was forbidden, they said. All love was banned. She and Rufus laughed at them, told them they were crazy. No one can live without love. They managed to escape, but their fears remained. They knew they'd be caught again, and they were afraid of what their jailers would do to break them. After all, they were only human. They could withstand only so much.

Claire shook her head, dislodging the beautiful, tragic dream from her mind. With a weary sigh, she sat on the arm of the sofa, unzipped her parka, and took another look around the room. Although his threadbare furnishings were a far cry from the gold and ivory, mahogany and zebrawood palaces of Rufus's ancestors, his aspirations and passions were the same.

She threw her arm across the imitation leopard pelt draped on the back of the sofa and stifled a sob. The anguish and ecstasy of their year-long love affair still permeated the air. Or was it her imagination? Did she dare hope they could start over, or was the magic gone, buried under a mountain of white dust?

THE LAST TRAIN TO MEMPHIS

A dark shadow eclipsed the rosy glow of memories. The lime-green Formica table where they had weighed their dream powder now held a catsup bottle and a loaf of white bread. The two-burner hot plate where they had cooked their heroin was now cold and guiltless. The chipped refrigerator, stained sink, and uneven wall tiles no longer held the mystical aura created by their freebased euphoria. The records, tapes, and CDs had doubled in number since the days they had lain on the floor, their bodies joined, male-female, and listened to the great Lester Prez Young reinvent tone and tempo for the tenor sax.

When she and Rufus weren't making love or getting high on booze and drugs, music was their passion, their release from the emptiness of nothingness. Desperately, she wanted to emulate Charles Mingus, her master, her teacher, on bass. She listened to his album, "Reincarnation of a Lovebird," a hundred times. She studied his technique, but her attempt to copy the bassist's style doomed her to failure. She didn't hear what he heard in his music: the cries of sorrow and defiance, the field holler, the blues shout. She had little satisfaction knowing the raging genius could constrain his bass but could never conquer it.

The heavy yoke of memories pressed down on her. She and Rufus could never go back to a life filled with erotic love games and drug-induced ecstasy. It had been a hell, not a heaven. The past was dead, the future dark and ominous. Only her love for Rufus kept her from running out the door and submerging herself in a line of snow. He was her strength.

A toilet flushed, and a moment later, Rufus shouldered his way through the beaded curtain hanging in the doorway. He had changed his clothes. Neither the faded black sweat pants nor the loose-fitting sweat shirt could hide his virility. She smiled. Depending upon his mood, his ebony eyes could flash in outrage or passion, his lips could pucker in annoyance or desire, his middle finger could stroke her arm or flick her clitoris. He was a magician, a chameleon, an obsidian gem: dark, glittering, unfathomable.

"I put your suitcase on the bed, but don't bother unpacking. You're leaving in the morning." His smile bridging the gap between malice and forbearance, he squatted in front of the refrigerator tucked under the sink. "You hungry? I got cheese and crackers. I can open a can of soup."

"You have any gin?"

"You sure you want another one? You're just out of rehab."

"You bought me one at Ella's. Why are you so worried about it now?"

"I didn't think." He shrugged, then stood up and slipped a pint of Harbor Lights gin hiding behind a row of canned goods stacked on a wobbly shelf.

"That's my bottle," she said in surprise. "You kept it all this time?"

"I don't drink gin."

"I know." She brushed past him, her leg hitting his thigh. She slipped a cup off a wall hook and poured herself a drink. She took one sip and tears sprang to her eyes.

"Wow! I better slow down. That sip hit my stomach, did an about-turn, and gave my head a mallet-sized punch." She made a face and set her glass on the table. "Mind if I take a shower? I feel really cruddy." She shot him a provocative smile. "You can join me if you want. I'll scrub your back if you'll scrub mine."

He impaled her with a dark glare. "There's a bar of soap on the rack. Don't stand under the hot water too long. Clarence makes ugly noises if I let it run more than a minute."

"Oh, please, spare me your idiotic excuses," Claire said, her voice heavy with sarcasm. "Tell me straight out you don't want to do anything physical."

"I thought I made that clear at Ella's."

"You were in shock. I thought you'd be in a better mood by now."

Rufus reached for a bottle of scotch, twisted off the cap, and took a swallow. "Forget it, babe. It's over. We're over. We can't go back, and I don't want to."

"I don't believe you. You couldn't 've forgotten all those nights we spent together making wild, passionate love."

He turned away and took another swig. "I'm tired. You're tired. Take a shower and go to bed. I'll see you in the morning."

She clenched her jaw muscles. His rejection didn't surprise her, but her reaction to it did. How could he still hurt? They'd been apart for a year. Could he actually hate her? Too confused and too hurt to argue, she stepped back, but as she turned to leave, she caught sight of his bulging erection.

Her shock gave way to an oppressive sadness. His erection meant nothing. It was a physical, not an emotional reaction to her presence. Her tears returned. She knew she had lost something exquisite and wonderful and doubted she would ever find it again.

She turned and walked into the bedroom.

CHAPTER THREE

Rufus watched until the beads hanging in the doorway stopped swinging, then reached down and adjusted his throbbing penis. He wanted Claire. He wanted to make love, but he didn't dare, or she'd be back in his life for good. Determined not to let that happen, he tried to analyze his obsession with her. He slogged through his mucked-up emotions and decided he was fixated on lust, not love, and this wasn't the time to go ballistics over a tight ass and two pointed breasts. Being in the same room with her always raised his testosterone level. It had nothing to do with sentiment or affection.

The memories of their carnal nights together swirled in his mind and sent blood rushing to his groin. Thoughts like that could raise a dead man's dick, but he had to chill out, forget the passion and those incredible orgasms. He wasn't some hot-blooded homeboy strung out on sex. In fact, he hadn't had sex since they separated. He'd had erections, but he blamed them on wet dreams or a full bladder. A cold shower or a few jerks took care of them.

He snorted in derision. Only a fool would make up stupid excuses for his sexual obsession. Claire had been more than a wham bam on a cold night. His love for her had been an obsession, but he had given up all his obsessions: love, sex, drugs. At least he thought he had. Her unexpected arrival hit him with a double blow: first in his heart, then in his groin.

He didn't want to believe a year's separation hadn't cooled his feelings for her, but apparently it hadn't. Their kind of love couldn't be turned on and off. They had had their tender moments, mellow with wine and roses and Billie Holiday's mood music, but the core of their love was hard, and deep, and eternal. It was an addiction a hundred times more powerful than a dime bag of junk or a quarry of crystal.

He had conquered his drug addiction in a lousy prison cell. Conquering his addiction to Claire should be easy compared to that. But it wasn't. He would never forget her, but he had to make her understand they were finished. No dillydallying, no pussy-footing around. Stringing her along wouldn't be fair, not with him heading to Memphis in a week, leaving everything, includ-ing his past, behind.

With a determined nod, he slipped into his nightly routine. Heedless, repetitive activities were the only way he knew to douse old fears and future uncertainties. Like he did every night fol-lowing an exhausting five-hour session at Ella's, he turned on his purple lava lamp and poured himself another drink. He placed a record of Lady Day singing "Big City Blues" on his stereo and fell onto his battered easy chair.

He peered out the dirt-streaked window. The arctic night's quiet beauty distracted him from his morbid thoughts. The heavy snow hid the cracked sidewalks and turned the junk-yard jalopies into humped white elephants. The cold had driven the whores and drug pushers into their sewers, and as yet the winos hadn't defaced the pristine whiteness with yellow curlicues. The scene filled him with an inner peace that was as unexpected as it was transitory. How could he relax knowing Claire was standing in his shower stark naked?

The sound of beads rustling in the doorway and the scent of gardenias turned his cock into an I beam and his balls into two stainless steel spheres.

"Damn," he muttered. So much for conquering addictions with self-control. If she was still naked, he'd be screwed literally and figuratively.

With a slight flutter in his throat, he turned to look at her. He would have laughed in relief when he saw she wasn't naked, but the g-string bikini and push-up bra under her see- through gown was no laughing matter. They covered enough to chill his fantasies and deflate his penis, but he knew his physical release was temporary. His snow princess knew how to relieve the lusty ache that plagued him whenever she was around.

"I can't sleep," she said in a flat tone.

"It might help if you went to bed."

"Wouldn't do any good. I'd just lie there and think of you. We haven't exactly been pen pals. I'd like to catch up on what you've been doing. No law against talking, is there?" Rufus adjusted his expression to fit his mood, which fluctuated between deceptive composure and open amusement. "There's nothing to catch up on. I've led a simple life since you left. I didn't win the lottery. I'm done with snorting and smoking, and I never took to the idea of sleeping around."

Claire eyed him speculatively. "That's hard to believe. As I recall, you always had a strong sexual appetite."

"I kept it under control. I never look for trouble, but that doesn't mean I don't find it. When I was in the joint, the lifers scared the hell out of me when they asked for a date—if you get my meaning. I tried to ignore 'em. When that didn't work, I told 'em I had some kind of oozing disease."

He returned his gaze to the window and continued in a bitter tone.

"Six months in hell's prison was a real downer, but I learned basic survival techniques real fast. For instance, I learned how to hate without showing it, how to draw blood without being caught, and how to die, if necessary, without a whimper. It took me a while, but I finally realized the dudes who had the least trouble followed their own set of rules. They never looked a guard full in the face, gave the hairy guerrillas the evil-eye, and crippled horny bulls with a quick kick in the groin."

"I'm sorry, Rufus. I didn't mean to bring up ugly memories."

"Memories like that don't go away, but don't get the idea I was a hero. I did what I was told, I kept my nose clean. To pass the time between one lousy day after the other, I read every book I could lay my hands on." He grinned. "For what it's worth, I have a jail-house degree in book learning and survival tips for dummies."

"How can you joke about something so ugly?" she asked, her voice choked with emotion.

"You laugh or you cry." He shrugged. "What about you? You must've had a few bad days."

"I had my share, but compared to your prison, my rehab center was a country club. Still, it took me longer than the usual six weeks to decide I could live without a hit. I missed you so much. There wasn't a day I didn't want to run away and come back here, but I knew it'd be a disaster if I did. I had to want you more than I wanted my nose candy."

Rufus tipped his head in understanding. He knew the white crystal's lure. A guy in the joint had sold his five-year-old daughter to a porno cult for one hit. He and Claire were lucky. They got clean before they lost their souls.

"I thought about you, about us." He smiled in a halting attempt to lighten up the grim atmosphere. "I thought about the band. I heard you on bass, Moon on drums, Lenny on piano. I even heard myself blowing my sax. We made some sweet, low-down music together." The muscles in his forearm hardened. "I stopped thinking when my body hit the cot. I had to. Watching you make love to me, even if it was only in my mind, would've dragged me down to no-where land."

"I remember the good times. Our first six months together were real fine, but not so the last six months. How did we convince ourselves everything was great? It's too late to sweat it now, but it finally dawned on me that the opposite of perfection is imperfection, and that translates into self-destruction. I'll never understand how we survived those endless binges of fucking, performing, and eight-balling coke and speed."

"We survived, but we paid a terrible price."

"I hope you're not blaming me. I'll take part of the blame, but it wasn't all my fault."

"Why would I blame you? We were too much alike. We had the same hungers, the same weaknesses. We craved drugs, and we craved a love frowned on by society and forbidden by the KKK. We didn't care. We were having too much fun. Like those Woodstock hippies, we middle fingered the rules and told everybody who didn't approve to fuck off. In the end, we learned we couldn't live in a straw house and survive on orgies and illegal drugs. A sadistic cop and a snoot full of coke blew our house down."

He stood up, stretched, and looked out at the snow, which was still coming down hard. A swirling wind had buried curbs and cars and fire hydrants under huge snowdrifts. The sound of a dog yapping in the frozen tundra sent a chill down his spine. Neither man nor beast should be out on a night like this, but they were. He saw the street people huddled under corrugated boxes, gripping their whiskey bottles. He was thankful for the roof over his head and the fifth of scotch on the table, but if he were one of them, he'd take a box in a doorway over a cell any-time.

In a perverse way, he envied their freedom. If he only had himself to think about, he'd keep his gig at Ella's, share his bed with Claire, and return to his free-wheeling, screwed-up past. Instead, he chose the steeper road. He was willing to give up everything he owned and everyone he loved so he could be with his son, Rufe Junior. After he boarded the train to Memphis, he swore, he'd never look back.

With his confidence restored and his goals reconfirmed, he pulled Claire to him. His eyes locked on hers, he wrapped one arm around her waist and massaged her back with the other.

"Sorry I yelled at you. I feel better now that we talked."

"I understand why you were upset. I'm sure the last thing you expected was for me show up during a snow storm and ask if I could stay the night. You know, I never considered the possibili-ty you could be living with another woman."

Her comment drained the blood from his brain, leaving behind guilt and confusion. Was this his cue to tell her he wasn't living with another woman at the moment, but he might be in another week? *Impossible*! No way could he tell her tonight, and since she'd be gone in the morning, he wouldn't have to tell her at all.

"It's good you came. I feel better knowing you made it, that you're okay, that everything's okay." He relaxed the worry lines on his brow. "By the time I was paroled and came back here, you were gone. I didn't know what happened to you, and I didn't have the guts to find out."

"I left a month before you returned. The whole time you were gone was pure hell. All I thought about was you rotting in prison and me living here alone. I was going out of my mind. Ella was great. She tried to help. She let me play with Moon and Lenny when I could barely stand up, but she cut me loose when I started weaving on the bandstand. She told me to get clean or get out. She'd had it with her drugged-out bass player. I thought she was the meanest bitch in the world. I hate to admit it, but I told her so. All the same, I knew I didn't have a choice. I had to stop sniffing or die. I called my father and told him I needed money to go into rehab. It was one of the hardest things I ever did."

"He gave it to you?"

"Of course." A cynical smile spread across her face. "He's always good for a touch but nothing else. He never visited me."

"Don't dis him. He sounds like an okay dude. He paid your bills, no questions asked." Rufus inclined his head in a thoughtful gesture. "I had help, too. Ella paid my rent while I was up the proverbial river. I was thankful I had a place to live when I came back." "Friends in need." She shrugged. "Damn, I don't know why I'm so suspicious of good deeds. I always think there's some ulterior motive behind them."

"Do motives really matter? I'd have had to hit the streets without Ella's help. I'd probably be dead by now. The same goes for you."

"I don't feel alive. I feel soulless, numb." She choked back an anguished cry. "I thought we could pick up where we left off, only on a higher level. I never thought about a future without you. I'm not sure I want a future without you."

"Come on, babe. Forget there was an 'us' and start thinking about you." He leaned down and brushed a kiss across her forehead. "You're beautiful, talented, and smart. I never could figure out why you tied up with a black dude who had no money and little hope of getting any."

"You're missing the point," she said in an angry outburst. "I love you. You're all I need, all I ever needed—except for my music. I need that, too, just like you."

Rufus dropped his arms to his sides. Needs and obligations lived on different sides of the street. He might need Claire, but his obligations to his son came first. He swore he'd do it right this time. Although he'd never seen his son and hadn't seen Salinas in ten years, he figured they'd get married eventually but not until he proved he had what it took to be a real father to his son.

His muscles tightened, and a wave of determination, even happiness, swept over him. He had a son to raise. He never thought he'd be able to say that. Although he was only nineteen, a street kid with no money and no future, he begged Salinas to marry him. It didn't matter that she was pregnant; he would have asked her anyway, but knowing she was carrying his baby made him all the more determined to spend the rest of his life with her. When Salinas left him, not telling him why or where she was going, he almost went out of his mind.

Maybelle, Salinas's mother, was so against the marriage. Who could blame her? She didn't want her daughter or her grandchild living from hand to mouth. But why did she have to take Salinas away? Why hadn't Salinas told him where she was going?

Rufus closed his eyes and tried to blot out the misery of the last ten years. The temptation to tell Claire about Salinas hit him again, but he kept silent. He had hurt Claire too much already. Better to let her think this was a simple parting of the ways. He wasn't worried about her. She'd come out all right. She had a home, two parents, and her music. Women bass players were rare. It wouldn't take her long to find a band that fit her style. She'd forget him. What choice did she have?

"Go to bed," he said. "I'm tired. We'll talk about this tomorrow." He turned his back and dismissed her with a flip of his hand, but the tension in his muscles didn't ease until he heard her walk away.

He sipped his scotch and listened to Billy Holiday's sultry voice mesh with Lester Young's cool sax in a passionate rendition of "The Very Thought of You."

Prez and Lady Day had had their basket of problems, too. Brilliant, talented outcasts, they knew all about police brutality, racism, and drug addiction. They found happiness in their music, their performances, and their fans, but it didn't last. Their excesses took their toll. They stopped fighting and died, destroyed by alcohol, marijuana, and heroin.

The thought both saddened and encouraged him. He would-

n't make the same mistakes they did. He wouldn't let that happen
to him.

CHAPTER FOUR

Rufus awoke to a frozen world that had been beautiful the night before but would turn into a slushy mess by noon. He rose from his chair, rolled his shoulders, and stared out at the blinding whiteness. The snow had stopped, leaving behind a foot of bleached powder.

He twisted his mouth into a cynical smile. Powder, snow, coke. He thought it was funny he hadn't made the connection before. Nature's mantle masked the hood's grime and poverty; cocaine masked a man's pain and despair. His nostrils flared. They might mask them, but they sure as hell didn't cure them.

He capped his scotch bottle, set it on a shelf, and grabbed the coffee pot. He filled it with water and dumped six scoops of coffee into the paper filter, double his usual amount. He knew he'd need the extra caffeine to get through the morning. After placing the pot on the hot plate, he leaned over the sink and splashed cold water on his face, but he didn't wake up completely until he heard the sound of footsteps brushing the floor, like a robin flapping its wings.

"Good morning," Claire said.

Rufus cringed, struck by the memory of her sleepy, throaty drawl. When she stepped behind him and began to massage his shoulders, he felt the pressure starting to build in his loins. He promised himself he wouldn't make love to her. It had nothing to do with principles or self-restraint; it had everything to do with survival.

He pushed her hands away, but her teasing laughter raised his sexual appetite to greater heights. He wiped the perspiration off his brow. What kind of game was she playing? She had to know what all her stroking and cooing and lip-licking did to him. He knotted his brows and spun around ready to lay into her, but his caustic words melted on his tongue at the sight of her.

The sun light streaming through the window turned her into a sensuous, seductive nymph. Her cropped brunet hair curled around her ears and framed her oval face. Whiskey brown eyes, once muddied by heroin, glistened under thick, arched brows. White teeth peeked from behind pouting lips.

Rufus groaned and dropped his gaze. She wasn't playing a game, at least not a new one. Sex games had been a major event in their relationship. But that was then, and this was now. He had to stop reacting like an oversexed, over-imaginative cat. He tried to swallow the hard rock of lust stuck in his throat, but it didn't budge. With a defeated shrug, he took in short, shallow breaths and watched her roll her shoulders and move her hips in sensuous, circular motions. The tie around her waist slackened, and her pink robe fell open. Two brown bull's-eyes crested on her firm breasts. Her torso, flat except for the soft pouch below her belly button, narrowed to a thatched triangle of dark brown hair.

He tried to grope his way through a torrent of emotions that rocked and rolled from romantic love to carnal desire. After much floundering and soul-searching, he was finally able to chill out and speak in a cool, authoritarian voice.

"Get dressed and get your stuff together," he said. "You're going home."

"How about a cup of coffee before you throw me to the wolves?" She smiled and made an unsuccessful attempt to close her robe.

A prickly sensation skittered from his fingertips to his groin. *How much more of this can I take?* To tame the monster roaring inside him, all he had to do was glide his hand down her belly, sift his fingers through her silken curls, and slide them into her moist, warm cavern.

"I told you to get dressed." His voice rose to an angry pitch. "We're leaving in half an hour."

"Where we going?" She fumbled with the front of her robe. This time she managed to close it.

"You're going home."

"Home? This is my home, here with you. I know we weren't good for each other before, but that doesn't mean we can't build a new relationship. I love you. I want to be with you."

"Where? How?" Rufus laughed. "Woman, look around my apartment. You don't see a cozy cottage and a white picket fence. And while you're looking, check out the mirror. White and black aren't hip anymore."

A cloud darkened Claire's expression. "Don't dump your racist crap on me. Love's got nothing to do with skin. Our hearts are the same color."

Rufus stared at her, perplexed. They could live in a cave, make love, play music, and get high, but there wasn't a cave deep enough or a drug strong enough to keep the hounds away. Why couldn't she understand love wasn't enough?

"I'm going to shower. When I'm done, I want you waiting at the door, dressed and ready to go."

He stalked into the bedroom, grabbed Jockey shorts and an undershirt from a drawer, then headed into the bathroom. Claire's scent permeated the small cubicle. Was there no getting away from her? He set his mouth in a hard line, turned on the water, and tested it to make sure it was cold enough to squelch his sexual urgings. He gritted his teeth and stepped under the pelting spray. Almost instantly, his passion ebbed, and he turned his thoughts to Salinas and Rufe Junior.

A rueful smile spread across his face. Months had passed since he received the letter from Salinas inviting him to come to Memphis. He shook his head. The letter was more than an invitation; it was a proposal. Her mother had died. She was alone. Would he be interested in picking up where they left off ten years before?

Rufus shook his head. *Ten years! What a waste!* If Maybelle hadn't been so all-fired determined not to let Salinas marry him, they could have been a family all that time. He would have raised his son; he would have loved Salinas; he would have worked day and night to give them a home. As it was, he had spent most of those years alone, spending time and money trying to track down their whereabouts. While he waited and looked and waited, he filled a lock box with momentos and what little money he could save so he could give it to his son when he found him. Now the long wait was over. He was finally going to meet Rufe, his beloved son.

He replied by return mail. Yes, he told her, he'd move to Memphis and do whatever was necessary to make up for the years their son had been without a father. And yes, he told himself, he'd made a commitment, and he'd stick by it. He also told Salinas he had signed a six-month contract with Ella, and she wouldn't release him from it. It was a lie, but it was better than telling her he couldn't leave until his parole was up.

In a week, he'd be a free man, ready to take on whatever the future had in store for him. He frowned. Was it possible to walk away from his past? Somehow, it always caught up with him. He knew he was taking a risk not telling Salinas the truth. Would she want to marry an ex-con whose only assets were five hundred dollars in the bank and a stack of CDs on a shelf?

Her mother had wanted better for her. After he saw the photograph Salinas had sent him, Rufus had to agree with Maybelle. Salinas was too beautiful to waste her life on an unemployed, teenage saxophone player. The naive girl he had loved and lost was now a stunning, self-assured woman. Age—hah, she was only twenty-six—had accentuated her high cheek bones, wide-set eyes, and sensuous mouth. Her skin gleamed with the satiny texture of polished topaz. He wondered why she hadn't married someone else.

Would she change her mind when she saw him? The thought nagged at him. They barely knew each other, and whatever emotions they had for each other had cooled over the years. He chided himself. She wasn't looking for a husband any more than he was looking for a wife. They were getting back together for their son. Rufus never dreamt he was the father of such a bright, fine looking young man, but he was, and he felt mighty proud of it.

Eager to get on with his life, Rufus finished his shower,

dressed quickly, and headed into the living room. Claire was waiting for him. He picked up her suitcase and opened the door. She picked up her bass and followed him into the hall and down the stairs.

CHAPTER FIVE

Rufus laid Claire's bass and suitcase in the backseat of his car, slipped behind the wheel, and shot away from the ice-packed curb. Half way down the street, he eased his foot off the accelerator and coasted to the stop sign. He started up again and tried to concentrate on driving, but Claire's silence had become too deafening to ignore.

"You going to stay mad the rest of the day?"

When she didn't answer, he hit the steering wheel with the butt of his hand. "Okay, I shouldn't have said it. I'm sorry. I know race doesn't have a damn thing to do with us. We had our problems, but they weren't black and white. If I had to put a color on 'em, I'd choose shitty green and firecracker red."

He gave her a sideways glance. He hoped his anemic attempt at humor would sweeten her sour mood, but her taut jaw muscles and cold, straight-ahead stare told him to try something else.

He remembered something about the best defense being a good offense and decided to attack headfirst.

"Sometimes hostility can be good for the soul," he said. "I, for one, don't like to show my emotions. When it happens, it can be exciting... and creative," he added. "Artists thrive on 'em. Especially musicians. Hell, Miles Davis was mad all the time. Billie Holiday, too. She cursed, gambled, drank, and fought like a man, but she made beautiful music when she sang."

Rufus paused, caught up in the imagery of the tragic life

styles he was pitching to Claire. "I'm not saying you got to be pissed off all the time to be great, but a lot of them were. Working with Mingus was like working in the cone of a volcano ready to erupt. The dudes who stuck with him knew he was a brilliant bassist and a great innovator of jazz, but they learned not to call him a jazz musician. Mingus said the word `jazz' meant back-of-the-bus and second class citizenship." He chuckled. "And then there was Ben Webster. That man never took a sober breath, but he…"

"Stop. Stop talking," Claire said. "I don't want to hear about Mingus or Miles or any of them. If you're trying to make me feel better by telling me they were drugged geniuses, it isn't working. I'm an ex-druggy, but that doesn't mean I'll ever play like Mingus. You're an ex-druggy, but that doesn't mean you'll ever play like Charlie Parker. We don't have to be like them. We have our own styles. We play our notes the way we hear 'em. And I don't give a shit if they were black, white, or purple. They were musicians, and they did what they had to do. So stop telling me how great they were because they were black and drank and shot heroin."

Rufus gaped at her in astonishment. "Is that what you were hearing? Oh, babe, that's not what I was saying."

"Then tell me, just what were you saying?"

"I don't know exactly. I said a lot of things. I got carried away." He averted his face and bit back a grin. He planned to draw her out of herself, to turn off her anger and start talking. He was only partially successful. She came out of herself, loud and clear, but she was still angry. He'd have to work on that, or, if he was smart, let her work it out herself.

"Let's cool it, babe." He reached over and patted her gloved hand. "What does any of this have to do with anything? We're ex-lovers who haven't seen each other in six months. We had a nice visit, but now it's time for us to go our separate ways."

"I didn't picture this kind of homecoming," she said with a hint of bitterness in her tone. "I thought we could patch things up, go back to the way we were before we got strung out on drugs. Why can't we do that?"

"Because things change. We can't go back. I don't want to, and if you'd be honest with yourself, you wouldn't either. Just leave it at that."

The car hit a patch of ice and started to slide into a line of cars parked helter-skelter along the curb. He pulled the car out of the skid and coasted until he reached the main road, which had been cleared hours before.

He took a deep breath and concentrated on his driving. The trip out of the city was a study in contrasts. Narrow, shotgun houses, barred liquor stores, used car lots, and revivalist churches gave way to gated mansions, fancy boutiques, domed synagogues, and spired chapels.

He wondered if Claire saw what he saw. He doubted it. Even if she happened to notice the neighborhoods change from poor to rich, she couldn't understand how the poverty of one and the wealth of the other affected the people living there. He knew better than to label her a liberal who thought the rich were morally decadent and the poor morally superior. Neither was she a conservative who blamed the ghetto's poverty on laziness and multiple births.

He didn't intend to open it up for discussion. Race or social class or rich or poor had nothing to do with their relationship.

None of it had mattered when they met, and none of it mattered now. He had rejected her and hurt her, and he hadn't had the guts to tell her why. He felt it was better that way.

The gated mansions and upscale subdivisions gave way to open fields that resembled farm land but had the feel of country estates. "Where are we?" he asked. "I feel like I've been driving for hours."

Still pouting, she pointed to an opening in a dense hedge row that lined the highway. "Slow down or you'll end up in a ditch."

Rufus nodded and made a sharp turn onto a narrow road that opened into a circular driveway. A quarter of a mile from the entrance, he spotted a white pillared mansion set in the center of a landscaped lawn festooned with oak and evergreen trees, marble statues, and an ornate gazebo. He let out a low whistle.

"Did I make a wrong turn, or is that hotel your home?"

"That isn't a home or a hotel. It's a magnificent mausoleum for the living dead." She snickered. "What did you expect, Uncle Tom's cabin?"

"I don't know what I expected, but it sure wasn't this."

"I hope you don't blame me because my parents live in that—that monstrosity?"

"What's to blame? You'll excuse me if I'm a little surprised. Your folks have to be loaded." He looked at her in astonishment. "What kind of game are you playing? You want to live in the ghetto when you can hang out in a pad like this?" He shook his head. "You have to be crazy."

"Who I live with is much more important than where I live. You can get mad and you can say I tricked you, but please, don't label me. I'm not a poor little rich girl looking for meaning in life.

I'm not searching. I know what I want."

"And just what the hell do you want?"

"I want you." She dropped her voice to a low burn. "I want to live with you, I want to play in your band. It'd be nice if we made enough money to buy food and put clothes on our backs, but if we don't, two pairs of jeans and a few shirts are all I need. And if we have to, we can get a meal at a Salvation Army food kitchen."

"What's with the 'we?' There is no 'we.' There's you and there's me," he said, his anger smoldering just below the surface of his skin. "Just for the record, when there was a 'we,' you never went hungry, you never had to beg, and you never slept on the street. Not to mention the six months I kept you supplied with coke."

"You're missing the point," she shot back. "All I'm saying is, I'd rather starve than live with my parents in that place they call a home. It's filled with so many ugly memories, it makes me sick to look at it. Oh, forget it. I'm tired of arguing. You can leave if you want. Drop off my bass and suitcase on your way out." She got out of the car and sprinted up the cobblestone walk.

"Claire, come back," Rufus yelled. "You can't run off and leave me sitting here. I'm not done talking."

He let out a string of curse words and darted after her. He caught up with her at the front entrance. He reached out, but before he could grab her arm, the huge oak door opened, and a tall, gray-haired man of color appeared. He took one look at Claire, wrapped his arms around her, and gave her a crushing bear hug.

"Girl, where you been? Flo and I been worried sick. We

expected you home last night."

Rufus stepped back, stunned by the man's friendly, yet commanding presence. Who was he? A friend? Definitely not a relative. His tailored black suit, starched white shirt, and regal bearing reminded Rufus of the traditional manservant in a white man's household. Whatever his job, servant or chauffeur or both, Rufus sensed he was definitely not a lackey.

Claire kissed his cheek. "I should've called, but it was so late when I got off the bus, I didn't want to wake you."

The man nodded and turned to Rufus. "And you brought her home. Much obliged, Mr…"

"Name's Rufus Johnson." He offered his hand.

"Henry Dent." He smiled and gave Rufus a hearty handshake. "Come inside. It's colder'n whatever out there."

He closed the door and stared at Claire, happiness sparking his eyes. "Girl, you're looking real good. You got a blush back in your cheeks, and you put on some weight." He grinned. "Mind you, I ain't saying you're fat, but you're sure not the scraggly-looking scarecrow you were when you left."

"I'm fit and healthy, and I'm going to stay that way. I sure don't want to go through that nightmare again." She rubbed her hands together and shot a hesitant glance at the winding staircase.

Henry followed her gaze. "Your mother's not well," he said. "Go on into the library. I'll brew a pot of coffee. Flo went shopping. There's no snow storm bad enough to keep that wife of mine out of the mall."

"Tell Mother I'm here," Claire said. "I don't want to upset her, but I would like to see her."

"I'll check." Henry smiled. "Guess I don't have to tell you where the library is."

"It's the only room in the house that has good vibes." She turned to Rufus. "Flo, Henry, and I did a lot of jamming there. Henry got me interested in playing bass. He beat those piano keys so hard I thought sure he'd break his fingers. Flo tried to keep up on her clarinet. I didn't even try."

"Not much music round here since you left." Henry sighed and walked away, his hesitant shuffle at variance with his imposing presence.

Claire took Rufus's hand and led him through an elaborately carved door.

He stepped over the threshold, stopped, and shook his head in disbelief. "I could put my whole apartment in here and have space for a dance floor, but who'd want to? It's just too much." He glanced around, dumbstruck by the room's luxurious decorations. Although the rows of leather-bound books on the wall, the exquisite oriental rug on the floor, and the baronial fireplace sandwiched between two floor-to-ceiling stained glass windows were astoundingly beautiful, he felt as if he were staring at a movie set or a look-but-don't-touch drawing room in a museum.

"I should be madder'n the devil at you," he said. "You're not rich, you're filthy rich. And to think I fell for that line you gave me about being the outcast daughter of an alcoholic mother and an arrogant father. Poor Claire! She had to beg for gigs so she could eat. Shit! If I'd 've known about this," he swung his arm out in wide circle, "I would've let you starve."

"I didn't beg for gigs," she said, her tone venomous. "I auditioned for them, just like everybody else. Guess it never dawned on you that a filthy rich chick would want to play in a band that gave its proceeds to a camp for needy kids." She glared at him with reproachful eyes. "Filthy rich chicks don't know a damn thing about compassion, right?"

"You telling me compassion was the only reason you auditioned?" He cocked his head. "Unh-unh. I don't buy that."

"Oh, and I suppose black and white dudes are filled with compassion when they perform at charity blowouts. Unh-unh. I don't buy that. Like everybody else, they want to get their names in the paper so they can make contacts so they can get a gig."

"So? What's wrong with musicians playing for charity? For some, it's the only way to be seen and heard and, with a little luck, discovered."

He ran his hand along the back of a beautifully upholstered rosewood chair. "Why did I have to bring that up? I hired you to play in my band, not because you were white or a woman, although a female bass player was a rarity, but because you're a talented, dedicated musician." He averted his eyes. He had thought they were compatible and would work well together. He sure didn't think they'd fall in love. He walked to the hearth and stared at the blue-red flames flickering on the gas logs. "It doesn't matter anymore," he said. "When I leave, I'll go my way, you'll go yours." A soft smile erased the tense lines on his face. "I feel better knowing you have a family to watch out for you. I don't have to worry."

"I never expected you to worry." Claire stuck her hands in her jeans' pockets and sighed. "I've done everything wrong. I made you angry. I tried to wedge my way back into your life, but I've done nothing but argue with you. Oh, nuts! I need a drink."

She walked to a cherry wood cabinet and gave the brass a yank. When it refused to open, she slammed her fist against the door. "I forgot. Henry keeps it locked, and only he has the key."

"Why? You got a bottle of rare brandy in there?"

"No. We keep it locked…"

A woman's squeal silenced Claire. Rufus spun around and stared at the spectacle stumbling toward him. His first thought was that a woman dressed like a clown had stumbled into the library. A pink satin negligee edged with dirty white feathers clung to her body and defined her shriveled breasts and skeletal torso. Orange hair, fuscia lipstick, black brows, and green eye shadow topped off her burlesque appearance.

"Mother," Claire said in a startled voice. Taking short, hesitant steps, she approached the woman, raised her arms as if to embrace her, paused, and dropped them to her side.

Rufus cringed. There would be no mother-daughter hug today.

"Claire, dear, how nice to see you. Where have you been? You haven't visited for such a long time." Mrs. Burton pointed to Claire's worn jeans and faded sweat shirt. "I wish you wouldn't wear that ghastly outfit. Really, dear, you look like a streetwalker. I'm sure if you asked your father, he'd give you the money to buy some decent clothes."

Rufus grunted. He felt as if someone had slammed a fist into his midsection. What was going on here? Claire just got out of rehab, and Mrs. Burton worried about how she looked. He held his breath and waited for Claire to explode in a fit of anger. When it didn't come, he looked at her. Instead of hostility, he saw tears glaze her eyes.

"Don't worry about it, Mother. I have a closet full of clothes in my room." She flicked a smile and pointed to Rufus. "This is my friend, Rufus Johnson. Rufus, my mother, Dixie."

"Forgive me. I didn't see you when I came in." Dixie acknowledged him with a silly laugh. "I have a terrible headache. I can hardly see." She turned to Claire. "Have you forgotten your manners? Fix Mr. Johnson a drink. While you're at it, fix me one, too."

"I can't," Claire said in a stammer. "Henry locked the liquor cabinet."

"Locked!" Dixie frowned. "Who gave him permission?"

"Mr. Burton. If there's a problem, you'll have to talk to him." Henry padded into the room and set the silver tray that held a coffee urn and three china cups on a table. He approached Dixie and led her to a chair.

"Let me pour you a cup of coffee?" he said. "It'll ease your headache."

"You know I hate the stuff unless it's flavored." Dixie sunk into the chair like a deflated balloon. "After I rest a minute, you can take me back to my room. I feel a little dizzy, not that anybody cares."

Claire rushed forward. "I'll get you a glass of water."

"Water! That's even worse." Dixie eyed her with a savage stare. "Stop harping at me. I'm not an invalid. If you really want to help, I'll tell you what would make me happy." She sucked in her cheeks, further distorting the clown mask on her face. "I'd like a civil word from your father and a martini, two olives, from Henry."

"Mother, please, be reasonable."

"Reasonable! You don't think my simple wants are reasonable?" She rose out of her chair like a phantom. Her red eyes glowed like neon signs. "Is it unreasonable for me to want my husband to talk to me, to share something besides my monthly allowance? Damn him. He'll let me buy a dozen fancy dresses but not one bottle of gin." She screeched, threw up her hands, and fell to the floor.

"Oh, my God!" Claire dropped to her knees and took her mother in her arms. "Are you hurt? Please, open your eyes. Talk to me."

Dixie's eyes fluttered open. "Claire, dear. You've come for a visit. How nice." She gripped her daughter's arm. "Please, help me up. I seem to have lost my balance."

"I'll take over now," Henry said. His expression a mask of stone, he eased Claire away, drew Dixie's arm around his neck, and pulled her to her feet. "The doctor warned you not to exert yourself," he chided.

"What does that fool know?" Dixie turned and gave Claire a wistful glance. "Do come back when you have more time. And bring your friend along."

Rufus watched Henry and Dixie stumble to the door, his thoughts jumbled, his emotions in turmoil. Was Dixie for real or was she acting out a role in a play? If so, was it a tragedy or a comedy? He turned to Claire. Her face was ashen, her cheeks scarred with tears.

"Is Dad home?" she called out.

"He left early," Henry replied. "Said he'd be home late tonight."

She nodded. "Tell him his daughter said hello."

"You're not staying?"

"I came by to grab a few things from my room."

She stood motionless until Henry and Dixie slipped into the hallway. She walked to the hearth and leaned her head against the mantle.

"Oh, dear God! Nothing's changed. It's the same old nightmare." She raised her head and looked at Rufus. "Who gives her liquor? Henry doesn't. It has to be Dad. He'll give her anything as long as she stays out of his hair. He's helping her kill herself."

"What can I do?" Rufus moved beside her and gripped her shoulders. "You and I have been down that road. We know the horrors of addiction."

"You know as well as I do she won't stop until she hits bottom or dies."

"I don't get it." Rufus shook his head. "Your mother has everything. A big house, servants, a beautiful daughter, and money, lots of money."

"You forgot one thing. She has a husband. He's around someplace. Only God knows where."

"I don't know anything about that."

"Let me fill you in. My dear father, Bernard, is a self-centered, money-hungry monster. He's responsible for mother's condition. In a round-about way, he was responsible for mine."

"Come on, babe. Nobody can turn a person into an addict. They do it to themselves."

"Maybe he didn't turn her into an addict, but he sure as hell screwed her up." With a snort, Claire pushed past Rufus, sat down on a chair, and stared at the flames dancing in the hearth. "He loved her once, but for the wrong reasons. She sang torch songs in a cabaret. She was a beauty, and she had some talent. Dad saw her perform, fell in love, and married her two months later."

"Sounds like a real love story."

"Some love story." Claire snorted. "They were attracted to each other because they were different, but their differences tore them apart. Mother was a nobody. Dad was the only son of a fabulously rich family that owned coal mines, lead mines, and half the state's legislators. Dixie DeVine didn't fit into their scheme of things. They rejected both of them."

"So they made it on their own," he said. "What's wrong with that?"

"Nothing, until Dad realized he couldn't live without his family's approval. He didn't need their money. He opened his own brokerage house and made tons of it. But he couldn't give up the family ties. When the petty jealousies started to pile up between him and Mother, blood lines became battle lines, and Dad withdrew from the scene."

"Blood lines? Does that include which side of the blanket a person's born on? Us black folks know all about that. Doesn't matter if you're ninety per cent white and ten per cent black, you got bad blood and you're the wrong color." The bitter edge of cynicism in his voice deepened. "If you're white, you're right; if you're black, stay back."

"That's exactly what happened. Mother was forced to the back of the bus." She took a deep breath and plunged on. "She became a fanatic. She checked her genealogy. She looked for an earl, a prince, a senator or two. Instead, she found a Jew. She bragged about it, like it was a badge of distinction. After all, aren't all Jews rich? Hard-line evangelicals didn't take that too well."

"The genealogy part makes sense to me," Rufus said. "African-Americans were cut off from their ancestors. It's like losing a hand or a foot. You never feel completely whole."

"The past doesn't interest me. The here and now is more important than the there and then." She picked at the last speck of nail polish on her index finger. "Dad bought her things, jewelry, clothes, fancy cars. Mother had problems, but she wasn't stupid. If he only gave her things, she'd get as many as she could. But we all know, things don't buy happiness.

"Water under the bridge." She jumped up and waved her hand in the air in a dismissive gesture. "I'm going to my room and grab some clothes and the three hundred bucks I got stashed under my mattress." She looked at Rufus with vacant eyes. "Will you wait for me? I'd appreciate a ride into town."

"Town is a big place," he said. "Just where do you want to go in town?"

"The Epson House'll do till I can find an apartment."

"Oh, shit! Why do you keep picking flea-bag flop houses?"

"Oh, and you live at the Ritz?"

"I change my sheets more than twice a year."

She met his angry gaze head on. "In that case, I'll just have to stay with you."

"You're setting me up, woman. You know I won't take you to a flea-bag bed-and-breakfast."

"I hoped you'd be cool and let me bunk with you." She smiled.

"Damn! I should've known." Rufus growled. "Okay, you can stay with me but only for a few days. Then you're out on your ass." He knitted his brows into a hard line. "We'll share the apartment, but we aren't going to shack up."

"I'll give Henry your address." Her smile faded, and a sadness settled in her eyes. "I don't understand why you want to get rid of me so badly. I thought you'd be happy to see me. I thought we could write some new songs, find us an agent, maybe head out to L.A. We're good together. Even when we were high, we never screwed up our music. When we were on stage, I felt like we were joined at the hip. I missed a beat, you filled in. What we had was beautiful. Why do you want to destroy it?"

"I didn't destroy it. We did. Way back when."

She shrugged. "You going to Ella's?"

"Yeah. Me, Moon, and Lenny got a practice session."

"Mind if I sit in?"

"You got to clear that with Ella."

"It'll take some doing. Luckily, she's a forgiving soul." She studied his expression. "I don't know what's going on with you, but right now it doesn't matter. Just remember, I love you."

"Get your stuff," Rufus said. "I'll meet you at the car."

CHAPTER SIX

Rufus held the door for Claire and scooted in behind her. Ella's Lounge was an oasis of warmth and congeniality after the cold drafts and brooding atmosphere of his apartment. As always, he felt a surge of excitement at the thought of jamming a few hours with Moon and Lenny, rapping with Bojay, and dissing Ella in a bantering give-and-take. Claire's anxiety was so noticeable, he decided to curb his enthusiasm rather than take the chance of aggravating an already intense situation. He hoped Ella didn't tell Claire to take a walk. He'd have to walk, too, and Moon and Lenny would be left hanging. He knew they'd manage; they'd play their sets and get through the evening, but it'd lay down some bad vibes between them.

He took Claire's arm and hustled her to the bar. Like a sluggish tide, the odors of liquor, smoke, and wet snow from the night drifted through the room and formed a blue haze overhead. He decided to ignore the foul air and Claire's apprehension, neither of which he could change, and sidled to the bar. He gave Bojay the high sign, and ordered a scotch and water and a gin and tonic.

"Coming right up, my man." Bojay mixed the drinks and set the scotch in front of Rufus and the gin in front of Claire. He paused and studied her with a curious intensity. "I see you's still draggin' your instrument around. Plannin' to play it soon?"

"Tonight maybe. Depends on Ella." Claire drew her lips into

a pinched smile.

"Ella ain't hirin'." He shook his head. "Business too slow this time a year."

"Ella hired the Rufus Johnson band. I say who plays in it." He grimaced. "Course, her vote carries a lot of weight."

Bojay laughed. "I figure her vote weigh ninety-nine percent. Your vote weigh one percent."

"Hey, it's nothing to get excited about," Claire said. "I'm not looking for a job. I'd like to play a set, but not if it causes hard feelings." She took a sip of her drink and made a face. "Ugh! This tastes bitter. Guess I'm not used to the taste of liquor." She slipped off the bar stool. "I'm going to check my makeup. I'll be right back."

Bojay pushed her glass aside and trailed it with a bar rag. "Man, what the hell you thinkin'? I don't like to butt into nobody's business, but I tell you, Ella ain't gonna be happy when she see her. Mind you, she got nothin' agin Claire personally, but business is business, and Ella don't want to lose no more. Things are different from the way they was six months ago. White customers done move uptown, 'n black sistas don't cotton to white chicks playin' in a black band."

"When the hell did you become an expert on race relations?" Rufus gave Bojay a hostile stare.

"Come on, man. Don't throw me no bullshit. I don't give a fuck about her color, but customers do."

Rufus downed his scotch and shoved the glass at Bojay. "This time, make it a seltzer and lime. I just got rid of one habit, don't want to start another."

"Shit, man. You hard a hearin'?" Bojay poured Rufus a fresh

drink and set the glass down with a bang. "Claire's trouble, 'n Ella don't like trouble. When she throws you and Claire out the door, remember I told you so." He snorted and joined the regulars at the opposite end of the bar.

Rattled by Bojay's fat mouth, Rufus hunched over his drink and mumbled profanities under his breath. What the hell was it to him if Claire played a set? Jeesh! She was a damn good bass player, and so what if she was white?" He shot an idle glance at the three brothas and two sistas sucking beer from long-necked bottles. They wouldn't care if Claire had green scales and purple hair as long as she played their kind of music.

He shifted on his stool. He knew Bojay didn't care either. He was speaking for Ella. Rufus rolled his eyes. As if she needed a mouthpiece. She had enough oil in her jaws to jack for a year. He slammed his glass on the bar and stood up. "Ah, the hell with it!" He grabbed her bass and his sax and headed into the lounge. He'd be leaving in a week to be with his son anyway.

A smoky blue haze cast a eerie glow over the dance floor, dark except for the colored lights strung across the ceiling. He paused at the door, struck by the shadowy image of Claire who stood in front of the bandstand and stared out at the empty tables. She was cool, and that surprised him. There was a time when she would have hit Bojay with a string of curse words and stormed out of the bar.

He hoped the white coats at the rehab center hadn't broken her spirit. It was okay by him if they bent it a little. Addicts' brains had to be reprogrammed. They had to be taught how to handle anger and ignore idiotic remarks. Sometimes they learned it the hard way. He had been beaten half a dozen times before he stopped reacting when a prison guard or honky inmate called him "nigger" or "darky" or any of the other catchwords in their long list of racial slurs.

He knew how important it was for junkies to lay back, to use their brains instead of their brawn, if they any brawn left after a steady diet of their poisons-of-choice. Emotion control was the one sure sign they were healing. That didn't mean they had to be zombies. They could argue, get upset, but they wouldn't scream or cry or jump out of windows.

He approached the bandstand, set the instruments on the floor, and wrapped his arm around Claire's waist.

"You okay?" he asked.

She responded with a smile. A sensuous light passed between them.

Rufus's heart fluttered. It was like old times, good old times. Why did life have to be so damn complicated? He had spent the last six months trying to forget her. Twenty-four hours after she came back, all the wanting, the hunger, the love hit him in the face and down south, too. When they split this time, it'd be for good. He knew he'd miss her, not because she was a sensational lover or a talented bassist, but because he loved her. Her lusty spirit and sexy sizzle ignited his senses. When they were high, they made love like wild tigers. When they were mellow, they made love like purring kittens. They savored passion's sensuous delights. They tasted its succulent juices, smelled its intoxicating scents, and stroked those hidden pleasure points and secret hollows unique to them.

Rufus's cock began to rise. When it felt as if the mercury in his genital thermometer reached a hundred and twenty, he took a mental chill pill. He didn't want Claire to know she could still inflate his libido.

His erection took a dive. He picked up her bass and handed it to her.

"Thanks," she said. "Think it'd be okay if I played a few tunes before Ella shows up."

"Why not? All she can do is shoot you." His grin soured into a frown. "Where the hell are Moon and Lenny? I told 'em to be here by two. Hell, they never could tell time. Moon's the worst. I'm surprised Ella puts up with it."

"They'll show. They always do," Claire said. She unsnapped her leather case and took out her bass. After a quick tune up, she pulled it against her body and started strumming. Like an engine warming up, she walked into her tune until she found the right feel and right notes and then broke out of a straight "four to the floor" by adding rhythmic accents to her lines.

Rufus grinned and tapped his foot in harmony with her beat. She was good, damn good, considering she wasn't a Charles Mingus or a Charlie Haden, but then, who was?

He leaned against the piano and let himself slide into her expressionistic interpretation of "Foggy Day." He had forgotten how much her playing affected him. His mouth twitched. He couldn't wait until they played a duet. Just like old times!

Claire's roving line sometimes complemented his sax solo and sometimes took off on its own, devoid of melody and rhythm. Her style straddled the line between composed and improvised, tender and harsh. The result was spontaneity of reflexes that thrilled and surprised him. It saddened him to think how much time and effort they wasted when they tracked onto the drug scene. He knew they weren't brilliant, but they had a flair for improvisations and beautifully structured ballads. If they had played it straight, they might have made it big in L.A. or New York.

He snorted. If he had a buck for all the "might haves" and "ifs" in his life, he'd be in New York signing million-dollar contracts. The fact was, they had buried their "might haves" under ten feet of powdered manure.

He took his sax from its leather case, hitched his butt on the edge of a stool, and ran his tongue across his mouth piece. A commotion at the bar caught his attention before he could play a chord. He looked up. Moon and Lenny stormed into the lounge, their angry voices ripping through the stagnant air like thunder across a prairie.

"Why the fuck didn't you call?" Moon shook his fist at Rufus. His dreadlocks bobbed like the accordion-pleated legs on a cardboard doll. "Lenny's been giving me shit all morning asking if we got practice today."

"What you talking, man?" Rufus shouted. "I told you we'd have a session this afternoon."

Moon punched Lenny's shoulder. "How come you don't never listen? You always dumping your shit on me. Do this, do that, get more gigs, make more money. You thinking I'm some kind of rocket scientist who know everything?"

Lenny stripped off his gray leather gloves and returned the punch. "You muthafucka! Only brain you got is hanging 'tween your fat-ass legs."

They stomped across the dance floor like two fire-snorting bulls.

Rufus stared at them in amazement. Moon, the trio's drummer, resembled a barrel of brown moonshine. At twenty-six, he was ten years younger, thirty pounds heavier, and two feet shorter than Lenny. Shoulder-length braids framed his round face. Buckeye brown eyes and a white smile animated his features. Rufus wondered if he ever took off his black sweatshirt, blue jeans, and black shoes. They were Moon's contact with the bebop generation. If he could go back in time, he'd play his drums in basement cafes and honky-tong bars right along with Bird and Miles, Monk and Dizzy.

Lenny, the trio's piano player, looked as if he stepped out of a 1920's speakeasy. Tall, thin, and balding, he was never seen without a three-piece suit, white shirt with monogrammed French cuffs, and pointed, two-toned shoes. As monogamous as Moon was polygamous, he never missed a chance to preach against the sins of the flesh. Fornication, masturbation, and fellatio were the top three on his list. He made sure Rufus knew his fornicating, drug-sniffing life was as unnatural as sodomizing a pig and a one-way road to hell.

Rufus had ignored Lenny's fire-and-brimstone sermons, but the anger he showed when he saw Claire exhausted Rufus's patience. He opened his mouth to tell Lenny to let it go, but Moon spoke out first.

"Holy shit! Look who's here." Moon grabbed Claire and planted a wet kiss on her cheek. "You looking good, woman. Nobody'd guess you just got done taking the cure."

"You're looking good, too, Moon." Her eyes misted. "I missed you guys. I missed our jam sessions." She ran her hand along the curve of her bass. "If Ella says it's okay, can I play a set with you tonight?"

"Always welcome, honey. Always welcome."

"Not so fast," Lenny said. "You been on a farm six months. How we know you can still pluck that bass?"

"I can pluck," Claire said in an emphatic tone. "Maybe I'm a little rusty, but I'll keep up with you cats. All I need is a little warm-up time."

"What about Ella?" Lenny said. "She know you here?"

"She knows I'm in town."

"Not the same as knowing you here." Lenny looked at Rufus, then at Claire, then at the worn velvet backdrop that covered the naked wall.

"Hey, man, you thinking this is Carnegie Hall?" Moon said. "What do it matter anyway? Claire ain't no stranger. She knows our style. I say we start riffing. If she's bad, she can try another time."

Moon's comment wasn't exactly warm and fuzzy, but Rufus appreciated his effort to cut Claire some slack. Lenny might be right about Claire's ability to play. She'd been gone a long time, but like Moon said, Ella's Lounge wasn't Carnegie Hall.

"I ain't gonna sweat it." Lenny sidled his way to the baby grand piano, sat down, and plunked a few chords. Moon squeezed into the space behind his drum kit, picked up his sticks, and beat out a snare-drum press role. Rufus blew a few scales, shifted to a simple melody and enlarged it. Claire, seemingly hesitant at first, plucked a few notes when Rufus opened with the song, "The Way You Look Tonight." He started with the melody, the familiar notes that could be hummed or sung. Moon, Lenny, and Claire joined in. When the rhythm section took over, the melody was lost under a barrage of notes and sounds. Rufus, Moon, and Claire faded out and Lenny began his piano solo. When he finished, Rufus took center stage and started his second solo with "Mood Indigo." Moon came in. Claire soloed. They switched back and forth, taking turns in a structured call-and-response arrangement that was neither arranged nor anticipated. When they finished the set with their improvised rendition of "Sophisticated Lady," Rufus was so impressed by their technical knowledge and improvisational skills, he asked them to bow when he introduced them to an audience that wasn't there.

Rufus and Moon congratulated Claire on her playing. Lenny kept quiet until Rufus asked him point blank if he changed his mind about Claire playing with the band.

"I never said she wasn't a good bass player," Lenny said in a grudging voice. "Just never figured she had soul."

"Mind explaining that?" Rufus said.

"I mean, she don't have soul." He shot Claire a critical look. "Ain't many white dudes got soul enough to jazz. Ain't no white chick got it." His antagonistic tone veered sharply to anger. "If you gonna play African-American music, you got to feel it. Quincy Jones done blend bebop, R&B, gospel, and African. Ice T rapped his way up the charts spouting ghetto talk. Ain't no white chick can say she gonna wrap her dick round a totem pole or fuck you daddy, and get away with it."

"What you talking, man?" Rufus glared at him. "I'm black, and I got a dick, but you won't see it wrapped around no pole." He sucked in a breath. "You got a problem with Claire, swallow it or learn to live with it. I don't want to hear your racist shit." He sucked in his breath. "What the matter with you and Bojay? This is Claire Burton. She played bass with the band over a year." He shook his head. "And just so you don't stay stupid forever, Ice T was called the street's Bob Dylan, and Bobby's a white dude."

"Oh, stop arguing." Claire grabbed Rufus's arm. "Lenny isn't mad at my skin. He's mad at me, and he's got a right. You didn't see the ugly stuff I did while you were gone. One night…I'll never forget it. I staggered into the club, stumbled to the bandstand, and upchucked all over Lenny's piano. Another night, I stood in the middle of the bandstand yelling and cussing like Charles Mingus on an acid trip. Ella's bouncer had to drag me away." She looked at Lenny. "Guess it won't change anything if I say I'm sorry, but I am."

Lenny focused his eyes on a rip in the velvet curtain and lapsed into a musing silence. As they waited for him to decide if he was going to wink or walk, Moon chitted on a cymbal, Claire chewed on her bottom lip, and Rufus held his breath. When the tension started to make sounds like a ticking bomb, Moon banged his snare. The "thwack" ricocheted off the walls.

"What are you waiting for?" Moon said. "Tell Claire what we're all thinking. She's a damn good bass player, she kicked her habit, and she paid her dues. Make up your mind. We don't have all night."

"Okay, man. I hear you." Lenny blinked and looked at Claire. "Ain't no sense pitching a bitch against you now." He flicked a smile. "Makes for a bad liver. Anyway, next week none of this gonna matter. The Rufus Johnson Trio's gonna be history."

"History?" Claire turned to Rufus. "What does he mean, history? Are you dissolving the band? You never said anything about it."

Rufus released the air constricting his throat. "Didn't see a need. It's got nothing to do with you."

"It's your band. You can do whatever you want." Her voice dipped to a strained whisper. "All the same, I'd think you'd have mentioned it."

"We'll talk about it later, babe," Rufus said. "It's complicated."

"She's been in town two days, and you ain't told her?" Lenny let out a cynical laugh. "Man, you in big trouble. Any fool'd know you don't keep a chick hanging 'round if you planning to marry a sista."

"Shut up, Lenny. Just shut up." Rufus jabbed his finger in Lenny's chest.

"Is this some kind of joke? Claire leaned her bass against the wall and approached Rufus, her expression thunderous. "What's going on? Talk to me, Rufus. Are you sleeping with another woman?"

"I'm not sleeping with anybody."

"You're not sleeping with anybody, but you're planning to marry somebody!" Claire looked at him in shock.

"I didn't say a thing about getting married."

She slammed her fist on the piano lid. "When you're done playing stupid word games, tell me what the hell's going on."

"I'm sorry, babe. I should've told you the first night you walked in, but I didn't plan on you hanging around. Remember, I said you couldn't stay with me. But you wouldn't listen. I was going to tell you, I swear. I was waiting for the right time."

"Quit with the doubletalk. Who is this woman you're not

going to marry?" She stared at him. Tears rolled down her cheeks. "I don't believe this is happening. I always thought... You and I... Are you in love with her?"

Rufus averted his gaze. Silence loomed between them like a heavy mist. No, he didn't love Salinas. He loved Claire, loved her beyond reason or understanding, but love had nothing to do with it. He had a chance to be a father to his son, to make up for all the years he had wasted. Salinas knew he was moving to Memphis to be with Rufe Junior. She accepted it. Now all he had to do was make Claire know how he felt and pray she would accept it.

"Please, try to understand," he said in a hoarse whisper. "This has nothing to do with you. It has nothing to do with us. It has everything to do with my son."

"Your son? What are you talking about?"

"I had a son. Ten years ago. Salinas, his mother, sent me a letter asking me if I wanted to patch things up between us and be a dad to my boy. When I agreed, you weren't around." His shoulders sagged. His troubled spirits quieted. "Even if you had been here, I wouldn't have said no."

"A son! You have a son? All this time you lied to me, treated me like I had AIDS." Her face flushed with anger and humiliation, she slapped him hard on his cheek, let out an anguished sob, and darted away.

In stunned silence, Rufus watched her run to the ladies room. He had hurt her, but he hadn't meant to. He harbored thoughts of his son deep inside him all those years, and he didn't want to share them, not even with Claire. The love in his heart and the unmailed letters in his lock box were his secret. Now he had to tell Claire; he had to make her understand Rufe was his future, and his future did not include her. He groaned. *What a lousy way for Claire to find out!* He knew it had cut her to the bone. Still, her fury had surprised him. They had shared a year of horror swilling booze, sniffing coke, smoking grass. They had screamed, cursed, and called each other every ugly name they could think of, but they never struck one another.

He jerked his head up and glanced at Moon and Lenny. They were staring at him, their mouths gaping.

He set his fiery gaze on Lenny. "This is all your fault, you muthafucka."

"Hey, man, take it easy," Lenny said. "How the shit was I supposed to know you didn't tell her?"

"It'd be a waste of time hitting the likes of you. It's no secret I'm leaving, but it's my business, not yours. I figure you're too dumb to know what your bad ass attitude just did, but I'm not going to break a sweat setting you straight." He kicked a chair aside and took off after Claire.

He hesitated outside the ladies room. He had to fix things between them before she did something crazy like get dusted on China white. One bad hit could kill her.

Sickened by the thought, he tensed the muscles in his upper arm, pushed the door open, and barged into the restroom.

CHAPTER SEVEN

Rufus stopped in the middle of the room and waited until she finished slapping cold water on her face before he spoke.

"You can't run away from this one, babe. We have to talk."

Claire spun around and leaned heavily against the sink as if she needed a prop to keep from falling.

"Get out of here," she said. "I don't ever want to see you again." She wadded a wet paper towel in her hand and threw it at him. "We have nothing to say to each other."

"You're wrong, babe. We have a lot to say. We been through a lot of shit together. I won't let it end like this."

"End what? Our affair?" She snorted. "Oh, such a fancy name for a fucking orgy. Screw the white bitch and move on, but not before you make a complete ass out of her. Maybe your bitches don't have to be white. They can be red or brown, or black as long as they keep your dick in shape." She locked her gaze on him. "Is this how you treated Salinas? Bam, bam, thank you ma'am between jam sessions?"

Claire's outburst lit a red flare inside Rufus. A fierce urge to slap some sense into her almost overpowered his reason. He took a step forward, then stopped when he realized she was making sense. He had betrayed her, and her fury was defensible.

He approached her cautiously. "You're pissed off. I'm pissed off, and we're both hurt. We're going to talk. We can do it here or wait till we get back to the apartment." He reached out and pulled her to him. "You can't believe I deceived you on purpose."

"Are you telling me you woke up one day and decided to move in with some woman or marry her, whichever came first?" She tried to push him away, but he tightened his grip around her waist and held on.

"That's crazy, and you know it."

"The only thing I know is you have a son, your son has a mother, and this is the first I've heard of them." She glared at him with reproachful eyes. "Maybe they weren't in your life, but you must have thought about them once in a while."

"Yes, I thought about them. I thought about Rufe Junior. Every year, I'd try to imagine how much he'd grown, if he had any hobbies, did he like music. All I could do was imagine and wonder."

"What about Salinas? You never tried to contact her?"

"She left before Rufe Junior was born. I didn't hear from her till I got her letter months ago asking me to come to Memphis. I couldn't believe it. I thought I was dreaming. I had looked all over for them. I wrote family, friends, anyone who might know where they were. Either they didn't know, or they were sworn to secrecy. So I waited and hoped. Now my dream has become a reality. I'm going to meet my son."

"Then it's settled. You're leaving, and I'm out of here." She pressed her palms against his chest and tried to push him away. This time he pinned her against the wall.

"Damn it, woman, it's not that simple. Not since you came back."

"I'm sorry if I ruined everything." She narrowed her eyes to slits. "But to quote you, I didn't do it on purpose."

"Quit acting like a bitch and listen. This isn't easy for me. It's tearing me apart. I love you. I've always loved you, and as far as I know I always will."

A contemptuous sneer distorted her face. "Oh, sweetheart, you got the wrong word. You're not talking love, you're talking lust. You know what lust is, don't you?"

Her eyes locked on his, she unzipped his pants, slipped her hand inside his shorts and fondled his penis.

"Damn it, Claire. What are you doing?"

A cynical smile cracked her lips. "Isn't it obvious? I'm seducing you. Isn't this all you want from me? A quick fuck?"

Her smirk ignited his fury. "If that's what you think, I'll be happy to oblige." Reacting to the challenge in her voice, he gripped the back of her neck and gave her a hard, crushing kiss. She sputtered and tried to break away, but he thrust his tongue into her mouth and smothered her protests.

He drew his head back. "Why are you fighting me?" He searched her face for a hint of compassion, a wisp of a smile, anything that would tell him she understood his sorry situation and forgave him. Her arrogant, mocking expression was a red flag being waved in front of an angry bull. The tension coiled in his gut erupted and shattered his waffling restraint.

His hot breath flowing through parted lips, he stripped her from the waist down, wedged her hips between two sinks, and submerged himself in the fire simmering in the black vortex of her eyes. Behind the anger and contempt, he saw a flash of passion and a ripple of excitement.

"This is what you want, isn't it, a fast fuck?" He grasped her hips and tilted her pelvis against his throbbing penis. When he felt her moistness, a geyser of erotic passion erupted in his groin and drenched him with a lubricious mist. The mild, tingling sensation of blood surging into his staff became a pulsating throb. He took her in his arms and gave her a hard, demanding kiss. When he felt her grow soft and malleable, he slid his hands under her buttocks and lifted her off the floor.

"No, Rufus, this isn't what I want," she said. She opened her eyes as if suddenly awakening from a dark sleep. "I don't want you to fuck me in this smelly rest room. I want you to make love to me on a bed with clean sheets and listen to Lena Horne sing 'Stormy Weather.'"

"Too late, babe. Too damn late." He pressed her back against the wall, gripped his cock, and steered the tip through her thick, brown pubic hair and into the mouth of her vagina. When he heard her short intake of breath, he knew it was too late for her as well.

The intensity of his passion and the effort it took to hold her up laid a film of perspiration on his skin. He hesitated and stared deep into her eyes. "I want you, Claire. Say you want me. Say it."

"Yes, yes. I want you. Oh, God, how I want you."

Only vaguely aware of his clammy palms and strained groin muscles, he penetrated her and began to move his pelvis, slowly at first, then faster. Claire was with him now, completely with him, bumping and grinding, lost in her own ecstasy. The erotic sensations were so intense, he came dangerously close to losing it. He stopped but only for a moment to catch his breath. He couldn't cheat her out of her orgasm any more than he could cheat himself. They had waited too long for this.

He felt the walls of her vagina squeeze his purple head, he

rocked back and forth and pulled in and out, each thrust sparked a flame inside him. When the flame turned into a raging fire, he plunged deep inside her. She opened her mouth and let out a cry of ecstasy.

"Rufus, oh, my God, Rufus, I'm on fire." She dug her fingers into his shoulders and spewed out crude, erotic utterances.

His climax building, he tightened his grip on her thighs, plunged deeper, withdrew, and plunged again. His legs shook, his muscles screamed, his cock swelled and gorged itself on her gamy juices.

He looked up and studied her expression. Her head flung back, her eyes closed, she glowed with the flush of raw, uninhibited sex.

"It's coming. The wave. It's, it's …"

Rufus kissed her hard and stifled her scream.

When the swell of her climax tapered to a ripple, he straightened and took one last stab. A rasping sound gurgled in his throat and exploded in an orgiastic shout. His virility drained, his passion spent, he lowered her legs to the floor. She slumped against him like a ragged doll, dropped her head on his chest, and sucked air into her lungs.

Rufus nuzzled his face in her hair and whispered, "That was fucking beautiful."

The door opened, and raucous laughter filled the room. "Lordy, Lordy, kiss my black ass if'n that ain't the dangest sight I ever seen."

Tess, Ella's matron, waddled in, her hips swinging from side to side like a windshield wiper.

"Oh, my God!" Claire jerked upright. Rufus yanked up his

trousers and positioned himself in front of Claire to screen her from Tess's startled gaze.

"Looks like we been caught in the act." He shrugged his shoulders in mock resignation. "Sorry if we embarrassed you."

"Ain't no cause to be embarrassed." Tess took a mischievous peek at Rufus's butt. "You done bring back memories long forgotten." She let out a pensive sigh. "If I was younger, I'd wait in line for that pecker to come back to life, but it be a waste. My coochie been dry so long, it'd take a downpour to get it back in working order."

"That you, Claire?" Tess cocked her head to one side and acknowledged Claire with a wave of her hand. "Heard you was back. Nice to see you and Rufus getting together again."

Claire stepped from behind Rufus and shook her head in dismay. "I can imagine what you're thinking. The tramp's back, and already she's fucking the band leader in the ladies restroom. It's okay. I'm thinking the same. Believe me, this was not planned." She shot Rufus a cold look. "It just kind of happened."

"Girl, I never thought that way 'bout you, and I ain't thinking it now." She smiled and shuffled to a stall. "You two get on with your business. I got to get on with mine." She opened the door and stepped inside.

Rufus turned to Claire and shook his head in disgust. "Hey, babe, I'm sorry. This is all my fault. I acted like a stupid fool."

"No, it's not all your fault. I egged you on." She flashed a cynical smile. "One thing for sure, we forgot about Memphis for a while." She gave him a push. "Get out of here. I need to use the toilet."

Rufus hesitated, unwilling to let things stand the way they

were. He heard Tess make noises and realized this was not the time or place to discuss the whys of his absurd behavior. "I'll meet you in the lounge," he said and walked away.

Safely ensconced in the men's room, a haven of tranquility compared to the x-rated scene in the ladies room, he hunched over the sink and took deep breaths trying to calm himself. What the hell had gotten into him? He hadn't made love to Claire, he had performed like an animal or an oversexed stud. He grunted in disgust. If he had stopped for a moment and thought about it, he'd have realized he had been goaded by anger, not love, not even lust. He unzipped his pants and stepped in front of a urinal. Who gave a damn now? The act, not the reason behind it, was all that mattered. After relieving himself, he returned to the sink, washed himself off, and zipped up his pants. As he started to turn away, he caught a glimpse of himself in the mirror.

He looked the same as he had yesterday, his expression was still cool and confident, but his emotions were in turmoil. There was no way getting around it. He was a bad-ass fool. Any time during the last two days, he could've made love to Claire, but he had kept his dick at half mast, locked securely in a vault of self-imposed restraint. He didn't have to be a psychic to know a quick lay would have long-term consequences that would scare the hell out of the simplest dimwit. It could ruin his chances of building a relationship with Salinas. If he so much as kissed her, she'd sense he was thinking of someone else. Somewhere down the road, women had acquired some sixth sense that told them their men were jerking them around. And, equally important, Claire might assume he had changed his mind, he'd stay with her and not get on that train to Memphis.

He knew he'd messed up, but he figured since he couldn't do anything to change it, he'd have to forget it. But would Claire forget? He cocked a brow, adjusted the lapels on his jacket and walked out the door.

He entered the lounge and saw Claire and Moon sitting at a back table, their heads almost touching, their hands jabbing the air as if accentuating a word or a phrase in their animated conversation.

Rufus debated whether he wanted to join them or head into the bar. He doubted if Claire was confessing his latest sin, but if she was, he didn't want to be around to catch Moon's reaction.

While he tried to decide what to do, Moon raised his hand and motioned for him to take a seat.

"Where you been, man?" He knitted his brows in a petulant frown. "Lenny took off. I hanged around to check if we was playing' tonight. So much shit going' on, I wasn't sure."

"We're playing." Rufus cocked a brow. "With or without Lenny."

"Oh, he come back once he get off his know-it-all soap box," Moon said. "Don't know what got into him." He reached across the table and took Claire's hand. "You didn't take the stuff he been throwing out personal, did you, girl?"

"No, I'm learning not to take anything personal." She looked at Rufus in surprise. "You sure you're going to play? Ella might kick us out when she hears what happened in there." She inclined her head in the direction of the restroom.

"What you talking, girl? You saying Ella be that mad cause Rufus brought you along tonight?"

Claire shrugged and threw out her hand.

"Ella runs hot and cold," Rufus said. "If she's got a fever tonight, it won't be because Claire's here." He averted his eyes. He knew Ella. She'd raise the roof when she found out what happened in the ladies room.

"Hey, man, if Lenny don't play, I don't play," Moon said.

"Ella isn't going to bag me or the band." Rufus looked at Claire. "If she gets testy, I'll take the fall for what went down in the throne room."

"Throne room?" Moon slapped the table and let out a roar. "Man, you're shucking and jiving if you're calling this place a throne room."

Moon's laughter melted the ice crystals in Claire's eyes. "I think we're talking about two different things," she said.

"Yeah? How so?"

"Never mind." Claire gave her head a shake. "Let's talk music."

"I know there's a lot going on 'tween you and Ella, but you never gonna have to worry 'bout being outta work. You got talent. Maybe Ella forgets that sometimes, but deep down, she knows. She knows we're good, otherwise why else would she keep the Rufus Johnson band on payroll?"

"You're right," Claire said. "I'll be better off if I concentrate on my music." She shot a sideways glance at Rufus. "But it won't be easy."

Rufus flinched. He had hoped that he and Claire could come to an understanding before he left, but her anger and hard-nose attitude told him it wasn't going to happen. In her mind, he was leaving her for another woman. No matter how many times he explained it, he doubted if she would believe he was going to

Memphis to be with his son. After that scene in the ladies' john, how could he blame her?

He checked his watch. "Looks like Lenny's gone for the afternoon. Might as well pack up so we can get back in time for our first set this evening."

He stood up and walked to the bandstand. As he started to disassemble his sax, he heard the click of high heels hitting the wooden floor. His heart sank. He didn't have to turn around to know Ella was fast approaching, snorting fire and brimstone.

"What you think you're doing? You done lose you motherfucking mind?" Ella grabbed his arm and spun him around to face her. "Less you want me to kick your sorry ass from here to kingdom come, get you black butt in my office now."

Anger crept up Rufus's neck and tightened his jaw muscles.

"I'm not hard of hearing, and I don't have a motherfucking mind. If you want to talk, all you got to do is ask."

"If it please you, Mr. Johnson, in my office." Ella narrowed her eyes and stalked away.

CHAPTER EIGHT

Rufus followed Ella into her office with a stiff dignity that concealed his muddled thoughts. Ella's temper was colossal, but, like a prizefighter on his way down, her punches stirred the air but hit nothing. One look at her blazing eyes told him this time she would aim for the jugular.

She stomped to her desk, spun around, and swung her massive arm at Rufus, barely missing his chin.

"You dumb ass nigger. If I weren't a lady, I'd break your mouth wide open, but it'd be a waste. You're so damn fucked up. You do six months in the white man's jail for using, then you gansta limp back home, swear you're going straight, then make a damn fool out of yourself humping a white chick in the ladies john."

"Get out of my face, woman. That white chick is Claire Burton. You know her. She played bass here in your lounge for over a year. If you got a gripe, amen, but cut the racist shit." He sucked in his breath and waited until his anger dissipated before he continued. "You got a right to chew my ass. I was an idiot, and I'm sorry. Blame me, not Claire."

"You're a proud man, Mister Johnson, but that pride gonna be your death. Less than a year ago, you were snorting white dust and sleeping with a white woman. It wasn't none of my business, so I kept my nose outta it. I figured you needed a woman, and she filled the bill. I thought you were done with each other when you and her rode different wagons outta town. Then she came back. I knew she was trouble, but I never figured you were looking for trouble. Don't know what you were thinking, but whatever it was, it came from that thing hanging between your legs, not from your brain."

"Since you're so all-fire set on dogging me, explain what I wasn't thinking?" Rufus pressed his tongue against his front teeth to keep from telling his bullheaded boss woman to buzz off. Trouble was, his messing around was her business.

"You couldn't been thinking when you nailed that snow bunny to the wall. You're right on one point. It wasn't her doing. No way she coulda nailed you. What really gets my blood boiling is knowing you weren't thinking about Salinas or Rufe Junior. You got a good woman waiting in Memphis and a son you never seen. Don't make sense you acting like a coochie-sniffing low life." She paused and took a deep breath before continuing. "You're a good man, Rufus Johnson, when you put your mind to it. If I didn't respect you, I'd call that Nazi pig Syd Garret, 'n tell 'im you done broke parole. That man hates you. He's waiting to put you back in the hole. But Salinas is waiting, too. She been hurt enough, what with her ma dying and you dumping her."

"You're wrong," he said, his voice simmering with barely checked anger. "I didn't dump Salinas. She dumped me. She could've contacted me over the years. Obviously, she's been keeping up with my whereabouts. She had to know I was looking for her. But that doesn't matter now. She did what she had to do." He paused long enough to curb his anger. "I can't excuse what Claire and I did in the ladies john, and I owe you an apology. Tess, too. Boot me out, but don't tell me you're going to call in the uniform. You give robo cop a foot in my door, I'll dis you and your club from here to catfish heaven."

"Now who's doing the threatening?" Ella snorted.

"I'm not threatening. I'm telling you the way it is. Word gets around you sold out a brotha, you better hire a disc jockey. No black band'll ever work here again." His rage mounted. "I won't go back to prison. I served my time. My parole's up next week. Only way I won't get on that Memphis train is if I'm dead. You want me dead, tell Garret how I made a jack ass out of myself. That blue light special would like nothing better'n to pump a slug in my skull. But before you give him my name, read Claude McKay's poem, 'If We Must Die.' Don't know it all by heart, but I remember some."

He ran his tongue over his dry lips and spoke out in his strong, masculine voice:

"If we must die, let it not be like hogs
Hunted and penned in an inglorious spot."

Rufus hem-hawed several more passages and then recited the last lines in soap-box oratory.

"Like men, we'll face the murderous, cowardly pack,
Pressed to the wall, dying, but fighting back."

Ella harrumphed and flicked a piece of lint off the tip of her massive breast. "Didn't say I was gonna do it. Just said I be thinking about it." She fell heavily onto her chair. "Benny Gees' band won't start till a week from Friday, two days after you leave for Memphis. All I ask is for you to blow your horn 'n stop acting like a river rat dragging your brain on you tail."

"You got a deal. I promise, no more screw ups." He headed to the door, turned, and looked at Ella with a sheepish grin. "It might not be the best time to mention this, but Claire'd like to play a couple of sets. It's your call."

Ella choked on her laughter. "You pushing me to the edge, but I ain't gonna jump. Your snow bunny ain't welcome in my club. She don't make trouble, she be trouble."

"I take that as a no," Rufus said.

"You is finally listening. Ain't that a bitch."

"I'm listening, but I don't like what I'm hearing. Come on, woman. Haven't you learned anything in your fifty years? Skinning Claire cause she's white doesn't even the score for all the years whitey was skinning blacks."

"I ain't skinning her cause she white. Nobody, black or white, gonna play my club if she's trouble."

"You let Claire play last year. Why are you against her now?"

Ella stared at her dragon-red thumb nail. "I ain't against her. She plays a fine bass, 'n if she stays off coke, I got no problem with her playing. But I gotta tell you, a couple red- necked coppers been sniffing around. They want free drinks and a ten under the table to keep things peaceful. For damn sure, they don't like black and white clubs. That white snakeroot Lieutenant Garret's the worst. He come by last week asking for a payoff. I pay him. I got to, but when he asks about you, I tell him to take a walk. He wanna know if you're clean. Shit! He don't know what clean is." She snorted. "I bet that motherfucker don't know to wipe hisself after he doodoo."

Rufus knitted his brows. "Ella, be careful. You shoot off your mouth, and that cracker'll get you for sure."

"I hates the man, 'n he scare the holy ghost outta me when he floats in like a vampire, but your neck's the one he wanna suck blood from." Tears clouded her large, brown eyes. "You're outta here in a week. Why you wanna mess with that white chick anyway?"

"Since when is letting Claire play in my band messing?"

"Don't know. Don't care. Just saying the way it sits with that blue devil." A twitch tugged her right eyelid.

"That isn't the way it is, and it's not the way it's going to be. That son-of-a-bitch isn't going to take me down. I'm clean, and I don't live on no fucking plantation. Tell me if he shows up again. I'll take him on."

"You and your stupid pride!" Ella shook her head. "You ain't gonna take nothing to nobody. I worry 'bout you as if you was my own. I know you're 'ornery 'n stubborn as a ghetto cur, but don't never forget the badge man got the power to ream your ass." She threw out her hand. "Hell, I'm sick a talking about it. Tell Claire she can play. Just don't be expecting me to like it."

"Thanks, sweet mama." He smiled. "I owe you." He ran his finger around his collar and took a deep breath. "And don't you worry about Garret. I'll be cool, but I won't let him hang me on a tree and watch me jerk like the dude in Billie Holiday's 'Strange Fruit.'"

"Don't talk like that. The devil'll hear you." She exhaled an asthmatic wheeze.

"Garret's the only devil I know, and he's deaf, dumb, and ignorant."

"Only takes one to mess up your life." Ella stared at the floor, a blank expression on her face.

Rufus bit his lip. He'd seen that expression so many times, it was almost a cliche: homefolks sitting in a car, the men in blue beaming their lights on them. Blood pounding in their temples, sweat glazing their upper lips, they sat mummy-like, their hands on their laps staring straight ahead, like deer frozen in position. A deflated feeling washed over him. He could handle her aggression but not her submission.

Rufus ordered a double scotch and sat at the far end of the bar. He wanted to be alone and sort out his thoughts before be returned to the bandstand. He had finished half his drink before he realized the alcohol made him feel worse. He thought about all the great jazz musicians who screwed up their lives with liquor and drugs. Miles Davis blew himself away on coke and coochie. Ben Webster drowned in a bottle. Lester Young swilled on gin with a sherry tracer and accompanied Billie Holiday on rocky mountain highs. Rufus took another swallow, then set his glass on the bar and stared at the amber liquid as if it were a crystal ball filled with ghostly images of a not-so-long-ago past. Jazz men played to the tune of a different drummer. They lived fast and died young, but before they took the high road to nowhere, they created sounds never heard before or since. With a groan, he gulped down the last of his drink and slammed down his glass.

What in the world was he doing? Trying to justify his free-wheeling life style? Take the cash, let the credit go. He gave his head a shake. He made mistakes. He paid his dues. When Salinas left him before their son was born, he thought he'd be unhappy forever. When he fell in love with Claire, he thought he'd be happy forever. He was wrong on both counts. He thought his slate was clean, but one problem remained. If he wanted to raise his son, he'd have to give up Claire. After seeing her again, he realized how hard that was going to be, but nothing in his life had been easy. Why should this be any different?

He returned to the lounge and was relieved to see Claire and Moon ragging on the bandstand. At least they had made peace with each other. He eased himself into a shadowy corner and listened. His relief turned into surprise. They sounded damn good considering they hadn't played together for half a year. Like diners skimming a buffet table, they sampled tunes, hip-hopping from blues to jazz and rag to rap with a little bossa nova in between.

Claire's fixed smile reflected the mental concentration and physical strain of playing a large, yet fragile, piece of wooden sculpture. Steel strings wrapped around gut formed calluses on her finger tips. The strain of pressing the neck strings to change the pitch built rock-hard biceps in her right arm. Her passion for the bass and her ear for notes and phrases came out loud and clear when she set the strong pulse and powerful vibrations that determined the rhythm's heartbeat.

Rufus's heart thumped when she finished strumming a solo of "Wrap Your Troubles in Dreams," and Moon, surrounded by his drum kit, joined in. Maintaining the tempo, he sshhhhhed and thwacked and jabbed, and ended the performance with a sensational flourish on the crash symbol.

Rufus stepped out of the shadows and applauded them, a grin stretching across his face.

"You cats aren't just grooving. You're digging a trench." He hit Claire and Moon with a high five and opened his saxophone case. "Now it's my turn."

He assembled his horn, fixed his mouthpiece, and improvised the mood-bending ballad "Moon River." He closed his eyes and saw himself drifting down a lazy stream, accompanied by silver notes and whitecapped licks. Claire and Moon came in, setting the groove to maintain the tune's lush sensuality.

Midway through the piece the music stopped. Rufus was so engrossed in his playing, several moments passed before he heard the silence. He looked up and saw Lenny walking toward them. His throat tightened. Was he in for another tirade on black is beautiful and white sucks?

He studied Lenny's features with a critical squint. The man's implacable expression told him nothing, but his disheveled appearance hinted at dissension. The blustery wind had ruffled his lacquered conk. Not until the overhead spotlight beaded Lenny did Rufus see the hint of a smile pinching his mouth.

Rufus released his tension with a mild expletive and offered his hand. Lenny shouldered past him, stepped in front of Claire, and gave her a hard stare.

Sweat beaded Rufus's forehead. What the hell was going on? Had he misread Lenny's expression? Had his smile been a sneer? When Lenny raised his arms, Rufus tensed, preparing to jump in if he tried to hit her. Instead, Lenny pulled her to him and gave her a rib-crushing hug.

"Figured all the jackasses don't live in Missouri." Lenny rolled back his top lip and mimicked a braying Missouri mule. "I'm standing at the bar hearing you groove, 'n it come to me I got no right to bra strap you cause you is a white chick." He smiled. His gold tooth sparkled under the spotlight's glare. "Don't matter what color folks is or what kind of pee-plumbing they got, talent's all that matters, 'n you got it, girl."

"Thanks, Lenny," Claire said. "Hearing you say that means a

lot to me." She laid her hand on his arm. "You and Moon and Ella remember all the carnival stuff I threw at you. I was walking a high wire and a free fall was the only way down. The mess it caused when I hit the floor splattered all over you. I'd be pissed, too, if the tables were turned." She took a deep breath and glanced at Rufus. "In less than a week, we'll be going our separate ways. I hope that's enough time for me to put things right."

Lenny shrugged. "We done enough talking. Let's jive." He hung up his coat and hat, then sat down at the piano. His gold grin burnishing his ebony skin, he left-handed a chord and right-handed the melody to the ballad, "The Way You Look Tonight." The others joined him. Moon spelled out the tempo. Claire "walked" in with a "four to the floor" beat, Rufus growled out the melody on his sax. Taking turns, they created call and response, melody-rhythm, and rhythm-melody phrasings.

Oblivious of time, they played two sets before Ella broke their magic spell by pointing to the empty tables and flickering flames on waning candles.

"Get yourselves on home," she said. "Ain't half dozen people come in. No sense playing to an empty house." She smiled at Claire. "You're not the fault. Weather's not fit for penguins. You're plucking a fine bass. Reminds me of old times. Makes me sad thinking it's got to end."

"You're speaking for all of us," Rufus said.

Everyone fell silent as if struck dumb by Ella's somber comment. Soon, too soon, all the time and work they spent perfecting their style and creating a whole out of four parts would come to a sorry end.

Long buried emotions welled up in Rufus. He prepared himself for the heartache of losing Claire forever, but he wasn't prepared for the loss of his friends, his band, and even Ella. The thought of building a new life when he got to Memphis overwhelmed him. He'd have to reestablish a relationship with a stranger, connect with his son, and launch a full-scale campaign to get gigs and hook up with booking agents, club owners, and critics—the battalion of white chiefs who controlled the jazz industry in Memphis.

"It's getting late," he said. "Time to pack up and hit the road." Shrugging in mock resignation, he disassembled his sax and returned it to its velvet-lined case. He high-fived Moon and Lenny, kissed Ella, and walked out of the lounge with Claire at his side.

Lost in thought, Rufus ignored Claire on the ride home. He helped her out of the car and walked silently up the stairs. He unlocked the door and pushed it open with his foot. The cheerless room reflected his dark mood.

Claire threw her parka on the sofa and set her bass on the floor. Like a bewildered child, she retreated to the far end of the room and crossed her arms in front of her. "Is it okay if I spend the night?"

He shot her a cold look. "Why 're you asking such a stupid question? You think I'm going to kick you out?"

"Last night you said you wanted me gone."

"You know as well as I do, you staying here is not good, but it's too damn late and too damn cold to take you home." He shrugged and headed into the kitchen. "Another night won't be the end of the world. For sure, I'll take you home tomorrow."

He grabbed his scotch bottle and filled a glass. He stood in front of the window and stared at the street lamp encircled in a halo of snow.

"Life can sure pitch a long ball," he said. "I thought six months in the joint was the worst, but damn if this isn't coming close."

"What does 'this' mean?" Claire stepped behind him and wrapped her arms around his waist.

"My life. What's happening. I'm so screwed up, I'm afraid to think. When I was in the joint, I lost everything, my name, my rights, my free will. As bad as it was, I knew it'd end. Six months in, six months out. What I'm looking at now won't ever end." He took a drink of scotch, savored its malty, pungent bite, and sighed, thankful some things never changed.

Claire released her hold and circled around to face him. "You saying you're going to lose your rights, your free will when you go to Memphis?"

"Hell, I don't know what I'm saying. It's hard to put feelings into words."

"Are you afraid?"

"Maybe." He took another sip and frowned. The scotch had lost its bite. "No, not afraid like I was when I went to prison. I'm worried. I'm taking on a new life. I'm not sure I can handle it." He looked at Claire, and a flash of loneliness stabbed his heart. She was everything he had ever wanted in a woman: sensual, talented, bitchy, lovable, warm, cold, good, bad. Most importantly, she loved him unconditionally and never tried to change him. He bit back a cynical smile. Why would she want to change him? They possessed the same traits and shared the same emotions. He leaned down and kissed her nose.

"I guess I am afraid... afraid of losing you, of going back to jail, of going to Memphis, of being a lousy father to my boy." He gave his head a hard shake. "Shit, I'm afraid of everything." He chugged the rest of his drink and poured another. "I guess a lousy father is better'n none. I would've been happy to have my old man around, even if he wasn't a story-book dad. But that's all beside the point. I'm going to love my boy like he's never been loved before." He clenched his hand into a fist. "That's got to count for something."

Claire exhaled loudly. "I envy Rufe. I know how much love you have inside you." She touched his arm. "Everything's going to work out, but you have to stop being afraid. Fear isn't a problem, but drinking yourself into a stupor is. You don't have to be a genius to figure out if you can't change things, you have to deal with them."

"And how does one deal with things without liquor or pot?"

"By talking. By getting your fears and hangups out of your system."

"It's not that simple."

"Oh, but it is." Claire sat down and tapped her index finger on her chin. "If you had told me you had a woman and a son waiting for you in Memphis, I would've been hurt and angry, but it wiped me out when I heard it from Lenny. You betrayed me. You betrayed my trust."

"I explained my reasons. You want me to go over 'em again?"

"Once is enough." She shook her head in exasperation. "I'm trying to explain why I stomped off like a jealous teenager. I wish I hadn't, especially in front of Lenny and Moon. They must've been saying to themselves, 'here we go again.'"

Rufus stared at her in amazement. He wasn't sure if it was her choice of words or the tone of her voice, but he understood what she was saying. She was still hurting, but her anger was gone.

"Let's drop it," he said.

"Fine with me." She shot him a speculative glance. "What now?"

"Same as last night. Go to bed."

"My suitcase is still in the car."

"I'll get it later. You can wear my pajamas. I got a pair some-place."

"Have you forgotten? I don't wear pajamas," she said in a deep, dusty voice.

"Damn!" he muttered. There it was again, that familiar flame of arousal. Didn't it ever go out? He studied her with a critical squint, hoping to find a hint of derision, disgust, anger... any emotion that would diminish the heat rising inside him. He groaned. No such luck! She was and always would be a cuddly, sexy, blissfully beautiful woman who could turn him on with the flick of her brow or the lick of her tongue.

Claire slid her arms around his neck and raised her eyes to his. "Come to bed with me. If nothing else, you can warm the sheets." She planted a flirtatious kiss on his lips.

A warning bell went off in his head. If they fell back into their old routine of sex, drinking, and performing, where would it end? How in the hell could he get on the train to Memphis knowing what he was leaving behind? He searched her face, look-ing for that dark cloud of hostility that would extinguish the tiny spark of desire. Instead, her sparkling eyes and flushed cheeks fanned the flame to a blazing inferno.

"It's taking you a long time to decide," she said. "What's the matter? Aren't you in the mood?"

He looked at her in astonishment. Couldn't she smell his arousal?

"Say something," she said. Her kittenish purr hardened to an irritable rasp. "Tell me, do you want to make love?"

His blood coursing through his veins like a river of bubbling lava, he locked his hand around her neck and kissed her with a savage intensity. His passion overriding reason, he thrust his tongue into her mouth and probed its velvety lining. His hunger satiated, he lifted his head and looked at her, his smile radiating a happiness he hadn't felt in months.

"Does that answer your question?"

"It's a start." She smiled back at him.

"No sense stopping now." His pulse quickened. He swept her in his arms, carried her through the beaded doorway, and laid her on the bed. After stripping off his clothes, he undressed Claire with slow, sensual movements. As he slipped between the cold sheets, she rose up on her elbows and looked at him, deep worry lines furrowing her brow.

"I love you, Rufus. I want you, but not if you don't want me." Her stare drilled into him. "What we did at Ella's. That wasn't love. It was a hard fuck, filled with anger and frustration. We messed up when we were living together, the fights, the drugs, the whole ugly scene, but we loved each other. We didn't even have to say it. I don't know what your feelings are now. You're going to move to Memphis, live with Salinas, raise your son. Where does that leave me?"

"I can't answer that." He met her accusing eyes, his misgivings rising to the surface of his consciousness. He knew what he had to do. He had to go to Memphis. Claire had to go home. They had to give up the past and plan for the future. He swallowed his anguish and ran his fingers through her short, curly hair. That was tomorrow; they still had tonight.

He gripped her waist and pulled her to him. "Would it help if I said I loved you?"

"It wouldn't hurt, but only if you mean it."

He lowered his head and brushed her lips with shivery kisses.

"I love you, Claire, but forget the dreams. They're dead." He ran his hand over her breast, down her belly, and parted her thighs. He responded to the passion radiating from her body like a flower seeking the sun.

CHAPTER NINE

Mingus, Miles, Leary, Lester. White powder. Purple haze. Mint dew. Claire. Drugs, music, sex. The story of his life. Rufus rolled on his back, opened his eyes, and stared at the dim rays of the winter sun seeping through the bedroom window.

He groaned and pulled a pillow over his face. *"This'll be the day that I die."* *If I'm lucky.*

He thought he could handle anything. He had survived six months in prison, gotten off dope, cut back on his drinking. Why in the hell couldn't he give up Claire? He reached over to touch her, but her side of the bed was empty. He bolted up and pressed his fingers on his throbbing temples. Where was she? Where'd she go? Damn! He did it again. Why the hell couldn't he make love once, maybe twice, and let it go at that? Shit! He had plunged in like a deep-sea diver, not caring if he ever reached the surface again.

Claire! He had to be driving her crazy with his on-again, off-again blues. He was driving himself crazy. He couldn't stay away from her, and he didn't want to. She was an obsession, a passion that wouldn't die. He rolled on his side and smelled the lingering, heady scents of sex and gardenias. He groaned. What the hell was he going to do? He threw back the covers and jumped out of bed. For starters, he was going to shower, shave, and put on an idiot's face. No more gloom and doom. What was the big deal anyway? They'd been separated for a year. Why, all of a sudden, was it so damn hard to leave her? Because this time their separation would be final, no wavering, no second thoughts. He was going to Memphis, and that was that.

He felt good after his shower, and good escalated to better when he smelled the aroma of freshly brewed coffee coming from the kitchen. He drew a T-shirt and cable knit sweater over his head, stepped into a pair of black, tight-fitting trousers and scuffed loafers, and burst through the beaded doorway with a smile on his face.

He approached Claire who was hunched over the table flipping through the latest issue of the *Rolling Stone*. Only the upbeat recording of Memphis Slim barrelhousing "Every Day I Have the Blues," moderated the glacial coldness radiating off her body.

"Good morning," he said, his strident tone demanding a response.

She nodded.

"How you feeling?"

"Okay."

He took a gulp of coffee. "Did you get a good night's sleep?"

"It was okay." She turned up the collar on her pink robe and turned a page.

"What the hell does okay mean?"

"It means the only time I woke up was when you jabbed me with your knee or elbow. You're used to sleeping alone, I presume."

"I could've told you that. In fact, I think I did." He pulled up a chair, sat down, and pondered his next move. Should he put his arm around her, kiss her, ignore her? He knew she was upset, but he didn't know why. He gave his head a shake. And he thought he had irrational mood swings!

"Okay. I get the message. You're mad. You're wishing you could cut my dick off and shove it up a dark hole. Maybe you got a right, but come on, give me some slack." He paused, then spurted out in a defensive tone. "It wasn't all my fault. You could've told me to stop."

"I don't know what you're talking about." Claire shoved his hand away and stabbed him with an arctic glare.

"I'm talking about last night, about making love, or screwing, or whatever in the hell you want to call it."

"Then you do know the difference." A cynical smile played on her face.

Rufus let out a low whistle. "If you're saying I slammed you just for sex, you're wrong. I was making love. I needed to feel you, touch you, devour you, but if you really believe I'm a selfish bastard who took care of my own needs, all I can say is I'm sorry and try to keep my hands off you."

"I'm not looking for an apology," Claire said. A jaded sadness crept into her voice. "All I want to know is how you can make love to me when you know you're going to go to Memphis and live with Salinas."

"Salinas has nothing to do with us. She's Rufe Junior's mother. I don't think about her romantically, and I'm sure she doesn't think about me like that either. Sure, I loved her once. We had a son, but Jeesh… that was ten years ago." He pushed the magazine across the table and gripped her chin, forcing her to look at him. "I know this is rough on you, and it's not a bed of roses for me, but we got to make the most of the time we have left. I want to be with you. I want to have good memories of our time togeth-

ELSA COOK

er. Last night, when we played our first set, we were making music like I never heard before. Shit, didn't you hear it? The tempos, grooves, and rhythms were right on. Everything we tried worked. It was so fine. Better than a snort of coke. We were playing the kind of vibes a musician looks for all his life."

"Yeah. I heard it. Too bad we didn't record it. All the same, what has that got to do with your sex drive?"

"You're not hearing me," Rufus said with a note of impatience in his voice.

"I hear words, but I don't sense their meaning."

"You been high before. You never want to come down. When you do, you can't handle the pain and you do crazy stuff. That's the way I felt when we were making love. I was missing you while I was holding you in my arms. Aw shit! I guess I was selfish. I was caught up in my needs and my pain." He fell silent and worked the muscles in his jaw. The butterfly touch of Claire's breath on his cheek eased his tension. "I never saw my son, but I've always loved him. I guess it's some kind of gene thing, hoping I passed on my good stuff and hoping I didn't pass on my shit. It scares the hell out of me. I know music. I don't know anything about being a father."

Claire's mood changed from cool to hot. "You telling me you put on a guerrilla suit when you slammed me against the wall in Ella's ladies room? That doesn't make sense. Even when we were high and licking the floor for powder, you never played the tough guy. In my mind, that made you a man. You're still a man. Why're you running scared now?"

"When we were together, I didn't worry about the future or sweat the past. Now I can't think about anything else. I'm so

85

damned confused. I got a whole list of stuff to worry about, you, my son, giving up my gig at Ella's, Salinas, finding work in Memphis. Rufe's my main worry. He must wonder why I haven't been around for ten years. Did Salinas and her mom blame it on me? My old man took off before I was born. I never would've done that to Rufe, but I couldn't stop Salinas and Maybelle from taking off. They made the choice then, now it's my turn."

"Listening to you makes me think I'm the one being selfish. All I can think about is losing you forever." She touched his brow and ran her finger down his cheek to his lips. "I love you. You're my Adonis, strong and muscular, virile and stormy, yet generous and loving. When you were arrested, and later, when I was in rehab, I never dreamt I'd lose you. I figured once we got our shit together, we could live a normal life, play music, make love, do whatever couples do… maybe even have a baby."

"You're living in a dream world," he interrupted. "I'm not an Adonis, and we're not going to have a baby. I'm going to Memphis, and you're going home."

"I can't stop you from leaving, but I don't have to go home." She brushed away the tears misting her eyes and stood up. "It's getting late. I'm going to take my shower. We'll barely have time to dress, eat, and get to the club for the first set."

"The club?" He looked at her, baffled. "Where'd you get the idea you were going to play tonight?"

"Ella said I could."

"And I said you were going home." Rufus gripped her hand. "It's not that I don't want you, but damn it, woman, this arrangement is not working. After you get settled, you can come to the club, you can play every night, but you can't stay here."

"Oh, I see," she said. "Screw the broad and send her packing. Is that the way it is?"

"NO, that is not the way it is. I told you …" He paused, stung by her absurd remark. He told her she couldn't stay; he explained why. Was she deaf or just stubborn? Either way, she hadn't listened. He glanced at the clock hanging over the sink. She was right about one thing; they were running out of time. Faced with the choice of arguing with her for another hour or explaining to Ella why he was late, he decided to let Claire stay another night.

He threw up his hands. "Go take your shower and don't use up all the hot water, or Clarence'll have my hide."

CHAPTER TEN

Rufus and Claire blew into Ella's on a gust of cold air and slammed into a wall of hip hop brothers and foxy sisters grandstanding their wares. Beefy grunts and shrill laughter filled the room.

"What the hell?" Rufus said with a growl. "Looks like we've been invaded by a pack of tail-twitching, hip-hopping Jack and Jills." He waved at Bojay to get his attention, but the man was elbow deep in an ice cooler bobbing for beers.

"Take a deep breath and keep your head down," he told Claire. "We're gonna blitz our way through this mess."

A bullnecked gorilla with mallet-sized fists stopped them at the entrance to the lounge. "Hold up there, man. You can't take that in with you." He pointed at Rufus's saxophone case.

"Who are you, and what the hell're you talking about?" Rufus said.

He looked up, studied Rufus's face, and backed away. "Sorry, Mr. Johnson. Didn't recognize you." He stepped back. "Name's Ish, Miss Ella's bouncer."

Rufus snorted. "You're not going to pat us down?"

"Just doing my job," Ish said, his words cold and exact. "Ella say I gotta check for Candy Cane. Blue boys been hanging around. She don't want no trouble." He flashed a courteous smile and offered his hand. "Glad to meet you, Mr. Johnson. Word out you the best sax player around." He inclined his head at the subdued crowd sitting around the tables. "Them cats got the fever for you. It's costing them a cover charge and two-drink minimum to hear you up front."

Rufus exhaled his tension. "Thanks for the plug." He introduced Claire and shot an approving glance at the audience. "We haven't had a crowd like this since winter set in."

Ish nodded and thumped them inside as the line began to lengthen.

Rufus walked to the bandstand and raised the velvet rope separating it from the dance floor. He and Claire slipped under and bumped into Moon who had come from behind his drums and hurried toward them.

"Hey, man," he said. "I'm thinking you ain't gonna show."

"What're all these cables doing on the floor? Who set up the electronic equipment? Is Ella planning a karaoke night?"

"Shit no, man. A super cat's coming to hear us." He sported a ragged grin. "He's gonna turn us into big-time celebrities."

"What kind of celebrities?" Claire asked.

"Wassa matter with you, woman? Didn't you never hear the word before?"

"There are celebrities, and then there are celebrities. Where do we fit in?" She glanced at Rufus.

He shrugged and threw out his hands.

"Don't you know nothing?" Moon pointed to a finger-snapping dude who stepped out from behind a curtain.

"What's up?" He peered at Rufus through smoke-colored shades. "Hey, you're Rufus Johnson, right?" He held out his hand. "Name's Harry Stump. Rhymes with hump. The Stumping Hump." He flashed a gold grin.

"Mr. Stump." Rufus took the man's limp hand and gave it a hard shake. "Mind telling us what's going on?"

Stump looked at Moon. "How come the man don't know what's coming down? Ella said everything was set." He frowned. "Maybe she forgot. But don't sweat it. You got an hour before we go on the air."

"Air?" Rufus cocked a brow.

Stump pulled him and Claire aside and downloaded his message. The NAACP regional chapter opened its semi-annual conference. The hotel canceled the kick-off party when a frozen pipe burst and flooded the kitchen. The entertainment director saw Ella's flier promoting the club's hot food and cool jazz available every night, no reservations required."

"Did you know about this?" Rufus asked Moon.

"Ella called me 'round three 'n says for me to buzz you. I tried four times. No answer. Finally decided your phone was dead. I figured you'd call in if you weren't planning to show."

"What about you?" Rufus looked at Stump. "You part of the act?"

Stump cocked his brow. "KRAP is the biggest Black owned radio station in the state. We're not an act. We're music, news, and politics. We're the voice of African-Americans." His expression sweetened as if he were looking at a simpleton who meant well but didn't quite get it. "Hear me out. At nine o'clock, we'll beam into folks' homes. I'll tell them we're transmitting from Ella's Lounge, give her a plug, and introduce the Rufus Johnson Quartet. You play a couple tunes. I break in, give 'em a rundown on jazz and black musicians, you play a few more tunes, we cut off. You go home. I go home. Maybe a record man hears your music, remembers your name. You'll make a few bucks. The NAACP cats'll have a good time. Everybody'll be happy."

For the next half hour, Rufus hung onto that thought as he and the band chose their music, keeping in mind the NAACP members were not improv, free jazz, rap fanatics. When they finished, Claire moved close to Rufus and tugged his arm.

"Is that guy for real?" she asked.

Rufus shrugged.

"Wouldn't it be great if he is? We could get..." She paused. "You could get national recognition. Maybe even make the cover of the *Rolling Stone.*"

He grinned and threw her a kiss. "You were right the first time. We'd get recognition. All of us. Moon, Lenny, you."

Before she could protest, Stump gripped the mike and announced the African-American Jamming Jive Music Hour. After giving the live audience a brief run down on their struggles to right the wrongs of America's native sons and daughters, he promised a short but genuine history of black music from plantation days to the present. "But first," he said, "a word from our hostess, Ella Edwards."

"Honey, I'll talk later. Right now, I'm gonna belt out a song so they know I'm not one of the fixtures." She grabbed the microphone from Stump and broke into an a cappella scat. Her gold-and-green chiffon caftan swirled around her body like a luminous vapor.

When she finished her solo, Rufus's heart swelled with pride. He wondered why she wasted her tremendous talent. He gave his head a shake. Maybe she hadn't wasted it. Maybe she set it aside when she bought the lounge and turned it into a jazz club. The entertainers, the audiences, and the steady money were more gratifying than a one-night gig in a two-horse town. He had to give the lady credit. She sure as hell knew how to work an audience.

Ella finished her overture with an airborne kiss and winked at Rufus. "It's all yours, baby," she whispered. "Show 'em what you can do."

Rufus tipped his horn and opened the session with the forlorn wail of a train hurling through a fog-shrouded night.

The rhythm section broke in with the melody, and Moon ended the romantic ballad "Body and Soul" with a hot lick on a the crash cymbal. Lenny followed with a solo rendition of Ellington's "Mood Indigo."

During the break, Stump rapped with the audience, took a few home calls, and pitched his history of jazz in a rapid-fire trill.

"Drumbeats send out the warning. White devil coming," he shouted.

"Tell it," the audience responded.

"Slave sounds—drumbeats, chains, howls—mingle in the ship's dark belly."

"Dark, brotha, dark."

"The harmony rises outta the belly of the whale and festers under the southern sun."

"No escaping hell's fire."

"We hears 'bout heaven. We picks cotton, cuts cane. We sings spirituals, but the sun get hotter, the rows longer. The man with the beard freed our bodies, but the man with the whip still owned our souls. We try to leave, but the tarred roads made travelin' slow. Our women grow old, our men bitter. We sit under the

Southern Cross and sing the blues."

Rufus and his band entered the lounge and walked single-file to the stage. Stump frowned, checked the clock, then continued his story double time.

He skimmed the ragtime era, swept through the Twenties jazz scene, hopped over the Forties big-band sounds, white-capped Bird, Diz, and Miles's bebop revolution, and etceteraed the artists who sired free jazz, rap, and hip hop.

It was two in the morning when they finished the jam session that followed the show's radio segment. By then, the most hip of the hoppers were gone.

Their throats raw, their eyes bleary, the band members stumbled out of the hot, smoky bar into the cold, morning air. They hung together in the parking lot, checking to be sure their cars started. Lenny fired up first. Idling his ten-year-old Cadillac, he stuck around until Rufus's engine turned. With a wave and a honk, he and Moon fishtailed across the ice-covered asphalt and skidded into the street. Rufus followed at a slower pace.

Claire leaned her head on Rufus's shoulder, mumbled something about a fabulous evening, and fell asleep. He glanced down at her, a rueful smile crinkling his mouth.

"You're getting old, babe. A year ago, you'd 've been good for another six hours." He rolled his shoulders and heard his joints snap and pop.

Rufus set his eyes on the road. He didn't like to think about it, but if Claire was old, he was ancient. In the past, he came out of a session feeling high or low, depending on how he played and how the audience responded. Lately, it seemed as if the highs barely passed the half-way mark, and the lows stuck to the bottom of the barrel.

He left Ella's on a high, but too soon he felt the blues coming on. He couldn't trust the good times. Something always went sour. Stump's radio show was the break he'd been waiting for. The band rose to the occasion, playing cool jazz and tender ballads. Even if a recording company executive caught their act, nothing would come of it. He was leaving. The band was breaking up. The thought paralyzed him until he remembered he had seen dark times before and survived.

Five years ago, he formed the Rufus Johnson Quartet: Lenny on piano, Moon on drums, and Otis Hamilton, a humming, strumming dude on bass. With youth on their backs and a smile on their faces, they headed South, following an updated chitlin circuit.

Because the country was desegregated, black, tan, and whites mingled in the bars, clubs, and roadside dance halls. They came to hear gut bucket blues and freestyle jazz. At the end of each session, they'd head out the back door and slip into a dark pine forest. With the owls hooting and the cicadas chirping, they chilled out on China white.

Otis was a bear with a wolf's teeth. His gold smile lit up the night and attracted sleek brown chicks and nimble white foxes. Rufus sat on a moss-covered tree trunk and watched them play ring around the rosy. When they became too lively and the bear too frisky, he lured Otis out of the forest by promising to stop at a cat house on their way out of town.

Otis's games and Rufus's prank worked as long as they played one-night stands. One night, a flash flood stranded them in a road house sitting on an isolated patch of red Alabama soil. After three dreary days of performing, drinking, and sleeping, Otis grew bored. He slipped out a side door while Rufus, Moon, and Lenny were packing up for an early morning getaway. When they realized Otis was gone, they checked the bar and the men's room, saw they were empty, and dashed outside. They flew across the muddy parking lot and stopped at the edge of the woods. Ominous sounds filtered through the foliage. His heart pounding, Rufus sprinted down a weed-choked path into the heart of the forest. Moon and Lenny followed. When the sounds grew louder and more distinct, he motioned for Lenny and Moon to stop, dropped his head, and listened. The yelps and snarls of frenzied hounds gorged the steamy night air and laid a layer of sweat on Rufus's shirt.

"What the fuck's happening?" Terror rippled across Moon's face.

"Shit, I don't know." Rufus peered into the dark void. "Maybe some hunters are bagging a deer."

"This ain't no deer season," Lenny said. "It's against the law."

Rufus rolled his eyes. "Just a guess, but I bet nobody in these parts gives a damn about the law." He walked on. "We got to find Otis. If that pussy-whupped crackhead's hitting on a groupie white chick, we better find him before some skunk-skinning posse does."

They plunged on, breaking their way through a tangle of vine suckers and wild briars. The cloying stench of fetid water and rotting vegetation mounted. So did the darkness. His arms outstretched like a blind man, Rufus slashed his way to a clearing brush and stumbled onto a scene out of a KKK enlistment brochure.

Five beer-barreled, hawk-nosed white men formed a half circle around a stately magnolia tree. They beamed their high-powered lanterns on Otis, who was strapped to the tree, his arms tied above his head, his eyes wide with fear.

"What the fuck's going on?" Rufus stared at faces malignant with hate.

A shotgun blast sent shock waves through the silent forest and started a din of yelps, croaks, and squawks. Rufus dashed into the open area and positioned himself between the jackals and Otis.

"Git your black ass outta here, boy, or the next shell will have your name on it," a man shouted.

"You planning to shoot me, you better do it now cause I'm not moving till you put those fucking guns down and crawl back into your holes."

The end man stepped out of line, then reached under a rotting tree stump and pulled a girl's quivering body into light. Her thin, cotton skirt was in tatters. Her transparent crop top twisted around her rib cage, exposing two pink nipples.

Blood gorged Rufus's temples and thumped a tom-tom beat in his head. "Otis didn't do that. He doesn't rape women."

"That nigger been messin' with our gals three nights straight," the man said. "Almost caught the bastard last night, but he gone afore we get here." He snatched a bloody handkerchief from his back pocket and waved it in the air. "We never found the gal, but this proof enough he raped her."

"Oh, God, I never raped nobody," Otis yelled. "I swear, I never hurt no woman like that."

"This gal say different." He shoved the frightened girl into the light. "We found her all bloodied and swollen. She says the darky raped her. That's all I got to hear."

Moon bounded into the clearing, dreadlocks flying. "You muthafuckas! Otis couldn't 've hurt her. He was with the band up till fifteen minutes ago. If you're thinking he's a big, bad stud, check his pecker. It'd still be wet if he stirred her juices." He raised his arm and shadowboxed the blank-eyed posse. "You crackerbillies like to go down on your own. No sweat to me if it pleasures you to fuck family, but you're not gonna put the blame on my homey."

Gin-scented squeals polluted the air.

"You slime dog! Nobody's gonna call me a liar and a pervert and get away with it." The man grabbed the girl's hair and threw her to the ground. He hunched his shoulders and charged across the open space. His eyes glowing red, he slammed the butt of his shotgun against Moon's head.

Rufus heard bone crack, an agonizing shriek, and a heavy thump. When Moon's body hit the ground, all motion ceased. The sound of footsteps bounding through the thick undergrowth broke the uneasy silence. Rufus looked up and saw Lenny standing beside a tree, his face frozen with fear. the narrow path that opened into the field. He waved his arms in warning.

"Lenny, get out of here," Rufus shouted. "Get the sheriff, anybody. Get help. Now."

It took Lenny several seconds to digest Rufus's warning. Finally he turned tail and darted down a narrow path that led to an open field.

Rufus waited until Lenny disappeared before he turned around. He expected to see one of the vigilantes run after him, but when no one moved, his stomach did a flip. He decided they planned to kill them quickly, or the sheriff was one of them.

He groaned. It didn't matter. He knew they'd be dead before the cavalry arrived. He kneeled beside Moon and pressed a handkerchief to his wound.

"Get up," he said. "You have to get out of here. Make a run for it. It's your only chance."

Moon placed his hand over his bloodied eye. "What the fuck you talking? I can't move. How the hell am I gonna run?"

"If you can't run, crawl," he said. "After I figure out a way to get Otis off the rack, we'll be right behind you."

"You fucking crazy? No way you can do it alone."

"You're wasting time. Shut your mouth 'n move your ass."

"What kinda shit you planning?"

"Don't have a plan. I'll do whatever's necessary." A snarl rode his lips. "Crackers love it when us darkies act the fool. I'll laugh and grin and do a fancy fetch 'n step. If that doesn't work, I'll grab my cock and wail, "Lord have mercy! How you figure a black man could rape a woman? Our peckers're so short, ain't no way we could please a white woman."

Moon looked at him in disbelief. "What you gonna do if they want to see it. Shit! You're hung like a horse."

"I'm not planning to cut it off, but those crackers don't know bullshitting from a hole in the ground."

The posse started to stir. Rufus pulled Moon to a sitting position, gave him a high sign, and stood up.

He rolled his shoulders and swung his hips in an exaggerated gangsta walk as he approached the main man.

"Lynching days are over, but that don't mean you got to go

home empty handed." He hunched his head between his shoulders and grinned. "What say we go back to the roadhouse and down a few? Drinks on me." He did a half turn and pointed at Otis. "Before we go, how 'bout cutting him loose. He never raped that gal. Shit! He got trouble peeing. Ain't no way he going to get it up without a lot of stroking."

The man cocked his head as if trying to decide which would be more fun: sucking some home brew or shooting a black man. He licked his lips and lowered his shotgun to half mast.

A bellow split the stagnant air. The end man ran forward and shoved his gun in the center man's face. "You thinking about drinking with a nigger, it'll be your last drink."

Rufus swallowed a groan. *Shit!* He picked a losing number. The main man was at the end of the line, not the center.

He glanced around and saw that Moon was gone. He mouthed a silent thanks. Somehow Moon had managed to crawl into the underbrush unseen. Now all he had to worry about was how to get Otis and himself out of there. From the looks of it, they wouldn't get a free pass from this holy hell.

The man stopped barfing threats at his fellow creatures and spun around to face Rufus. "Your shit-ass hustle don't fool me none. We gonna teach your coon friend to stay outta the wood shed, and I'm gonna start the lesson."

With the spasmatic jerks of a marionette, he raised his shotgun, pointed it at Otis, and pulled the trigger. A barrage of pellets hit Otis's face, burning his skin and peppering his eyes. He lifted his head and cried out for mercy.

His blood boiling, Rufus kicked the gun from the man's grasp and slammed his fist into the man's jaw. He squealed, fell to his knees, and writhed in pain.

"You fucking son-of-a-bitch. You can't shoot a man and walk away, not today. We got laws."

"You're wrong, nigger. The center man grabbed him from behind and threw him to the ground. "This is white man's country. I'm the law here." He brought his shotgun down on Rufus's skull, raised it, and hit him again. Rufus struggled to remain conscious, but the excruciating pain shut down his body. His vision blurred, his hearing muffled, he released the tension in his muscles and closed his eyes. He didn't fight the darkness. No sense postponing the inevitable. He was going to die.

He awoke to a dusty dawn and smelled nature's sweet, earthy scents. He heard a rooster crow, a dog bark. Tears slid down his cheeks. He'd survived. What about the others?

A loud, rattling noise coming from under the hood of his car brought Rufus back to the present. He looked out the window. He was half a block from the apartment. He eased his foot off the brake, coasted to a parking space, and turned off the ignition. The engine sputtered and died. He leaned over and woke Claire with a kiss.

She opened her eyes, and a frown skittered across her brow. "Why'd you do that? I was having such a wonderful dream. You and I were in this sun drenched garden perfumed with flowers and filled with romantic music."

"Later, babe. I'm tired and cold as hell." He smiled, opened the car door, and flipped her the keys. "I'll grab the instruments. Go on up and unlock the door."

Claire waited for him at the top of the stairs. Wordlessly, she opened the door and stepped inside. She threw her jacket on the sofa and rubbed her hands together to warm them. The tension in the room was audible.

"You coming to bed?"

"Later," he said. "I got some thinking to do."

"I don't get it," she said. "We had a great session. Everything was cool. Why are you acting like some doom-and-gloom preacher man all of a sudden?"

Rufus walked to the sink. He poured himself a scotch, sunk heavily onto his chair, and stared out the window.

He felt her anger. He understood her frustration, but he couldn't cope with the mess of thoughts warring inside his head. His future was vague, his past haunting, his present volatile. He pressed the glass to his lips. With the scotch slowly trickling down his throat, he let his thoughts slip back to the blood-soaked killing field.

Lenny, the hero of the day, made it back to the roadhouse, told the owner there was a black-rock lynching going down, and they better stop it fast unless the man wanted the United States army, the Alabama militia, and the CNN brigades swarming around for the next six months. They arrived in time to save Rufus and Moon, who had fallen into a culvert and passed out, but too late to save Otis.

Rufus poured another drink, trying to lobotomize the gruesome visions of Otis's butchery, and the moratorium on justice when the butchers walked away free.

He felt a hand touch his shoulder. He turned. Claire looked down at him, tears glazing her eyes.

"You thinking about Salinas?" she asked.

He shook his head and sighed heavily.

She took a step back, her eyes boring into him in mute expectation. "Love me," she whispered. "I feel so alone, so afraid."

Rufus rose and pulled her to him. The delicate scent of wildflowers and the musky scent of passion banished his dour thoughts and lit the flame of unrestrained lust. He gripped the back of her neck and kissed her. In a frenzy of desire, he pulled off her robe and lowered her to the floor. His eyes locked on her naked body, he stripped off his pants and shorts and stood over her, his throbbing penis hard and erect like a phallus on an ancient God.

He dropped to his knees and stuck his finger inside her and stroked her until she grew wet. He lifted her buttocks and guided his penis inside her. They clung to each other, groaning and writhing until unbearably rapturous waves smashed over them. The squall receded, and they floated to shore.

CHAPTER ELEVEN

Loud, militant squawks struck Rufus's ear and reverberated inside his head.

"What the hell!" He opened an eye and peered out his bedroom window. A black crow, bloated with the food scraps rotting in the hood's garbage cans, streaked past. It squawked again and returned on the same flight path. Its glossy, blue-black feathers cut an ebony swath across the gray sky.

Rufus threw his arm over his face and recalled his mother's warning, "Black bird squawking, white bird pimping." He touched his forehead, mouth, and heart and mumbled the voodoo incantation she taught him to ward off evil.

He cocked an ear and waited for the crow to squawk again, but all he heard was the wind battering the trash cans in the alley.

He stared at the water marks splotched on the ceiling and chastised himself for acting like a fool. What kind of stuff was he tripping? He wasn't into omens and spells and white-faced devils. Bad luck came and went, and there were too many two-legged devils to put all the blame on a stupid crow.

Smoke-filled air drifted in from the kitchen. He jumped out of bed and grabbed his trousers. By the time he pulled them on, he realized Claire was cooking breakfast but apparently having a tough time of it.

The smell of charred bacon, burnt toast, and boiled coffee followed him into the bathroom. He relieved himself, brushed his teeth, and slapped his face with cold water, but he didn't feel any better than he had before. If anything, he felt worse. Something was wrong. Claire knew how to fry bacon and toast bread, and she took pride in making a good cup of coffee. Was she screwing up on purpose? He stuck his hands in his pockets and walked into the kitchen.

"Good morning," he said with a forced cheerfulness. He filled his coffee cup and sat down at the kitchen table. He strangled a groan when Claire handed him a plate of watery eggs and charred bacon.

"I'll stick with coffee this morning." He eased the plate away and flashed a cautious smile.

"You won't like that either," Claire said.

"You saying the coffee's no good?"

She fell onto a chair and propped her chin in her upraised hands. "It tastes horrible, but it doesn't matter. You'll be leaving next week. You won't have to put up with my cooking anymore." She turned and gazed out the window.

Rufus gripped her shoulder and forced her to look at him. "Last night, everything was fine. This afternoon, nothing's fine. What's going on?"

"I love you. That's what's going on. I love you, and I'm going to lose you. When I think about it too much, and the hurt lasts too long, I want to kick and scream and curse. It's not fair you leaving me for Salinas."

"What's fair? Life's not fair, but if you can't change it, you got to ride it. Getting uptight makes things worse."

"Is that right, doctor know-it-all?" She shot him a defiant look. "It's nice to know you never get funky."

"Why are we arguing? We're up shit creek, and there's no way out." He ran his fingers through Claire's hair. "We've been through this a dozen times. We talked, we cussed, we cried. Why can't you give it up?"

Claire hooted and pushed his hand away. "We're talking about my life," she said. "Let's suppose I'm on death row. I'm going to be executed in four days. You think I'm going to worry about what I'm going to get for my last meal, or what I'm going to wear on my last walk."

"Where the hell do you get these ideas? Death row. Executed." He exhaled loudly. "Woman, you have one hell of an imagination."

"Maybe so, but at least I'm in touch with my feelings. You've managed to bury every emotion except guilt and lust."

"Oh, great! All of a sudden, I've been downgraded from a handsome Adonis to a guilt-ridden creep who wants to ride every woman he sees."

"That isn't what I said."

"That's what I heard."

They pulled away from each other like two prize fighters withdrawing to their separate corners to regroup and fight again.

After a prolonged silence, Claire was the first to speak. "I'm sorry. I shouldn't have said those things. I figured I could do or say anything in the name of love, but love has many faces, and it doesn't exist in a vacuum. Fear, fear of the future and of being alone, can be as powerful as love. Both can make a person do weird, even cruel things."

"What about guilt? You have a real hang up on that."

"I know what guilt can do to a relationship. My mother spent her life trying to be something she wasn't. She ended up drowning herself in a vat of booze." She coughed and swallowed and coughed again, as if trying to expel a lump in her throat. "Of course, I blamed myself for her drinking. I was her daughter. I should've been able to help her. It was my weakness, not hers."

"I hope you know better now." Rufus came out of his corner and took her hand. "Kids have a funny way of looking at the world. That's why I have to go to Memphis. I don't want my son thinking I'd be there if he could run a little faster, or jump a little higher, or sing a little louder. In other words, I'd be there even if he wasn't perfect."

"Stop," Claire cried. "I can't handle this anymore. I can't feel sorry for you, your son, my mother, and myself. I only have so much pity to go around. I have to hoard it. After you leave, I'll draw on it every day. I'll get out my bass and pluck every blues song I know. I'll cry and feel sorry for myself, for whatever good it'll do."

"Come on, babe. You're not going to do any of that," he said, lightening his somber tone. "I'll give you a month before you're catwalking down Malibu beach in a white bikini."

She swiped away her tears and shook her head. "I don't like beaches. I don't tan. I burn."

"Then you'll be doing something else, but for sure, you won't be crying and moaning over me." He stroked her arm and studied her face. "You're smart, talented, young and beautiful, not to mention rich."

"You're wrong," she said. "I'm not rich." She grinned, grabbed his plate, and stood up. "I'll start over. This time, I won't burn the bacon."

He started to protest, but a loud knock on the door silenced him.

"Who can that be? Clarence?" She shook her head. "Can't be. We're not using his hot water."

"Open up, Johnson," a man shouted.

Rufus was on his feet, clicking off the lights inside his head, mentally rejecting what his gut was telling him: bad shit was coming his way. "Garret? What the hell you doing here?"

"You ain't as dense as I thought. You remembered my voice."

"I remember a lot of crap about you, none of 'em good, Garret."

"Lieutenant Garret to you." A hiss slithered through the transom. "I'm here on official business. Open the fucking door."

"'Less you got a search warrant, take your tired old ass back to your sewer and leave me alone," he said.

A growl fragmented into spurts of contemptuous laughter. "That's the trouble with you Africans. You ain't got brains enough to blow your nose, but I'll blow it for you in your own private cell if you don't let me in."

"Like I said, the door stays closed 'less you got a warrant."

"Don't need no warrant. You're on probation. I'm checking out a rumor you been dealing on the side."

"That's bullshit, and you know it. I never dealt, not even when I was using." Fear and anger tied a knot in Rufus's gut. He knew it was a waste of time to argue with Garret. The man had the law on his side and a relentless hatred in his heart. Garret's venom frightened Rufus the most. Like evil, he couldn't see it. He couldn't fight what he couldn't see, but he knew it was there.

"Guess they didn't teach you no manners when you was in

prison, otherwise you'd know how to speak to your betters, especially them that wears a badge," Garret said. "I'll take care of your Goddamn manners later. Right now, you open the door, or I call headquarters and tell 'em I need help to subdue a black dude high on coke. After they take the door off its hinges, can't promise I'll be able to control 'em."

Like a trapped animal, Rufus stood motionless and tried to decide what to do. He could split, but the only way out was through a window. Even if he survived the two-story drop to the alley littered with broken glass, he wouldn't leave without Claire, and she wasn't dressed. He shrugged. Garret had a score to settle. There was no place to run where he wouldn't find him.

Rufus grabbed Claire's arm and pulled her close. "Go in the bedroom. Get dressed and stay there. Don't come out no matter what happens or what you hear." He tightened his grip until he saw her wince. "Do you understand?"

"Yes, I understand." She yanked her arm free and looked at him, a thread of hysteria darkening her eyes. "No, I don't understand. Garret has no right to threaten you and scare us to death. You have rights. Call the police."

"Babe, he is the police." He gave her a push. "Do what I tell you, now, before things get nasty."

"Johnson," Garret shouted. "I'm counting down from ten."

"Shut the fuck up. I'm coming."

Rufus walked to the door, threw the locks, and yanked it open. He stared at the short, squat man, standing under a naked light bulb dangling from the hall ceiling. He was still the ugliest man alive with his pocked face, bulbous nose, and corpulent body heaving under the strain of being alive. A battered felt hat was pulled low on his head, as if trying to hide the lousy dye job visible on the strands of hair protruding around his ears. Spaghetti sauce and beer stains spattered his ankle-length trench coat. Brown juices oozing from the cigar butt clenched between his teeth stained his lips and settled in the crevices around his jowls. But it was his ruthless expression more than his solvenly appearance and rancid stench that defined his character. To Rufus, Lieutenant Syd Garret was the physical embodiment of a Biblical plague.

"Door's open, Garret," Rufus said. "Pitch your spiel, then get the fuck out of here."

Garret tongued his cigar to the corner of his mouth.

"Only a stupid homeboy'd make things hard for hisself. Another two minutes, and I'd 've had a squad coming in behind me." Garret shoved his way in and glared at Rufus. "You're a murderer and a liar. Never figured you to be stupid."

"I asked you what the shit you wanted. That too hard to understand?"

"Checking out a rumor you're planning to leave town."

"What happened to the rumor I was dealing?" Rufus sneered. "Crime must be slow if all you got to do is listen to scuttlebutt about Rufus Johnson."

Garret turned up his top lip and brayed like a mule. "I check all rumors on parolees, especially if I hear they're planning to skip town. Ain't no way you're gonna screw the justice system a second time."

"Justice system!" Rufus laughed. "You shouldn't use words you don't know how to spell."

"There's white justice, and then there's nigger justice." Garret stared at him, his face flushed with a sadistic smile. "Least there was before that nigger judge and nigger jury let you get away with murder. When they said not guilty, I figured the justice system needed some tuning, and I'm the man gonna do it."

"You're talking ancient history, but ancient or not, check your facts before you make asshole statements." Rufus's jaw muscles tensed. "Eight out of twelve jurors were white. The judge was Hispanic. And the murder charge never would've gotten beyond the precinct's latrine if you hadn't colored your report with fucking lies and racist shit."

"You killed my partner. His blood's on your hands." Garret's eyes narrowed to reptilian slits. "I'm here on official business, and I'm telling you right out, you ain't leaving town."

"You flat-footed son-of-a-bitch. I did my time. Next Wednesday my parole's up, and I'm out of here. Nobody's going to stop me, not you, not your white justice system."

"How old are you, Johnson? Figure you're old enough and black enough to know what good cops do to smart-mouth niggers." Garret took the cigar butt from his mouth and tongued its soggy tip. "We could make your life ugly if you're serious about moving to Memphis and taking up with your bastard boy and his hoochie mama." He snorted. "Does your white ho know you're gonna dump her?"

The rage fermenting in Rufus's belly erupted. He picked up a chair and raised it over his head, prepared to throw it at Garret.

The click of a .38 stopped him in mid-stride.

"Drop the chair, or I'll send your Goddamn cock flying through that fucking window."

Like a fast-moving storm, Rufus's rage slipped away, replaced by the survival tactics he learned in prison. A tense silence enveloped the room as he weighed his choices. He wanted to strangle Garret. It'd be easy for him to knock the gun out of his hand and choke him to death, but three minutes of pleasure wouldn't be worth spending the rest of his life in a cell or being strapped to a gurney with a needle stuck in his arm.

He dropped his gaze and stared at the revolver pointed at his groin. In Garret's meaty hand, it looked like a harmless toy, a plastic facsimile of his cowardliness. But the pressure of his index finger on the trigger made Rufus realize he was a hair's breath away from being a dead man. He looked up. Garret was staring at him, his expression blank.

He wondered why Garret didn't pull the trigger, get it over with. One glance at his glittering, reptilian eyes answered his question. Garret hoped that by throwing out the words "bastard," "hoochie," and "ho," Rufus would come at him, and he could shoot him in self-defense.

Knowing his freedom and possibly his and Claire's lives were on the line, Rufus let Garret make the next move.

"I'm not gonna kill you." Garret shot him a dirty grin. "Not yet, anyway." He returned his gun to his leather holster and backed to the door. "Just came by to tell you don't plan on leaving. You and me are gonna butt heads one of these days. I say when and where." With a snort, he turned and walked away.

Rufus watched him go, his relief tempered by a gut feeling that their next meeting would be in the vicinity of a lynching tree.

CHAPTER TWELVE

Rufus waited until he heard the dull thud of Garret's uneven gait recede before he dropped the chair to the floor. His mind muddled by rage and shock, he stared at it for a silent moment, transforming it into his image of hell: its yellowish-green color reminded him of a prison's putrid walls; its chrome legs iron bars. A cold sweat beaded his skin. He swore he wouldn't go back to prison. He'd did his time, and in a week, he'd be a free man. Free? Would he ever be free with Garret hounding him? He kicked the chair half way across the room.

"Rufus. My God! What're you doing?" Claire grabbed his arm. "You're acting like a madman."

"Leave me be. I don't want to talk. I don't want to feel. I can only take so much shit."

"Shit! What shit?" Claire took a wary step backward. "Why are you so angry? Why are you shouting?"

"I'm not shouting." He dismissed her with a flip of his hand. "Let it go, damn it. Just let it go."

"It's Garret, isn't it? You're letting him get to you." She knitted her brows in a worried frown. "Don't waste your time on him. He's a buffoon blowing hot air."

"He's a cop with a license to kill Blacks, no questions asked." Rufus sat down and looked out the window, his shoulders slumped, his eyes fixed on the hood's harsh landscape. The poverty, the grime, the trash-filled gutters sickened him. The offal of human despair reflected his grim mood. His life, the hood hadn't always been ugly. He had glimpsed some beauty, some good—Salinas, his first love, Rufe Junior, his son, and Claire, the great passion of his life—but Garret had defiled them all with his obscene slurs and racist gibes. Demoralized by the cop's hatred and vindictiveness, he slipped into a morass of self-pity and self-deprecation.

In the past, Claire and jazz made him forget the ugliness, but Garret's visit had rung a warning bell inside his head. Enmity and trouble were always lurking in the shadows, and happiness was as fleeting as a snow storm in the tropics.

She pulled up a chair and sat beside him. "Please, talk to me. I hate it when you disconnect."

Rufus sniffed the air. The scent of gardenias and spring rain that drifted off Claire's damp skin thawed the icy edges of his pessimism, but the frigid core around his heart remained intact.

"Why do you keep messing with me?" He glared at her. "There's a ton of bullshit floating around us, and all you want to do is talk. I'm done talking."

"Okay. We won't talk bullshit. We'll talk about something else." She laid her hand on his arm. "What'll it be? The weather? The gig? We're going to have a hard time trying to top last night's performance. Tonight, maybe we should lighten up on the improvisations and stick with the standards. You know, songs like "Night and Day" and "The Way You Look Tonight." If the audience starts snoring, we can liven things up with a few African-Caribbean rhythms."

"Sometimes you can be a real bitch," he said.

"See, you can express your feelings when it gets right down to it." A cynical smile rippled across her face.

"You want feelings? You want to know how much a man can hate?"

"No, that isn't what I want," she said in a cold, exact voice.

"I'm going to tell you anyway." He gripped her wrist. "You heard this a hundred times. A pitiful, punk policeman with a brain as limp as his pecker comes sniffing around like a nigger-hunting sheriff. When he catches the arrogant darky, the statue of justice dumps her scales, the judge and jury wink, and the black man fries." He paused and waited for his hand to stop shaking. "He got me once, but he's not going to get me again."

"Garret's a eunuch, a sadistic pervert. His gun and his badge make him feel like a man, but he doesn't have the guts to take you on. He's playing you, hoping you'll make a mistake." Claire flinched. "All the same, I think we should leave town, now, today. I have friends in Los Angeles. It's a big city. He'll never find us."

"You're not hearing me." His voice rose to an angry pitch. "I'm not running. I'm staying here till my parole is up. I promised Salinas and Rufe Junior I'd be on that train. I'm keeping that promise."

"Let's assume for an instant that Garret is planning something. He thinks you killed his partner during that stupid drug bust. He swore he'd get revenge. We'd be fools to ignore his threats."

"Make up your mind. Is he playing a game, or is he playing for keeps?"

"How should I know?" She sucked in her breath. "He's crazy enough to kill you. The thought of you leaving me is almost unbearable, but it's better than the thought of burying you. Why are you so damn stubborn? Call Salinas. Tell her an insane police-man is out for your hide, and you have to lie low for a while. She'd understand. She's waited this long. What's another month or two?"

"Maybe she can wait, but my boy can't. A ten-year-old needs his father, and his father needs him." Rufus rose and stared down at her, his eyes blazing. "Forget L. A. I won't let that son-of-a-bitch scare me into running."

"Oh, aren't you the big man? You won't run. It's not macho." Her tone veered sharply to anger. "Maybe you never heard about Moses leading the Israelites out of Egypt. Wasn't that running? Or how about Sojourner Truth, the black woman who set up the underground railroad and led hundreds, possibly thousands of slaves to freedom. Wasn't that running?"

"Maybe you haven't heard about computers and FBI files and racist state cops that make catching fugitives child's play." A sneer caught on Rufus's lips. "I'm not going to stop playing my sax. No way am I going to hide in a fucking cellar. Shit! I'd be better off rotting in a prison cell."

"Rufus, you have to face reality. We're talking life and death, a bullet in the back of the head."

"I been facing reality all my life. My idea of reality is handling problems, not running away from them." He wanted a drink, a snort, anything to take the edge off his anger and help get him off the damn fence. He could only teeter so long before he fell into a pit crawling with vipers and scorpions with human traits. He decided months ago to move to Memphis and be with his son. Even though he had concerns about his career and qualms about Salinas and what she expected from him, the decision had been easy. All of a sudden, complications set in. Claire came back into his life. Just when he thought she was finally accepting the inevitable, ass-hole Garret crawled out of his sewer snorting hatred and revenge. He'd heard about a person's past catching up with him, but this was ridiculous.

He shoved his hands in his pockets and stared out the window. He felt like a straw man devoid of all emotions except guilt and confusion. He hurt Claire. He hated Garret. He loved his son. In the distance, he heard the whistle of a train and the clack of its wheels. Would it stop? Would he ever get on the train to Memphis?

He heard Claire step behind him and felt her arms wrap around his waist.

"Hear me out," she said. "I'm sorry. I'm being a real bitch. All the advice in the world isn't going to change things. You have to do what you think is best. We've been through a lot together. We dug our way out of a lot of pain, most of it was our own doing. What's happening now is not our doing. All I'm asking is for you to be careful. Don't give Garret an excuse to kill you."

She released her hold. Rufus turned and brushed a gentle kiss on her lips. "I know you're upset," he said. "Hell, I am, too. But there's nothing we can do. We can't run. We have to ride this one out." He shrugged. "Please, stop saying you're sorry. Even if you had something to be sorry about, it'd be a waste of energy. What does it mean when people say they're sorry? Do they think it gets them off the hook? I'm sorry I'm a drunk. I'm sorry I killed your dog. I'm sorry I gambled away the rent money. Right now, all I want to hear is that you love me."

"If I didn't love you, I wouldn't be here."

He smiled. "Funny how those three little words can make a guy mellow."

"Works on gals, too." Claire stood on her tiptoes and gave him a bruising kiss. She pulled back and flashed a provocative grin. "See what I mean?"

"Humm, don't see much sense stopping with a kiss." He swept her into his arms and walked into the bedroom. "We don't want to chill out too soon."

He laid her on the bed, stripped off his clothes, and fell beside her. "You in the mood, or do you want me to stop?"

She grinned. "How can you stop? You haven't started."

"How right you are."

He opened her robe and kissed her neck, her breasts, and flicked his tongue over her swollen nipples. She arched her back and soft moans flowed from her throat. He raised his head and looked at her in astonishment.

"Slow down, babe, or we'll be through before we start."

"I can hold on as long as you can," she said. "Shut up and make love to me."

"Ooh, I like a woman who knows what she wants." He gave her a lecherous look and gave her a hard, punishing kiss.

"Easy, darling," she said. "You're bruising me."

"Is this better?" He brushed his lips across her stomach and stroked her inner thighs. She took his rod in her hand. Her gentle squeezing motion lit a fire in his groin. He felt his cock swell and start to bob.

"Slow down, babe," he said. "My emotions are too damn raw for any long-term foreplay."

"Lie still. I'll take care of it." Claire straddled him and eased herself onto the top of his cock.

He slid inside, slowly at first, then with one violent thrust, he was deep inside her. He felt her muscles tighten. His lunges intensified. He gripped her hips and began to move. She dug her nails into his back and uttered wild little cries.

He slowed to a rhythmic push and pull. The friction sent a river of hot lava through his groin. New sensations rose from the molten bedrock. Claire rode with him as prickly spasms and flapping wings seeded his passion. When it reached its apex, his body grew rigid, his mouth opened, and earthy, visceral moans rippled out.

"I'm coming, babe. Hang on. Hang on." His warm juices erupted inside her like a volcano spitting hot lava. He held his body rigid until his smoldering, earth-shattering orgasm waned and finally died.

Not until she rolled off him and nestled her head at her side did he notice the flush of passion tinging her skin. He grinned.

"You okay?"

"Better than okay," she said.

"You sure. I heard a gasp but no scream."

She nodded. "We came off together, but I guess you didn't notice. You were someplace in the stratosphere, riding a star or circling the moon. I met you on the way down."

"That's good. I wanted you with me, but I wasn't sure we'd meet up. Anger can do stuff to your mind. Make it hard to feel pleasure."

"Then I suppose we shouldn't waste time getting angry."

He rested his head on his elbow and gazed down at her, his heart filled with love and hopelessness. He had found a woman who understood his hungers and shared his passions. It saddened him to think he was going to lose her.

He kissed her nose, laid on his back, and closed his eyes. In less than a week, he'd be gone, and Claire would be out of his life. He'd never forget her, but he vaguely remembered thinking the same about Salinas. Time had obscured his memories of her, but the fleeting images he did recall were good as were the letters and pictures she sent him. Her sparkling eyes and high cheek bones set in a perfect oval face gave her an exotic look. The rich hue of coffee and cream glowed on her flawless skin. Even standing rigid for the camera, her narrow waist, fine hips, and shapely thighs gave her a willowy, graceful appearance.

From the brief account of her accomplishments, a college graduate, a managerial position in an insurance company, treasurer of the local NAACP, he knew she was intelligent and ambitious. Her picturesque anecdotes of Rufe Junior's talents and achievements told him she was a loving, nurturing mother.

On paper, she was the perfect woman, but was she perfect for him? What did she and an ex con, a saxophone player, a live-today-starve-tomorrow drifter have in common?

His brows slanted in a frown. They had their son, Rufe Junior, in common. She knew what to expect. In the letter he wrote accepting her proposal to move to Memphis, consider marriage, and be a father to Rufe Junior, he described his life in detail, leaving out the time he spent in prison. Hollywood wasn't knocking on his door, recording companies weren't offering him million dollar contracts, and top agents weren't standing in line to sign him up. There were times when he barely had enough money to pay his rent. Whether he ate or not depended on Ella's kitchen staff. His accumulated wealth consisted of floor-to-ceiling records, tapes, and CDs, a stereo system, and a worn out coffee pot. On the plus side, he loved basketball and music; he was honorable and trustworthy.

Her response: Rufe Junior needed a father. Everything else was negotiable.

He groaned. Everything was negotiable: love, sex, even life and death, at least for a while. That was the crux of his problem. Everything was negotiable, but nothing lasted forever. With that dire thought swirling in his head, he brushed a kiss on Claire's nose, got up, and headed to the bathroom. "I'm going to shower, babe. We'll grab something to eat on our way to Ella's."

The bathroom was still warm and steamy and perfumed with lush, tropical scents from Claire's shower. He smiled, appreciative of the civilizing aspects of a woman's presence. God, he loved her. He'd miss her. With a shake of his head, he stepped into the shower stall and turned on the hot water.

A blast of lukewarm water raised goose bumps on his skin. He jumped back and barked, "Clarence, you tight bastard. When you going to get your damn plumbing fixed?" He gave the faucet a slight spin, took a deep breath, and stepped under the shower. The steady trickle allowed him to work up a lather, but he had to increase the pressure if he wanted to rinse off the soap.

He tensed his muscles and turned on the faucet full blast. Cold water spurted from the shower head and pelted his body with frozen buckshot. He stood there, mummified, waiting for the hard water to rinse away the soapy film.

The sound of a fist battering the wall raised another layer of bumps on his skin.

"How many damn showers you gonna take?" His landlord's shrill voice cracked the ice glazing the shower stall. "And quit all your damn screwing. Ain't you got nothing else to do?"

"Screw you, Clarence," Rufus yelled back. "I'll shower and fuck whenever I want."

"Not in my apartment, you ain't. I'm sick of hearing you bucking and shouting like a mule in heat. If I hear your shit one more time, I'll call the cops and have you thrown out on the street. We'll see how much you'll like screwing in the snow."

"I'll have a hard time telling the difference," Rufus said.

Clarence appended his profanities with another round of threats and fell silent.

Rufus turned off the water and wrapped a towel around his shivering body. As hard as he tried, he couldn't figure out what was going on. First Ella and then his landlord had threatened to sic the cops on him. He growled an obscenity. Since when was fucking a felony, especially in his own home? He paid his rent. Maybe not always on time, but he did pay it. He dried himself with rough, frenzied swipes and stepped out of the shower. His mind still racing, he wondered when colored folks decided to call the fuzz to settle an argument. That was as stupid as asking a hyena to bury a carcass rather than eat it.

He shaved and cut himself three times. He dressed and popped a button off his jacket. By the time he joined Claire in the living room, he was a mass of incandescent anger.

"Get your coat," he said. "We're out of here."

She jerked her head up and stared at him in dismay. "Half an hour ago, you were all smiles. Now you look like you're ready to kill somebody."

"Don't push me. I'll tell you later."

She grabbed her coat and slipped it on as they were going out the door. "Apparently our discussion on anger control didn't register."

He slammed the door, shot her a nasty look, and pulled her along behind him.

"Where you want to eat?" he asked.

"How about a hardware store? We'll buy a box of nails and chew on 'em." She darted down the ice-covered steps and plowed her way through a mound of snow on her way to the car.

Rufus shook his head. "Damn!" he muttered. Why did women have to be so temperamental?

CHAPTER THIRTEEN

Rufus white-knuckled his way along the snow-packed streets and slid to a stop in front of the hood's most popular grill. Even before he stepped out of the car, he smelled the earthy aroma of rancid grease, draft beer, and fried fish. He glanced at the lime-green facade, the dirt-streaked window. The red sign hanging precariously above the door boasted Chicken and Chitlin's deep-fried chicken, blackened catfish, and crispy French fries as the best in the world. Below it was a picture of the mayor eating a chicken leg as big as his arm.

"Is this okay, or you want to go someplace else?" he asked Claire.

"This is fine." She smiled.

"When you're hungry, there's nothing like down-home food. Sticks to your ribs."

"And a few other places."

A waiter followed them to the farthest booth from the door and tossed two menus on the table. "Name's Blade." He cocked a hip and pointed at the starred items. "Most folks get the blue-plate special if they real hungry."

Claire blanched. "Half a fried chicken, boiled greens and pork rinds, coleslaw, and a slice of sweet potato pie." She looked at Blade. "All that food goes on one plate?"

"Corn bread go on the side." He grinned and shifted his weight to the other hip.

"We'll take two specials, two beers, frosted glasses, small heads," Rufus said.

Blade stuck the menus under his arm and walked away, both hips swinging.

Claire unzipped her jacket and leaned her head against the booth. "You're a strange man, Rufus Johnson."

"How so?"

"The blue-plate special. An hour ago, you were snorting like a dragon, now you're grinning like a cat, a fat one at that."

"You think so?"

"I know so. Your eyes get all glittery thinking about all that food." She frowned. "A grilled cheese would've filled me up."

"My mama done told me, 'Son, don't you never turn down no meal cause you don't know when you gonna get another.'"

"She was a wise woman, but I never had to worry about my next meal."

"You were never hungry."

"Just the opposite. My substitute parents Henry and Flo made nasty sounds if I didn't eat. I had a touch of anorexia in my teens."

"You must've done something right. You look mighty damn healthy to me." He reached across the table and laid his hands on hers. "Guess neither of us had great childhoods. For sure, we went through some tough times together." He grimaced. "Not many couples share such fine memories of drugs, rehab, and jail."

"That's one way to look at it." She inclined her head thoughtfully. "Personally, I feel as if we're actors in a bad play. It'd be nice if it had a happy ending."

"If I wrote the script, I'd see to it."

Blade shuffled to the booth and set down two beers and two platter-sized dinners.

"Yell if you want dessert." He nodded at the picture-perfect drafts. "How you like that, man? I poured it myself."

Rufus saluted him, then waited until he gangsta limped away before digging in.

He barely paused for breath until he cleaned his plate, leaving behind a residue of grease and bones." He looked at the food on Claire's plate and showed his disapproval with a shake of his head."

"You're not eating. What's the matter? Aren't you hungry?"

"Not really." She pushed the greens and pork rinds to one side and took a long drink of beer.

"Something's eating you, and it's got nothing to do with food."

"How do you know? I haven't said one word."

"You don't have to. Your hunched shoulders and sad face say it all."

"We're having a good time. Why spoil it?" She shoved the beer away and took a sip of water. "I don't like beer. Gives me gas."

"You're worried about Garret, aren't you?"

Claire exhaled. The fear and anxiety she had tried to bury rose to the surface, presenting Rufus with an image of raw, primitive fear. "Why did he show up all of a sudden? He's not your parole officer. He had no right to check on you, much less threaten you."

Rufus shrugged. "Maybe he remembered my parole is up next week." His lips twisted in a cynical smile. "It must be driving him crazy knowing I'll be a free man come next Wednesday, and he won't be able to hassle me anymore."

"Hassle?" Her voice held a trace of hysteria. "Kids hassle. Cops like Garret go for the jugular."

"Hey, don't sweat it, babe. I can handle him."

"How can you handle him?"

"He's a mad dog. If you got a weapon, you face up to him. If you don't, you ignore him. Black folks have been dealing with honky cops and red-necked sheriffs a long time. We got an instinct for 'em. They're like omens. 'Red moon rising, hound dogs baying. Watch out.'"

He fell silent, trying to control his overwrought emotions. He was talking centuries of bigotry that even he had difficulty understanding. People were separated by race and culture. To him, chitlins and greens, sweet potato pie and corn bread weren't just food. They were a way of life. They were the soul of black folks.

He was aware of black and white distinctions when he met Claire. He didn't like to think he was bigoted, but he knew every ugly cliche blacks pinned on white chicks. They were either stud hunters looking for a stray piece, or inside-out sandwich cookies looking for a house nigger to drape on their arms.

He remembered the day she walked into the civic auditorium, lugging her bass, and waited in line to audition for a six-week stint in the Music for Life program sponsored by Friends of the Symphony. As artistic director, he listened to the amateurs, knowing three-fourths of them were musically challenged and had no idea how to teach music appreciation to inner-city children. He wanted her to play a standard piece and leave. Instead, she insisted she be allowed to play a medley of classic-to-rap tunes with a fifteen-year-old pianist she had met at another audition. Reluctantly, he agreed to her demands. When she finished, he hired her on the spot and gave her top billing at the closing recital.

Six weeks later, she moved in with him. He tried hard to think of her as a white chick slumming for thrills, not as a gifted bassist who loved music as much as he did. When that didn't work, he decided she was a temporary distraction from his humdrum existence. That didn't work either. Finally, he ran out of denials and excuses and admitted he was in love with a white female bass player with exceptional talent.

Loving Claire had all the excitement and danger of a roller coaster ride. His highs came in waves of passion; his lows came from an inner voice floating across a Louisiana cotton field telling him to watch out for the white-sheeted overseer who was watching and waiting.

He ignored the inner voice and made Claire a permanent fixture in his life. She helped him with a project he'd been thinking about for years. It hadn't been easy, but they had rephrased standard tunes such as "My Old Flame" and "Embraceable You" and linked them to jazz.

Miles, Duke, and Bird had done it with great success. What came naturally to them was a blood-sweating chore to Rufus. His attempt to redefine Coleman Hawkins's classic version of "Body and Soul" on tenor sax floundered when he tried to balance long stretches of inspiration with endless hours of copulation. He realized now he should have considered his efforts a noble experiment. Instead, he considered himself a failure. In the dark hours between midnight and dawn, he slipped into the quiet world of alcohol, snow, and dust. Eventually, Claire joined him, and their *tete-a-tetes* turned into Mad Hatter's tea parties.

The six months he spent in prison away from his music gave him the perspective he needed to understand that jazz musicians didn't score improvisations, they played them. Rufus swallowed his sour grapes and stopped wallowing in self-pity. He might not reach the summit of jazz stardom, but he knew he had talent. The important thing was to never stop learning.

He checked the time. "Hey, we got to move. We're going to be late. He hustled Claire out of the booth and flipped Blade a ten-dollar bill on his way out the door. The man's wide grin told him he probably over tipped, but hell, he thought, where else could he gorge himself for ten bucks?

Half an hour later, they walked into Ella's Lounge, got a high-five and a frown from Bojay.

"Where you been, man? Ella looking for you."

"Is that good or bad?"

"Can't say. She fly into the bar then fly back to her office. She's talking to some dude."

"Good dude or bad?"

"Wasn't a copper. Other'n that, can't say."

"I'll check with her later."

He took Claire's arm and ushered her into the lounge. They meandered around the tables on their way to the bandstand and waved at the regulars who had grabbed the tables closest to the dance floor. Rufus felt a twinge when he saw Moon and Lenny riffing to kill time until he and Claire arrived. Moon pounded out bass drum strokes. Lenny did a Fats Waller stride on the piano. To the casual listener, their improvisations would sound brash and incoherent, like two deaf people having a musical conversation, but to Rufus their sounds were inspired genius. He was in the mood for genius, but if they came up short, it was okay, too. The atmosphere, the music, their performances were all that mattered. The only time the world was right and he was at peace with himself was when he was on the bandstand blowing his sax.

He knew Lenny, Moon, and Claire agreed. They were virtuosos who separated their private lives from their professional ones. They prided themselves on their ability to play their best anytime, anyplace.

"Hey, guys! How's it going?" He greeted them with a smile and nod. "Ready to rock and roll?"

"You're late. Folks been waiting twenty minutes." Lenny slammed his fingers on the keys. The shrill notes set Rufus's teeth on edge.

"I'm sorry. I lost track of time. Stay cool. I'll be ready in a minute." He opened his sax case and quickly assembled his horn. When he finished, he noticed Lenny's scowl and Moon's sulk. He knew something was wrong, but since he didn't have time to find out what, he turned to the audience and introduced the band members.

After a polite round of applause, the band opened with their rendition of "The Way You Look Tonight." Well into the piece, Rufus noticed Lenny and Moon played every note, turning the romantic melody into a dirge. Subtly, he tried to alter the phrasing, but Moon ignored him and spelled out the tempo in a straight fashion. Lenny's accompaniment on the piano was as dreary as a droning bee.

He glanced at Claire. She looked as bewildered as he was. He tolerated Lenny and Moon's constipated syncopation until the queasiness in his stomach started to corrode the base of his throat. He ended the song with a wail and bowed to the audience who looked as if toxic fumes had fried their brains. He turned to Moon and Lenny.

"What's going down here? Jeesh! That was the sorriest piece of shit I ever heard. This is a jazz club, not a funeral parlor."

Lenny responded with a hostile glare. Rufus looked at Moon. His teed-off expression was disturbing but not deadly.

"You dudes can't be this pissed off because we were late," Rufus said. "What the hell is it?"

"Ask Ella," Moon said. "All your jack jawing and honey cooing done finally pay off."

"What the hell you talking about?" Rufus threw up his hands. "Never mind. We'll talk later. Right now, I'm asking you to play like the professionals you are. Folks out there are waiting for a show. We owe 'em."

Moon and Lenny exchanged glances. At some point in their eye-ball-to-eye-ball trajectory, their heated emotions deflated. Lenny nodded. Moon shrugged. Rufus sighed.

Five minutes later, Rufus ran his tongue around his mouth piece and blew the first notes of "I Got It Bad and That Ain't Good." Heads rose, shoulders moved, eyelids fluttered as the rhythmic beat of Ellington's sophisticated anthem struck the right chords in their heads. Rufus's mood shifted from gloom to jubilation. He raised his thumb in the air. They were grooving again. When they shifted to a bluesy rendition of "Mercy, Mercy, Mercy," they sounded so fine, Rufus thought he heard snatches of lush harmony reminiscent of the incredible sounds produced by Ben Webster on bass, Art Blakey on drums, and Herbie Hancock on piano. Even though they lived in a different time, he often imagined joining them at New York's Blue Note or Village Vanguard. He wondered if today's generals ever dreamed about fighting under Napoleon or Julius Caesar. He shrugged. It was just a thought.

When the set ended, he stepped up to the microphone and introduced Lenny on piano, Moon on drums, and Claire on bass and waited for the applause with the tenseness of an accused man waiting for a jury verdict. He would have been happy with a courteous response. The rowdy cheers and stomping feet that followed a moment of silence was beyond his expectations.

He called for a short break. In an instant, waiters appeared, pen and pad in hand, ice clinked in near-empty glasses, and Ray Charles wailed "A Rainy Night in Georgia." Rufus studied Lenny and Moon, hoping to read their mood. If they were still pissed, they didn't show it. They smiled, rolled their shoulders, and slapped Rufus a high five on their way to the bar.

"Hold up." Rufus grabbed Claire's arm and hustled after them. "I'm buying."

After Bojay delivered their drinks, Rufus raised his glass in a toast. "To jazz. To the Rufus Johnson Quartet, the best in the business." He glanced at Lenny and Moon. I mean it. We were always a team. But something's going on now, and I want to know what it is. I know we were late, but Jeesh, is that any reason to ruin a set?"

Moon took a drink of beer, set his glass on the table, and stared at it under hooded eyes. "Lenny says you're jerking us around."

"Jerking you! Humm." Rufus cocked his head. "How about putting some meat on that statement?"

"What you mean 'meat?'"

"Explain how I'm jerking you around."

Moon drew his lips into a persimmon pucker. "I ain't mad or nothing. You got a right, but all the same, it ain't fair you cheating us outta our due."

"I'm still not reading you."

"Read this." Lenny snagged Rufus in a combative stare. "I figure we wasn't supposed to know nothing about this, but when you was late, your honky dude told us about your deal."

"Deal? Honky?" Rufus rolled his eyes. "I don't know a deal or a honky dude. Just in case I missed something, explain what kind of deal I'm supposed to be dealing."

A hand tapped his shoulder. He spun his head around and froze when his nose skimmed Ella's monumental breasts. He lifted his chin. Her angry expression sent a chill down his spine until he realized she was looking at Lenny, not him.

"Why you making trouble when there ain't none to make?" She stiffed Lenny with an angry frown and glanced at Rufus. "Come on into my office. You got business to take care of."

Rufus scanned Claire's face. Her blank expression made him feel a little better. For whatever reason Ella was hot, it had nothing to do with them. He took a deep breath to compose himself, but his eyelid continued to twitch. He knew from experience nothing good ever came from a trip to Ella's office.

He trotted behind Ella across the dance floor, through the bar, and down a hallway. They stopped in front of a door that held a plaque with Ella's name on it emblazoned in gold. He reached out and turned the knob. Before he could open it, she stepped back and shook her head.

"I'm not going in, but don't you sweat it. You're gonna do just fine." She flipped a hip and sauntered away.

He watched her walk away and felt the sweat rise on his forehead. What fine thing was he supposed to do? Since there was only one way to find out, he opened the door and stepped inside. Whatever he expected, it certainly wasn't a copycat image of Duke Ellington wearing a long, camel-hair coat, black felt hat pulled low over one eye, and fingering soft leather gloves.

"Names Drew Wiley. I own AF Record Company." He strode toward Rufus, his hand outstretched. "Got a minute? I'd like to talk."

Rufus responded with a vigorous shake, a limp nod, and a direct question. "What's on your mind?"

"Money," Wiley said. "You interested?"

"Interested enough to listen."

Wiley motioned for him to sit down and followed suit. "Like I said, I own AF Recording Company. I can see from your expression, you never heard of us."

"Sorry to say, I never did."

"We're a small company, just starting out. We're always looking for talent. A while back, I heard you on a CD. Soundtrack wasn't the best, but it was good enough to catch my interest." He pulled a cigar from a silver holder, snipped off an end, and lit it with a gold-plated lighter. "I caught your act tonight. You blow a damn fine sax."

"Thanks. I can see you have a good ear for music." He smiled. "As much as I appreciate compliments, I don't imagine you dropped by to smoke a cigar and pump me up." Rufus frowned. "What's up?"

"Your music." Wiley blew a perfect smoke ring and watched it dissipate before he continued. "Would you be interested in cutting a TEMP? If you are, I'll set up a recording date tonight."

Rufus let out a low whistle. "I've been waiting a long time for a break like this." He grinned. "Moon, Lenny, and Claire are going to have a hard time believing me when I tell 'em about your offer."

"I hear you, man. A lot of talented musicians wait a lifetime for that one big break that never comes." Wiley cleared his throat. "But before we go on, let me kick around some facts about the situation. AF Recording doesn't have the big money to publicize a band. We're checking out musicians who have special talents like yours, but, you understand, we have to be careful. We make too many wrong choices, we're out of business. You got to know, the Rufus Johnson Quartet isn't filling clubs in New York or LA."

"I'm not following you. Do you want to sign us up or not?" Rufus leaned back in his chair and stared at the cigar smoke glutting the room with a blue-gray haze.

"I want to sign you up. We have our own band. We need a tenor sax player."

"That puts a different spin on things." He sat up and shook his head. "We been together a long time."

"Hey, don't worry about Moon and Lenny. I talked to 'em.

Told 'em just what I told you. We need a sax player, not a quartet."

His jaw muscles went slack. Suddenly, he knew why Moon and Lenny were so constipated. They figured he had sold them out. He chewed on his bottom lip, stunned by the thought. They should've known he wouldn't do that.

He rose out of the chair. "My mouth's watering, but I got to say no. I have got too much going on right now. I'm leaving for Memphis this coming Wednesday."

"You sure? This could be your big chance."

"I'm sure."

Wiley pulled a gold-plated case from his pocket and handed Rufus his card. "Call me after you get settled. I have connections in Memphis. We'll talk."

Rufus palmed the card and headed for the door.

"What about your bass player, Claire Burton? She leaving too?"

"Not with me."

"She's talented. I'm surprised you don't want to hang onto her. A black sax player and a white bassist could be a draw in some circles."

"We're musicians, not freaks," Rufus said with a hint of sarcasm in his voice. "How would you bill a black sax player and a white bassist? The bearded lady and the elephant man?"

"Didn't mean to insult you." Wiley shrugged. "It was just a suggestion."

"Yeah, yeah." Rufus strode to the door. "It doesn't matter. Claire and I are splitting. We'll be traveling separate roads."

"No problem, man. I'll talk to her. I can always find a spot for a talented, fine-looking bass player."

"You do that, man, but don't hold your breath. Claire has other plans." Rufus opened the door and walked out.

CHAPTER FOURTEEN

In the early hours before dawn, Rufus groped his way from the bathroom to the bedroom, stripping off his clothes and dropping them willy-nilly on the cold, gritty floor.

"Damn, I'm freezing," he said. "Clarence turns the heat up one hour a day. Doesn't the idiot know pipes and people turn into icicles when the temperature hits thirty-one degrees?"

Claire peeked at him over the edge of the blanket. "Don't you dare touch me till your feet and hands get warm," she said.

"You're my heating pad, and it's your job to warm me up." With a malicious grin, he slipped under the covers and ran his icy fingers down her spine.

"Stop that right now, or I'll give you a kick in your you-know-what."

"Oh, babe, you are one bad lady. You could put me out of commission for a week."

"By next week, I won't give a damn. Your problem will be somebody else's problem, not mine."

"You want to explain that?" Rufus flinched. He felt a storm coming on.

"You'll be sleeping with someone else." She flung the words at him in a reproachful voice.

"Dammit, woman, why do you keep jabbing me with stupid stuff like that? You know the score. I'm not skipping to Memphis to slam-bang Salinas. I'm going there to be with my son."

"So okay. I hear you, but don't get the idea you being with Rufe makes it any easier for me."

He pressed his body to hers and planted butterfly kisses on her neck and shoulders. "Hey, sweetheart, come on. Don't bury yourself in a sand trap. We have a lot of living to do between now and Wednesday."

"Then what?"

"Then who knows?"

"Who, indeed?" She pulled away and looked at him, a sadness staining her face. "You have somebody to go to. Somebody to share your life with. I won't have anyone. It's the difference between traveling alone or with someone you love. Everything that means anything to me will go puff the minute you get on that damn train. And don't tell me how talented and beautiful I am. I'm a female bass player. Agents aren't standing in line offering me gigs."

Rufus let out a cynical chuckle. "I don't hear any agents knocking on my door."

"You'll get a gig before I will. Guys can always get gigs. Or you can call Drew Wiley. Tell him you're interested in cutting that demo."

"I have to work if I want to eat. And if anybody's going to cut a demo with Wiley, it'll be you. His parting words are still ringing in my ears. 'I can always find a spot for a talented, fine-looking bass player.'"

"Sounds as if he's looking for a piece of ass, not a bass player," Claire said, an impassive coldness in her voice.

"If he was after your tail, he wouldn't have messed with me. Lighten up, babe. I don't like seeing you so unhappy."

"I'll be unhappy if I want to."

"I have a better idea." He rolled over, drew her on top of him, and gave her a long, passionate kiss.

Claire straddled his hips and returned his kiss with a breathless hunger.

Her abrupt change in mood from sadness to lust startled him. Their love making had always been exciting and confrontational, but the intensity of their passion had escalated since she came back into his life. Memories of their first night together brought a smile to his face.

Like most first nights, it had elements of the best and worst in the art of love making. Actually, it wasn't an encounter, it was an adventure filled with mystery and anticipation and doubts. He wondered if he could please her, if he could rouse her passion before he blew his head. Later, he realized he shouldn't have worried. The thrill of the quest and the ecstasy of discovery turned a one-nighter into a romantic coupling of two people who had fallen in love but didn't know it.

He knew it now. Dismissing the bittersweet memories flitting through his mind, he cupped his hand around her breast and fondled it until it grew firm and hard. He made love to her slowly, gently, taking time to explore, arouse, and give her pleasure as he had before the anger, the arguments, and the drugs tore them apart.

He traced a path across her belly and down her thighs to her ankles, stopping to knead her pleasure points until she was moaning and writhing in ecstasy.

He parted her thighs and entered her with an urgent thrust. She lifted her hips and mimicked the rhythmic motion of his penis, kindling her passion.

They climaxed together in a burst of fiery flashes and clapping thunder.

Her lids fluttered open, and she gazed at him, her eyes glowing with wonder and love.

He pressed his lips to her ear and whispered words of love. When she smiled and closed her eyes, he dropped his head on his pillow and sighed. He didn't have to tell her he loved her. His passion said it all.

After she fell asleep in his arms, he tried to relax, but his fears of a future without her unleashed a tidal wave of misgivings.

He turned on his side and stared at her. He heard her whimpers and saw the dreamy smile on her lips. Was she dreaming of him or some future lover? What kind of man would she choose, someone like him, a nighthawk, an itinerate saxophone player, a pub crawler who went to bed with the sun and rose with the moon? Or would she shed her rebellious nature and return to her upper-class roots? He could see her falling in love with a butcher, a baker, or a white-collared money maker but not a guy who wore starched pajamas and wool socks to bed.

He rolled on his back and focused his bleary eyes on the dirt-streaked window. He was tempted to lie there and feel sorry for himself, but he axed the urge when he realized he had nothing to feel sorry about. He was leaving Claire not the other way around. And who gave him the right to decide what kind of guy was best for her? It would be her choice. He wanted her to be happy whoever the bastard was.

He and Claire had fallen in love and shared their passion for music, but love and music weren't enough to keep them together. They'd been happy for a while, but eventually their drug habits had torn them apart.

He didn't know Salinas's values, but he believed they were similar to his. They both grew up in the ghetto and were straddled with Saturday night fathers. But Maybelle had tried to protect Salinas from the debilitating effects of poverty, ignorance, and racial segregation, while Nettie, his mother, hadn't had the time to raise him. Dead-end jobs and worries about money had drained her spirit and sapped her strength. Early in life, Rufus knew he'd have to hustle to stay alive. When he was ten years old, Rufe Junior's age, he cleaned toilets at local taverns and dragged their trash to the dumpsters. Always on the lookout for a deal, it didn't take him long to realize that what was trash to some was a treasure to others. Before he dumped, he scrounged. Bingo nights were his Christmas days. Once he found a twenty dollar bill and two hand guns. On off nights he found a box of Trojan condoms, a thong bikini, and souvenir picture of the governor signed "To Latice with love." Politically ignorant at the time, he threw it away.

His most prized treasure was a saxophone he found in a pile of garbage. He took it home, replaced the missing mouth piece, polished the pitted metal, and took it to the *Three Balls You're Out* pawn shop, hoping to make a fast buck. When the owner offered him five dollars, he walked out. Rather than waste the time and money he had already spent on it, he had it repaired by a sax player who played for tips in a local bar, bought a how-to-book, and taught himself the scales. What started as a curiosity grew into an obsession. Under the guidance of his grade school music teacher, he spent the next six years practicing, studying, and honing his talent. He divided his days between work and school and filled his nights with music and dreams.

Nettie died on Rufus's seventeenth birthday. Music and the night sustained him. Sex and booze consoled him. He met Salinas at a Black Knight picnic where he played with a group called the Blue Devils. Salinas was young, pretty, and awe-struck by his seductive

smile, bulging biceps, and growling saxophone solos.

He was bewitched by her innocence and sincerity, qualities sorely lacking among the local prostitutes who roamed the neighborhood. Since he had only a murky concept of virginity and no concept of its importance to a woman, he made love to Salinas with all the gallantry of a dude on the make. When he learned she was pregnant, he looked for a job, hunted for an apartment, and, with a nod at honorable intentions, asked her to marry him.

Salinas was thrilled. Her mother was furious. Maybelle swore he would never see Salinas or his baby as long as she was alive. She kept her promise.

Rufus slammed his fist on the mattress. Why the hell was he traipsing down memory lane? Only an idiot would want to rehash his ugly past. He forced the unbidden thoughts from his mind, closed his eyes, and eventually dozed off. When he awoke, his bladder was full, and Claire's side of the bed was empty. He dropped his feet to the floor with a thud and groped his way to the bathroom. He opened the door and entered a sauna clogged with hot, steamy air.

"What're you doing?" he asked in a disgruntled voice.

"And good morning to you," Claire shouted from the shower.

He flipped up the toilet seat lid and relieved himself. "How many showers you take in a day?"

"As many as I need." She peeked around the curtain and grinned.

"Don't use all the hot water." Rufus tucked his semi-erect penis into his shorts. When she stepped out of the shower, he grabbed a towel and buffed her skin pink.

"Oooh, babe! You are one luscious peach."

"Get your hands off me. A night of wild sex might not faze you, but I'm sore as hell."

His brows joined in an affronted frown. "I thought women didn't dry up till they were middle age."

Claire shrieked and stomped out.

He stripped, stepped into the shower, and turned on the water. A blast of ice water slammed him against the wall.

"What the hell!" He spun the hot water faucet from low to high and slammed his shoulder on the wall. "Clarence, you miserable excuse for a landlord, turn on the damn water heater," he shouted. He turned on both faucets full blast, grabbed a bar of soap, and scoured his body. It took him ten seconds to rinse off the suds, two minutes to dry, and five minutes to dress.

He walked into the kitchen, madder than a hound dog infested with fleas. His anger took a nosedive when he heard the familiar thump, thump of a bass. He spun around and saw Claire hunched over her bass, plucking strings, walking chords, beating out the melody to "Just One of Those Things."

When she finished, he raised his hands to applaud her performance, but he held back when she drifted into the bittersweet ballad, "For All We Know." Caught up in the song's wistful melody, he leaned against the wall and sang the opening line. "For all we know, we will never meet again."

Claire flinched. "Get your sax. You play better than you sing."

"Ah, come on! Can't a guy get sentimental?"

"Later, darling. We've had enough sentiment for now."

He assembled his saxophone and riffed chords while Claire walked her way through "After You've Gone." Captivated by her melodic sensibilities, he waited until she finished her solo before edging into the groove.

They played for an hour. African and Caribbean rhythms melded into bebop improvisations of Cole Porter and Duke Ellington classics. They were half way through Thelonious Monk's "Round Midnight," when a fist hit the wall.

"Clarence, what the hell! Don't you have anything better to do than pound on walls? Rufus snarled. "We're not in the shower, and we're not using up all your fucking hot water."

"Watch your mouth, man. I ain't said nothing 'bout water. I got my woman with me. She wants to hear some sweet music, not a lot of screeching. You sound like a horny cat trying to screw its mama."

Rufus caught Claire's grin. "Looks like we got us an audience." He chuckled and shouted at the wall. "Sounds like we're not the only horny ones. What do you want to hear? Cool and sweet or hot and sexy?"

"My woman likes Nat King Cole's "Unforgettable" and Ray Charles's "I Can't Stop Loving You." He snickered. "What the hell! Play what you want long as it keeps us in the mood."

"You saying you don't want to hear a jazzy bass-sax duet?"

"Ain't you hearing me? We want music not screeches."

"In that case, I'll play the real stuff." Rufus laid his sax on the sofa. He rippled through a stack of CDs, dropped four in his stereo and turned it on.

He turned to Claire. "May I have this dance?"

She smiled and wrapped her arms around his neck. Their bodies touching, they danced in place, swaying in unison to the Ray Charles's sensuous rhythms.

"Is this our last dance before Memphis?" she asked.

"Don't talk. Just enjoy." Rufus nuzzled his face in her hair and held her close.

A knock on the door shattered the intimate moment. Reluctantly, Rufus drew away from Claire's embrace and stalked to the door.

"What the hell's the matter now?" He stomped to the door and mumbled under his breath. "I thought he was taking care of his woman. How can he be in bed and outside my door at the same time?"

Rufus touched the door knob and paused. His hair bristled on the back of his neck. Something was wrong. Clarence didn't knock; he pounded.

He tensed his muscles and turned the knob. When he opened the door and saw the tall, imposing man standing under the naked light bulb dangling overhead, he froze. Bilious gasses erupted in his gut and settled in his throat. He didn't have to ask his name. He would have recognized those steely blue eyes anyplace.

"Mr. Burton," he said barely above a whisper.

Burton nodded and returned Rufus's stare. Rufus, stunned

into silence, studied the man, trying to decide if he should slam the door in his face or welcome him in. Despite Burton's imposing height and rigid stance, he didn't appear threatening. If anything, his grim expression suggested he was flying a mission without a parachute.

"Is Claire here?" Burton asked. "I have to talk to her."

Rufus chilled. Recalling the stories Claire had told him about her father, he was tempted to tell him he got the wrong address. The cat house was up a block. He held back. Burton was, after all, Claire's father. And he might be rich and powerful, but he sure as hell didn't have any street smarts. Nobody with an ounce of sense would make a trip to the ghetto wearing a cashmere overcoat, designer watch, and gold cuff links. If the gangstas in the hood sniffed him, they'd strip him down, chop him up, and feed his sorry hide to the mangy curs roaming the alleys.

"I'm looking for Claire Burton," he repeated. "I was told she's staying here. I have to talk to her."

"Hang on a minute. I'll see if she's available." He started to ease the door closed. "It's all right. I'll talk to him." Claire stepped in front of Rufus and looked at her father, her expression dark and inscrutable.

"What do you want?" she asked.

"I want you to come with me. Your mother... We have a crisis. I need your help, now."

CHAPTER FIFTEEN

Claire's adamant refusal to ride with her father angered Bernard and exasperated Rufus. He didn't go so far as to empathize with Burton for his daughter's obstinacy, but neither did he understand why Claire insisted he tag along. And tag along was all he intended to do. He was more than willing to comfort Claire and give her support, but he drew the line at her insistence that he attend a family crisis meeting.

A quick glance at her pale face and shaking hands told him she wasn't being stubborn, she was afraid. After all, she had been out of rehab less than a week. Still confronting her own demons, she was ill-equipped to handle any more. Her mother's illness was like a cancer that was growing larger and more destructive every day. She needed him if only to have someone standing in the wings in case she fainted.

"I'll drive Claire. We'll be right behind you," Rufus said. He motioned for Bernard to go on. Ten minutes later, he and Claire were heading to the suburbs.

Burton met them in the grand hall of his baronial manor. "We'll talk in the kitchen." He gripped Claire's arm. "There'll be fewer interruptions."

"You're coming, too, aren't you?" Claire gave Rufus a pleading look.

"You go on. I have to call Ella and tell her we'll be late, again." He flicked a weak smile.

He waited until Claire and her father turned left and disappeared down a shadowy hallway, then walked to the telephone blinking on an ornately carved console table. He was confounded by the flashing lights and thirty-four plastic tabs that accessed everything from voice mail to video conferencing. He wanted to make a phone call, not contact the Pentagon.

Daunted but not defeated, he lifted the receiver and punched in Ella's number. The sound of her growly voice made him wish he had dialed the wrong number.

"Don't you know how to tell time, you fool? Moon 'n Lenny 'n me are ready to boil you in oil. Shit! What am I gonna tell 'em when you don't show?"

"Sweet Ella. Tell 'em I'll be a little late. I have to handle some fast changes going on in my life."

"What changes you talking?"

"Illness in the family."

"Ha! Hard dick in the pants more'n likely."

"Not so, baby. I promised I wouldn't let my dick get in the way of my better judgment. You and me got trouble enough." He sugared his tongue and cooed. "Don't go off on me. You know how to work an audience. Sing a few of sexy ballads. They'll love you, and I'll owe you."

"I know you're fucking with me, but I ain't got time to talk." A sigh followed a string of obscenities. "Okay, I'll sing, but your fat ass better be here 'fore I lose my voice."

Rufus hung up, then looked around for a bathroom. Two doors, one labeled HIS the other HERS beckoned. He groaned. Four people in the house, and they got segregated toilets!

He entered the HIS door and flipped on the light. He gasped.

This wasn't a toilet; it was an alpha male's crapper. With the morbid curiosity of a Peeping Tom, he eyeballed the ornamentations, noting the ceiling's brass and wood chandelier, the chocolate suede walls, and the streaked beige and gold marble floor. A massive mahogany wardrobe, a clothes tree, matching wash basin, toilet, and urinal filled the space in between. He unzipped his trousers and assumed the pose in front of the johnny pot. He watched the yellow spray splatter the shiny porcelain. When he finished, he shook his penis and tucked it away. Then, feeling guilty for messing the "number one" icon, he hit the flush button twice.

He washed his hands twice and studied himself in the mirror. "Why in the hell did I let Claire drag me with her?" He knew if she and her father got into it, he'd be as out of place as an atheist at a Baptist convention.

He slapped cold water on his face, grabbed an orange-pumpkin towel branded with a B and wiped away the moisture, but he couldn't ax the guilty feeling gnawing at his insides.

Like it or not, he had to stop procrastinating and join Claire and the man in the kitchen. He caught a flashing red light when he turned to leave. Another telephone! He would've seen it when he walked in if the chocolate walls hadn't camouflaged the phone's chocolate case. He snorted. Couldn't Burton even take a crap without his umbilical cord to the financial world? He opened the door and followed the sound of human voices drifting down the hall.

He paused at the fringe of a light beam streaming through the kitchen door. He tipped his head and peered inside. Several seconds passed before his eyes adjusted to the blinding glare of

THE LAST TRAIN TO MEMPHIS

white on white, and he could differentiate the white cabinets from the white appliances.

Claire and Burton faced each other across a butcher block table, the wood's beige tones and the red flares flashing in their eyes the only colors visible in the sterile room.

Tuning out their accusatory wrangling, he concentrated on Burton's appearance. His arrogant expression and sharply defined features labeled him an opinionated, influential tycoon, but his slouched shoulders and bowed head implied a wariness and physical exhaustion. Rufus cocked a brow. He knew looks could be deceiving, but at that moment, the hood's street-corner capitalists were more intimidating than Burton.

Rufus entered the kitchen with slow, easy strides. Burton shot him a cold glance and then turned his gaze back to Claire and continued his diatribe.

"What the hell did you want? I gave you everything money could buy. The best schools, finest clothes, latest cars, prestigious friends. What did I get in return? A derelict daughter, living in a squalid tenement with a drug addict, ex-con and a penniless, lazy slam."

"How dare you say such horrible things about Rufus! He's the kindest, most honorable man I've ever known." She picked up a salt shaker, threatening to throw it. "You take it back, or I'll…"

"Cool it, babe." Rufus grabbed her wrist and pried the shaker from her clenched hand. He looked at Bernard and struggled with his conflicting emotions. Should he pity the man or light into him? Deciding to take the high road and not make matters worse, he set the salt shaker on the table and sat down beside Claire. "This is your father's house," he said. "He's got a right to speak his mind."

"Speak, yes, but he was slandering you."

"I've heard worse. Can't say I like hearing it, but sometimes it's better to know where a person's coming from." He gave Burton a twisted smile. "Don't take it personally if I don't ask you to write my obituary. For the record, the word's Sam, not slam. You know, like in Little Black Sambo."

Burton's face flushed. He crossed his arms over his chest, and slipped into a silence that hung in the air like a Damocles sword.

Claire took several deep breaths. When her hands stopped shaking, she leaned across the table and gave her father a hard, blistering stare.

"You can call me a whore, a penniless bass player, an ex-addict, a ghetto debutante, but no way will I let you put down my friends. And never Rufus."

Burton sneered. "You don't have the sense you were born with. I didn't invest a fortune raising you only to have you live in a neighborhood swarming with rapists, murderers, and drug dealers."

"That's it." Claire threw out her arms in defeat. "You came looking for me. You said you needed help. All I've heard is what a sorry daughter I am." She rose and reached for her parka. "I'm out of here. You don't need my help. You need a laxative."

"Who taught you to talk to your father like that? I never thought I'd hear such filthy language come out of your mouth." Burton sat up in his chair, drawing his slouched shoulders ram-rod straight.

"I'm sorry if my language upsets you, but I asked you not to insult Rufus or condemn the way I live." She slipped an arm into her jacket and turned to leave, but Rufus reached out and pulled her back.

"Let me handle this," he said. He turned to Burton and spoke in a slow, measured cadence.

"There was a time when you and I would've settled our differences outside, but I learned violence and name calling only make matters worse. You came to my apartment and asked Claire for help. Whatever the problem, it's between you and her. It doesn't concern me. You can tell me to get the hell out, but if you do, Claire goes, too, and you still have your problem. How about forgetting the past and present crap you're flinging at Claire and tell her what's going on. If you're ready to talk, we're ready to listen."

Rufus waited for Burton to bury him under a mountain of fire and brimstone. When the volcano didn't erupt, he leaned back and assumed the watch-and-wait attitude of an interested but uninvolved observer.

"You staying or going?" Burton spoke to Claire, a slight hesitation tempering his belligerent tone.

"I'll stay, but only if we stop arguing. I hate it when we fight. If it makes you feel better, I admit I was never your poster daughter, but then, we were never a poster family. That's okay. Every family has problems." She lifted her chin in a defiant gesture. "You went to a lot of trouble to find me. You said there was a crisis. What is it? I know it has to do with mother." Her expression darkened. "It must be bad. You never asked for my help before. You always took care of things." She looked down and stared at her quivering hands. "What do you want from me?"

Burton glanced at Rufus. "I'd rather he wasn't here. I'm not going to discuss family problems in front of strangers."

"Rufus isn't a stranger," Claire retorted. "Just get on with it."

"She tried to commit suicide." The dark cloud on Burton's face accentuated the anger and disgust flaring in his eyes.

"She. Dixie. My mother." Claire slammed her fist on the table. "You're telling me Mom tried to kill herself, and we're discussing it as if it were an everyday occurrence? What did you do to her? Where is she?"

"I didn't do anything to her, and she's upstairs in her bedroom," Burton said.

"Is that all you have say? She's in her bedroom. Doing what? Having a drink, celebrating her pitiful attempt to be rid of you and be free at last?" Claire's outburst dissolved in a wail of tears.

"Here we go again. First the sarcasm, then the blame, then the tears."

"Claire's upset, Mr. Burton," Rufus said. "It might help if you didn't shout." He put his arm around Claire in a protective gesture. "Stay cool, babe. Don't get your back up. You're stronger than that. You don't want to lose control now."

"She lost it a long time ago," Burton said. "I thought she'd want to help, but I was wrong." He stood up and looked at her with burning, reproachful eyes. "Get out of my sight. Go back to your black ghetto and miserable crack house. I don't know what I expected but certainly not this."

Rufus released Claire and stood up, his six-foot-two frame eclipsing the man who sat hunched over the table. "Chill out, man," he said. "This isn't the way you want to go. You need help. Mrs. Burton needs help. If you cut Claire now, she's gone for good. Somebody has to give. From the looks of things, it'll have to be you."

Burton hooked his brows together in a baffled frown. "I don't know what business this is of yours, but if you're saying we have to work together…" He rubbed his eyes and let out a weary sign. "I can't do this alone. I never faced anything like this before. My family hid their emotions. You always said we were cold and detached. Maybe we were, but detached sure beats the hell out of chaos and madness."

"Madness!" Claire screamed. "Are you saying mother's insane?"

"I'll tell you what happened, and you can make up your own mind on that," he said with a note of impatience in his voice. "Your mother slashed her wrists. Flo found her. I wasn't home."

"Is mother all right? I mean, she's not…" Claire threw her hand to her lips.

"She's all right. Flo found her in time."

"Flo! That poor woman. She must've been terrified. What did she do? She couldn't handle something like that alone."

"She buzzed Henry, and Henry called me. I didn't believe him. Henry and Flo are housekeepers, not doctors."

"Oh, for Chrissake, you don't have to be a doctor to see someone's wrists are bleeding. That's immaterial right now. But mother! My God, tell me what happened."

Burton ran his fingers across his brow. "I called Dr. Ashley and hurried home. By the time I arrived, the doctor had bandaged Dixie's wrists and sedated her. He insisted I take her to the hospital."

"Why didn't you?" Claire yelled.

"Your mother rose out of her bed like Lazarus rising from the dead. She kept screaming, 'No hospital, no hospital.' I want my baby. I want Claire.' She wouldn't calm down until I promised to find you and bring you home. Dr. Ashley didn't like the idea, but he finally agreed but only if someone stayed with her around the clock."

The telephone rang, jolting the trio into a glacial silence. Burton thawed on the second ring. He shifted his eyes to the red phone. Rufus wondered if he would answer it, or stay with Claire to console her and ease her fears. He saw the nervous tick in Burton's cheek, he started to count down from ten to see how long it took before he responded. On the fifth ring, Burton hurried across the room. On the sixth ring, he lifted the receiver.

Claire turned to Rufus, her face livid with rage. "You see that? He's talking on the damn phone. He cares more about his damn profits and losses than he does about me or his wife. I can't stand it anymore. I'm leaving." She jumped up. Rufus reached out and grabbed her.

"Goddammit, woman. Put your ass on that seat and cut all this crap about how good you are and how bad he is. So he loves money. Who doesn't? You came here to help your mama, not reform your daddy."

"It isn't crap. It's the truth. He's a self-centered, money-hungry miser."

"Don't you understand? He can't help himself? Money may be his life, but he came looking for you. He took the first step. Who knows if he'll take a second? Be thankful for small favors. I'd have done anything in the world if I could've helped my mama, but I never got the chance."

Claire simmered, sniffled, and finally fell silent.

"I'm going to have to leave," Burton said when he returned

to the table. He looked at Claire. "It has nothing to do with making money. One of my clients, an older woman, gets confused. She worries about her investments. She calls me all hours of the day and night. I know it's hard for you to believe, but even hard-nosed capitalists can be angels of mercy."

"What about mother? Doesn't she need an angel of mercy?"

"She has you. My client has no one. I'll go upstairs with you and check on Dixie before I go."

Rufus took Claire's hand. Side-by-side, they followed Burton into the foyer, up the grand staircase, and down the hall to Dixie's room, the Oriental carpet muffling their footsteps.

The door was ajar, but even if it had been locked, a deaf man could have heard Dixie's wails.

Claire jerked her hand free and darted inside. She came to an abrupt halt and stared terror-stricken at her mother straddling a window sill. Black mascara streaked her gaunt cheeks. Purple lipstick bled into the lines around her lips.

"Mother, get away from the window. My God, you could fall and kill yourself."

She started forward, but Henry stepped in front of her and forcibly held her back.

"Don't scare her," he said. "Give her space. She's been sitting there for fifteen minutes. She's not going to jump."

"How do you know?" Claire glared at him. "I can't wait. I won't take that chance." Jerking free, she approached Dixie, a tepid smile on her face.

"Mom, it's me, Claire. You said you wanted to see me. Come, sit with me on the sofa. Please. We'll talk. Tell me what's wrong. I want to help."

"Stay away," Dixie shouted. "Nobody can help me. Nobody cares if I live or die. I don't care either." She teetered on the edge of the sill.

"No. You're wrong. I care." Claire darted to the window and yanked her inside. With a thud, Dixie fell to the floor. Terrified, she clawed the air and cursed God.

Rufus and Henry ran to them. Henry restrained Dixie. Rufus drew Claire into his arms, and their eyes locked on the wasted shell of what had once been a beautiful woman.

When Dixie's body finally went limp, Henry glanced up and barked, "Claire, throw me the comforter on the bed. Rufus, get the limo out of the garage and park it in front of the house. Mr. Burton, call Dr. Ashley. Ask him to contact the Clearwater Rehab Center and tell them we're bringing Dixie in. You'll have to go along. They'll want personal information, proof of insurance, and a medical history."

Roused by Henry's commanding tone, they rallied instantly. Claire helped Henry tend Dixie. Rufus pocketed the car keys Henry tossed at him, and Burton hurried out the door, mumbling that he would use the private phone in his office to call Dr. Ashley and his client.

His emotions wired, his thoughts disjointed, Rufus plunged down the stairs and along the dark hallways to the garage. He paused at the door and caught his breath. He couldn't decide if he was running from something or to something. Probably both. He knew if he hung around Burton too long, he'd take a swing at him. Although he felt sorry for Dixie, he couldn't understand how a woman who had everything could end up with nothing. All of a sudden, he understood what the term dysfunctional meant. In Burton's circle, it meant families were angry and alienated. In the ghetto, it meant families were fucked up.

He pulled open the fire door and entered the four-car garage. Minutes later, he parked the black limousine in the front of the mansion.

When Henry and Claire emerged, with Dixie tottering between them, Rufus scrambled around the front of the car and opened the doors on the right side. With Dixie and Claire in the back, and Henry in the front, Rufus eased the car around the circular driveway and picked up speed when he reached the highway.

Half an hour later, Rufus braked in front of a massive red brick structure, its wings curving out like open arms in welcome.

A woman and two men wearing the uniforms of their profession burst through the glass doors, down the walk to the car. With robotic efficiency, they transferred Dixie to a wheel chair and whisked her into the marble foyer where another woman, in a stiffer, whiter uniform acknowledged them with a scowl.

"I'm Nurse Pratt. Dr. Ashley gave us orders to admit Mrs. Dixie Burton," she said in a rote, humdrum tone. "As night supervisor, I don't usually deal with routine paper work, but Dr. Ashley specifically asked me to take responsibility for the patient and report to him personally."

She checked her watch and shot a disparaging glance at Dixie who sat slumped in the wheelchair, her eyes closed, her chin touching her chest. "Is this the patient?"

"Yes," Claire said. "She's my mother."

Pratt lowered her head and peered over the rim of her glasses. "I know you. Weren't you a patient here?"

"Yes." Claire crossed her arms in front of her and shivered slightly. "The hallway's freezing. Can't we take her to her room?"

"We can't admit Mrs. Burton until we see her insurance card. That's the rule." Pratt arched a brow. "You know we always follow the rules. We don't make exceptions."

"I believe in rules, but as far as I know, only ten have been written in stone." A man's voice ricocheted off the stark, plaster walls. "You don't have to worry about getting your money. I'm Mr. Burton. I'll take care of it."

"Bernard, is that you?" Dixie raised her head and peered at him through narrowed eyes. "Where am I? Why am I in this wheelchair?" She sniffed the air, pungent with the aroma of medicine and bed pans and despair. "This is a hospital. I begged you not to bring me here. Please, oh God, please take me home."

"You belong here," Claire said. "They're going to help you get well. I promise. I'll stay with you as long as I can."

"Shut up," Dixie said. "I don't want you. I want my husband." She reached out and grabbed the hem of Bernard's overcoat. "You'll take me home, won't you, darling?"

"Stop making a fool out of yourself." He twisted his mouth in disgust and turned his gaze to Pratt. "Is this the way you take care of your patients? How long does she have to sit in a dark, drafty hallway before you take her upstairs?"

Pratt responded immediately. She snapped her fingers and pointed to an orderly. "Room two-twelve."

Tears rolling down her cheeks, Claire watched as the man wheeled Dixie away. She stepped beside Rufus and slid her arm around his waist. "Let's go," she said. "We can make it to Ella's in time for the second set."

CHAPTER SIXTEEN

Rufus and Claire made it to Ella's in time for the second set. He stepped onto the bandstand and planted a kiss on Ella's cheek.

"Thanks for standing in for us." He winked. "I wish I could've caught your act. I bet you wowed 'em."

"Them folks so hungry for entertainment, they'd a been wowed by a monkey act."

The sarcasm he heard in her voice contrasted sharply with the excitement he saw in her eyes. He knew how much she loved the spotlight. She was a trooper from the chitlin circuit, and he had heard her belt out a song with such power and passion, it would've made a Baptist choir hand in their robes. Her heaving breasts and frazzled expression tempered his enthusiasm. The chitlin circuit had been a long road back, and time had taken its toll. He was glad he and Claire arrived in time for the second set.

"If they're looking for an animal show, we could do worse than make sounds like the Monkees. You remember 'em, the pop group from the Sixties?"

"Course I remember. They recorded 'I'm a Believer' and 'Last Train to Clarksville.' I ain't senile, but I got trouble figuring what they got to do with you."

"Forget it. They got nothing to do with me. I'm making noise."

Ella pointed to his saxophone case. "Make noise with that. I'm going to the bar and tell Bojay to mix me a tall one."

Rufus greeted Moon and Lenny with a hesitant smile. When he got the same back, he breathed a little easier. They might not be happy with him, but they weren't ready to stomp off stage. He assembled his sax, grabbed the microphone, and introduced the band and the first number.

Rufus soloed "Bye Bye Blackbird." Claire, Moon, and Lenny comped. Moon soloed "Umbrella Man," and the others comped. They continued their round-robin musical medley through eight more songs before Rufus called for a break. It was almost midnight. The group had to be dragging. He wiped the perspiration off his forehead, did a half turn, and glanced at Moon and Lenny. If they were tired, he didn't see it. Instead of dying, they looked good to go and ready to jam till dawn.

Rufus understood how they felt. Like food and drink, music was a need, an obsession. He read someplace that Artie Shaw, a famous band leader in the Forties, supposedly said playing music was better than sex. He thought that was a stretch, but he did believe playing jazz got rid of the blues faster than sniffing coke. A glance at Claire confirmed his belief.

She stood a few feet in back of him and a little to the right. She leaned into her bass and waited to lay down the basic notes needed to coordinate the harmony.

If she was upset or anxious, he didn't see it. Her body poised, her expression serene, she had somehow suppressed her anger against her father and the shock of seeing her mother being wheeled down a dark, antiseptic-smelling hall at the Clearwater Rehab Center. He knew her heart was broken, and her sorrow would return, but for now, the band, the music, and her talent were all that mattered.

Rufus opened the last set with the ballad "Sweet and Lovely." Lenny joined in, his fingers splayed across the keyboard. Finally, Moon and Claire established the groove. They swung into a bluesy rendition of Ellington's "Mood Indigo" and finished with a mixture of traditional and modern favorites that included rhythms from Africa to the Caribbean, from Brazil to Harlem.

Bojay closed the bar at two o'clock. The stragglers stumbled out half an hour later. No one turned down Ella's offer of a late dinner or early breakfast, whatever they preferred to call it. The group sat around a large table and sipped drinks until Bojay arrived carrying a tray heaped with food. Like a cocaine high, the pungent odors of hot wings, greasy fries, greens, and corn bread awakened their senses and made their mouths water. Conversation was limited to grunts and nods until the platters were wiped clean.

"Mighty good fixin's," Moon said. "Gonna take me a while 'fore I can get my butt off this chair."

"Take your time, son," Ella said. "It's still early. Folks like us hang 'round till the sun come up." She grinned. "If it's a cloudy day, we sit till it do."

"Marathon drinking bouts are a long time past," Rufus said.

"Ain't saying we should. Just saying we did," Ella said. "They was good times, but we paid the piper in the end."

Claire looked up. "Everybody pays the piper in the end, and the bill is always higher than we thought."

Rufus looked at her in surprise. She hadn't said ten words while they ate. He thought she was exhausted, now he realized she was depressed. He had to take her home. Despair and low self-esteem could be disastrous to recovering addicts. A snort was the only way they knew to ease the pain. Just one. But one was never enough.

"Time to hit the road, babe," he said in a smooth voice. "We'll pick up on this later."

"I don't want to go," she said. "Moon, Lenny, and Ella have a right to know why we were late." She turned to Ella. "Don't blame Rufus. It was my fault."

"I ain't blaming nobody," Ella said. "I knows you two got problems, 'n you got to work 'em out."

"Thanks," Claire said. "You put up a lot with me. I appreciate it."

"Don't you go making me into a saint. When you showed Tuesday last, I was ready to kick your ass outta here. I figured shit was gonna happen. You didn't give me no shit, so I ain't gonna give you none."

"I wouldn't have blamed you if he had kicked my ass out the door. I thank God you didn't. You saved my life."

"Lawd amighty, I'm a church-going woman, but I ain't no missionary. I know problems when I see 'em, and you and Rufus got more'n your share. Ain't no secret he got feelings for you. I figure the good Lawd got His reasons for putting you together and then tearing you apart. It be His doing, not mine, so I'm gonna sit back, cross my arms, and wait for the Lawd to tell me what I got to do."

Claire gripped Ella's hand. "I wish my mother had your faith and your strength. Sometimes I wonder if she even knows what they mean."

"Them's hard words coming from a daughter."

"I don't mean to sound disrespectful, but I'm angry. Falling-down-drunk is the only image I have of my mother. She should've known how terrible it was for a little kid to watch her slowly kill herself on alcohol." Claire clutched her fingers into a tight fist. "She's messed up real bad. I didn't know how bad till tonight. I guess she got tired of waiting to die, so she decided to commit suicide. Rufus and I took her to Clearwater Rehab Center." She wiped away the tears streaking her cheeks. "You understand we had to get help."

In the silence that followed, Rufus studied Ella, Moon, and Lenny's expressions as they mulled over Claire's family tragedy. He saw surprise and shock, disbelief and denial. If they had thought about Claire at all, she was another rebellious white chick who wagged her tail at a ghetto rooster for the fun of it. It wouldn't have dawned on them that her mother was a drunk, and her daddy was a fuck-up. As far as they knew, Claire and her family lived in a glass house, ate dinner at a table, and paid the rent on time.

Moon was the first to respond to Claire's pain. Like a mourner at a wake for someone he barely knew, he offered his sympathy in a hesitant voice. Ella and Lenny did the same. When their moods took a downturn and the tension became palpable, Moon jumped up, circled around the table, and stopped beside Claire.

"This ain't no way to end the evening." He took Claire's hand and pulled her off the chair. "Come on, babe. You and me's gonna dance."

"No, Moon. I'm not in the mood. Anyway, there's no music. We can't dance without music."

Moon snapped his fingers and yelled at Bojay. "Hey, man, lay a record on the turn-table and wire it in here. Something cool and jazzy."

"I know you're trying to cheer me up. I appreciate your concern, but, please, don't force it," Claire said. "I promise, I'll be in a better mood tomorrow, but right now…" She turned to Rufus. "I want to go home. It's late. You said so yourself."

"You have time for one dance. We all have time for one dance." Rufus rose and offered his hand to Ella. "Will you do me the honor?"

Ella smiled like a school girl at her first dance. "You handsome dude. Can't think of nothing better I'd like to do."

The Latin rhythms of Cole Porter's "Begin the Beguine," filled the room. Moon swept Claire in his arms and broke into a wild, hip-swinging rumba.

Rufus and Ella followed them around the dance floor. He tried to imitate Moon's exotic moves and intricate steps, but after a while, he realized what a difference age makes. When he slowed down, the room came into focus, and he saw Lenny and Bojay sitting at the table having a heated conversation. When they finished talking, they stood up and headed to the dance floor.

Rufus looked at them in astonishment, positive he had never seen anything like it. Lenny and Bojay were doing the rumba. Bojay led, Lenny followed. Rufus smiled. Bojay was grooving and seemed completely oblivious of his partner's constipated attitude.

An hour later, Rufus pulled into a parking space directly in front of his building, turned off the ignition, and whooped. "This is my lucky day," he said. "I've never found an empty spot this close till mid-morning when folks go to work or hit the street."

He helped Claire out of the car, grabbed her hand, and pulled her with him across the ice-covered sidewalk and up the steps. She stopped and burst out laughing.

"What's so funny?" He growled. "It's colder'n hell out here. Get your butt inside before it and I freeze."

"Stop being such a crab. Look around. See how beautiful it is. Everything's so quiet, so peaceful." She turned and faced the bitter wind that roared down the ghetto canyon. "It feels so good to laugh." She squeezed his hand. "It feels so right, you and I, together. Thanks for helping with mother. Thanks for letting me play in your band. Thanks for loving me."

"Cut it, babe. You don't have to thank me for anything. Whatever I gave you, you gave it back doubled." He tilted her chin up and looked at her in amazement. "I love it when you laugh. Your whole personality changes. Laughter becomes you. I wish you could be happy forever."

"Nothing lasts forever." She brushed her mouth across his lips, then opened the door, darted into the foyer, and up the stairs.

Rufus sprinted after her, a playful puppy nipping at her heels.

They made love and fell asleep as the first rays of light burnished the eastern horizon. When Rufus awoke hours later, the sky was overcast, the air heavy with the promise of snow. As quietly as possible, he slipped out of bed, showered and dressed, and headed into the kitchen. He reached for the coffee pot, paused, and shook his head. They needed more than coffee to charge their batteries. They needed a rib-sticking breakfast. He believed Ella's banquet had raised Claire's spirits more than Moon's rumba. Simply put, they had to eat to live.

He checked the refrigerator and wasn't surprised to see it was empty. As much as he hated grocery shopping, he knew he had no choice. If he wanted to eat, he had to buy food. He put on his coat and slipped his wallet into his back pocket. On his way out the door, he scratched a note to Claire telling her where he went and not to worry.

He grumbled all the way to the car, protesting the cold wind slapping his face and the slush soaking his shoes. He scraped the ice off the windshield, opened the door, and slid behind the wheel. He turned the ignition key. Nothing happened. He turned it again. The engine sputtered and died. Gasoline fumes seeped inside the car and gagged him.

"Damn!" He growled. What the hell happened to his luck? He checked the hoarfrost glazing his car. No doubt it was lost somewhere between the Arctic Circle and his street. He counted to ten and tried again. No sputter, no chug, no luck.

He laid his head against the seat and aimlessly gazed out the window. It was empty except for the usual string of junk-yard cars. The scene was so familiar; he almost missed the late-model sedan parked half a block away. Dark thoughts put him on instant alert. Either a drug deal was going down, or the men in blue were tracking a high-rolling cat.

He was hip to the black man's survival tactic to vacate before shit started to fly. He didn't want to be caught in the middle of a shooting match, but neither did he want to be the only target. If he made a sudden move, and the dudes were trigger happy, he could find himself on the wrong end of a firing range.

Go or stay? While he weighed his options, the car pulled away from the curb and coasted down the block. He smelled trouble. In his neighborhood, only gold-toothed hustlers and prowling cats toured a scene, and then only in the summer.

The car pulled alongside his. The driver stuck his head out the window and motioned for him to do the same.

Rufus's heart did a wingover. Although he didn't see a badge or a uniform, the man's pasty, white skin, ragged brows, and lethal stare were standard features on the local fuzz. Rufus's uneasiness rose a notch.

"Need some help?" Whitey asked.

"I'm cool," Rufus said. The steady tone in his voice surprised him. "In fact, I'm damn cold. So's my car. It's a stubborn bastard. I'll get it started eventually."

Whitey slid out of the car and approached Rufus. Three mastodons followed.

"Open the window and hand me some ID," he ordered. "No fast moves. Take it slow and easy."

"I'm not showing you nothing till you tell me who you are."

"Officer Mullins." He cocked his head at the mastodons. "Them's Tom, Dick, and Harry."

"I knew you were badge men. Problem is, you're not wearing 'em." Rufus sneered. "I guess you didn't have time to dig 'em out of a cereal box."

"Okay, nigger, that's it." Mullins yanked the door open and thumbed him out of the car. "Hands over your head."

Rufus slid out of the car and pointed his finger in Mullins' face. "You call me nigger again, and I'll spread your nose over your ugly face." He sucked in his cheeks and narrowed his eyes. "You got nothing on me, but that doesn't matter, does it? You can always find something. If you're into racial profiling, you should have at least waited till I got my car started."

"Shut your fucking mouth, Johnson." Mullins slammed Rufus against the car and ordered him to take the position. After he patted him down, he yanked his arms to his back and cuffed him.

Rufus's blood went cold. Mullins knew his name. This wasn't racial profiling, it was a set up, and that bastard Syd Garret had to be the pimp.

"Okay. You know who I am, and you know where I live. Now what? You going to arrest me? This won't mean shit to you, but for the record, you got to read me my rights, and somewhere down the line, you got to charge me with a crime. You'll have to make that up since I haven't committed one. I'm a God-fearing man. Shit, I don't even spit on the sidewalk."

"Is that right?" A smile cracked Mullins clam-shelled face. He pulled a bag from his coat pocket and dangled it in front of Rufus. "How the hell you explain this, for the record? Looks to me like a twenty-cent bag of marijuana."

"You motherfucker, you can't pin a dope deal on me. I'm clean. I don't trade the stuff, I don't smoke it."

"Quit shitting us, Johnson. One of your buddies dropped a dime on you."

"You quit shitting me. That's not mine, and you fucking know it."

Mullins raised his arm and backhanded Rufus's mouth. The blow knocked Rufus against the car. He swallowed the blood pooling in his mouth and checked his anger, another survival tactic. If he called Mullins a lying bastard, he'd end up mincemeat at the police kennel. He couldn't take another hit. His cracked lip and the pain shooting up his arms were close to intolerable.

He was almost relieved when two members of Mullins' crew shoved him in the back seat and sandwiched him between them.

Mullins shifted the car into motion and drove down the street keeping well within the speed limit.

Rufus knew something bad was coming down. He didn't know what, but he did know he couldn't fight his way free. He had to figure a way to outwit them. He might not be a brilliant strategist, but he was a hell of a lot smarter than Mullins and his mastodons combined. All he had to do was stay alert and get one lucky break.

He pressed his tongue on his lip to stem the bleeding and looked out the window. If he escaped, he'd have to know where he was so he'd know where to go. By checking street signs and prominent landmarks, he realized Mullins was heading north into the ghetto's soft underbelly. He frowned. His hope for a lucky break went sour. He assumed Mullins would take him to headquarters and book him on a trumped-up charge. Then he would've called a legal defense lawyer and walked out in a matter of hours. When Mullins turned into a trash-littered alley and stopped in front of a burned out shell of what had once been a solid, two-family duplex, Rufus knew no lawyer would be inside, and the only walk he'd take would be on a short plank, unless elusive lady luck blew in and decided to stay awhile.

The doors opened and burly hands dragged Rufus from the car. Like mendicants in front of an altar, they stood four abreast and stared up at the rotting structure.

Rufus tried to bring the building into focus, but pain and stress blurred his eyes.

"How come you ain't thanking me?" Mullins elbowed Rufus.

"I went through all kind of trouble to bring you here. Thought you'd like to see your old crack house again. Ain't much to look at no more, but it never was real fancy, was it?"

Rufus felt a stirring in his gut. That motherfucker couldn't have ... What was the point? He raised his head and forced himself to take another look. This time he not only saw a building, he saw a scene more grotesque than anything hell had to offer.

"You fucking asshole," he bellowed. "What kind of shit you putting on me?"

"Watch who you're calling asshole. I'm just an inch away from hurting you bad." Mullins sucked in his temper and grinned at Rufus. "Thought you'd like to see your old stomping grounds. Couple years back, it was the crack house of choice for scum like you. But that ain't why you remember it, is it? You remember it cause it's where you murdered a cop."

Rufus looked at Mullins in disbelief. "I didn't murder anybody, and you know it."

Mullins grabbed Rufus's throat. "I could kill you right now, but I promised Garret you'd be breathing when he got here." He released his hold and looked at him in contempt. "You murdered Lieutenant Ronnie Feldon. Garret was there, he saw the whole thing. But you got lucky. Some fucking judge let you walk."

"A jury cleared me, not a judge," Rufus said. They heard the facts, saw the truth, and found me innocent."

"A jury found O. J. Simpson innocent, but that don't mean shit to me."

Rufus looked at the mastodons staring at him with hate-filled eyes. "Didn't figure it would."

"Figure this. Garret and the rest of us guys had our own trial.

Our jury said you're guilty. We don't have no prison, so we sentenced you to death. It ain't going to be quick. Garret decided to kill you the same way you killed Feldon. That's going to take a little time."

Mullins glanced down the deserted street. "Where the hell's Garret? He said he'd be here by now." He shivered and rubbed his hands together. "Damn, it's cold. Take the spook upstairs and dump him on the floor. We'll wait for Garret in the car."

The two men grabbed Rufus's arms and dragged him through the door and up a flight of stairs. When they reached the second floor, they dropped him on a wooden plank as if he were a bag of potatoes.

As they turned to walk away, Rufus called out for them to stop. "How about showing a condemned man a little mercy and unlocking these cuffs? My arms are aching, and my hands are numb." He sensed their hesitation and held his breath. Maybe they weren't brainless goons after all. Maybe they still had a spark of humanity left despite Garret's indoctrination. "What's it going to cost you? Hell, I'm not going anyplace. Only way out of here is through that window or the front door."

"Whatdaya think, Tony?" The older, gruffer man looked at his partner but didn't wait for an answer. He looked down at Rufus and shook his head.

"You know what the trouble is? You got nothing to think about 'cept the pain in your hands. I can do something about that." A perverse smile distorting his face, he lifted his foot and kicked Rufus's groin, chest, and head.

Rufus closed his eyes, clamped his mouth shut, and waited for the pain and nausea to subside. He opened his eyes and saw the expectant looks on the men's faces. They wanted him to cry out in pain, to beg for mercy. Rufus smiled. They'd have a long wait.

"What the fuck you idiots doing?" Mullins's bellow thundered up the staircase.

"Having a little fun." Tony chuckled.

"I hope to hell you're not funning with Johnson. Garret wants him wide awake and in one piece when he shows. Now get your asses down here. I'm freezing mine off."

Rufus was glad for the cold air blowing in from the open window on the far side of the room. The icy blasts kept him from passing out. He, like Mullins, hoped Garret showed up soon. He didn't know how much longer he could hang on. He maneuvered himself into a sitting position, leaned against a post, and glanced around the barren room.

Disquieting thoughts raced through his mind. This is where it all started, and this is where it would end if Garret carried out his threat to kill him. At the moment, Rufus couldn't think of any circumstances that would make him change his mind. He had a mission. He was going to avenge his partner's death.

Rufus played the scene in his mind and tried to see it the way Garret did. He couldn't remember everything that happened on that awful, fateful day two years ago, but he remembered enough to know he didn't kill Ronnie Feldon.

He would, however, agree with Garret; he had been a fool. He frowned. Weren't all drug addicts fools? He didn't think so when he walked into the hood's prime-time crack house, paid his entrance fee, and joined the mad hatters sniffing their way into oblivion.

No one expected a raid. Before a big party, prime-time dealers made a large donation to the Blue Shirt Benevolent Association. In return, the policemen on the take agreed to protect and defend the guests' right to snort, smoke, or shoot their drug of choice.

Rufus never knew why Garret decided to break the contract. Maybe he hadn't gotten his fair share, or maybe he needed a bust to get a promotion. It didn't matter either way. Rufus remembered he was tripping like Little Red Riding Hood when Garret and his handpicked crew showed up.

He remembered thinking he was watching a bad movie, or this was somebody's idea of a joke. Three cops carrying assault weapons didn't storm into a drug house, announce their names and ranks, and threaten to shoot anybody who didn't drop to the floor. He decided it was a joke, but a burst of gunfire aimed at the ceiling changed his mind.

Rufus would never forget the hatred he saw in their eyes. Nor would he forget their names. Syd Garret, Ronnie Feldon, and Freddy Worth would stick in his mind until he died. Rufus dropped to the floor. His legs crossed, his eyes blurred, he peered at Garret through the smoke-filled haze. "This is shit, man," he said. "We's having a par-tay. We paid big do, re, mi to keep you dudes away. What happen? Our main man forget to pay?"

A gun butt landed on the right side of his head. He raised his arm to ward off a second blow and accidentally knocked a candle off a table. It hit his thigh, burned a hole through his jeans, and singed his skin in a matter of seconds. He slapped at it, but his wild, frantic motions missed the target. Positive he would be burned alive, he darted across the room, grabbed a pitcher of water, and emptied it on the burn.

"What the shit you doing, you shine-faced nigger?" Garret shouted. "Quit your damn jigging, or I'll blow you away." He aimed his gun at Rufus's heart.

Rufus stared at the gun. If he didn't know before, he knew it now. Garret planned to kill him. He had to get out of there. If he could reach the staircase and run like hell, he might make it to the street before Garret realized what was happening. He shook his head. He'd never make it, not with blurred eyes and rubber legs. He wasn't alone. If a couple of brothers started yelling, Garret would have to deal with them. He glanced down. They weren't going to help him. They were lying on the floor face down, too scared to move and too high to care.

He glanced over his shoulder and saw the open window directly in back of him. As an escape route, it had a lot to be desired, but it was all he had. He stretched his head and peered out. He turned away. He'd rather be shot than taking a dive out of a window two stories up. Dying was dying but not that way.

Feldon stood beside Garret, his face flushed with rage. "What the fuck! You hard of hearing? The lieutenant said for you to drop. If you're not face down in two seconds, I'll shove your nose in the rat droppings and make you lick 'em up with your tongue."

"Won't do it," Rufus said. "Don't see no sense in it. If you're going to arrest me, then do it. I'm not going to lick no rat shit."

Feldon's flush darkened to a deep purple. "Ain't no fucking coon gonna say 'won't' to me. 'Bout time somebody taught you some manners." Line an enraged bull, he hunched his shoulders, lowered his head, and bounded towards Rufus.

Rufus froze. In seconds, the son-of-a-bitch's solid oak head would ram into his stomach. He knew he had to get out the way, but the drugs had muddled his thoughts and rooted him to the spot. An instant later, his survival instincts surfaced. When Feldon was less than a foot away, Rufus finally dropped to the floor. He heard Garret holler at him to stop. The next thing he heard was Feldon's shrieks as he flew out the open window. His cries reverberated off the brick walls and stopped abruptly when his body hit the pavement two stories below.

Silence, like a deadly gas, filled the room. Garret stirred first. Like a hibernating bear awakened from his lair, he let out a low growl and humped across the room, his flat feet stirring the dung and dust on the wooden floor.

He leaned out the window and let out an ear-piercing howl. When he finally stumbled away from the window, he told his sergeant to check on Feldon and call for an ambulance. Hate glistening his eyes, he bent over Rufus and pressed his gun on Rufus's forehead.

"You fucking bastard. You killed Feldon," he said. "You killed my partner." With the cold, unseeing eyes of an assassin, he drew back the trigger.

Rufus closed his eyes and said a prayer. This was it. He was going to die in a rat-infested drug house. He thought of Claire and Ella, Moon and Lenny. They'd know he wouldn't kill a man, but they'd never know the truth. He waited for the click. When it didn't come, he opened his eyes. Garret had dropped his arm. His gun dangled at his side.

"No. It's too easy, too fast," Garret said. "I got other plans for you. I promise. You'll pay for this. You'll pay, one way or another."

CHAPTER SEVENTEEN

Rufus shifted his weight and rolled his shoulders in an attempt to bring feeling back into his arms. It didn't help. His muscles were locked and his bones solidified. He knew he wouldn't get any relief until he got the cuffs off his wrists, and he didn't know when that would be.

He cast a wary glance around the room. The filth and the litter were still there, but the room looked darker and more foreboding. He peered through the dust mites floating in the air and concentrated on the light coming through the window. He sucked in a gritty breath. As bad as things were now, he knew it would get worse. When the sun went down, he'd be trapped in the rat-infested tenement with no light, no heat, and little hope of getting out alive.

"Not so," he shouted. As long as he was alive, there was hope. He forced himself to think good thoughts. *Claire?* He shook his head. That wasn't a good thought. He knew she'd be frantic by now. *Rufe? Yeah. My boy. I got to remember he's waiting for me. My God! What would he think? His dad killed in a drug bust! No, no, no. I won't let that happen.* He fought down his panic and concentrated on what he knew best. Ella, Moon, Lenny? Yeah. That was better. He saw himself standing on the bandstand, playing a saxophone solo. He heard the melody. His spirit inched up from the cellar. He hummed the tune, "Into Each Life Some Rain Must Fall." A wave of nostalgia hit him. The song had gotten him through some rough times. He sang it to chase away the prison cell blues. He sang it when he was sitting in the hole, lonely, hungry, and helpless. He was still hungry and helpless, but this time he was hurting real bad.

Unable to sustain his optimism, he dropped his head and his mood veered sharply to anger. He brought this ugly mess upon himself. If he had had any sense, he would've recognized Garret's posse the minute he saw the unmarked car.

To make matters worse, he had ignored Garret's warning to watch his back. But Garret said a lot of stupid things. Who'd believe a cop who said he was going to murder you? Shit! He might do it, but even a nut case wouldn't advertise it.

The sound of an engine kicking over brought his head up. He figured Garret's lackeys had turned on the heater in their car. Lucky bastards! He was freezing while they were sitting in an unmarked patrol car, sipping on a whiskey bottle in a brown paper bag, the temperature on high.

He knew they were waiting for Garret, waiting for orders. His temper flared. Why didn't the son-of-a-bitch kill him and get it over with? Only a sadist or a man filled with hate would drag a man to a garbage dump and kick the hell out of him for fun. Any normal shithead would be home picking last night's cooties out of his crotch or dry fucking a prostitute of choice.

The sound of a car screeching to a stop clobbered Rufus with a mixed bag of emotions. The bad news was Garret had finally showed. The good news was that no matter what grisly games Garret had in store for him, he wouldn't freeze to death.

He heard muffled voices drift in from the street, then silence, then the thump of booted feet on the stairs. His adrenal gland shifted into high gear. He counted each thump. On the thir-teenth, Garret appeared at the top of the stairs. Rufus felt the blood rush through his veins.

"You should take better care of yourself. You look like a mangy dog." Garret greeted Rufus with a malicious grin and a raspy growl.

"You must be looking in a mirror," Rufus retorted.

"You want me to shut him up?" Mullins raised his fist.

"You some kind of sadist?" Garret laughed. "Cops don't beat up hog-tied Africans. You know the rules. If they get too uppity, shoot 'em."

"That's it! You just gonna shoot him." Mullins shook his head. "We coulda done that when we picked him up. Because of him, I missed the football game."

"Quit bitching." Garret flicked a smile. "You like football, that's what we'll play. Think of this as the first quarter skirmish. We'll skip the second and third quarters. On the fourth, I'll take the ball over the line."

Mullins frowned. "You saying we ain't done with him yet? I'm cold, I got a hangover, and I feel like shit. Sometimes you push this cop stuff too damn far."

"Shut your mouth and pay attention." Garret motioned for the sergeant to move forward. "Take off his cuffs."

"You crazy? I seen cops beat raggedy-ass bastards till they're red with blood. The minute they get untied, they start swinging."

"Quit wasting time." Garret gave the sergeant a shove. "I don't want to see any heavy bruises or deep cuts on his body. What I got planned has to look like an accident, a bad accident." He chomped down on his cigar butt. Brown juice trickled down his chin. "Johnson ain't gonna give us no trouble. He's a patsy horn blower, not a heavyweight boxer."

Rufus listened to the men's jabber, and a sliver of hope broke through the dark clouds of despair. If he had any chance of talking himself out of this nightmare, he'd have to concentrate on the sergeant. Rufus decided the youngest of the three liked the graft that came with being one of Garret's boys, but the poor bastard didn't have the stomach for murder. He tensed when the sergeant squatted beside him and unlocked the cuffs. From his light touch, Rufus knew he was trying not to hurt him, but that didn't minimize the pain shooting up his arm and exploding in his head like a gigantic fireworks display.

After the cuffs were off, Rufus pressed his back against the wall and eased himself up to a standing position. His eyes blurred. His stomach was about to jump ship. He sucked air and swallowed hard until he felt his stomach, lungs, and head get back into line. When his wrists stopped throbbing and feeling returned to his arms, his confidence spiraled upward.

He shifted his gaze and covertly assessed his situation. Garret stood in front of the open window, his back to him, and fumbled with a black leather case on the sill. Mullins and the sergeant stood sentinel in front of the staircase. For a moment, the unexpected calm unnerved Rufus, but if it was the calm before the storm, he decided to take advantage of it.

"Okay, Garret," Rufus said in a cool, yet authoritarian tone. "You've had your fun, but now the game's over. I'm out of here." He pulled himself to his full height and sauntered toward the stairs. "I'm a little woozy, but I'll survive. Don't worry about me squealing on you. I got enough sense to know no one would believe me. Even if I could find somebody who did, I couldn't prove anything."

"You ain't going no place," Mullins said. "You're our pigeon, and we're gonna pluck you." He touched the gun attached to his belt.

"Listen to the man," Garret said. "In a couple minutes, you ain't gonna give a shit where you are." He spun around and waved the hypodermic syringe he held in his hand. "This is your one-way ticket out of here."

Rufus stared at the hypodermic. Fear coiled around his heart. "What you planning to do with that?"

"I'm gonna send you on a trip, and it ain't gonna be to Memphis." He let out a scornful laugh. "But you been there before so there won't be any surprises."

"No way I'm going to let you pump some stinking poison in me." Rufus shoved past Mullins, but the sergeant grabbed his neck and threw him to the floor.

His head hit a gangrenous beam on his way down. Dazed and inert, he listened to the bees buzzing inside his head.

A well-placed kick roused him. He opened his eyes and saw Garret standing over him.

"You're gonna die. Might as well get used to the idea." He waved a hypodermic syringe in front of Rufus, a sadistic smile on his face. "Much as I'd like to kill you right now, I gonna stick to my plan. I started working on it the day that fucking jury let you walk." His escalating rage jiggled the flaccid skin under his neck. "You killed my partner Feldon. Now you're gonna pay. An eye for an eye. Setting this up took some doing. For sure, I was gonna kill you, but not until I hurt you real bad. Then I had to figure out how to make it look like an accident or a suicide. After I worked them two problems out, the rest was easy."

Garret snapped his fingers. Mullins and the sergeant jumped. "Take off his jacket and hold him down."

The men grabbed Rufus's arms and tried to yank off his jacket, but Rufus fought back. He kicked, punched, and finally landed a blow. Blood spurted from a deep split on Mullins's mouth and dribbled down his chin.

Mullins stumbled back and bellowed a string of curses.

"What the hell's the matter with you?" Garret kicked Mullins's leg. "You idiot. Johnson gets one lucky punch, and you fold like a thumb-sucking pansy. You call yourself a cop! Take out your gun. If he moves, shoot him. Just don't kill him."

Rufus stared at them like a panther eying its prey. He smelled their fears and uncertainties. They were dimwitted jackals. He knew he could take all three of them down, if... He shook his head. If they didn't have guns and if he had full use of his arms. As it was, he felt damn sure he was the one going down, but for sure he'd go down swinging.

Garret approached him, his eyes narrowed, his mouth taut. Rufus reared back. He figured Garret would retaliate, but he didn't see it coming. Garret's fist smashed into his face, his knee jabbed his groin. The impact sent him reeling. On his way to the floor, Rufus grabbed Garret's leg and gave it a hard twist.

"You motherfucking s.o.b." Garret squealed and fell on Rufus with unrestrained fury. Rufus tried to protect himself, but pain and exhaustion had drained his energy and his will to fight. He rolled on his side and welcomed the semidarkness that spread over like a shroud.

Garret gave him one last kick and turned to Mullins. "Think you can handle him now?"

Mullins nodded. He and the sergeant stripped off Rufus's jacket and clamped his arms to the floor. Rufus didn't bother to open his eyes until he smelled Garret's rancid breath and felt a needle touch his skin. He turned his head and glared at Garret.

"Is that how I'm going to die, a drug overdose?"

"Oh, no. That's too easy. We're gonna to kill you the same way you killed Feldon, with a few exceptions. You tripped Feldon, and he flew out the window. We're gonna pitch you out head first. Of course, you'll have coke in your blood. My buddy was clean."

"You're insane. You can't toss me out the window like a bag of garbage. You'll never get away with it." He looked at Mullins and the sergeant. "You in this with him? What're you getting out of it? You're cops."

"Yeah, we're cops, and you're a cop killer," Mullins said. "Cop killers got to be punished."

"I didn't kill Feldon. Sure, he went out the window, but I didn't trip him or push him. It was an accident. I was standing in front of that open window. I was strung out. I said stuff I shouldn't 've. He got mad. He dropped his head and came charging at me like a wild bull. I dodged the hit, and he flew out the window. You think I'm going to stand still and let him bore a hole through me?" Rufus turned to Garret. "Tell your buddies the truth. Tell 'em you made up that crazy story." He rolled his head back to Mullins. "Check the transcripts of the trail. A cop, one of your own, swore on a Bible that I didn't touch Feldon. Why would he lie? Sure as hell not to save my neck." Rufus fell silent and studied Mullins and the sergeant's faces. Did they hear him? Did they care?

Rufus swallowed a cheer when he saw Mullins and the sergeant's expressions change from certainty to doubt. They weren't killers. Deep down, they had to know this was wrong. A few more reminders of the injustice of their cause, and they might tell Garret to forget it. Before he could open his mouth, Garret jabbed the needle in his arm.

"Ain't no way you can fuck up my plans now, so quit trying. Your ass is mine now. You ain't gonna walk out of here alive." He looked up at Mullins and the sergeant. "Don't you idiots get any ideas about walking. You're in this with me. It's too late to change your minds."

He shot the cocaine into Rufus's vein.

Rufus felt the rush, the familiar high that was so terrifying, so incredibly fantastic. His mouth went dry, his pupils dilated. Hallucinations materialized. The demons followed. A whore covered with maggots winked at him, urging him to follow her.

"NO!" His roar frightened the whore. She fell into a cesspool and disappeared beneath its murky depths. Rufe Junior appeared. He grinned and waved. Two women moved beside him: Salinas on his right, Claire on his left. Tears streaked their cheeks. He heard music. A mixed chorus of African-Americans sang "Nobody Knows the Trouble I Seen." A saxophone growled Billie Holiday's classic, "Bitter Fruit." In the distance, he heard a train speeding southward, its clattering wheels and lonesome whistle wailing "The Blues in the Night." His body went limp and blackness engulfed him.

Rufus awoke in a room streaked with red, green, and silver

lights. He lay motionless until he could decide if he was dead or alive. The cold air blowing through the open window cleared his mind and swept away the fog that clouded his eyes. He raised his head and saw the neon sign flashing on the derelict hotel across the alley and the silver moon suspended on a telephone pole. He dropped his head and sighed. He had to be alive. As far as he knew, neon signs didn't exist in the afterworld. His pounding head and bucking stomach confirmed his deduction; he let out a triumphant cry.

"That muthafucking Garret didn't kill me. I'm going to walk out of here alive." He pushed himself to a sitting position and took a deep breath. He was thankful to be alive, but the effort to stay alive was giving him a lot of grief.

His grief grew to gargantuan proportions as he struggled to his feet. He sucked air into his lungs, but it didn't help. He felt his body weave, his stomach do somersaults, and his legs turn to butter. He grabbed a post to keep from falling. A wave of panic swept through him. What made him think he could get out of there before Garret came back. He couldn't stand, much less walk. He wanted to sit down, close his eyes, and...

"And die," he shouted. "Die like a pig."

His outburst numbed his pain and gradually revived his spirit. He could make it. He had to make it. He stumbled to the stairs, gripped the handrail, and placed his foot on the top step. When his leg held, he dropped his other foot and continued down the stairs, one at a time. Although he was weak, nauseous, and his whole body hurt, he realized every breath he took and every muscle he moved made him a little stronger.

He took the last step, paused, and peered out the open door.

He had to make his way into the street and find someone to help him. He knew the chances of that happening in this neighborhood were close to zero.

He looped a cynical grin around his swollen lip. A couple hours ago, the chance of him getting out of Garret's rat hole alive were close to zero. He'd beaten those odds. He'd beat the rest. His smile broadened. Garret screwed up. The greedy bastard must have grabbed a bag of coke from the NARC unit, but knowing its street value, he milked it before he shot it. His grin deepened into laughter. Garret's greed saved his life. He tottered to the door. His laughter drifted away on a gust of ice-chilled air. If he wanted to stay alive, he had to move faster than this. Garret and his men could show up any minute.

He staggered out the front door onto the sidewalk. "Damn," he yelped. Cold, frigid, and icy didn't begin to describe the arctic blasts slapping his skin. He crossed his arms over his chest and felt skin.

He yelped again. He had left his jacket lying on the floor. He shrugged. He didn't have a choice. He'd have to endure the cold; he didn't have the time or the strength to go back after it. His shoulders hunched, his head lowered, he moved to the end of the building. He peered around the corner. Seeing no unmarked police car, he continued down the block, his body hugging the buildings for safety and support.

With nothing but a throbbing head, freezing feet, and the howling wind to keep him company, Rufus carried on a conversation with himself.

"What the day is it?"

"Saturday, I think."

"Wonder what Claire's doing?"

"Going out of her mind wondering where you are."

"Claire, get out of the apartment. Garret might come after you."

"What about Rufe Junior? You going to make it to Memphis?"

"Got to. He's my boy. I owe him. More importantly, I love him."

"Salinas?"

"She's his mom. She's a good woman. She'll do what has to be done."

"Rufe! Claire!" Tears glazed his eyes. He wasn't going to make it. He was at least a mile away from the apartment, and he wasn't sure he could make it to the end of the block. Garret and his blue boys would be back soon. Wouldn't take them long to find a derelict druggie stumbling down a deserted street.

The sound of an approaching car sent him into a panic. He glanced around looking for a place to hide. He spotted a narrow entryway leading into an empty building. He slipped inside and pressed his back against the wall.

A wet snow had begun to fall. The cold wind made his nose run and his teeth chatter. He clamped his lips together and willed himself to hang on. He counted the seconds it took for the car to coast half a block, stopped at the count of ten, and cocked an ear. The engine's ping and chug were as familiar to him as the wail of his sax. A flicker of hope stabbed his heart. It had to be … There was only one … He stepped onto the sidewalk and stared at the rusted, broken down car pulling to the curb.

"Rufus! My God, Rufus, what happened to you?" Claire ran

to him, her mouth open, her eyes red and puffy. Without speaking, she unzipped her jacket, threw it over his shoulders, and led him to the car. She turned up the heater and sped away.

She covered half a mile in thirty seconds, slowed, and zig-zagged through deserted neighborhoods until she reached an abandoned warehouse. She drove to the back and cut the engine.

"Rufus, thank God you're alive. I've been looking all over for you. Ella and Moon and Lenny, too." She took his raw, swollen hands and rubbed them.

"How did you know?" he asked.

"Know what? That Garret grabbed you?" She heaved a sigh. "I suspected it, but I didn't know until I talked to Ella. I woke up around ten. You were gone. I figured you went to the store. When you weren't back by noon, I started to worry. By one, I was frantic. I called Ella at two and told her you were gone. She said she'd make a few phone calls. I almost lost it when she told me the grape vine had it that Garret was looking for you. Her contact at the police station said there was going to be a hit. We all took off, she and I, Moon and Lenny."

"How'd you know where to go?"

"I knew about the crack house. It was a lucky guess."

"I wouldn't have made it." He held his hands in front of the heater. "I thought about escaping. I didn't dream I'd be rescued." He touched her cheek. A hot ache throbbed in his throat. "You got a lot of guts. If you had found the crack house and stumbled inside, Garret would've killed you, too." He shook his head. "You must have been under a voodoo spell."

"Nothing that exotic." She smiled. "Even before I called Ella, I knew you were in trouble. You left your keys in the car. That wasn't very smart. Anybody could've taken it."

He ran his hand along the curve of her cheek. "Thanks," he said simply and fell silent.

CHAPTER EIGHTEEN

Claire helped Rufus up the stairs and into the apartment. He stumbled halfway across the living room before his head began to spin and nausea rose in his throat. He paused and closed his eyes.

"Man, I am one sorry mess. What doesn't ache, hurts, and what doesn't hurt, aches."

"Sit down before you fall down. I'd never be able to get you up." Claire helped him to a chair, threw a blanket over his shoulders, and sat beside him.

"Would a glass of water help?"

"No, nothing, or you'd have something else to pick up off the floor." He took her hand and sucked air into his lungs. "The room's spinning. My stomach's rebelling. Woman, it's been a long time since I felt this much pain."

"Please, don't pass out on me." Claire ran to the sink and returned with a wet towel. She dabbed his forehead and gently wiped away the blood caked on his bottom lip. "Let me take you to a hospital. You could be bleeding internally. You could die."

"No." Rufus reared up. "No hospital. They'd take my blood. They'd find …" He shook his head. "I can't let them find it. I'm still on parole."

"Find what?" Claire's voice hardened to a shrill. "I know Garret beat you. What else did he do?"

"He shot me up with coke and took off. He planned to come back later and finish the job when he thought nobody'd be around."

"Finish the job?" Claire cocked a brow. "What do you mean?"

"He was going to throw me out the window."

"Oh, my God, Rufus, why would he do something that horrible?"

"He planned to kill me. But he wasn't going to shoot me or whack me with a club. It was going to be a ritual death." Rufus snarled. "That s.o.b. must've gotten a hard on just thinking about it." He coughed several times, bridled the quiver in his voice and, as calmly as possible, recounted everything that happened from the time Garret's men forced him into their car until she found him staggering down the street.

Claire's face paled and tears flooded her eyes. "You can't let him get away with it. Report him. Have him arrested."

"Oh, that'd do a lot of good." He sneered. "Who's going to believe me? I can't prove it. It'd be Garret's word against mine. And he's got two witnesses who'll swear they were watching TV and drinking beer. I don't remember how long it takes for coke to get out of my system, but you can bet they'll look for it. I'll end up in a prison cell, and Garret'll be able to get at me anytime he wants." He paused and sucked in his breath. "He won't stop. He'll figure another way to kill me. And I can't do a thing about it."

"Yes you can." Rage flared in Claire's eyes. "You can kill him first. It's your life or his."

A cynical laugh sputtered from Rufus's mouth. "Sounds good, babe. I'd love nothing better, but I wouldn't be on the street five minutes before Mullins picked me up. Dead is better than prison. No way am I going to spend the rest of my life in a crummy cell. I have to play it cool a few more days. This'll end once I get to Memphis."

"How can you be sure? What if he follows you there? What if he goes after Rufe Junior and Salinas."

After a moment's thought, Rufus raised up and locked his eyes to hers. "In that case, I wouldn't have a choice. I'd have to kill him. I'd do the same if he came after you."

"Okay. Let's not talk about that." She laid the towel on the table and gripped his arm. "You have to rest. Come on. You're going to bed."

"In a minute." A chill racked his body. "Call Ella. Let her know I'm safe and tell her I can't play tonight."

"She'll be relieved to say the least." Claire reached for the telephone and dialed the lounge. Ella answered on the second ring.

"Yeah, he's here," Claire said. "He's not great, but he'll live." She paused. "Yeah, Garret had him." Another pause.

Rufus listened to her broken conversation with a casual indifference until she started to describe his harrowing experience in more detail. Her vivid choice of words hurtled him back to the drug house, and his racking chills returned. Somehow he had survived the beatings, the coke, and the cold. Would he survive if Garret came after him a second time?

The sudden shift in Claire's voice from courteous to patronizing drew him out of his tormented reverie.

"No," she said repeatedly. "No broken bones. No concussion. No, he needs to rest more than anything. No, he hasn't eaten." A pause. "If you insist, I'm sure he'll be glad... Twenty minutes. Fine."

She dropped the receiver on its cradle and looked at him, her cheeks stained with a crimson blush. "I'm sorry. She's coming over. I told her you were all right. She insisted. I guess she wants to see for herself."

"It's cool, babe." Rufus smiled. "Ella's family. We don't have to entertain her."

"At least sit back and relax. You look like you're going to faint." She took a calming breath. "Can I get you something? Tea? Coffee? I think we have a couple cans of soup left."

"A sip of scotch would be nice."

"Oh, I don't think so. You haven't eaten since yesterday. And the coke's still in your blood. You don't want to OD, not after all you've been through."

The sound of a fist banging on the door impaled Rufus's gut. For a nerve-racking second, he saw Garret standing in the hallway, a gun in his hand, murder in his heart. He grabbed Claire's arm and motioned for her to go into the bedroom.

"No," she whispered. "He won't kill both of us."

"Don't argue. He's not sane. He doesn't care who he has to go through to get to me."

Another bang followed by a man's shrill voice burst the suffocating tension in the room.

"Clarence, you are one evil muthafucka," Rufus shouted. "You just scared the hell out of me."

"Sorry, my man. I just come off the street. I was out looking for you. Ella said some blue devils grabbed you. I figured you were in deep shit." Clarence eyed Rufus with a critical squint. "Man, they did a number on you. That ugly mug of yours looks like a blinking Christmas tree, all green and red and puffy."

"Thanks, for noticing," Rufus said. "I'll pack it in ice and be fine in the morning."

"Yeah, well, like I was saying, I saw your light, and me being suspicious and all, I decided to check it out. I was hoping I wouldn't find no dead cat on the line." Clarence narrowed his eyes and studied Rufus's face. "You sure you're okay? They didn't do nothing real bad to you, did they?"

"No, man. Nothing real bad. And thanks for checking. I appreciate it." Rufus cocked a brow. He had no idea so many homefolks cared about him. And Clarence, of all people! The man was a puzzle. He bitched about him using too much hot water, then risked life and limb looking for him.Go figure!

"Better call Ella 'n tell her you're alive," Clarence said. "She's one strung out lady."

"She's coming over."

"That don't surprise me. She don't believe nothing till she scope it out. And don't worry none about them honky cops knocking on your door. I done padlocked the whole house. They want in, they better get a bulldozer." Clarence harrumphed. "I done turned up the heat, 'n there's plenty of hot water. Take all the showers you want, but if I was you, I wouldn't overdo. Too clean ain't healthy."

"I hear you, man," Rufus said.

"Yeah, well, you take it easy." Clarence rapped the door and walked away.

The next rap was lighter, quieter, but the voice was higher, more urgent.

"Rufus, Claire, open the door. It's me, Ella."

"As if we didn't know." Claire sprinted to the door and threw back the deadbolts. Ella blew in like a tempest and headed straight for Rufus. She dropped her purse and a large basket on the floor. She threw her arms around his neck and planted a kiss on his cheek. Rufus grimaced. "Easy, woman. I'm one sore dude."

She pulled away and stared at him, laughter mingled with her tears. "Lawd, you is one sorry sight, but for sure, I expected worse." She tossed her fur coat on the back of a chair and sat down. "You put a scare in us. I never figured I'd see you alive again."

"I thought the same, but, lucky for me, I had some bull-headed friends out looking." He took Claire's hand and pulled her beside him. "If it wasn't for her, I'd be an ice man by now."

Ella looked at Claire with affection. "You're a good woman. You're loyal, and kind, and you love that man. I know you're hurting what with Rufus going to Memphis and all, but I know you gonna handle it. You ain't the same gal what walked outta here six months ago. You got your shit together. You're gonna be okay."

"I hope so," Claire said. "Right now, I'm not worried about Memphis. I'm worried about Rufus staying alive."

"I hear you." Ella glanced at Rufus and let out a startled cry. "Lawdy, we're standing here rapping, and you're in pain."

"I'm cool." He stifled a groan. "Maybe lukewarm. My head and my stomach keep going in different directions."

"Time for you to lie down," Claire said. "Can't imagine how you managed to stay up all this time."

"I have to shower first. I smell like shit. I won't be able to sleep until I scrub all this dirt and dried blood off my skin." He tried to stand, but half way up, his legs buckled, and he fell back onto the chair.

"Wow! Guess I'm weaker than I think." He lowered his head so he wouldn't see the shock on Ella and Claire's faces. They had never seen him so vulnerable. The pain that traveled from the top of his head to the bottom of his jaw and from his rib cage to his groin was so intense, he couldn't even pretend to be strong and invincible. At the moment, the extent of his injuries worried him more than the decline of his superman status. In prison, he had had his share of beatings, but the pain hadn't been as severe as it was now, and it hadn't been that long ago. He was still strong and virile; he was still a man. Why was he so weak? He thought for a moment. A light bulb switched on. In prison, no one had shot him up with coke, and although the assaults were brutal, his attackers hadn't hated him or intended to kill him. The anger that gushed through him like a surging river washed away his apprehensions. With sheer determination, he pushed himself to a standing position and stepped away from the table.

"See, I'm fine," he said. "I just have to take it slow."

"If you say so." Claire drew a blank expression on her face.

"You take it mighty slow." Ella flicked a tentative smile, lifted her basket off the floor, and set it on a chair. "I got to get back to the club. I'll leave this here. Use what you can." She slipped on her coat. "Don't you worry 'bout the show tonight," she said. "The boys 'n me gonna make out just fine."

"Thanks for everything," Rufus said.

Claire walked her to the door, kissed her cheek, and promised to call if they needed help. After she locked the door, she headed back to the table.

"Ready for your shower?" she asked.

ELSA COOK

"After we check Ella's basket." He sniffed. "Hope she brought food. I'm starving."

Claire lifted the towel and peered inside. "You're in luck. Chicken soup, crackers, cheese, coffee, and a bottle of wine." She reached for a small red bottle and read the label. "Antiseptic for cuts, sores, and minor injuries." She chuckled. "Think it'll work on major injuries?"

"Not mine," Rufus said. "You're not putting that stuff on my scratches. It stings like hell."

She touched the lacerations on his cheek. "If those wounds get infected, you might miss that train to Memphis after all."

"And if I don't wash this crud off my body soon, nobody'll let me on the train to Memphis."

He shot Claire a look of disdain, turned, and managed to take half a dozen steps before he started to sway. He growled. It bugged him to think Mother Nature was stronger than male pride, but he had no choice; he had to surrender or end up on the floor.

"Mind if I hang onto you?" He turned to Claire. "I can make it on my own. I'm just being cautious."

"Cautious is good." She smiled.

He draped his arm around her shoulders and tottered into the bedroom. He leaned against the chest of drawers until his dizziness passed. He took off his clothes and kicked them across the room.

"Throw 'em out," he said. "I never want to see 'em again."

Claire stared at him, her mouth gaping. "Oh, Rufus! You look…" She caught herself and continued in a lighter tone. "Don't look in the mirror, or you'll want to throw your body out,

199

too."

"I would if I could. I don't know what's worse, the stink or the pain."

"You can wash off the smell in ten minutes. The pain'll take a little longer." She glanced at his clothes and shook her head. "You sure you want to throw everything away? You could have 'em cleaned." She picked up his shirt, sniffed, and threw it back down. "What were you lying in, dog doodoo?"

"Shit. Dog shit," he corrected her. Stark naked, he shuffled into the bathroom and turned on the water. A warm mist filled the room and wrapped him in its soothing vapor. Feeling better already, he let out a tranquil sigh and stepped into the stall. His bellow ricocheted off the walls.

"What is it?" Claire called out. "What's the matter?"

"I'm being stung by a thousand bees. I can't move."

"Bees!" She entered the bathroom, holding a rolled magazine over her head. She peeked inside the shower. "There aren't any bees here. Don't scare me like that. I'm so upset, I'll believe anything. If it hurts that bad, get out and take a sponge bath."

He grimaced and groaned but held his ground. "I'm not an invalid. I can handle it."

"Stand still and let me wash you. I'll try to be gentle, but you will tell me to stop if the pain's too bad."

"Loud and clear, babe." He handed her the soap, gripped the faucets and took a deep breath. The first two swipes were the worst. After that, her hand's soothing touch and the soap's clean smell sedated his skittish nerve endings. When she finished, he felt as if he'd been reborn.

His elation was short-lived. When the cold air hit his body

and the towel's coarse nap grazed his skin, the pain returned. He didn't protest when she helped him to the bed and drew the covers over him.

"Don't go to sleep yet." She leaned down and kissed him. "I'll open a can of soup and see if I can find some aspirin. You'll need both to get through the night."

Rufus tried to relax, but the minute he closed his eyes and cleared his mind, the nightmares swooped in and filled the vacuum. He saw Garret's evil face, heard his menacing voice. He felt the coke surge through his veins and tasted the blood congealed in his throat. His hand shook. He could live with his memories of Garret and what the man did to him as long as he thought it was over, but he knew it wasn't. He wouldn't leave for Memphis till Wednesday. Garret had four days to finish what he started.

Rufus sneered. Unless Garret shot him at long range, he'd be ready for him. In a sick sort of way, he hoped Garret did come after him. He'd tear the man's face apart and hang the consequences.

He heard Claire part the beads in the doorway and enter the room. He put his negative thoughts on hold. Until Garret made his next move, all he could do was wait.

"You're still awake. It's nice to know you listen to me once in a while." She smiled, sat on the side of the bed, and set a tray on the night table. "Scoot up a little. I'll feed you some soup."

He glowered and pointed to the tray. "Put it on my lap. I can feed myself, thank you."

She glowered back and transferred the tray from the table to the bed. She sprawled across the foot of the bed, propped her head on her arm, and stared at him.

"Okay, Miss Nightingale, you can take your shower now."

"Later. I'd rather watch you eat."

"Women! They don't give a man a minute's peace." Intending to slurp and smack his lips, he dipped the spoon in the soup and carried it to his mouth. After the first sip, he forgot about bugging her and devoured it in less than a minute. Like a scavenger, he consumed the crackers, cheese, and sliced apple, then looked up, a contrite expression on his face.

"I ate it all. I'm sorry. I was hungry."

"Don't sweat it. I took a few bites while I fixed your tray." She handed him a small pink pill and a glass of water. "Take this. It'll ease your pain and help you sleep."

He shook his head. "No more drugs. I still have Garret's poison in my blood."

"It's a pain pill from Ella's basket of goodies. She wouldn't have brought it if she thought you'd get hooked."

Rufus weighed the effect a powerful pain killer would have on his nervous system. Faced with the possibility of a long, sleepless night, he popped it in his mouth.

"Pain is a great motivator." He handed Claire the tray and stretched his body the full length of the bed. "I'm ready to see if it works." He grinned. "Turn off the light on your way out."

"We have one more thing to do before you go to sleep." Claire set the tray on the floor and reached for the antiseptic bottle and cotton balls she had placed on the night stand. "Roll over. When I washed your back, I saw a few open cuts."

"No way, babe." He threw out his arm in a restraining gesture. "I told you, no hot sauce. I've had all the pain I can handle."

"Tell that to the doctor when he has to scrape out all the pus and muck when they get infected."

"They don't do that anymore," he said flat out. "They give you a shot of penicillin."

"If you say so. But just in case you're wrong, and you end up in the hospital for two weeks, remember, I warned you."

"You know, you can be a real pain when you put your mind to it." He glowered, he snarled, he rolled on his stomach. "Okay, get out your poison and put it on my wounds, but please, dab, don't dig."

"Lie still. It won't take more'n a few minutes."

His jaw tensed, his fists clenched, Rufus waited for what he hoped would be a slight sting. What he felt was a red hot rod searing an open wound. He raised up like a cobra and let out a grating, rasping shriek.

"Will you please hold it down? Guys aren't supposed to yell and holler over a little discomfort."

"A little! Mullins's kicks didn't hurt this bad." He dropped his face into a pillow. "For your information, I didn't yell and holler while he was beating me."

"Why not?"

"You think I'd let Garret know I was hurting? I'd have bitten off my tongue first."

"My macho man." She swiped the wounds one more time, dropped the bottle on the tray, and kissed the nape of his neck. "You can roll onto your back now."

Rufus grimaced and grunted on his way over. When he was finally settled, he gazed at her, his liquid eyes caressing her with love.

"I'm going to miss you, babe. You know that, don't you?"

Her eyes misted instantly. She nodded.

"Promise you won't hang around Ella's after I'm gone."

"I can't walk away and not look back. I'll need someone to talk to. It took me six months to kick my drug habit. It'll take a lot longer to get over you."

She gave him a long, lingering kiss. She lifted her head and stared at him, her heated breath brushing his cheek.

"I love you." She parted her lips and seared a path down his chest to his groin with her tongue.

Rufus moaned. "No, babe. Not tonight."

"You don't have to move. I'll do all the work." Straddling his legs, she flicked her tongue around his swollen crown, then plunged down and sucked his cock like a hungry infant sucking a tit.

Rufus closed his eyes and lay rigid, desperately trying not to move. He had focused his thoughts on his captivity and torture and the pain and mental anguish that followed. He never even considered having sex. But the more he thought about it, the more he liked the idea.

He grunted, and a gurgling sound rumbled in his gut. Moments later, his abdominal muscles tightened and a hot, stinging sensation gorged his penis.

"Claire," he croaked. "Yes, yes. Jesus, baby, don't stop." He arched and groaned. Claire's tongue was touching nerves, already super sensitive, that sent him into an erotic ecstasy.

He pressed his hand on her head and thrust his penis deep into her throat. He shuddered, threw back his head, and ejaculated his juices inside her mouth.

Claire swallowed, wiped her lips, and fell onto the bed, her body contoured around his.

Rufus kissed her forehead and stared into her eyes, so dark, so brilliant, so unbearably beautiful.

"I love you," he said.

He pulled the blanket over them and closed his eyes. He fell asleep, the steady beat of her heart thumping in his ear.

CHAPTER NINETEEN

Rufus awoke to the sound of splashing water and the scent of gardenias. A hint of a smile tugged at his mouth. Outside, the winter wind howled and sleet splattered the window. Inside, Claire was taking a shower, he was lying in bed, the room was warm, the light mellow.

"Ah," he sighed. Life could be good. He wished he and Claire had found this kind of peace and contentment their first time around instead of getting caught up in drugs and ego trips. His smile took a downward turn. It was stupid and a waste of time to fantasize on what-might-have-been when they could build good memories in the time they had left.

He raised his head to check the time. A wall of pain crashed down on him, a vivid reminder that his life was not and never had been on track. After noting it was three in the afternoon, he fell back on the bed and waited for Claire to finish her shower. He knew he couldn't stand up until she gave him one of Ella's little pink pills.

No matter how much he hurt, he was going to perform tonight. He owed it to Moon, Lenny, and Ella. Twice they had carried the show without him and Claire, but no more. He'd make it to the lounge if he had to crawl. If he didn't have enough strength to blow his sax, he'd introduce the trio, Moon on drums, Lenny on piano, and Claire on bass.

With Claire's help and encouragement, he crawled out of

bed, ate a five p.m. breakfast, rested, dressed, rested, and they headed out the door two hours later.

When Rufus entered the carnival atmosphere at Ella's Lounge, he forgot about Garret, his bruised body, and his uncertain future. This was where it was at. This was where he wanted to be. He brushed the ice crystals off his hair, took Claire's arm, and strolled into the bar. The noisy crowd, the neon jukebox, the smoky haze and barroom smells maxed him out. There were no strangers here, no cockroaches, no drugs, just good times, good music, and hip homefolks.

"Hey, Rufus, my man," Bojay shouted. "You is one bad muthafucka. Git your ass over here and gimme five."

As Rufus and Claire made their way through the crowd, a cheer went up, and the patrons raised their glasses in a salute.

"What's going on?" Rufus asked. "Did I win something?"

"You won a gold medal," Bojay said. "Word's out 'bout what went down 'tween you and that bad smelling honky cop. Guess you showed him them bad days are over when the muscle boys could split a brotha's head, take a leak, and walk away. We're proud of you, dude."

"You sure you got the right man? I wasn't a hero. I was glad to get out alive."

"That ain't what we heard." Bojay set two drinks on the bar.

The crowd parted like the waters to let Rufus and Claire break through.

"Rufus you done show dat muthafucka how to spread his legs," one man yelled.

"Dat ofay ain't gonna mess wit a brotha no more," another followed.

"No way. No way," came the response.

"Tell it! Tell it!"

"Rufus twist the bastard's balls."

"Throwed him off the mountain."

"Rufus done wit dat peckerwood PO-liceman."

"Ain't gonna bother us no more."

Rufus laid his elbow on the bar and leaned into Bojay. "What is going on?" he asked.

"I told you. Word's out. You're the Man."

"What word is that?"

"You put Garret down. Ain't one of them cats ain't had a run in with a racist cracker cop. They got the cigar burns and cuff marks to prove it."

Rufus took a drink of scotch. "I didn't put Garret down. He's still out there, alive and kicking."

"And you're here, alive 'n kicking. That's what counts." Bojay winked. "Come on, man. Talk to the folks. Tell 'em how it went down. They wanna hear it outta your mouth."

"This is ridiculous. I wasn't brave. I was lucky." He lowered his gaze. A sense of inadequacy swept over him.

Claire nudged him. "Doesn't matter," she whispered. "You beat the odds. They want to know how."

"Okay, okay, I hear you." He took a swallow of scotch and blotted his sweaty palms with a napkin. He was a musician, not a public speaker. Even if he'd done something great or courageous, he wouldn't have wanted to talk about it, but since he had to, he decided to give them a short but descriptive account of his day at the crack house in the company of three sadistic cops. He'd thank the brothers and sisters for their support, and hightail it to the safety of the bandstand. He hoped they didn't intend to pin a real medal on his chest. He took another swallow of scotch and turned to face them.

The chatter, laughter, and shouts died. Rufus stared at them dumbfounded. He saw their expressions change from animated expectation to dreamy abstraction. He realized they were home-folks who harbored Martin Luther King Junior's dream of free-dom and equality in their hearts. They wanted to know if the dream was still alive.

Rufus assured them it was. He reminded them a lot of folks took a lot of beatings and shed a lot of blood for freedom, and the struggle wasn't over. African-Americas were still being execut-ed for crimes they didn't commit; voting rights were politicized; policemen were prejudiced, racists and hate mongers sold their wares on courthouse steps. And yes, he said, he had survived his ordeal, but he'd have to watch his back for the rest of his life. Garret or someone like him would be standing just around the corner looking for a head to crack.

Emotionally charged by his speech, Rufus thrust his fist in the air. The crowd roared "black power." And then it was over. Laughter and smoke filled the air, beer caps popped, and "A Rainy Night in Georgia" came over the loud speakers. Rufus fin-ished his scotch. He and Claire headed into the lounge.

Moon looked up when Rufus and Claire stepped onto the bandstand. He laid down his sticks and smiled broadly.

"You lay out a good story," Moon said.

"Aw, come on, not you, too." Rufus groaned. "I'm not a hero, and you know it."

"Far as I'm concerned, anybody who walks away from a

lynching's a hero. Guess you forgot what that bull-neck sheriff 'n his stone-eyed monkeys did to a brotha in that Alabama swamp. I ain't never wanna see nothing like that again."

"I hear you, but I don't want to think about that now." Rufus opened his sax case, assembled his horn, and introduced the band. He opened the set with Thelonious Monk's ballad, "'Round Midnight." He played it slow and pretty, no flourishes, no jarring licks. Claire and Moon broke in and defined the rhythm and the groove, but Claire's quiet bass pulse and Moon's light brush on the cymbals emphasized Rufus's lackluster tone. When the song ended, he realized the cats weren't tapping their feet or snapping their fingers. Their polite applause confirmed his suspicion. He was putting them to sleep.

"What the shit you doing?" Moon said in a hoarse whisper. "We're supposed to be playing jazz, not funeral music. Man, that's the way Lenny 'n me were playing couple nights ago, 'n you jumped down our throats."

"Cool it, man. I hear you." Rufus shook his head. What *was* he doing? A sax player in a high school band could have played the ballad better than he did.

He looked out at the audience. Their blank expressions and ho-hum response chilled Rufus. He realized he had played his solo with the enthusiasm of a dying cat, but he expected more than a nod and a yawn from the folks sitting at the tables. They were the same ones who had cheered him earlier. He was their hero, an African-American who had outwitted a pack of white racist dogs. Now they merely looked at him.

What do they want, a hero or a sax player? He answered his question even as he asked it. They wanted to hear jazz, they wanted to hear him swing and swoop, twist and roar, raise 'em off their chairs.

Rufus knew the cats in the audience didn't go out on a bitter cold night unless they were looking for something special. To a crowd of funky fans, jazz was the only music worth getting out of bed for. Rappers rapped, country twanged, hip hopped. It was good music played by talented musicians, but it lacked the tension and excitement of a creative jazz session. Jazz musicians believed innovation and inspiration were more important than structure. Like Ornette Coleman, who is credited with coining the phrase "free jazz," Rufus believed performers could express themselves any way they wanted. He had to admit there were limits to that freedom. The cats in the audience didn't want to hear a standard ballad without riffs and flourishes. Rufus regrouped his thoughts. He had played it straight to protect himself. He knew if he improvised, he would be on his own. There were no rules. Without rules, he might swing down an uncharted road and never come back. He didn't want to take the chance. He didn't want to bomb. He didn't want to lose his audience. For this one night, he wanted to be a hero, not a musician. Heroes, he realized, were as fleeting as yesterday's newspapers. The home-folks gave him a hero's welcome, but the cats wanted to hear jazz. He had almost lost them, but the night wasn't over. He still had time to rearrange his thinking and salvage the set. He started by introducing Lenny's solo.

Lenny started the ballad "Tea for Two" with a basic succession of ideas based on the melody. Slowly, he began to reword the old favorite into an improvisational extravaganza. He improvised the melody with his right hand, and spelled out the rhythm and harmonies, normally provided by the bassist and drummer, with his left. The power and texture of his improvisations and harmony brought the audience to its feet. Their shouts, "go, man," and "do it," grew to a roar.

Rufus beamed when Lenny rose and took his bows. He was a talented soloist and an expert accompanist. He glanced at Moon and Claire. They were equally talented, but, more importantly, they played together so well, they could have been joined at the hips.

By the end of the first set, Rufus knew something special had happened on stage. No matter what they played, ballads, blues, or show tunes, they ignored chord structures and relied on inspiration. The rhythm section communicated spontaneously with Rufus when he explored new territories during a sax solo.

Backed by Claire's bass, Moon's drums, and Lenny's piano, Rufus strained to break out of his groove, but eventually the pain he'd been trying to ignore all evening became too intense. Reluctantly, he lowered his sax and let the rhythm section finish the set.

Rufus felt sad and nostalgic as he listened to them play. His band was breaking up. In a few days, they'd be going their separate ways. It happened. All the great bands broke up eventually. The Ellington, Basie, and Goodman bands were revolving doors through which musicians came and went. Rufus knew once his band walked through the door, no one else would come in.

He'd give Moon and Lenny a week before they got new gigs. A little longer if they left town. Maybe they'd form their own group and sign on Claire as their bassist. The thought of them moving up and him moving out gave him a kick in the gut. But since that's the way it was going down, he had to roll with it.

The session ended and Rufus stepped forward and introduced the band with a wave of his hand. "Claire Burton on bass. Moon Shakaan on drums. Lenny Richardson on piano." After the applause died and the lounge emptied, Moon took off for the bar, Lenny and Claire headed to the restrooms, and he began to disassemble his horn.

He didn't have to look up when he heard the staccato click of high heels strike the wooden floor. He knew it was Ella. He had heard that sound often enough. Depending upon the situation, it had either raised a sweat on his forehead or brought a smile to his face. This time it brought a lump to his throat. Damn! He was going to miss her, too.

He greeted her with a smile. "Woman, where you been hiding? You missed a real cool session. We were swinging."

"I was in the office, but I heard you. You sounded real good." She adjusted the pink boa around her neck, tugged at her pink sequined gown, and ran her tongue over her glossy pink lips. "Never figured you'd last the night after the beating you took. You gotta be one fast healer."

She walked to the back of the stage and pulled Rufus with her. "Ain't often I see you this happy, but I gotta warn you, two of Garret's hangmen come sniffing round looking for you."

"What the hell those muthafuckas want?" Rage exploded inside his head and momentarily blinded him. "Whatever Garret's got planned is between him and me. If he sends his hit men after you, I'll kill all of 'em. I swear I will."

"You some kinda fool? Garret's been hassling me for years. I been paying him and his boys protection money long as I can remember, and I ain't the only one. He passes around the collection plate to every bar owner, cabbie, and ho house in Dark Town. But he ain't gonna mess with me long as I pay my monthly dues. You're different. He figures you're some kind of devil. Ain't your fault, but that doesn't change nothing. He showed his long tail and black horns when he took you to that drug house to kill you. Lucky he messed up, but that don't mean he won't try again."

She harrumphed and put her hands on her ample hips. "You're a good man, Rufus Johnson, but you got bad luck. I wanna help, but you ain't the only one I got to worry about."

"I told you to stay out of it," Rufus said. "You stick your neck out, he'll chop it off."

"Stop interrupting and listen." Ella bore down on him with a hard, unrelenting stare. "I'm talking 'bout Salinas and your son. Ain't no way you should go to Memphis with this Garret business hanging over you. He's planning to kill you. He ain't gonna care if he has to take Salinas and the boy, too."

"Quit with this gloom and doom talk. I will not hide in a sewer cause some muthafucking cop wants to bust my balls."

"That's fine for you to say, but what's Salinas got to say? Did you tell her 'bout Garret? Does she know what kinda mess you're in?"

"There's nothing to tell. When I get on that train, it'll be over between me and Garret. If that nazi comes after me, he'll come alone. His rat squad'll party in their own backyard, but they won't go into foreign territory to kill some Afro dude who ain't worth a nickel to 'em."

He shoved his hands in his pockets and paced the floor, trying to relieve the tension building inside him.

"If what you're saying's true, then you only got to worry about the next three days. That ain't a long time, but with your life on the line, it can seem forever." She opened a desk drawer, pulled out a gun, and handed it to him.

"Take this. Nobody owns it. Nobody can trace it. I ain't saying for you to shoot the bastard. Let him see it. Maybe he'll think twice 'fore he messes with you again."

"Woman, you want to get me killed?" Rufus speared Ella with a steely gaze. "If Garret knows I have a gun, he has two choices. He can shoot me, or he can give me a one-way ticket up river."

"A cell's better'n a bullet in the head."

"Not so. I'm dead either way. If he kangaroos me back to prison, he'll make sure I get a shiv in my back before the week's out." He pushed the gun away and headed for the door. "That dumb ass has got to be wondering what happened to me at the drug house." He let out a cynical laugh. "If the cats at the bar heard I broke out, the boys at the station heard it, too. If he's got any sense, he'll lay low for a while or forget the whole thing."

"Rufus, you are a fool. Garret ain't gonna stand around knowing his boys are laughing at him. Next time, he'll make double sure he does the job right." Ella dropped the gun in the drawer and turned the key. "Do it your way. But you're wrong if you think he's got a conscience and won't shoot you in the back."

Rufus stepped into the hallway and leaned against the wall and let out a tired sigh. He knew Garret wouldn't give up. The thought shattered Rufus's self-confidence but not his ability to reason. He knew a dozen guns wouldn't stop Garret. What was the sense in carrying one? He had survived prison, the drug scene, the crack house beatings. He was tired of fighting, tired of running. His bones hurt, and the shadows deepened. He needed some R&R. He needed a drink.

He joined Claire at the bar minutes before two hulking men lumbered in, their snow-covered baseball caps pulled low on their foreheads. The arctic wind had frozen sinister sneers on their faces and colored their eyes blood red.

Rufus stared at them in amazement. He thought he'd be raging mad the next time he saw Mullins and his side-kick, sergeant something or other, he couldn't even remember his name, but he wasn't even angry. He was wary. He knew it wouldn't take much effort on their part to stir up some hatred.

They made their way to one end of the bar and ordered two beers.

"Bar closed," Bojay shouted. "Ain't allowed to serve no more drinks."

"You serve us, or I'll padlock this darky dive for good."

Bojay grabbed two warm beers and set them on the bar. Mullins waved him away. A smirk pasted on his thin lips, he peered through the blue haze at the group sitting at the other end.

"Looking for Rufus Johnson? Anybody seen him?"

"Last time I seen him, he was at a PO-lice banquet honoring some fat-ass lieutenant. Maybe you knows him, PO-liceman Sydshit Garret," one of the regulars said.

Laughter rattled the bottles behind the bar.

Mullins turned three shades of red, grabbed the neck of his beer bottle, and threw it at the man. The man ducked. It hit the floor with a thud.

"That's what's gonna happen to your head you get smart with me." Mullins stood up and glared at the stone-mountain faces staring back at him. "You got thirty seconds. I don't get an answer, I call the vice squad and take you to the station for soliciting, pimping, doping. You name it, we'll pin it on you."

No one spoke.

Mullins grabbed the sergeant's beer and threatened to throw it at Bojay. After a tense moment, he took a long drink and set it on the bar.

"Two more beers, nigger," he bellowed. "And this time, you better be sure they're cold."

Bojay stood motionless, his rigid stance shouting defiance.

A thin line of perspiration rippled across Mullins's forehead. "Okay, you scum. Have it your way." He drew a cell phone from his jacket and started punching in numbers.

"You looking for me?" Rufus stepped out of the shadows and confronted Mullins with icy contempt.

"You bastard, you been here all the time," he said in an unsteady voice.

"You're out of your territory, Mullins," Rufus said. "If I was you, I'd be scared shitless to show my face in Dark Town without some heavy artillery protecting my ass."

"You're under arrest." Mullins slipped his hand inside his jacket. "You give me trouble, I start shooting. You won't be the only one to go down."

"I don't want trouble, but I'm not going with you unless you tell me why and what for. I don't remember breaking any laws. Course, that doesn't mean shit to you, does it? You don't know what the law is."

"Lieutenant Garret says to bring you in. That's all I know."

"In other words, you don't have an arrest warrant, a bill of sale, nothing but an invitation."

Mullins looked at the sergeant. The sergeant looked at the floor. Rufus smirked. He had guessed right. If he got to Memphis, this whole nightmare would end. Garret's crew wouldn't back him, and Garret wouldn't come after him alone. Rufus studied the officers' sallow faces and quivering lips. He wondered how the hell they had ever gotten on the force. There were some good men in the department, all colors, black and white, and brown, who were proud of their uniforms and the work they did in the community. Stretching a cliche, Garret's apples were not only rotten, they were brainless and gutless. But they understood power and strength. They knew Rufus had escaped after they had beaten and drugged him. The fact that he had beaten impossible odds had to make them wary and gave Rufus an aura of indestructibility.

Rufus took a threatening step forward. "Before something bad happens, you better get your fat asses out of here. If Garret wants to talk, tell him I'll be waiting for him. And tell him to come alone."

"Garret ain't gonna like this. If he has to come after you again, ain't no saying what he'll do."

"Who's gonna do what to who?" Ella entered the bar accompanied by two hulking heavyweights. Their bald heads glistened under the single overhead light, their black jackets pulled tight over their massive shoulders. Despite their large builds, they walked with the agility of a gymnast and the swagger of a boxer.

She stopped in the middle of the bar, shot a slanted look at Rufus, then thrust out her ample breasts and glared at the two uniforms. "Club's closed. If you want a drink, move your asses to another joint."

"Lieutenant Garret said we was to bring Rufus Johnson in," Mullins said. "If he doesn't come peaceful like, we'll have to…"

"Have to what? Kill him, here, in my bar, in cold blood?"

"Nobody said nothing about killing," Mullins stammered.

"Don't have to say. You tried once. You'll try again." She jerked her thumb at the two men standing beside her. "This here's Ham Bone and this here's Ish. "I pay 'em to get rid of rats and vermin that crawl in from the sewer. Course I ain't talking about you boys. You come in here through the front door. If you got sense, you'll leave the same way." She narrowed her eyes. "You understand. The club's closed."

"We don't go less Johnson comes with us. We're the law. You mess with us and …"

"That's it," Ella said. "I'm damn sick of you boys coming in here threatening me, my customers, and my help. You get a warrant, I get a lawyer. Till then, you're gone."

She snapped her fingers. Ham Bone and Ish approached the policemen, their steps synchronized, their shoulders touching. They stopped a hair's breadth from their noses. After a two minute wait when no one moved and no one spoke, Ham Bone grabbed Mullins' arm and escorted him to the door. The sergeant followed. Growling menacing threats, Ham Bone pushed Mullins out the door. He and Ish slipped out behind them and vanished in winter's white night.

CHAPTER TWENTY

Rufus unlocked the door to the apartment and stepped aside to let Claire enter first. He relocked the door and paused before turning around. Claire's mood had been bleak when they left the Lounge and had grown steadily worse on the ride home. He tried to figure out what level of bleak she was on and what had caused it. She wasn't angry. She wasn't good at hiding that. Depressed? Maybe. Denial? He shook his head. She might not like what was going on in her life, but she always faced up to them, eventually. He shrugged. Maybe she was exhausted. He felt bushed, too.

He turned on the light, took off his jacket, and rubbed his hands together until he felt the ice crystals begin to melt. He glanced at the beads on the door leading into the bedroom, the coffee pot sitting on the burner, and the blanket thrown across his chair. He could go to bed, brew some coffee, or wrap himself in the blanket and listen to Bird's matchless rendition of "Dark Shadows." Any one of them could warm his body, but only Claire could warm his soul. Did he dare approach her? He knew he couldn't sleep until he found out what was bothering her. Could he sleep if he did find out?

Claire walked to the window. She folded her arms over her breasts and gazed out at the swirling snow. Her blank expression mirrored the emptiness he felt looking at her.

He stepped behind her and locked his arms around her waist. "Want to talk about it?"

"I can't. I'm one breath away from bursting into tears."

"Crying's okay if it makes you feel better." He kissed her neck.

"It won't make me feel better. Nothing'll make me feel better." The sob waffling in her voice erupted. She spun around and laid her cheek on Rufus's chest. "I feel like we're trapped on an ice floe in the middle of a lake. It's melting, and we can't get off. We're going to drown. We're going to die."

"Stop thinking stuff like that, babe." He massaged the back of her neck. "It makes you feel lousy, and it doesn't help."

"Oh, Rufus, I've never felt so awful in my life. Ever since I came back, we've had so many problems and so much pain. I thought life would be perfect when I walked out of rehab with that damn monkey off my back. I didn't know there were so many monkeys around. It feels as if I have a dozen wrapped around my neck. Mother's fighting for her life, Dad's still acting like nothing's wrong, and then, of course, there's you." Sadness crept over her face. "I thought getting off drugs was the worst hell imaginable until you told me you had a son, and you were going to Memphis, and I'd never see you again. But none of them come close to the horror I felt when I saw the hatred in those policemen's eyes. It was like looking into the face of evil, and they were only the devil's messengers. Garret is Satan himself. How can you fight pure evil? Even God hasn't figured that one out."

"I don't know about God, but I've been giving this a lot of thought, trying to make sense out of senselessness." Rufus took her hand and led her to the table. He sat her down, grabbed two glasses, and poured two drinks.

"Garret's a maniac, a hate-filled wacko," he said. "I don't

know if his hate triggered his madness or if his madness triggered his hate. Either way, I don't think his obsession to kill me has a damn thing to do with his partner flying out the window. It has everything to do with whatever monsters he sees when he thinks about me."

He paused and took a long drink. The smooth, malt liquor awakened his taste buds but did nothing to temper his hostile mood. "Why am I wasting time trying to figure him out? Even if I cared, I couldn't change him. Hell, he's so sick in the head, a brain transplant wouldn't make him human, if he ever was."

"What you're saying makes sense," Claire said, her tone suddenly animated. "Garret doesn't give a damn about Feldon's death or how he died. He's trying to kill those horned creatures jumping around in his head." The excitement in her voice faded. "The trouble is he sees your face on those creatures." She picked up her drink, looked at it, and put it down. "I'm afraid, Rufus. Don't tell me I'm emotional and to get over it. I never thought I'd say this, but I won't stop worrying until you get on that train to Memphis."

"I'm not leaving so I can get away from Garret," he said. "You know that, don't you?"

"Of course I know that. My God! We've discussed this a dozen times." Tears glazed her eyes. "You have a son you've never seen. Do you have any idea how blessed you are? If I had a son waiting for me, wild horses couldn't keep me away."

"I thought about him a lot over the last ten years. I knew his mother loved him. His grandmother, too. But too much mother love can be as bad as too little. He needs a father. He needs me."

He lifted Claire's hand to his lips and kissed her palm. "That doesn't mean I don't need you, too, babe."

"I'm tired. Tired of talking, tired of worrying. I'm going to bed." She withdrew her hand and stood up. "You coming?"

"In a minute. I want to finish my drink."

"You can have mine, too. I'm already depressed. I don't want to make it worse." She leaned down and lightly brushed her lips over his. "I love you," she said. She smiled and walked away.

He watched her go, his heart filled with an inexplicable sadness. He rarely felt sad, but lately it was his constant companion. He knew he was losing something precious, something beautiful, something so unique he would never forget it. Claire was his joy, like a balmy day in winter, a rose bud at its peak, a cooling rain in an August drought. He knew his sadness and loneliness would fade with time, but the memories of her would remain, an eternal flame that might flicker but never die. He finished his drink and walked into the bedroom.

Claire spun around. "You scared me. I didn't think you'd come in so soon."

Rufus stared at her. His sadness vanished. She stood in the room's dim light wearing only her bra and bikinis. She looked back at him, her eyes lustrous, her cheeks flushed.

Without speaking, he strode across the floor and took her in his arms. She lifted her face to his. They kissed. The pressure of her lips on his sparked an erotic flame inside him. He coaxed her mouth open with his tongue and then drew it in and out in a teasing, tantalizing motion.

"No," she said and pulled away. "Not now. Later, after you've rested."

"No," he said, mimicking her tone. "Later may never come.

Now is all that matters."

He waited for the tension in her muscles to ease before he unhooked her bra and fondled her breast until he felt it swell to the intimacy of his touch.

"You feel so good." He kissed her ear, dropped his head, and suckled her nipple gently, hungrily.

Claire stiffened. A breathless cry slipped from her mouth.

"Oh, babe," was all Rufus could utter before his passion hurdled down on him like an avalanche of hot ashes and bubbling lava. He swept her in his arms and carried her to the bed. After stripping off his clothes, he laid his body on top of hers and gently moved back and forth, back and forth. The friction of his hard, bare chest rubbing against her satin-soft skin sparked a fire in his groin that was soon raging out of control.

A hot tide of passion flowed from his throat to his feet. He rolled onto his back. Claire mounted him. He thrust his cock deep inside her. She gasped and held herself deathly still. She caught her breath and began to move her hips, slowly at first, then faster and faster until he felt her muscles contract and she cried out in a wild frenzied voice, "Hold me, love me, oh, please, love me."

"I'll love you forever." Rufus gripped her hips and held on as the pressure on his engorged penis continued to mount.

"Oooh, babe!" His shout lapsed into a groan. He ran his hand over her breasts and trailed a sensuous path to her hips. He felt the dampness on her skin and the wetness between her legs. He was lying on a sun-bleached shore, the ocean waves lapping over him. The gentle swells grew more turbulent and finally erupted in a torrent of erotic rapture.

She dropped her head and sucked air into her lungs before she rolled over and laid beside him, her arm flung over his chest. He raised up and covered her lips with slow, fluttery kisses.

He felt a dampness on his lips, followed by a sharp pain that shot across his jaw and surged up his cheek to his eye. He released her and dropped his head back onto the pillow.

"Oh, my God! You're bleeding." Claire gasped and took a second look. "I didn't do that, did I?"

"No, not you. Garret. I thought it had healed, but kissing you and blowing my sax must've opened it up." A smile eased the furrows on his forehead. "What's a little pain? It was worth it."

"Don't move. I'll get some cotton and dab peroxide on your cut. You don't want it to get infected."

Before her feet hit the floor, Rufus grabbed her arm and pulled her back onto the bed. "You and your infections! You're obsessed. Believe me. That's the last of my worries."

He sat up and threw off the covers. "I'll wash it with soap and water. You go to sleep. I'll be back when my lip stops throbbing."

"You sure?"

"I'm sure."

"I won't be able to sleep till I wash my face, brush my teeth, and put on my flannel pajamas." A twinkle flashed in her eye. "I'll need something to keep me warm if I have to sleep all by myself." She pushed him back on the bed, drew the covers up to his chin, and kissed his nose. "Rest a minute. I won't be long."

"Hurry up." He touched his lip and moaned. "I need a pain killer bad."

"How about a couple of aspirin?"

He shook his head.

"A dose of scotch?" She cocked a brow.

"Now that you mention it."

"Hang in there. I'll see what I can do." She slipped off the bed and sprinted into the bathroom.

Rufus lay flat on his back and gazed out the window. The street lamp's somber light filtered through the glass and permeated his soul. A raw and primitive loneliness eclipsed the warm flush that followed their fantastic love making. His future looked as dim and shadowy as that hour before dawn when the night was ending and the day was only a premise. In two days, he would be leaving Claire, his music, his gig, everything he loved. Would the world stop spinning if he didn't get on that train to Memphis? Would Salinas curse him? Would Rufe Junior hate him? Not as much as he'd hate himself. He knew he'd self-destruct eventually, either from guilt or from the drugs he took to suppress it.

He got out of bed, pulled on his clothes, and went into the kitchen. He poured himself a scotch and water and flinched when the liquor passed over his cut lip. He gulped it down and poured another. The liquor dulled the pain but failed to relieve the loneliness, strain, and discontent.

He heard Claire leave the bathroom, switch off the lamp, and call out good night before she hit the sack.

"Sleep tight, my love," he said. He stared at the beaded doorway and debated whether he should join her. In his juiced state, he was afraid he'd toss and turn and keep her awake. He grabbed a blanket, fell onto his battered easy chair, and closed his eyes.

Sleep came first, then the dreams, then the nightmares. The first scene in his visionary journey was a whirlwind orbit of the universe where he traveled from the past to the present to the future.

On a distant star, he saw Salinas walking hand-in-hand with a young man. He couldn't see the man's face, but he knew it was him. He touched her swollen belly. She was smiling. They were happy. Without warning, a meteorite swept across the sky, and a torrent of cosmic dust rained down on them. They clung to each other for protection, but a gale-like wind tore her from his arms and threw him to the ground. When the storm passed, he pushed himself up and looked around. Salinas and the star were gone, and he was on the bandstand at Ella's Lounge, playing a sax solo with Claire, Moon, and Lenny improvising in the rhythm section. They were smiling. They were happy. A tempest blew in from the west. The wind howled; the building shook. All was chaos. They tried to run, but Mullins suddenly appeared, a gun in his hand, a sneer on his face. He pointed his pistol at Rufus's head and slowly pulled back the hammer. Rufus shouted at the others to take cover a second before the blast exploded in his ear.

Rufus awoke with a start, his warning cry still quivering on his lips. For several minutes, he sat in suspended animation as he tried to separate fact from fantasy. When he finally realized he had been dreaming, he bolted up and reached for the bottle of scotch. He poured what was left into a glass and paced from window to door and back again, sipping, pacing until his heart stopped thumping and his mind cleared.

He finished his drink, walked to the window, and stared out at the pale dawn that had replaced the ebony night. "*Damnable dreams, fucking nightmares.*" Would there ever be a time when troubles didn't whack him in his sleep? If not, he wondered how long a person could stay awake. Whatever the record, he was sure he could top it.

He ran his tongue over his lip. He felt only a twinge of pain, but his foul breath and the stale taste of cheap liquor and dried blood gagged him. He switched on a table lamp, more for its warmth than its light, and made a pot of coffee. He found a shriveled lime in the refrigerator's vegetable drawer. He quartered it and sucked on one of the pieces to cleanse his mouth until he could get into the bathroom and brush his teeth. He realized he also had to relieve himself, but he didn't want to wake Claire. He figured he could hang on for another hour. If she wasn't awake by then, he'd have to chance it.

Restless and irritable, he circled the room, drawing his hand along a row of CDs, wondering how in the hell he'd get everything packed in time to catch the train to Memphis. The aroma of brewed coffee drew him into the kitchen. As he passed his ugly chrome table, he saw his unopened mail lying behind the catsup bottle. He picked it up and flipped through it, hoping there wasn't a last-minute bill he forgot to pay. His eye caught on the edge of an envelope mixed in with the usual junk mail.

Now what! His heart skipped a beat. He knew it wasn't good news. Not with the luck he'd been having. He slanted his brow downward. Could be a telephone bill. Or a court summons. A poison-pen letter from Garret, assuming the nazi knew how to write. He turned it over in his hand. The second he saw his name written in a child's scrawl, a torrent of conflicting emotions washed over him. The first was excitement. He was holding his son's letter. It seemed so unreal it was almost a mystical experience. Until that moment, Rufe Junior had been an illusion, an obligation, now, suddenly, he was flesh and blood; he had a heart, a brain, a soul. Awed by the significance of his revelation, Rufus understood the inscrutable bond that existed between a parent and a child, a father and a son. He heard women had the same feeling the minute they learned they were pregnant. Men, on the other hand, weren't fathers until the baby was born, or in his case, until he received a white envelope with his name printed in block letters with a lead pencil.

A muscle flicked in his jaw. He felt anger and envy, anger at Salinas because she left him before his son was born and envy because of the ten years she and Rufe had shared without him.

He slumped onto a kitchen chair, opened the envelope, and drew out the letter. He read the greeting, wiped away the moisture in his eyes—a speck of dust must have irritated it—and read on.

Dear Dad:

Mom says you're gonna come live with us. I never saw you, and I don't know nothing about you except you play the saxophone and you're real famous. I like music. I'm happy you're coming. My friends at school think it's swell. When you get here, Mom said I could have a party so they can meet you. We're going to be at the station when you get off the train. It'll be late. Way past my bedtime. If Mom lets me, I'll stay home from school the next day, and you and me can shoot some baskets in the back yard if the snow goes away.

Love, Rufe Junior.

P.S. Mom helped me with this letter.

The moisture in his eyes trickled down his throat and formed a lump. What kind of kid did he have? Not a word about his father's ten-year absence. Not a hint of fear that his life would change. Not a trace of jealousy at having to share his mother with a stranger.

Rufus laid the letter on the table. He had no idea how to be a father. Was it something he could learn? If so, he'd have to learn fast. He knew he'd make mistakes, but, by God, he hoped he'd get an A for effort.

He reached for the bottle of scotch, capped it, and pushed it away. He started to rise, but a hand touched his shoulder and pushed him back down.

"You look like a man possessed." She pointed at the letter. "Bad news?"

"It's from Rufe. He wants to see me."

"Did you think he wouldn't?"

"I didn't know."

She tightened the blanket wrapped around her, sat down, and took Rufus's hand. "Are you afraid?"

"A little."

"Don't be." She smiled. "Everything'll work out. You're going to be the best father ever. Your son'll love you the minute he sees you. Boys, and girls, need their fathers, and fathers need their sons and daughters."

Rufus looked up in surprise. "You giving me permission to go to Memphis?"

"Permission?" She rolled her eyes. "Are you saying you won't go unless I give you my okay?"

"No, damn it. That's not what I'm saying." He frowned. Don't play games with me, and don't say you want me to go unless you mean it."

"I'm not playing games." Her expression softened. "You know I'd do anything to keep you with me, but it's too late to worry about that now. The train's on the track. You'll be gone in two days. I will not spend what little time we have left walking around like a zombie." She leaned her head to one side in a musing gesture. "Of course, I'll be a basket case after you're gone. I'll miss your smiles, your frowns, your kisses. You'll be gone, but the love we shared will always be with me. It got me through the hell of rehab. It'll get me through this. Doesn't matter if you go to Memphis or the moon. I'll always love you."

"I know. You don't have to say it. I sense it, I feel it. The feelings we have for each other are buried deep inside me, too. Every time I hear a bass or smell a gardenia I'll think of you." He paused and averted his gaze. "Shit, I'm not used to saying all this flowery stuff. I'm a sax player, not a singer belting out some bluesy love song."

"I love bluesy love songs." She smiled. "There aren't a lot of guys who'd even try to put their feelings into words."

He leaned close and studied her face feature by feature. He concentrated on the subtle flicker of an eyelash, the quirk of a smile, knowing that in time the slight tilt of her nose, the dimpled chin, and the long neck would fade from his memory, but for now, it was all he had, and it was enough to make him happy. He reached out and ran his hand across her flushed cheek with a tender, sweeping motion.

"What's going to happen to you?" he asked. "No way can I say thanks for the memories and walk away."

"You have a choice?" She shot him a musing glance. "Don't sweat it. I'll be okay. I'll hang around here till Mother goes home, then I'll hit the road, work my way out to L.A., playing gigs in Kansas City, Denver, Vegas."

"No way. A female musician on the road, alone, lonely! You'll be a drifter. God knows what kind of trouble you'll drift into."

A warm smile tugged at her lips. "You're something, Rufus Johnson. Something special. I don't remember anyone ever worrying about me before. It makes me feel good. It also makes me feel sad. I don't want you to worry about me. I may be a drifter, but I'll never be alone, not as long as I have my music and my memories of you." She blinked away the tears misting in her eyes. "Right now, I'm going to drift into the bathroom, take a shower and dress, then head out to Clearwater and check on Mother. If I can borrow your car…"

"Let me take you. I'm the only one who can move that bucket." He shrugged. "That is if you want company."

"I can always use company." She threw him a kiss and walked away.

CHAPTER TWENTY-ONE

Rufus parked in a spot marked "for visitors only," cut the engine, and stepped from the car. He sprinted around to the passenger side and opened the door for Claire. While he waited for her to get out, he glanced at the Center's imposing buildings. Old fears and apprehensions hit him in his gut.

In the bright afternoon light, the Clearwater Rehab Center looked more hospitable than it had on that cold, blustery night when they arrived with Dixie, but not even the sunlight dancing on the ice-clad trees could temper the institution's foreboding atmosphere. He shuddered. He hated all of them. Hospitals, prisons, reform schools were coops where the poor, the weak, the jinxed were incarcerated and dehumanized. The inmates' only distinguishing mark was the number branded on their souls.

"You okay?" Claire nudged his arm. "You don't look like you want to do this. You can wait for me in the car. I won't be long."

"I don't like buildings with bars on the windows, but I'm cool."

Claire touched his cheek with a mittened hand. "I have the feeling wild horses couldn't get you inside if you weren't with me."

"I've had my fill of institutions." He grimaced as if he had bitten into a tart apple. "I can't stand the sickening odors of urine, fear, and despair."

"I know. I hate it, too, but this is it if you want to get well," she said. "I kicked my habit here. It was a brutal, wrenching nightmare. A day didn't go by that I didn't think about leaving. My bass and my memories kept me from running. I knew I had to get clean if I ever wanted to see you again. But good intentions and a handful of memories would've been worthless without help, tough help." She frowned. "I thought a pack of hyenas hired the staff and set up the program. They actually laughed at me when I cussed and kicked and begged for a fix. Later, I found out the hyenas never left the room. They sat on the window sills and waited for me to die."

Rufus nodded. "I saw snakes. They hissed and coiled and flicked their tongues. They scared the shit out of me. I didn't think anything could be terrifying until I realized they were inside my head."

"You were stronger than I was. I'd have killed myself if I had had to do it alone." Claire sniffed the fresh air as if trying to banish her nightmarish visions. "The day I walked out, I swore I'd never put myself through that again."

With a trembling hand, she pointed to a third-story window. "That was my room. I used to look out that window every evening and watch the dark shadows slink across the grounds and coax me to join them. Between them and the hyenas, it's a miracle I didn't kill myself."

Rufus reached out and pulled her to him. "It's over, babe. They're gone now."

"Are they?" Claire gave her head a dubious shake. "How do you know they're not hiding inside?"

"Inside what?" he asked. "The building or our heads?"

"Either. Both."

234

"We'll find out soon enough." He released her, took her hand, and led her down the brick path to the front door.

After they signed in, the receptionist told them to go into the waiting room. Nurse Platt would be with them shortly.

They entered the Spartan room and sat down on the chrome and plastic chairs nearest the door. Their backs rigid, their feet planted firmly on the tiled floor, they stared straight ahead, silently, motionlessly, as if afraid a whisper or a shrug would contaminate the sterile environment.

Rufus glanced at the clock ticking away the seconds. After five minutes had passed, he shifted in his chair and studied the portrait of a white-coated man hanging below the clock. He was holding a Bible in one hand and a tablet in the other. By straining his eyes, he read the Twelve Steps engraved on the stone.

The words were encouraging, the spiritual message inspirational, but Rufus knew they were mere words to an unremorseful alcoholic living in the twilight world of booze and despair. He knew it wasn't a matter of "kicking the habit." That was too easy. Not until the pain was worse than the pleasure did a drunk take that first step.

He shot a sideways glance at Claire. His heart filled with pride and love. She had survived the trip through hell when she got off the roller coaster ride of coke and alcohol. He knew neither of them should get near a bag or a bottle. He promised himself he'd stop tempting fate and quit drinking his scotch. He'd ask Claire to lay off the gin. He knew it'd be hard to give up their last crutch. They were musicians. They played in bars, cabarets, and honky-tonks, where ever they could get a gig. Bird, Miles, the Prez, Billie couldn't climb that wall. They tried, but like Bird said when he described his hell, he could get the stuff out of his body, but he couldn't get it out of his mind.

Rufus felt a particular kinship with Charlie Parker. Maybe it was because they both played the sax. The only difference was, Bird was a genius who created sounds never heard before or since. Like a lot of aspiring sax players, Rufus tried to imitate Bird's dazzling technique and frantic tempos. The only thing he managed to copy was Bird's addictions. There were some sax players who came close. Some critics claimed Coltrane outplayed him. Rufus shrugged. Both were great jazz musicians. Both created their own style. It didn't matter if he was playing bebop or free jazz, he knew he couldn't duplicate their wails and growls. Maybe he never got high enough or drunk enough. Lucky for him and the jazz world, other musicians, Miles Davis, John Coltrane, Dexter Gordon, Art Blakey, Sonny Rollins managed to move jazz from the cellar to the roof before they died.

Rufus grimaced. He hated to admit it, but Garret saved his life when he and his posse hit the drug house. A couple more trips to the rock-candy mountain, and he'd have been the one diving out the window instead of Ronnie the Rube Feldon. Garret saved Claire's life, too. Together, they might've shot up till their veins collapsed, or they overdosed. He went to prison. She went to Clearwater. They were alone and miserable, but they got off drugs. Through it all, they loved each other, and they survived. Too damn bad Garret didn't see it that way.

He reached over and rubbed Claire's cold hand until her skin warmed to his touch.

"You okay?" he asked.

"Yeah, for now, but I don't want to sit here all afternoon?"

"This is an institution. The people who run it don't bother with time except when they're checking patients in and out." He tweaked a smile and pointed to a plaque hanging off center on the drab, beige wall. "Read that. It might help."

She frowned and mumbled the words in a weary voice.

"'God grant me the serenity to accept the things I cannot change, courage to change the things I can, and wisdom to know the difference.' That's not for me." She let out a derisive snort. "I'm tired of accepting things, I'm not wise, and I'll never be serene. If I thought about every piece of shit that hit me in the face, I'd end up back here, a gutless, spineless chicken. As far as accepting things, hell, that's the story of my life. I accepted Mother's drinking. I accepted Dad's love affair with his inner self. I've even come to terms with you leaving. One of these days, something's going to happen that I can't accept, then watch out. I won't think. I'll act. Maybe it'll be stupid and foolish and ill-advised, but it'll be my decision."

Rufus heard the quiver in her voice and saw her troubled face. He wanted to comfort her like she had comforted him, but he held back. He knew she didn't want comfort. She wanted understanding, approval, and acknowledgement of her unique-ness. She wasn't only a dutiful daughter, a sensuous lover, and a doer among drifters. This lady was a shrewd, street smart woman with an indomitable spirit.

Rufus noticed her spirit quickly returned when Nurse Platt entered the waiting room, wearing a crisp uniform and a dour expression.

"Miss Burton. Mr. Johnson." She shook hands and took a seat across from them. "I'm glad you came. I meant to contact you, but everything's been so hectic." She swung her head at the reception desk and then glanced down at the clip board lying on her lap. "Dr. Ashley is sending your mother home tomorrow. There are a few things we have to discuss."

"Home?" Claire frowned. "That can't be. I was here for months. She hasn't been here for a week."

"Yes, I know." Nurse Platt assumed the stiff, competent pose of a veteran adviser. "Alcoholics and drug abusers go through different treatment programs."

"Different! How? What? I don't understand. An addict's an addict." Frustration stoked the pitch in Claire's voice. "If she goes home too soon, she might never get well." She clasped her hands together and laid them on her lap. "Please understand. I'm not questioning your knowledge and training, but Mother's been drinking half her life. By drinking, I mean she was a raging, fall-down drunk. This is her first time in a rehab program. If you toss her out now, send her back home, I know she'll start drinking again."

"We can't keep her here forever." Pratt's thin lips puckered in annoyance.

"Forever? Of course not. But she should stay long enough to get the booze out of her system and be sober for at least a month."

"Oh, you think a month'll do it?" Nurse Platt exhaled her frustration. "Tell me, Miss Burton, how long have you been free of drugs?"

"Four months. Maybe longer. I was so messed up, I can't be sure." Claire shrunk back as if cowed by Pratt's authoritarian tone.

"Please, relax. I didn't mean to put you on the spot. I was trying to make a point."

"What is your point?" Rufus asked, annoyed by Pratt's patronizing tone.

"I'm getting to it, Mr. Johnson." She sucked in her cheeks and turned to Claire. "Do you still crave drugs?"

Claire nodded.

"How often do you have these cravings?"

"A couple times a day." She shrugged. "Sometimes more, sometimes less."

"And when do you think the cravings will stop?"

Claire's eyes widened. "Probably never."

"How do you handle them? How do you keep from going back?"

"I remind myself how painful it was when I was using. I remember the indescribable torture of coming down. I don't ever want to go through either hell again."

"That's where we want to get your mother," Platt said. "She has to pick her hell: keep drinking or stop drinking. Neither choice is easy, but if she stops, she'll have a chance to survive and maybe even be happy again."

"She can't do it alone."

"She won't do it alone. She'll have help."

"Who's going to help her? Me? My father?" Claire shook her head. "Impossible. In many ways, we're sicker than she is."

"No, you're not. You're much stronger than you think." Pratt's lips parted in a friendly smile. "You already know alcoholism is a disease. You didn't cause your mother's problems, and neither did Mr. Burton. On the other hand, you're right when you say she needs help, but the burden won't fall on you completely. Mrs. Burton will have to admit she's an alcoholic, take responsibility for her behavior, and join an organization that will help her over the rough spots. We recommend AA, Alcoholics Anonymous."

"That's it?" Claire looked at Pratt with an iffy stare.

"No, Miss Burton, that's not IT. That's only the beginning." She picked up her clip board and rose from her chair. "In fact, the beginning has already started. "Come along. I'll take you to your mother's room. Keep in mind Mrs. Burton is still very sick. Be positive, cheerful, and supportive. Don't argue, accuse, or pamper her." Pratt shot a curt glance at Rufus. "You can come along, if you wish, Mr. Johnson. As a friend of the family."

Rufus stood up. Claire took his hand. Together they followed Pratt out of the room, keeping two steps behind.

The institutional smell accompanied them up the elevator, down the hall, and dissipated slightly when they reached Dixie's room. Pratt knocked on the door, announced their presence, and entered the room without waiting for a response.

A woman's startled cry hit Rufus in the pit of his stomach. He was Claire's lover, not a friend of the family. Convinced that his presence would intensify an already tense situation, he told Claire he'd wait in the hallway.

"You'll do no such thing. I want you with me." Anger sparked in Claire's eyes. "How dare that nurse intimidate you!"

"I'm not intimidated," Rufus assured her. "I don't want to complicate things. Your mother doesn't know me, and she sure as hell won't be in any condition to socialize."

Claire fumed. Rufus held fast. Thirty seconds later and fully aware his determination was no match for Claire's when she dug her heels in, he compromised. He would go in but only as far as the door.

Placated, Claire straightened her back and entered the room. Rufus slipped in behind her, sidled to a shadowy corner, and took a quick glance around the room. The luxurious furnishings amazed him. With the cherry-wood furniture, satin drapes, and decorative pictures, it could've been a suite at the Hilton, but he knew it wasn't. No furnishings, no matter how expensive, could eliminate the anguish and despair that permeated the atmosphere. He caught a glimpse of Bernard Burton. No where was the anguish more apparent than on his grim face.

Rufus heard a twittering sound. He turned. Dixie stepped from behind a wing-back chair and staggered to the center of the room. He gasped. Her narrow shoulders, hunched back, and frail limbs reminded him of an injured bird.

Her hands in constant motion, she fluttered from the window, to a table, where she opened a book, closed it, spoke to Claire, stopped in mid-sentence, then turned to Bernard and finished the sentence with a question. Would he pick her up in the morning, or should she call Henry? Would he bring her favorite blue dress? She wanted to look her best when she went home.

Rufus waited for Bernard's answer her questions, but instead of words, he responded with stilted nods and awkward simpers. Rufus shook his head. Was this the same man whose hot temper and commanding presence had intimidated and enraged Claire only days before?

He shifted his gaze from Bernard, to Pratt, to Dixie, and stopped at Claire. The shades of anger, fear, bewilderment, disgust on their faces made him feel as if he was in a madhouse filled with tormented souls.

Pratt was the first to break the heaviness that had enveloped them. She paced in front of Dixie's bed, checking her mustering-out list. She urged them to contact AA, offer Dixie candy when she felt the urge to drink, keep a bottle of water handy, keep her busy and never let her have just one little swig of liquor. To an alcoholic, there's no such thing as one little swig.

Rufus acknowledged Pratt's recommendations with a nod. When he glanced at Dixie, he realized she hadn't heard one of them. She was too busy flitting from Claire to Bernard, talking incessantly, checking her makeup each time she passed a mirror.

Claire followed her mother's migration around the room, praising her progress, commending her courage, and assuring her of her love.

Dixie paused and looked at Claire full in the face. "Love!" she said in a strained voice. "Oh, no! I'm not lovable. I'm a drunk, an unhappy, miserable drunk, and I've made everyone else unhappy." She dropped her arms to her sides and stood there, alone, defenseless, heartsick. "I wish I could die so you and your father could get on with your lives."

Pratt spun around and drew her thick brows together, the long, black line resembling the wings of a raven silhouetted against a chalk white sky.

"We'll have no talk of dying," she said. "Have you forgotten our last session where we discussed self-pity? You have a family who loves you and friends who support you, but it's much more important for you to love yourself."

"I love my daughter and my husband," Dixie said. "I didn't

turn their lives into a living hell on purpose." Tears streaked her cheeks and settled in the crevices around her mouth. "Why shouldn't I want to die? It's the one thing I can do to make up for all the hurt I've caused." She glanced at Rufus. A cheerless smile tugged at her lips. "Claire found a man who loves her." She spun around and looked at Bernard. "When I'm gone, I want you to find a woman who can make you happy."

Bernard bolted from his chair. "You have it all wrong. I don't want another woman. I want you to get well."

The room grew silent, the tension weighty.

"That's not true. You never wanted me. I was never good enough. Please tell me I didn't make your life so miserable you can't stand the thought of living with another woman."

Bernard strode toward her, his dark eyes searing the space between them. He took her hand. The glow of his smile filled the room with an unexpected warmth.

"I'm tired of hiding," he said. "I'm tired of living a half life. I listened to too many people who gave me all the wrong advice, but I don't blame them. I blame myself. At last night's meeting here at the Center, I learned that a person makes his own heaven or hell. It's true. It's my fault if I'm lonely and afraid. If it's not too late, I'd like to patch things up between us. I'll help you. You help me."

The chilly silence returned. Pratt's hand, poised over her clip board, froze in midair. Claire let out a choking sob, and tears tumbled down her cheeks. Dixie stared at him in mute bafflement.

"You mean it?" Dixie asked. "You truly love me?"

He nodded. "It won't be easy. We have a lot to make up for,

but we have to start sometime."

"Yes, we must start. I'll try, but promise me you won't get angry if I stumble." She smiled and the twittering in her hands eased.

Rufus drifted out of the shadows and wrapped his arm around Claire's waist. "Let's go," he whispered. "I think your parents would like to be alone."

"No, I'm not leaving." She shoved him away. "He's lying. Nobody changes that fast. He wants us to feel sorry for him. I won't let Mother be alone with him. She couldn't handle it if he called her a weakling and laughed at her after we leave. He did it before. He'll do it again."

Bernard shot them a fretful glance, as if he were aware of a slight disturbance, but unaware of the bomb he had just dropped in the room's close, stagnant atmosphere.

"Claire?" Bernard looked at her with a strained expression on his face. "You're still here? I thought you left. Do you want to talk to your mother?"

"I think we've done enough talking for the day." Pratt donned her authoritarian pose and approached Claire. "Visiting hours are over. It's time for you to leave."

"What about him?" Claire pointed to her father.

"Don't worry. I'll handle it." A plastic smile froze on Pratt's lips.

"Come on, babe." Rufus took Claire's arm and tried to pull her to the door, but she broke away and ran to her mother. "I'll take care of you. Tell me what you need. I'll get it for you. Please, don't send me away."

"I don't need a thing, but thank you for your kindness."

Dixie worked up a smile. "It means so much to me."

"Kindness! I'm Claire, your daughter, not some social worker."

Pratt approached Claire, her brows slanted in a warning frown. "Mrs. Burton should rest now. She's doing so well, but too much tension could hurt her at this stage of her illness." She gripped Claire's arm, marched her across the room, and handed her over to Rufus. "Be careful when you leave. The sidewalks are still very slick."

Outside, the brittle wind whistled through the barren limbs of giant oaks and bowed the Scotch pines, their long needles tumbling to the earth like a widow's tears. Gripping Rufus's hand, Claire walked to the car, the hard ground crunching and moaning under her feet.

Rufus opened the car door and motioned for her to get in. Instead, she turned and stared at the bleak wintry scene, a desolate expression distorting her features.

"Oh, Rufus, I'm feel so lonely. You're leaving me. My parent's don't want me. What am I going to do?"

"You're going to do what you've always done when life got shitty. You're going to pack a suitcase, your bass and bow, and hit the road." Rufus pulled her to him, then leaned down and kissed her forehead, her cheek, and her lips with a light, feathery touch.

"But I'll be alone. So alone."

"No, you won't, babe. You got your music and your talent. That's all you need. The rest will come. The friends, the laughter, the love."

"No, not love. I'll never love anyone the way I love you." She wrapped her arms around his waist, and they clung to each other, oblivious of the wind and snow dappling their eyelashes and flushing their cheeks.

CHAPTER TWENTY-TWO

On the drive back to town, Rufus started to suspect depression was the rule rather than the exception in Claire's life. It was like a festering sore that never healed. She was only happy when they were making love or playing jazz. He looked up. A pothole the size of Yankee Stadium was coming up on him at fifty miles an hour. He swerved around it and straightened the car seconds before he hit a fire hydrant. He relaxed his grip on the steering wheel, exhaled, and returned to his dismal thoughts.

Depression! He was right there beside Claire when it came to gloom and doom. And like her, sex and music brought some relief, but he couldn't make love or play his sax twenty-four hours a day.

Neither could he make excuses for all the shit life dumped on them as well as the shit they dumped on themselves. They could find a dozen reasons to justify taking drugs. Didn't all musicians drink or snort or shoot? Black musicians had to put up with racism and poverty. Female musicians had to put up with sexism and, in Claire's case, wealth. He knew that passing the blame was a cop out. If snorting coke wasn't their fault, they didn't have to stop. On the other hand, they had to quit blaming themselves for other people's screw-ups.

Rufus shot Claire a sideways glance. Her mute, wretched expression hit him in the gut. She was depressed, but it was a legitimate depression. She had gone through too many changes in too short a time. Losing him, losing her gig, and struggling with her parent's botched lives had hit her in the gut big time.

Rufus shook his head. They had had a rough, supercharged day. He was hungry and Claire probably was, too. Since the heart and the stomach were in contact, he decided if they fed one, they'd feed the other.

He smiled and nudged her arm. "You hungry for Chinese?"

She grimaced and shook her head.

"Come on, babe. You gotta eat at least once every few days. You don't want to crash while you're standing in front of an audience playing your bass, do you?"

"What I don't want is for you to bug me about eating." Claire shot him a brittle glance. "I'll have a drink at Ella's. If one doesn't work, I'll drink another, and another, and another."

"Great. That's just what you need. Go to the cabaret. Have a few drinks. Forget your troubles." Rufus sneered. "In case you've forgotten, that kind of thinking is what got you and me into drugs."

"Well, excuse me. I guess I'm not as strong as you. I like to drink. But that's no surprise, is it? I come from a long line of drinkers. No reason why I shouldn't follow in my mother's footsteps."

"You're talking stupid now, but if that's what you want, go to it, babe. I won't stop you. It'd be a waste of time to try, but I'm going to get something to eat."

He made a sharp left turn, drove two blocks, and stopped in front of the House of Wong. "Well, what do you want to do, sit out here or go inside? It's your call. I'm not going to beg."

"And you shouldn't have to beg." Claire gave him an apologetic smile. "You've been great, and I'm acting like a jerk. And you're right about the liquor. So far, I've been okay with one drink at Ella's or at the apartment, but if I start drinking to drown my sorrows, I may not stop."

"You're fine, babe. Don't sweat it." He leaned across the seat and kissed her. "You'll be even better after you eat." He reached for the door handle. "Come on. Let's go in before we freeze or starve."

Claire frowned and shook her head.

"Now what? You change your mind already?"

"Not about eating. I'd rather eat at home. Is carry-out okay?"

"More than okay." He switched on the engine. "Stay warm. I'll be back in a flash." He stepped out of the car, spun around, and motioned for her to crack the window. "You want your usual?"

"Chicken fried rice and wanton soup." She grinned. "Do they make anything else?"

"I hope so. I'm up for sweet-n-sour shrimp, egg roll, and a bucket of rice."

He winked and walked into the restaurant with a smile on his face and a spring in his walk. While he waited for the waitress to fill his order, he tried to figure out why he felt so happy. It didn't take a lot of deep thinking to realize there was little to be happy about. His life was like a boat caught in a typhoon. Claire's wasn't any better. Even when they were hanging on by their nails, they found an inner strength that kept them going. He thought their inner strength would be stretched thin during the next few days, but he knew it wouldn't break. After all, what else could happen to screw up their lives?

His up mood stayed with him on the drive to the apartment, the walk up the dimly lit staircase, and into the cold, dark room. He flipped on a light before the darkness affected Claire's mood, but he needn't have worried. Her ready smile and eager expression told him she was as determined as he was to enjoy what little time they had left together.

She glided around the room like a ballerina, collecting candles, setting them on the table and lighting them after she made a wish. When Rufus reminded her that most people blew out the candles then made a wish, she laughed and reminded him that their lives had been upside down and inside out for so long, society's rules didn't apply to them. Slipping into madcap spirit, he set the table, opened a container, and wafted it under her nose. "Will this be satisfactory?" He responded to her smile with a wink and a smile. "Will you be using a fork or your fingers, ma'am?"

"Oh, for God's sake! Give me that." Claire grabbed the box and dumped half the carton of fried rice on her plate. She snatched two chopsticks from the bag and used them to shovel food into her mouth.

Rufus sat down, filled his plate, and picked up a fork. "By the time I figured out how to hold those things, there wouldn't be any left as fast as you're eating." He studied her fluid hand-wrist movements intently. "Who taught you how to use chopsticks?"

"I taught myself." She eyed him uncertainly. "Don't you remember? We lived on Chinese food when we were flying."

"I dumped those memories a long time ago. Who wants to remember trips to hell?"

"Sorry. I shouldn't have brought it up. I don't want to ruin our party." With a perverse smile, she speared one of his shrimp and stuck it in her mouth. Rufus managed to jab two shrimp before she attacked again. Like two jostling knights, they deflected each other's weapons with a hit and a lick and let out a victory shout when they snared a bite. Their laughter ricocheted off the plaster walls and ice-fringed window and filled the air with its rich sonorous tone. Rufus and Claire laid down their weapons, pushed away the empty boxes, and stared at each other across the table. Captivated by the sensuous glimmer in Claire's eyes and the candle light's romantic glow, he reached across the table and took her hand. "Damn, I'm going to miss you, woman."

Rufus paused when he saw her bottom lip quiver. He had a sinking feeling in his gut. Why had he said he'd miss her? Of course he'd miss her, but did he have to keep reminding her he was leaving?

He leaned back and shot her a cautious glance. He wouldn't have been surprised if she stalked off and didn't talk to him the rest of the evening. Instead, she rose, walked around the table, and stood beside him.

"You're all that matters to me. I know I'll be miserable after you leave, but you haven't left yet, so there's no reason why I should wallow in self-pity. That's what it would be, nothing but self-pity." She leaned down and brushed a kiss across his forehead.

The touch of her moist, firm lips on his brow quickened his pulse and gorged his mind with erotic thoughts. He caught his breath, shocked by his instant response to her gentle kiss. Making love was the last thing he had on his mind when they left the rehab center. Suddenly, it was all he could think about. He gave his head a disparaging shake. *Damn! This was a hell of a time to realize sex could be as addictive as cocaine.*

He averted his eyes, embarrassed by his thoughts. He loved Claire. It upset him to know sex and love weren't a duet. For that reason, he decided he wouldn't take her to bed. He wanted their sex to be like it had been: filled with a magic that touched their souls as well as their bodies. Would she feel shock, anger, dejection if he told her his thoughts? He looked up and searched her face, trying to reach into her mind. He was stunned when he realized he didn't have to probe. The lusty shimmer in her eyes and the slight flare of her nostrils told him she felt the same physical hunger and sensuous desire he did.

The heavy rock of passion lifted, supplanted by a rapture he had never experienced. He stood up, swept her into his arms, and carried her into the bedroom.

They undressed and stared at each other's bodies as if they had suddenly acquired a uniqueness and a beauty visible only to them. Although Rufus had explored every inch of her body and knew every sensuous spot, her full breasts, taut belly, and the thick brush of brown hair filling the triangle between her thighs sent his libido soaring.

He saw her eyes widen at the sight of his throbbing penis. His passion flared. He reached out and pulled her to him. He kissed her hard on her mouth.

Rufus heard her whimper. He started to release his hold until he felt the slight shudder of her arousal. They fell onto the bed. She thrust her pelvis against his groin in silent expectation. Rufus entered her. Instantly, he saw the play of erotic sensations flutter across her face. Slowly moving in and out, he saw the first flush of passion stain her cheeks. He saw her lips part and her jaw muscles tighten. As he quickened the pace, he felt the slight arch of her back and the soaring potency of her rhythmic thrusts.

Rufus felt his orgasm advance from some mysterious abyss and consume him. He tried to resist it, to let it linger a moment longer, but it was too powerful. He lost contact with the world and was carried away on a massive cosmic wave. Moments later, Claire's gasps exploded, and she let out a frenzied cry.

They lay together, his penis still inside her, his hardness spent but his desire still intact. He buried his face in the curve of her neck. The lush scent of gardenias mingling with the musky odor of sex rekindled his hedonistic thoughts. He rolled her over, raised his body on top of hers, and moved his chest across her breasts. The friction of skin against skin ignited fiery sparks, and he felt his penis throb and harden.

"No, please, no more," she whispered. "I'm tired. I want to sleep."

"Was I too rough?" He looked at her in alarm.

"No, oh, no," she whispered. "It was fabulous." She smiled and stared at him, her eyes filled with love. "I want to go to sleep and dream about you. When we're together like this, we're always happy. There's no Memphis, no Garret, no gigs."

"Happy dreams." He kissed her lips, rolled onto his back, and drew her into his arms. They slept for a brief time. When they awoke, they slipped out of bed, showered, and dressed in silence, their thoughts and feelings buried deep inside once more. When the tension became too intense, he gripped her arm and forced her to look at him.

"What happened? You're not happy anymore. Did you have

a bad dream?"

She nodded. "A real lemon."

"Damn! What's left if you can't depend on a dream?" He grinned.

"It's not funny."

"It's not the end of the world either."

"How do you know? Bad dreams can be omens, warnings of things to come." She grabbed her coat and stormed out of the apartment.

Rufus followed her down the stairs and out the front door. "Come on, babe. Don't go getting angry on me now. We're going to have a good time tonight." He threw his arm around her shoulders and gave her a kiss. "We're going to Ella's. Trouble won't find us there. Remember the song from 'Cabaret?' Remember the words?" He hummed the melody and belted out the last lines: "Life is a cabaret, old chum... Come to the cabaret."

He caught the hint of a smile on her face. "See what happens when you're thinking good thoughts? Stop messing with your mind, and keep your emotions under control or you'll always be unhappy."

"Okay, I hear you. No more fantasies. Just hard, cold reality." Claire zipped up her jacket and tripped down the steps to the car.

Rufus stood at the top of the stoop and glanced up and down the street. If Garret or one of his hound dogs were hanging around, he wanted to see them before they saw him. He felt a sudden burst of anger. He expected to be hit by winter's frigid blasts and to see shadows playing hopscotch on the deserted street, but he didn't expect the fear that gripped his heart.

ELSA COOK

Was Garret out there, waiting? He narrowed his eyes and
looked for an unmarked sedan, a lone man, an armed assassin.
He sniffed the air, expecting danger to have an odor. He listened
for the click of a hammer being drawn back, the firing of a bullet, but his senses caught nothing. He darted down the steps.

Claire stood at the curb and looked at him in alarm. "You saw
Garret, didn't you? Where is he?" She glanced over her shoulder.
"I don't see him. Is he alone?" She reached down and opened the
car door. "Come on. Let's get out of here."

"He's not here." Rufus shook his head in bewilderment.
"Shit! What the hell's the matter with me? I told you to get hold
of yourself, and here I am, acting like one damn scared rabbit.
I'm having nightmares, and I'm wide awake."

"How do you know he's not watching?" Claire protested. "He
could be…"

"He could be, but it doesn't matter if he is or isn't. I won't let
him turn me into a zombie, afraid to move, scared of my shadow." He got in the car. With a twist of his wrist, he switched on
the key, pumped the accelerator, and forced the sluggish engine
to cooperate.

A short time later, Rufus and Claire walked into Ella's
Lounge. The handful of people in the bar was hunched over their
drinks watching Monday night football on the TV. Rufus walked
to the far end of the bar and punched Bojay's arm.

"What the hell's going on?"

"What the shit you think's going on?" Bojay rolled his eyes.
"We're watching the football game. You got a problem with
that?"

"This is a lounge, not a sport's bar. They want to watch football, tell 'em to go to the game."

"Don't sweat it, man. I'll turn it off when you guys start play-ing." Bojay ran his rag across the bar and nodded at Claire. "How do you put up with that dude? He can be one sorry ass when he wants to."

"It's been a long day." Claire tweaked a smile and ordered their usual.

When Bojay reached for the glasses, she touched his arm and shook her head. "Make those two seltzers with lime," she said. "We're on the wagon, starting right now."

Rufus wanted to protest but decided he didn't want to aggra-vate Bojay anymore than he already had, and he sure as hell did-n't want to discuss the pros and cons of drinking liquor with Claire. Instead, he shot a sideways glance at the glassy-eyed patrons staring at the TV. "Don't tell me this batch of homeys is tonight's audience."

Bojay set the drinks on the bar. "Case you ain't got the brains you was born with, it's gonna start snowing, and the tempera-ture's gonna drop way below zero. The regulars and a few dudes wanting to take a break from their women and kids is the only ones crazy 'nough to come out on a night like this."

"Why didn't Ella close?"

Bojay shrugged. "I ain't got the foggiest."

"Did Moon and Lenny show?"

"Yep. They're here."

Rufus took a sip of seltzer, coughed, and gripped his throat. "What is this stuff?" He set the glass on the bar and pushed it away. "This is going to be one sorry night."

"Quit with the complaining," Claire said. "We're here. We're ready to do a show. What difference does it make if we play to ten people or a hundred? I'd rather be in a half-empty lounge filled with live music than a cold apartment filled with dead memories."

"Okay, okay. You're right. Anything's better than that." He slipped off the stool and stretched to his full height. "Let's do it. Maybe if we start early, Ella'll let us leave early." Claire nodded, grabbed his drink, and followed him to the lounge.

When they reached the bandstand, Moon did a drum roll, stood up, and bowed from the waist. "Welcome to the Eskimo suite." He grinned. "Thought you guys'ed be hunkering down at your pad on a bad night like this."

"It never entered our minds," Rufus said, his tone rife with sarcasm. He opened his case and assembled his horn. Then, as if he was a jazz high priest performing a set of rituals, he licked his mouthpiece, fingered the keys, and blew a few notes. Assured that he and his horn were in tune, he introduced the first set to a sparse audience.

"Instead of playing our standards, we're going to jam for our special audience."

He bowed, introduced the band, and opened with a muted statement of the melody to "I Could Write a Book." Claire came in on bass. He bobbed his head to her strong, pulsing thumps. When Lenny charged in, his fingers tripping up and down the keyboard, they were off and running.

Half way into their collective improvisation, Lenny took the spotlight with a solo rendition of "Round Midnight."

Rufus answered with a breathy rendition of "The Way You Look Tonight." Moon accompanied him on the snare.

Moon and Claire grooved through a galaxy of musical periods: swing, soul, free jazz, Latin jazz, bebop. They recycled Ellington's "Satin Doll," Gershwin's "I Got Rhythm," and Monk's "Little Rootie Tootie" by stamping the melodies with their unique styles and creative improvisations.

Rufus studied Claire's technique, listened to her pluck the notes, then concentrated on her tone with the objectivity of a music critique from the *Chicago Tribune* or the *Rolling Stone*.

Her quest for artistic perfection was the most obvious. Although it seemed effortless, her ability to sustain the songs' structure, accommodate a soloist's maneuverings around chords, and swing when she plucked and walked and improvised her own solos was fantastic. When she and Moon finished their set, Claire picked up her bow and played a succession of romantic ballads. Her solos of "When I Fall in Love" and "April in Paris" were filled with raw emotion and musical streams of consciousness. Rufus closed his eyes and heard Billie Holiday and Bessie Smith's melancholy despair, infinite loneliness, and rootless existence.

The distinctive sounds of jazz and blues, their wails and cries, thumps and chords filled Rufus's heart with a crushing sorrow. As difficult as it was, he was prepared to leave Claire and his band and start a new life in Memphis, but he wasn't prepared to give up his music. He didn't know what he would do if Salinas insisted he put away his saxophone and get a real job. The thought stunned him. If it weren't for his son, he would let the train to Memphis leave without him. But he had made a promise, and he intended to keep it. He wanted to keep it.

Claire and Lenny finished the set with the pensive love song, "They Can't Take That Away from Me."

She played her bass with the intensity of a woman making love to her man, her sounds shifting from light and romantic to loud and sensual. She might have dedicated the song to him, but she was playing to anyone who had ever loved and lost, who would never forget "the way you hold your head, the way we danced till three…"

Rufus cycled his emotions into memories and stored them in a secret place inside his head. He would let them out at night when he was alone or in a smoke-filled bar, or during the day when he heard car wheels thumping on a rain-splattered street, or caught a sun beam dancing on a frosted window. A pensive smile settled on his lips. *No, no one can take that away from me.*

The band finished the session early and headed to the bar. While Bojay emptied ash trays, collected beer bottles, and transferred the night's receipts from the register to a money pouch, they rehashed their past and outlined their future.

Moon was the most exuberant. His enthusiasm cheered the group and kept the party from becoming a dirge.

"Come Friday, I'm heading' south." Moon took a drink of his draft beer and shook his body, miming a shiver. "The good Lord put Adam in a jungle where there weren't no bugs or mosquitoes or snow plows or ice scrapers. Course that snake come along and cause trouble, but I ain't going to no jungle. Florida look mighty fine to me."

"How you gonna get there?" Lenny asked. "You ain't got two dimes to rub together."

"I got a cousin in Tallahassee. She gonna send me bus fare, and I'm gonna use my last pay check to ship my drums to a dude in Miami."

"Don't know how far it'll get you," Rufus said, "but I figured I'd give you my car. I won't need it…" He caught himself before he added that Salinas probably had one, and he'd make do till he got his first gig.

He glanced at Claire, wondering if she completed his sentence, but her blank stare told him nothing.

"Thanks, man," Moon said. "I'll get that bucket to Florida if I got to push it." He tipped his glass and nudged Claire's arm. "You got plans?" he asked. "You'n Lenny're welcome to come along for the ride. We can cut loose when we get to sun country or anywhere in between."

"Thanks, but I think I'll hang around here for a while. After I settle some family problems, I'll be heading west." She looked at him, a weary smile pasted on her lips. "I hate the cold, too."

A morose silence settled over them like a pall of polluted air. They sipped their drinks, shifted in their seats, and averted their eyes, the strain of breaking up the group visible on their bleak faces. They had been together too long and cared about each other too much to pretend this was simply another phase in their rambling lives.

Bojay turned off the bar's back lights, approached the table, and laid his hand on Rufus's shoulder.

"Time's up," he said.

"So soon?" Rufus gave him a grudging nod and glanced at Moon, Lenny, and Claire. The song "Breaking Up Is Hard to Do" flashed in his mind. He knew all about breaking up, and it was never easy. When Salinas disappeared, carrying his unborn son, he'd searched for them, but no one would help him where to look. He needed money to live and keep looking, so he played his sax in honky-tonks and roadside taverns in dozens of nameless, forgettable towns. At each stop, he wrote a letter to his son and put it and a little money in his lock box. Now he would carry that box to Memphis and read the letters to Rufe.

The group rose, set their glasses on the bar, and collected their coats. They walked out into the cold night and scrambled to their cars, their heads bowed low against the wind.

CHAPTER TWENTY-THREE

Rufus awoke from a nightmare in a dark, frigid room where one-eyed demons covered with blue scales floated across the ceiling. Like an exorcist, he flailed his arms and ordered them to leave but not until he was fully awake did they disappear on a beam of light that seeped through the grimy window.

He sat up and glanced around the room with a critical squint. Once he assured himself the demons were gone, he leaned his back against the headboard and tried to untangle his jumbled thoughts. He didn't believe dreams foretold the future, but it was possible they revealed high-tension anxiety he couldn't or wouldn't face when he was awake.

It had been so terrifying, so vivid, he thought he could replay it from start to finish. Instead, it came back in bits and pieces. He remembered struggling to get his head above water, but it wasn't water. It was blood, white blood. And it was cold, freezing cold. He sniffed the air and smelled hatred.

He checked the time. Five o'clock. He had caught three hours sleep, enough to take the edge off his exhaustion but not enough to make him feel rested. He dropped back onto his pillow and closed his eyes. He heard the early morning sounds of a neighborhood waking up: a yelping dog, the crunch of footsteps, a chugging engine, the screech of brakes.

Like clarions, they called to him, luring him outside. His imagination took hold, and he felt himself float out the window and follow their shrill summons. He saw himself standing on the edge of a vast, barren land. In the distance, a long line of white flags flapped against a jet black sky. What did it mean?

Curious, he stepped into the void. Frigid winds and searing fear gripped him. He spun around but saw nothing. Frightened by the unseen force, he tried to run, but he couldn't move. Finally, a light appeared in the distance. Like a brilliant star, it streaked across the ebony sky, its golden radiance a beacon of safety.

He summoned all his energy and forced his legs to move, slowly at first, then faster and faster. When he reached the light, he tried to grab onto its golden rim, but a loud, cracking noise boomed in his ear. The noise awakened him. He bolted up and sat motionless until his heart stopped pounding and his lungs filled with air.

He leaned over and brushed his hand down Claire's cheek. Her gentle breathing and peaceful expression calmed him. She was safe. He had had two bad dreams, nothing more. Not wanting a third, he slipped out of bed and headed into the bathroom. After emptying his bladder, he showered and shaved. He tiptoed around the bedroom collecting his clothes and dressed in the kitchen. He stood in front of the window and basked in the rays of the early morning sun. It felt good. He relished the moment even though he knew it was as fleeting as the snow.

He was tempted to wake Claire and share a rare moment of peace and solitude, but knowing how quickly the reality of his leaving would set in, he decided to let her sleep.

He made a pot of coffee. While it was brewing, he grabbed three empty boxes and started packing records, tapes, CDs, and his collection of frayed biographies of the famous and not-so-famous musical greats who revolutionized jazz. It took him an hour to clear off three shelves. Two more shelves remained, but he only had enough boxes to clear one. He gritted his teeth. Which ones should he take? Which ones should he leave behind?

"Damn!" He gritted his teeth. How many more choices would he have to make? He had already decided between Rufe Junior and Claire. He wanted to be with both of them, but knowing that was impossible, he chose his son.

He didn't kid himself. He knew the choices he made between Coltrane and Rollins, Dizzy and Miles, Sarah and Billie were comparatively insignificant, but it was still difficult. If he sent his whole collection to Memphis, he'd have to put them in storage. They'd be exposed to dust, moisture, and changing temperatures. If he kept them, they'd end up in a trash can. Moon and Lenny had their own collection. Claire would travel light when she headed to the West Coast. His only alternative was to destroy them himself in a solemn ritual, a visible severing of his past and future.

He divided what was left into two piles. He put one in a shipping box and dumped the other into plastic bags. When he finished, he taped the boxes and printed Salinas's address on the tops. He dragged the bags to the door. He planned to drop them in the trash on his way out, but a moment later, he knew he couldn't do it. He was a musician. No way could he exterminate his own.

His frown eased into a smile. He'd give them to Ella and tell her to donate them to a charity or a library. They were, after all, jazz classics.

He returned to the kitchen and poured a cup of coffee. He opened the refrigerator to check for cream. The sound of tingling beads caught his attention. He glanced around the open door and smiled.

"Good morning, sunshine." He snatched a carton of cream that smelled like last week's garbage and kneed the door shut. "I'm pouring this morning," he said in a staid English-butler tone. "Would you care for a cup?"

Claire sat at the table and dropped her chin in her upraised hands. "Two cups, but hold whatever foul stuff is in that carton."

Rufus laughed, poured the curdled liquid down the sink, filled her cup, and joined her at the table.

"You look like a wilted sunflower." He studied her expression to discern her mood. He saw a remoteness in her dark eyes but not anger and definitely not cheer. "When I got up, you looked so calm and peaceful—nobody messing with you, nobody giving you lip. Why the change?"

She peered at him over the rim of her cup. "Maybe I'm dead and don't know it."

"I think I'd know it." A grin crinkled his eyes. "More'n likely, you were whipped."

"Not too whipped. I heard croaks and groans and a few cuss words. I felt all this movement in the bed, like a frog was jumping around." She eyed him suspiciously. "I wonder who could've been causing all that commotion."

"I had a bad dream."

"Want to tell me about it?"

"I have too much to do to try and unravel a senseless fantasy."

"Exactly what do you have to do?"

"Finish packing." He pointed to the boxes. "I crated the records and CDs I'm going to take with me, but I still have to pack my stereo, speakers, and clothes."

A dark cloud settled on Claire's face. "Oh, I see."

Rufus swallowed a groan. He knew from this moment until he got on the train, everything he did, or said would be a reminder that time was running out.

"You have to pack, too," he said in a matter-of-fact tone.

"Yeah, I know." Her glance sharpened. "I have one suitcase. It'll take me all of five minutes to throw my stuff in and snap the locks." She sighed. "I know you're leaving, and I know you have to pack, but there are some things that are too raw for me to face. Just ignore me if I get upset."

"Hey, babe, I can't ignore you. I don't want to ignore you. If you're upset, we got to talk."

"Talking won't change anything." She flicked away the tears pooling in her eyes. "What're you going to do with your dishes and furniture?"

"I ought to pitch 'em, but I'll give 'em to Clarence." He chuckled. "He can make a few extra bucks renting out this fine suite of rooms fully furnished. Maybe he'll get enough to buy a new hot water heater."

"Oh, I hope not. Think of all the fun and excitement the new tenants will miss when they take their morning shower." Her jesting tone faded to a somber sigh. "Let me help you pack. I have to keep busy, or I'll go crazy."

"You sure? Empty closets can be damn depressing." He cocked a brow. "Every time I move, I get this spooky feeling like somebody died. I guess moving is kind of like dying. You leave one place and move to another."

"Stop. I'm depressed enough. I don't need to hear about moving and dying." Her dour expression in tact, she headed toward the stereo. "I'll start on that."

Together, they padded and taped the turn table and tonearm to keep them from moving. They slipped the record player and auxiliary equipment into boxes, filled them with "popcorn," and sealed them.

When they finished, Rufus glanced at Claire. She seemed relaxed. The hint of a smile he saw on her face made her look almost happy. He rose from his squat, took her hand, and helped her up.

"That didn't take long. Ready to tackle the bedroom?"

"Why not?"

Rufus turned on the radio, and they listened to oldies from the 60's and 70's as they packed the last of his personal belongings. He carried the drawers holding his underwear and socks from the dresser to the bed. While Claire separated and folded the clothes, then laid them neatly in a suitcase, he tackled the shoes, trousers, and jackets hanging in the closet. It took him longer than he expected to decide what he would take and what to leave. After singling out the too-tight trousers, faded shirts, and worn loafers that would go to charity, he ended up with one good jacket, two white shirts, and two pairs of shoes.

He checked his watch. It had taken him close to an hour to do what he thought would take twenty minutes. He heard his stomach growl.

"I'm hungry. How 'bout you? Ready to take a break?" He

waited a moment. When she didn't respond, he turned to face her. He saw Claire kneeling beside the bed, mumbling under her breath. Confused and disoriented, she shifted his socks from one side of the suitcase to the other.

He never saw her like this before. He didn't know how to react. Should he ignore her? Show concern? Comfort her? Joke with her? After a moment's soul searching, he decided to listen to his heart. He knelt beside her.

"What's going on, babe? He kissed her ear and pressed her head on his shoulder.

"I thought I could do it," she said with sob. "I wanted to help." She lifted her head and looked up at him, her eyes red and swollen with unchecked tears. "I meant to put the brown socks on the right and the black on the left, but they're all mixed up. I guess it's the light. It's hard to see. Give me a minute. I'll get it right."

"Oh, babe! What was I thinking?" He laid his head on hers. Anger and self-contempt rose inside him like mercury in a thermometer. Too late, he realized that asking her to help him pack was as cruel as asking a condemned man to tie his own noose. He wasn't going on a trip; he was leaving her. Consciously, she knew he had to go; he had to be with his son; he had to raise him, love him, do all those things a father did with a son. But subconsciously, she rebelled at the thought of him going to another woman, maybe loving her, maybe marrying her. He'd feel the same way if their situations were reversed.

The sun wasn't shining on any of them, he thought. Salinas had to be having her doubts, too. She hadn't seen him in ten years. It was possible they wouldn't even like each other. She was taking a big chance on him. All he knew was that they both want-ed to do the right thing for their son.

Rufus gathered Claire in his arms and stood up. He kissed her and wiped away the tears streaking her cheeks.

"Let's get out of here. We'll eat and then do some shopping. I need to pick up a few things."

"Yes, I'd like that." She withdrew from his arms, leaned down, and closed his suitcase with a bang.

Minutes later, they headed out the door, mummified under hats, scarfs, coats and gloves. While they waited for the car to warm up, Claire turned to Rufus, her brow knitted in a frown.

"What do you have to pick up?" she asked.

"It's a surprise."

"For me?"

He grinned. "Maybe."

"What? Tell me." A glint of wonder lit up her face.

"It won't be a surprise if I tell you, but I'll give you a clue. It's a gift, and you're going to love it."

"A good-bye present?"

"Stop thinking about good-byes." He squeezed her hand. "I don't like seeing you sad all the time. You've been down too long. You deserve to be up for a while."

"You don't understand." She smiled. "I know all my emo-tional ups and downs are hard on you, but you have to remem-ber, women don't hide their feelings. We wear them. They're out there for everyone to see. Sometimes I get overwhelmed by the thought of losing you. I've had my moments of self-pity, but I'm in control now. Let's do something fun. Like buying me a pres-ent. And while we're out, you should buy something special for

Rufe Junior. Salinas, too."

"Great idea. Why didn't I think of it?" He paused and looked at her warily. "You want me to buy Salinas a present? You did say that?"

"I know. It doesn't make sense me telling you to buy my competitor a gift." She let out a cynical snort. "Makes you wonder if I'm a martyr or a fool. Actually, it's like an alcoholic giving up liquor. When I finally detach myself from you, I want to do it with love in my heart, not jealousy or self-pity. This is my first step in letting go. Just think, I only have nine hundred ninety nine more to go."

"You're something else. Just when I think you're sinking fast, you pop up and swim to shore." He laid a kiss on her cheek. "It helps, babe. I die a little every time I think about leaving you."

"No more talk of dying." She slipped her arm through his. "And don't worry about me. Shopping's a great mood lifter and one of my better talents."

"One of many." He winked, and his lips parted in a sensuous smile.

CHAPTER TWENTY-FOUR

Rufus and Claire hopped over frozen slush and mounds of snow on their way from the parking lot to the front entrance of Goldman's Department Store. Rufus downgraded his enthusiasm to a low three out of ten when they entered the store.

Immediately, he noticed the aisles were almost empty, and the handful of shoppers who had braved the cold seemed more interested in looking than buying. One glance at the dresses crammed on racks and the perfumes and jewelry spread out in glass cases made him wonder how long it took for anyone to pick one thing over another. A frown wormed its way across his brow. He couldn't say he hated to go shopping because he never went; he ordered his clothes by mail-order, and if it wasn't in a catalog, it didn't exist.

He slowed to a crawl and shot a wary glance at Claire. "I got a great idea," he said. "I'll find the sporting goods department and buy Rufe Junior's present. You can look around and buy something for Salinas."

"Oooh no you don't," she said. "This has to be your gift, not mine. And keep in mind, just being here while you're buying Salinas a present isn't easy for me."

"Hey, babe, I know that. I appreciate what you're doing, but can't you have a little pity for me? I don't have any idea what to get her. I don't know her size, tastes, what colors she likes." He shook his head and withdrew into a grumpy silence. Claire was not being fair. How could she expect him to know what to buy a woman he hadn't seen in ten years? Salinas had sent him a picture. Was she still tall and willowy, or had she put on weight, spread out in the lower regions? Did she have hobbies? Wear jewelry? Carry a purse? Was it large or small?

His shoulders slumped. He could buy a gift for Claire with his eyes closed. She loved fisherman sweaters, bangle bracelets, and loop earrings. She wore size four jeans and 34-C bras, satin with lace trim. A knot formed in his throat. He had no intention of buying anything that personal for Salinas.

"Are you going to stand here all day?" She crossed her arms and sighed in exasperation.

"No, I'm not going to stand here all day." He mimicked her sigh and gripped her elbow. "Come on, let's get this over with."

He headed down the main aisle and scanned the leather goods, lingerie, sweaters and blouses. Overwhelmed by the quantities and styles, he moved on. He was ready to give up when he saw the small stationery department.

"There it is, exactly what I was looking for."

"There what is?"

"Salinas's present."

"Where? I don't see…" Her mouth dropped open. "You're not thinking about buying her a box of stationery, are you?"

"I'll give her a pen, too," he said in a peevish tone. "What's wrong with that? People still write letters, don't they?"

"She wrote to you," Claire said, "but a box of stationery isn't the message you want to give her."

"Message! What're you talking about?"

"A gift is more than an item. It expresses a thought, a feeling.

You want it to be personal but not intimate. Impressive but not costly."

"Translate that for me." He groaned. "Or just tell me what to buy?"

"Poor Rufus!" She bit back a smile. "You don't understand the intricacies of buying a gift for a woman."

"I didn't have any trouble buying you one," he said in a forbearing tone.

"That's different. You know all about me but very little about her." Claire's expression lost its luster. "A year from now, it'll be the other way around."

Unable to think of anything to refute her statement, he fell silent.

Momentarily, Claire clenched her jaw, as if imposing an iron control on her emotions. "Sorry. I swore I was going to be strong and not think about you and Salinas and next month or next year."

"It's cool, babe." Rufus smiled. "You're doing great, considering."

She gave her head a quick nod, headed down an aisle, and stopped in front of a glass case holding a selection of silk scarves.

"I bet Salinas would like one of these." She sifted through the pile and pulled out a satiny black and white scarf. "This would be perfect." She looped it around her neck and modeled it for Rufus. "Well, what do you think?"

"You like it?"

She turned to a mirror and flung an end over her shoulder. "I don't wear scarves, but Salinas is a professional woman. They always wear accessories. Makes 'em look so together."

THE LAST TRAIN TO MEMPHIS

Rufus studied the scarf with a probing gravity. He saw that it was black and white and silky. He knew he wasn't seeing the whole picture. He imagined Claire saw it as an accent piece around the neck of a woman who was wearing a black suit, white blouse, gold earrings and medium heeled pumps. Hell, he thought, the outfit would look just as good without it.

Anxious to buy Salinas's gift and move on, he smiled and nodded and then heaved a sigh of relief when Claire read his gestures as signs of approval.

Buying a gift for Rufe, Junior would be a no-brainer, he thought when entered the sporting goods department. His optimism faded as they made their way through a maze of merchandise for athletes of all ages.

Rufus looked around in bewilderment. Was Rufe, Junior an athlete? He played soccer. Did he like basketball? Baseball? Maybe he liked to roller blade. Maybe Salinas didn't want him to roller blade. His eyes settled on a poster showing LeBron James slamdunk a basket. He remembered that Rufe mentioned ball in his letter. Taking that as his cue, Rufus grabbed a regulation-sized basketball from a wire container and held it up for Claire's inspection.

Her eager response fueled Rufus's enthusiasm for shopping. After paying for the ball, he hustled Claire into a book store where he flipped through a biography of America's most famous African-American musicians. Not only were all the jazz greats mentioned, their lives and the writing were appropriate for a ten-year-old.

"Where to now?" Claire said, tongue-in-cheek. "Electronics, clothes, shoes, pianos, toys? How about a toy saxophone? Can't get him started too early."

"When I buy him a sax, it'll be a real one." He grinned. "You know how sax players feel about tone. He won't get it blowing plastic."

She inclined her head and smiled. "What if he asks for a bass?"

"I'd say right on." He looked at her, his eyes gentle and contemplative. "I'm going to have Rufe's book gift wrapped, then I have to pick up one more thing. Won't take long. You might as well head over to the deli across the street. I'll meet you there."

"You sure you don't want me to go along while you pick up that one more thing?" She smiled mischievously.

"I'll be there in twenty minutes."

"Okay, okay, twenty minutes." Laughing, she flipped her hand in the air and sauntered away.

Rufus watched her go, his gifts in his hands, his heart in his throat. He didn't know what to make of her rapid mood changes. He was struggling with his own emotions, and her roller coaster rides from resentment to acceptance, from sadness to joy, from distant to seductive made his anguish all the harder to deal with. Maybe, like him, she still didn't believe they were going to separate. Even now, with a little over twenty-hours left before he got on the train, it didn't seem possible, not after all they'd been through. In a matter of seconds, his mood veered from distress to anger to acceptance of the inevitable.

No one was forcing him to go to Memphis. His decision had been instant and irrevocable. His obligations and his love for his son took precedence over his love for Claire. And it wasn't as if they were only lovers who had to part. It had always been and always would be the soul message in music, movies, literature, and art. Frankie and Johnnie, Rick and Ilsa, Romeo and Juliet. Blues and women. Blues and men. Wanderers, cheaters, drinkers, lost loves. "Saint Louis woman with her diamond rings."

The sound of a woman's voice startled Rufus. He looked up and saw the saleslady staring at him with a critical squint.

"I'm sorry. Did you say something?"

"Can I show something else?" She handed him a bag holding Rufe's gift, then gestured at the shelves jam-packed with books. "We have a large selection of biographies."

Rufus thanked her and made a quick exit. He didn't want to keep Claire waiting. He didn't know what her mood would be if she had too much time alone, too much time to think.

He found Claire sitting in a front booth sipping a beer when he entered the deli. He slipped onto the seat opposite her and focused on her smile, a beacon in a moonless sky. He managed to curb his excitement long enough to order a beer and pastrami on rye for himself, a roast beef for Claire, and wait until the waitress waddled off before pulling a small box wrapped in silver and festooned with gold from his pocket and laid it on the table.

Her eyes bright and playful, she snatched it up. Like an over-eager birthday girl, she tore off the wrapping and lifted the lid. A gasp rose in her throat.

"Oh, Rufus, it's beautiful." The light from the candle caught on two charms dangling from a gold-link bracelet. She fingered the tiny gold bass and studied the flower, a diamond in its center, its petals in full bloom.

She locked her gaze on Rufus's face. "It's a gardenia, isn't it?"

"I know it's your favorite flower. I always meant to buy you

276

one so you could put it in your hair so you could look Billie Holiday."

"I could never look like her. She was so beautiful." A winsome smile crept over Claire's lips. "I'll feel beautiful every time I wear it. And I'll think of you." She gave her head a shake. "What am I saying? I'll wear it all the time. I'll never take it off."

Rufus saw her eyes grow misty. He took the bracelet and put it on her wrist. "When you think of me, know I'll be thinking of you, but we can only have happy thoughts."

The waitress arrived with their order, and Rufus made a point of opening his napkin, taking a sip of beer, and finally chomping into his sandwich even though he had lost his appetite. He noticed that Claire was also going through the motions. For whatever reason, they profiled confident and cool and ate their meal in silence. Rufus grimaced. And life went on as usual.

The huge crowd at Ella's was unusual for a Tuesday night, Rufus thought as he and Claire elbowed their way through the packed bar on their way into the lounge. Laughter and high fives generated a holiday spirit and bolstered Rufus's mood.

"Don't know what's happening, but whatever it is, I say, right on," he shouted in Claire's ear.

"Looks like Ella's throwing us a farewell party. See there." She pointed to a banner stretched across the bandstand.

"I dig it, woman." He peered through the smoky haze at the three black and one white silhouettes hunching over their instruments on a red satin bunting. Printed underneath were Ella's grade-a, rap-a-riddle words: "We're swinging tonight. Bug out. Bump up. Adios, brothas and sistas. We love you."

Rufus threw back his head and roared with laughter. "No sad

songs tonight. We're rockin' 'n rollin'."

He grabbed Claire's hand and bolted to the bandstand where Moon, Lenny, and Ella waited, their faces beaming.

"Is this your doing?" Rufus wrapped his arms around Ella waist and gave her a bear hug.

Ella pulled herself free, then stepped back and stared at him, a tremulous smile touching her lips. "I ain't much on saying good-bye, so I figure swinging's better'n sighing." She moved her gaze around, catching on Moon, Lenny, and Claire. "I'm sure gonna miss you."

"We're going to miss you, too." Claire gripped Ella's hand and sucked air into her lungs as if trying to hold back the sobs gurgling in her throat while conveying her intense love for the woman. "You've been a real friend. You sure didn't have to be considering what an ass I was." She averted her eyes. "The drugs, the liquor, the tantrums! I'd 've kicked my butt out in two seconds flat."

"Guess I saw something I never saw before, like how much you love Rufus. At first, I thought it was all about sex. Not that I fault you for that. Rufus is some bad looking dude. But I'll tell you the truth, I was damn mad when you showed up out of nowhere. I was thinking, 'ah shit, here we go again. She's gonna fuck things up just like she always did. I figured you'd find some way to keep Rufus from going to Memphis, but I'll be damned if you didn't prove me wrong."

Ella ran her finger down Claire's cheek with a feathery touch. "You done a lotta growing up this week. Ain't sure I could've let my man go without a fight."

Oblivious of the commotion swirling around them, the two

women stood in the center of the stage, holding hands and staring at each other through tear-glazed eyes.

"Enough of this blubbering," Ella said. "It's time for your first
set. Don't forget. You're gonna stay with me after 'The Man' gets
on that train." She turned to Rufus, misery roosting in her eyes.
"I'll see you at the station. After I wave you off, I'll bring Claire'll
home with me."

"You're a sweet woman." Rufus grinned. "And a long-suffer-
ing one, too." He gave her a big hug.

"Get outta here." She drew herself up and gave him a
scathing look. "I ain't paying you to mess with the boss."

Rufus took center stage, tapped his foot, and blew his horn,
starting the first set. Wailing and wiggling through "Loverman,"
he sweated to reach the emotional heights and tormented beauty
of Charlie Parker's rendition when he cut his album, *Charlie
Parker on Dial.*

Silver sparkles reflecting off a revolving strobe light shed an
eerie glow in the dark, haze-filled lounge and created an aura of
exotic anonymity.

Caught up in the magical atmosphere of light, sound, and
mood, they played a medley of earthy love songs, boisterous
rock-and-roll, soul-clapping blues, and abstract, improvisational
jazz.

Claire and Rufus finished the last set with a duet, strumming
and blowing the ballad, "One for My Baby." Caught up in the
song's emotional intensity, the audience joined in, at first humming and tapping the tune, and finally belting out the restrain,
"One for my baby, and one more for the road."

In that moment of awed silence, after the music stopped and

before the applause began, a metallic sound drew Rufus's attention to Claire's wrist. He noticed when she moved her arm to adjust her bow, the bass and gardenia charms made a clicking noise. He froze, its metronomic rhythm reminded him of the passing of time. Click, click, tick, tick. The clock was ticking. The train to Memphis was on its way.

He looked up and saw Claire staring at him, her face chalk white, as if she, too, heard the clicking, ticking sounds and felt the wheels rumbling on the track.

The audience rose and gave the band a thunderous ovation. Amid the swell of clapping hands and stomping feet, Rufus and Claire's eyes met. Was it his sadness or hers he saw in the dark brown depths? A moment later, they smiled and bowed to the crowd.

CHAPTER TWENTY-FIVE

Rufus and Claire walked into the apartment with their arms wrapped around their chests to ward off the cold that followed them inside. He flipped on the light and stood motionless for several seconds, basking in the warm air flowing through the vent.

"Is it my imagination, or is that heat I'm feeling?" He let out a full-hearted laugh. "Clarence must've found some duct tape for the furnace. The apartment hasn't been this warm since last summer's heat wave."

"Feels good." Claire took off her jacket and nuzzled her head against his shoulder. "We won't have to go to bed right away to get warm for a change."

"Quit messing with my mind." A lecherous grin lit up his eyes. He took her into his arms and kissed her hard on her mouth. Like a candle over an open flame, her body melted into his.

"Forget the furnace. I know a better way to heat up." He drew her sweater over her head and traced a sensuous path down the nape of her neck. He stopped when he reached the curve of her breast. Something was wrong. Was it his imagination, or did he sense a hesitancy in her response to his foreplay? In the past when she didn't want to make love, she told him right out, and that was okay with him. After all, she wasn't a hoe ready to perp an organism at the flip of a dime. But she was his lover, the woman he loved, and she could turn him on with the cock of a brow.

Hell, he thought, it had to be his imagination. A shudder of anticipation raced through him, and he slid his hand under her bra and massaged her taut breast. A hot ache grew in his throat. He lowered his head and flicked his tongue on her nipple. The electric charge that surged down his spine to his groin short-circuited when she pulled away and gave her head a hard shake.

"No," she whispered. "I don't want to make love. I'm sorry. I can't. I just can't."

"What's wrong?" He looked down at her and saw a dark cloud settle on her face. When it lifted, and he saw her tear-glazed eyes and the rigid set of her chin, he pulled her close and stroked her back in a comforting gesture.

"This is a hell of a time for both of us. I know how you feel, and it's okay."

"You don't know how I feel, and it won't be okay." She pulled away and stared at him, her anger amplifying her gaunt, pinched expression. "How can you want to make love after what happened tonight? How can you turn off and on so fast?"

"Turn what off and on?" He let out an exasperated sigh.

"Mullins. Garret. Threats. Hate. Just thinking about them makes me want to scream."

A wisp of a smile tugged at his lips. "Oh, babe, haven't you figured it out yet? Mullins, Garret, and the whole bag of shit are the reasons we should make love. We need each other. We need to share our feelings, to feel the warmth of another human being, to know there is love in the world. If it wasn't for that, we'd all be like Mullins and Garret."

"Maybe so." She pushed out her bottom lip in a pout, but her expression remained wary.

"No maybes about it." Rufus grinned and motioned for her to come to him. When she hesitated, he threw his hands in the air, conceding defeat. "Now what's the matter?"

"I'm afraid." She flushed and turned her head aside. "I know it's silly, but if we make love, it'll finally hit me. You and I, us, will be over. I'll know it's for real. I won't be able to pretend any-more."

"So what do we do?" Rufus grabbed her arm and spun her around to face him. "I say we chuck it all and take off. Disappear off the earth. We could do it. It's not too late. Who'd blame us?"

"If I thought you meant it, I'd hitch my wagon to your star in a minute." She let out a weary sigh. "But I'm not into science fiction or fantasies, and neither are you. With our luck, we'd land on a planet swarming with little green toads with the name Garret flashing in their beady little eyes." She slipped into his arms. A wistful smile played on her lips. "Hold me. Tell me you love me. Tell me everything's going to be okay. It might not be true, but I want to hear it anyway."

She laid her head on his chest and cried.

He didn't try to console her. What could he say? She didn't want to hear about the plans he had for his son and for himself. He would be the ideal father. Rufe Junior would be the ideal son. No hassles, no second thoughts, just pure happiness. He had great plans for Claire, too. She would move to L.A., get a gig with a rap band, and hit the charts with a smash CD. *Fly me to the moon, why don't you?*

He nuzzled his face in her hair and massaged the muscles

knotted at the base of her neck.

"You okay, babe?" he asked.

"Yeah, I'm okay." She looked up and studied his face feature by feature. "I'll never find a man half as handsome as you. You're so sexy. Your lips, and your smile. It's so white. You should do toothpaste commercials."

Rufus laughed. "Where you coming from, woman? You are one rolling stone. One minute you're crying the blues, the next you're shuckin and jivin."

"I don't want to cry anymore. It doesn't help, and it makes for a lot of misery." She withdrew from his embrace, turned, and headed into the bedroom. "As they say in the movies, I'm going to change into something more comfortable. How about you making us some coffee?"

"Coffee? It's four in the morning. Wouldn't you rather go to bed?"

"We can do that later." A sensuous smile played on her lips. "Right now, I want to talk. Nothing morbid or sad. Fun talk. Maybe take a walk down memory lane."

Rufus waited until she disappeared through the beaded curtain hanging in the doorway before he switched off the overhead light and entered the kitchen. He turned on the radio to an all-night jazz station, lit a small table lamp, and fixed a pot of coffee. Soon, the dim light and soft jazz eased him into a mellow mood. He ambled to the window and contemplated the wintry landscape. A light snow was falling. Like a magician's wand, the street lamp's yellow glow tinted the white crystals with a golden hue.

He tried to hang onto the scene's beauty and serenity, but gloomy thoughts kept seeping inside his head. The muffled hush of the snow-clad street evolved into an eerie silence; the street lamp shed the same shadows as the yellow light bulb hanging in his prison cell. He groaned. Why was he so edgy? He knew he had to control both his anger and his apprehensions. Those were not what he wanted to feel when he met Rufe Junior at the train station.

He poured a cup of coffee and returned to the window. A slight movement caught his attention. He squinted and tried to pierce the mantle of falling snow. Seeing nothing, he chided himself again. If he was seeing moving shadows, what else would his mind conjure up? Devils? Winged serpents? He started to turn away, but he saw the shadow move again. This time, he knew it wasn't his imagination. He saw a two-dimensional figure emerge from the murky surroundings. He sucked in his breath. Only a lunatic or an idiot would be out at this hour in this weather. Syd Garret was the only lunatic-idiot he knew. A nervous tick pulled at Rufus's eye. The bastard hadn't forgotten. Today, Wednesday, Rufus's parole was up, and he was heading to Memphis.

Rufus's first thought was to move away from the window. With the light at his back, he made a perfect target. Something inside of him, possibly a streak of irrational bravery or his pure hatred of the man, kept him glued to the spot.

He saw Garret step out of the shadows and position himself in the middle of the street. His arrogance and bluster reminded Rufus of a fool play-acting a scene from a Western shoot-out, a pre-dawn *High Noon* without its noble principles.

Despite the darkness and the snow, their eyes locked. Garret's cocky stance and hate-filled gaze told Rufus what the man was thinking. *I'm here. I'm coming to take you down.*

"Think again, you motherfucker," Rufus yelled. "You don't have the guts to try it alone. Where are your sorry-ass desperadoes? In a flop house, sucking dick?" He snarled in contempt. "You want a shoot out? Come on, baby. Come get me. I'll take you down in two seconds."

"Rufus, what're you doing? Who're you talking to?" Claire stepped through the beaded doorway and stared in at him in bewilderment.

"Go back into the bedroom," he said, his tone hard and ruthless.

"What are you looking at? Was there an accident? Is someone hurt?" She rushed forward, fear glittering in her eyes.

"Get away from the window." He gave her a push and then turned his gaze back to the man standing under the street light. "He's out there. That son-of-a-bitch is out there waiting for me."

"Who's out there?" She peered out the window and followed his gaze through the snow-spattered glass.

"Garret! Oh, my God! What's he doing out there?" She took a second look and yanked Rufus's arm. "Don't stand there. You're a perfect target. He could shoot you, and who'd know? Who'd care? It'd be just another shoot-out in the hood."

Rufus finished his second drink and set the glass on the table. "If he planned to kill me, he'd 've done it already." He pushed Claire away and stomped to the door, grabbing his coat on the way. "I'm sick of him spooking me. You stay here. I'm going down and have it out with him. We'll see how brave he is when we're face-to-face, one-on-one. He'll probably shit in his pants."

"If you're going down, I'm going with you," Claire said, her voice cold and exact.

Rufus stared at her dumbstruck. "Think about that, babe. If he can shoot me, he can shoot you, too."

"He can't kill us both and hope he can get away with it, but it's your call. Stay or go. Either way, I'll be right beside you."

"Oh no you won't. This is my problem. I got to handle it my own way."

She crossed her arms in front of her and gave him a defiant look.

He looked away. Bullheaded woman! He knew she was capable of doing something really idiotic like going after Garret with a frying pan. He knew he had to calm her down, but first, he had to get his own emotions in check. He took a deep breath and shrugged offhandedly. "Don't sweat it, babe. Can't you see he's bluffing?"

"Maybe he is, maybe he isn't. There's only one way to find out." She gripped his hand and gave him a satanic smile. "Let's go."

"You know I can't take that chance." He stomped across the room and threw his coat on the sofa. "You're blackmailing me, and I don't like it one bit."

"Listen, to me, you bullheaded fool. If you're going to walk out of my life, you're going to do it on your own two feet. Think about your son. How will he handle it if you don't get off that train? I'm sure it'll make his day when his mother tells him you got popped by some lunatic cop."

"Okay. You made your point." He stared at her with a thunderous expression. After a moment, he swallowed his anger and returned to the window.

Garret was still standing in the middle of the street, his seedy trench coat covered with snow. When Rufus reappeared, he raised his arm and thrust his middle finger in the air. Rufus stared at him a moment longer, turned, and headed into the bedroom.

"I'm dead tired," he said. "Let's hit the sack."

CHAPTER TWENTY-SIX

Rufus awoke late in the afternoon, his mind boggled, his body stiff. He tried to get up only to discover he could barely move. He hadn't been this tense since his first night in prison. His future had looked dark and uncertain, but he knew he had to face whatever lay ahead. He stretched his legs and rotated his shoulder muscles. Getting little relief, he let his body go limp and mindlessly stared at the brown water stains streaking the gray ceiling.

Zero hour minus five had finally arrived. No more tomorrows, no more yesterdays. He cocked a brow. Actually, he had less than half a day before he got on the train. Depending on his and Claire's mood, each hour could seem like an eternity. He could spend what little time he had left worrying about Garret, Claire, Rufe Junior, and Salinas, but that would only make him more uptight.

"Move your sorry ass," he mumbled to himself. If he took his shower, dressed, and finished packing before Claire woke up, they could spend the rest of their day doing ordinary things lovers did before they went their separate ways.

He eased himself to the edge of the bed. Before he could drop his feet, Claire swung her arm across his chest.

"Where you going?" she whispered.

"I was getting up, but I guess I'm not." Her sensuous, velvety tone relaxed him. He didn't have to worry about her. She was one strong woman, and she had more guts than he gave her credit for. He rolled on his side and saw her smile. Her eyes sparked with expectations that only a lover could decipher.

Wordlessly, he took her in his arms and kissed her mouth. He stroked her breasts. The friction ignited lusty flames in his loins and shed a luminous glow on Claire's skin.

His passion tempered by the dull ache of memory, he made slow, sensuous love, he trailed his fingers across her stomach and down each thigh. She pushed his hand away. She went down on him and flicked the crown of his throbbing cock with her tongue.

"Do it, baby," he yelled. "Ooooh, do it."

His body stiffened when she took his rod into her mouth and flicked her warm, moist tongue around its throbbing crown. She sucked and toyed with it until he was on the verge of losing it. His ragged growl mingled with her rasps and moans. He twisted his hips and flexed his pelvis trying to find some relief from the perverse ecstasy roused by her sexual manipulations. Blinded by passion, he ran his hand across her ass until he found her opening. He thrust two fingers in as far as they would go. Her body jerked, and her moans deepened.

She raised up, threw her leg over his groin, and straddled him. Their eyes locked. He watched as she spread the lips of her vagina and guided his cock inside her. A smile touched her mouth, and she started to move, and grind, and push. He threw his head back but kept his eyes focused on her face. He loved seeing the flush of passion redden her cheeks and cast its florid glow across her breasts and down her stomach to her triangle of thick, dark hair.

Minutes passed, hours, an eternity of pure ecstasy. But too

soon he realized that nothing, not even eternities, lasted forever. When the pressure inside his engorged penis became intolerable, he grabbed her hips, dug his nails into the soft flesh, and stabbed her with hard, deep thrusts. They went over the top together.

Like two lovers whose bodies were carved in stone, they held their position until air returned to their lungs and blood surged through their veins.

Rufus took her into his arms and pulled her beside him. He kissed her eyes, her nose, her lips with a gently, brushing motion. He dropped his head on his upraised hand and stared at her. His heart was filled with love, but his mind was in turmoil.

"I love you, Claire. You and I shared something special. A lot of people never feel what we felt toward each other."

"I'm thankful we had that," she said.

"You going to be okay?"

"Sure. I'm going to be fine." She exhaled. "Whatever it takes to get through the day."

"Whatever it takes." He kissed her again and slipped out of bed. "I'm heading for the shower. Wanna join me?"

"And after the shower, then what?" She looked at him with wide, soulful eyes.

"Then you and I pack our bags, walk out the door, and never look back."

"I'm hungry. Do I get a last meal?"

"You name it, babe."

"How about catfish and red-eyed beans?" she said. "Or maybe you'd rather wait till you get to Memphis. I imagine they eat a lot of catfish there."

"Watch it. You're getting close to the edge."

"I fell off a week ago. I'm hanging onto a tree but only by a twig."

Rufus smiled. "I always said you were a lot stronger than you put on."

"Strength has nothing to do with it. Giving you up is something I have to do, like dying." She gave her head a shake. "Oh, go take your shower. Don't use all the hot water."

In their last hours together, Rufus and Claire packed away the last of their memories over a platter of fried catfish minus the beans. During the lengthy lulls in their conversation, Claire picked at her thumbnail and toyed with the charms dangling from her wrist. Hesitant to make the final break, yet agonizingly aware of the passing time, Rufus glanced at the wall clock and then at her, a halting expression lining his face.

"I know. We have to go. You don't want to miss the train."

"I'll have to drive slow. The roads are bad, and my tires are bald."

They walked out of the restaurant and entered a winter wonderland of powdery snow and crystal icicles. A blast of brittle air struck Claire's face. She flinched and pulled her hood over her head.

"I'm cold, Rufus. I don't think I'll ever be warm again," she said, the misery of the night furrowing her brow.

"Hey, none of that." Rufus brushed away the tear that had escaped from the corner of her eye.

"I'm sorry. I promised myself I wouldn't cry till you got on that, that train."

"It's okay, babe. If I could, I'd cry, too, but men aren't supposed to let go like that."

She looked up at him, and flicked him a bitter smile. "Maybe later, when nobody's looking."

He nodded and helped her into the car.

The train station was a jumble of sights, sounds, and smells, but mostly it was a bleak, empty space.

Rufus skidded to a stop on the snow-covered parking lot. He reached over and squeezed Claire's hand.

"Wait here," he said. "I'll pick up my ticket and be right back." He opened the car door, jumped out, and dashed across the icy walkway that led to the derelict station house. Snow clogged the corrugated metal siding, and a yellow lantern dangled above the front entrance. Its rusted metal cord creaked in the wind, and its dim light created eerie shadows on the polar snowscape. He hurried inside and followed the worn pathway to the ticket counter.

"One way ticket to Memphis," he said in a forceful voice.

The dozing ticket taker jerked his head up, a baffled expression darkening his face.

"Ain't no call to yell. I ain't deaf. You got time enough to get your ticket 'fore the train comes. You don't have to worry none about gettin' a seat. You'll have a whole car to yerself. Ain't nobody goin' to Memphis from here 'cept you. Fact is, train ain't stoppin' after tonight. No passengers, no service." He managed a wry grin. "Guess there ain't much to do in Memphis 'cept maybe take in the blues joints 'n see Elvis's fancy house."

"Seeing as how I like blues and fancy houses, Memphis is the place for me." Rufus leaned against the counter and laid down his money.

The agent handed him a ticket and pointed to the clock.

"The train'll be on time, but you better move fast when you hear the whistle. What with the weather 'n all, old Ed'll barely brake."

"Thanks." Rufus headed for the door. When he stepped outside, a blast of frigid air struck him broadside. He paused to catch his breath. Moored in an eddy of swirling snow and howling wind, he thought he heard a car engine. Could there be another passenger going to Memphis or points beyond? He lowered his head and ran to the car. He slowed when he saw a black Lincoln Continental idling next to his. Ella! He'd know that car anywhere. It had to be twenty years old, yet it was always as bright and shiny as a newly minted silver dollar. He snickered. Thanks to the elbow grease Bojay put on it. He exhaled a frosty breath, yanked the door open, and stuck his head inside.

"Ella! Are you crazy or what, coming out on a night like this?"

"Had to say good-bye to my sax man." A broad smile lit up her face. "Keep in touch, you hear, or I'll come down to Memphis 'n give you the evil eye."

"Don't want that." Rufus leaned across the seat and planted a kiss on her plump cheek. "You get yourself back to the club before the roads turn into an ice rink."

"Ain't no call to shout. Claire done blow me out already. I told her there ain't no way she's gonna drive your bucket home. She's gonna ride with me. Moon can pick up your ole jalopy in the morning." She blinked and set her gaze on the ice-glazed windshield. "Now go say good-bye to your gal. I'll wait here with the heater on."

The forlorn wail of a train whistle pierced the night air and unleashed a hot panic in Rufus's gut. He sprinted to his car and skidded to a stop in front of Claire who was leaning against the front fender holding his saxophone case in one hand and Rufe Junior's basketball in the other.

"Here, you don't want to forget these," she said.

"Hang onto them a minute." He snatched his duffel bag from the back seat. "I want to drop this off on the platform." He cracked a smile. "I don't want to have to juggle everything in case I have to make a mad dash for the train."

In a flash, he was back. He placed his saxophone and basketball on the hood of the car and swooped Claire in his arms. She wrapped her hands around his neck and held on.

"You take real good care of that son of yours," she said.

"Ask me something hard," he said.

"Take care of yourself."

"You, too, babe."

She raised her chin and looked at him, all her pain and misery etched on her beautiful face. "I figure you'll write to Ella. Is it okay if I check with her and see how you're doing? I won't do it often. Maybe once a year at Christmas time. I don't want to lose total contact." She dropped her arms to her side. "I love you, Rufus."

The angry clatter of metal wheels and the shrill wail of an engine whistle drowned out Rufus's reply. He touched her cheek and gazed at her one last time. With a shake of his head, he grabbed his sax and the basketball and headed toward the station platform. Half way across the parking lot, a black shadow emerged from the white curtain of snow.

Rufus's heart did a double flip, but in less than a instant, anger displaced his shock when Syd Garret's hate-filled face came into focus.

"What the fuck you doing here?" Rufus sneered. "I thought I heard a car pull up. I had a notion it might be you, then I thought, naw, couldn't be. Garret's a nickel-slick, muthafucking Charlie, but he doesn't have the guts to throw his shit around on a night like this."

"Keep talking, Johnson." Garret's eyes narrowed to a slit. "You're gonna make it easy for me to drag you down to the station in irons."

Rufus glanced over Garret's shoulder and shrugged his contempt. "I see you don't have your posse with you. Who you figure's going to put the irons on me?"

"This is all the posse I need." Garret drew a pistol from his coat pocket and pointed it at Rufus. "You're under arrest."

"Oh, yeah? Since when is it a crime to wait for a train?"

"I got a tip you're selling dime bags of marijuana and some snow, and it ain't this shit wetting my neck freezing my balls."

"Didn't your mama tell you you don't have balls?" Rufus pointed at Garret's pistol. "Put your fucking toy back in your pocket and quit wasting my time. My parole's up. I'm a free man. I can come and go as I please." He glowered at Garret, turned, and proceeded on at a casual gait.

"Hold it right there, Johnson," Garret yelled. "You take one more step, and you're down."

Rufus hesitated. He wasn't sure if Garret's threat was a last-ditch effort to intimidate him, or if he would shoot him to prove a point.

The roar of a train engine grinding to a stop tied a cord around Rufus's chest and indecision tugged at each end. If he moved, Garret might shoot him in the back. If he didn't move, he'd miss the train.

The cord tightened. What the hell should he do, go or stay? Die or make a run for it?

He heard the whistle, the last warning before the train left the station. He heard Claire call his name. He spun round and saw her running toward him.

"Get on board," she yelled. "He won't shoot. He's bluffing. He's so drunk, he can't see."

"No. I can't leave you here alone with Garret."

"I'm not alone. Ella's here." Claire slid to a stop in front of him. "Please, Rufus, go. Your son's waiting. You can't desert him. Move." She clenched her jaw and rammed her fists into his chest. The impact knocked Rufus off balance. Claire grabbed his arm, twisted him around, and gave him a push forward.

"I love you, but you have to go. Please."

Rufus shot a glance at Garret who was standing in back and to the side of Claire, his corpulent body swaying in the wind. He waved at Claire, motioning her away. "You got to get out of here before Garret comes out of his drunken stupor."

"I'm out of here," Claire said.

Rufus threw her a parting kiss, gripped his sax and Rufe's basketball, and took off.

"Johnson, where the fuck you going?" Garret shouted in a voice thick with liquor and hate. "Get your black ass over here."

Claire turned and glared at him. "Too late, Garret. He's gone."

"Shut up and move your fucking ass outta my way. I'm gonna take him in." Garret lurched forward, his shoes slip-sliding on the icy surface. "I see you, Johnson. Stop, or by Christ, I'll blast your head off."

Claire followed Garret's gaze. Rufus was reaching for his suitcase. The lamp hanging above the platform swathed him in a circle of yellow light.

"Rufus, watch out. He's going to shoot."

He spun around and saw Claire make a lightning dash toward Garret. He shouted for her to stop, but the wind tossed his warning into the swirling air. He dropped his duffel bag and sax and darted back, holding the basketball over his head like a missile, ready to throw at Garret.

Claire reached Garret first. She lunged at him. The impact knocked the breath out of him. He clutched his stomach and let out a bellow. He straightened. His eyes glowing with hate and anger, he raised his hand. A second later, the crack of a firearm rent the air.

"Nooo," Rufus raged and began to run. When he reached Claire, he dropped to the ground and lifted her in his arms.

"Claire, my God! Why?" He rocked back and forth, tears streaming down his cheeks.

She smiled. Her eyes closed. Her head lolled to the side.

Rufus kissed her lips and held her close. He felt a hand on his arm. He looked up. Ella was staring at him, her tears falling on Claire's hood.

"Is she…"

Rufus buried his face in her hair. Today, the music died.

CHAPTER TWENTY-SEVEN

Rufus stared down at Claire's open grave. He felt as if he were on a threshold of a dream. On one side of the threshold, he felt the serenity of the cemetery with its expanse of knolls and turf and swaying brown willow trees interspersed between rigid white tombstones. He thought of Claire's grave as a sanctuary of everlasting peace, not as a refuge for the dead.

On the other side of the threshold, he relived the horror of Claire's death which was intensified by its pointlessness. He saw himself kneeling in the snow, clutching Claire's lifeless body, willing her to open her eyes, yet knowing he was asking the impossible. He saw the station master running toward them, waving a gun, spotting Garret, and ordering him to drop his pistol.

A cacophony of sounds roared in his ears. He heard Ella's screams, her frantic call on her cell phone, and Garret's incoherent mumbling. He saw the red stain on Claire's jacket and the yellow puddle crystallizing at Garret's feet.

Rufus lifted his head and glanced at the mourners standing at the edge of Claire's grave. Ella, Moon, and Lenny held hands and swayed to the sing-song cadence of the minister's oratory as he read the familiar passages from the Bible. If they were meant to comfort the bereaved, one look at Dixie and Bernard's wretched expressions and swollen eyes told Rufus the man was failing miserably.

A flash of wild grief surged through him. He leaned down

and placed Claire's bow and a gardenia on top of her coffin. He raised up quickly and took a deep breath. He could only handle so much pain without breaking down. He couldn't do that with young Rufe looking on. How could he explain his sorrow to a boy who had called him "His Man and had followed him around like a puppy, love and adoration lighting his beautiful face?

He hadn't meant for the boy to see any of this. When he called Salinas and explained what had happened, he asked her not to come to the funeral, but she insisted. She agreed it would-n't be an auspicious beginning for them, but she understood his pain. She, too, had lost someone she loved. She wanted to assure him his past would have little or no bearing on their future. And, she confessed, she wanted to assure herself they were making the right decision. She didn't want him to come to Memphis and build up their son's hopes, only to have them separate again.

Rufus had his doubts, too. Salinas hadn't known about Claire, but the empathy he heard in her voice told him she could live with the memory of a woman who died to save him.

Soon after she and young Rufe arrived, he realized he was glad they were there. Shooting baskets with his son and talking to Salinas about Claire had kept him from slipping into a dark hole of depression or seeking revenge.

The thought of killing Garret was a festering sore inside his head. After the ambulance had taken Claire's body away and the police had taken Garret away, he swore he'd kill the bastard. He had to kill him if he ever wanted to sleep again. Ella, Moon, and Lenny had stayed up all night talking to him, reminding him of his obligations to his son. They told him Claire's death would have been in vain if he ended up in prison.

Rufus breathed a sigh of relief when the minister ended his oratory with the affirmation, "In God's hands we commend Claire Burton's spirit." He wanted to leave the cemetery before the full impact of her death hit him. In his mind, she was still alive, still sensuous, exuberant, and yes, even bitchy. But before he could pull himself away, the children's choir from Ella's church began to sing "Amazing Grace."

Their youthful voices broke the heavy silence that gripped the bleak landscape. Grasping hands, the mourners swayed from side to side and joined in, their grief-filled voices cracking under the strain.

The song ended, and the crowd began to stir. Ella, Moon, and Lenny circled Rufus, paused to embrace him, and nodded their condolences to Claire's parents before heading to their cars.

After the crowd dispersed, Rufus approached Dixie and Bernard. He stared at them, trying to find words to express the sorrow in his heart.

Following a moment of tense silence, Dixie pulled away from Bernard's protective grasp and embraced Rufus.

"I thought we had time," she said. "We were going to make it up to her, all the misery, the drinking, the fights. I loved her. I always loved her. My sweet, beautiful daughter." She stepped back and wiped her eyes with her gloved hand. "Her father loved her, too. He thought money…" She broke off and shook her head. "Now she's gone. She'll never know."

"She knew. Deep down, she knew." Rufus reached out and took her hand. "You didn't fail her. Sure, she knew heartache, but she also knew love. I know. I heard it in her music. I felt it in my heart." He dropped his head and fell silent.

Bernard clasped Rufus's shoulder, his despondency mirrored on his pale, drawn face. "You gave her love. You let her play in your band. You encouraged her when no one else did. You were good for her because you were there for her."

Good for her? A choked laugh rose in Rufus's throat. *She's dead because of me.* He thought for a moment and then let out an anguished sigh. No, that wasn't true. Garret killed her. The crazy bastard murdered her. Bernard would make sure he'd pay for it. He'd end up in prison, and he wouldn't be at a country-club variety. He'd do hard time in the pen. The brothas he kicked and beat before he took them to the station would be waiting for him. What goes around comes around. There'd be one less murdering SOB on the street.

"I'm moving to Memphis," Rufus said. "I have a son. His mother and I have decided to make a home for our boy."

"We didn't know," Bernard said.

"They're here. I'd like you to meet them." Rufus turned and waved to Salinas and Rufe, motioning for them to join him.

Dixie's eyes brightened when Rufe scurried to his father's side. "Such a strong, handsome young man." She turned to Salinas and offered her hand. "How lucky you are to have him. Love him. Make a good home for him. Children need their parents. It sounds easy, but it's so hard. I'm sorry. I sound like I'm lecturing. But it hurts so bad." She covered her face with her hands.

"Please, don't apologize," Salinas said. "You've suffered a terrible loss. My heart goes out to you."

"Thank you," Bernard said. He wrapped his arm around Dixie's waist. "It's time to go."

Dixie leaned heavily against her husband, and together they walked to the limousine idling on the snow-swept road edging the cemetery.

"We better get going, too. Looks like we're in for some more snow." Rufus smiled at Salinas. She was a classy lady. He had no doubt that she had felt the same despair and loneliness he had felt when her mother forced her to leave him and go to Memphis, yet she had summoned the strength and courage to have their son, to raise him, and to love him. She wasn't bitter or angry. If anything, she was exceptionally warm, compassionate, and understanding. He knew people reacted to misfortunes in different ways. Some became petty and cynical while others became more caring and humane. Salinas was in the latter group. He knew she might never fully understand his relationship with Claire, but she wouldn't dwell on it or let it affect his relationship with Rufe. He was thankful for that.

Rufus stepped between Salinas and Rufe, took their hands in his, and together they headed toward their car.

A sadness and a terrible sense of loss struck Rufus. He quirked an ear, trying to catch the rhythm of life. He heard the twittering birds, the rustling wind, the thump of boots striking the frozen earth. He also heard a band playing: a bass, a sax, a drum, a piano. The music transported him back to Ella's Lounge. They were all there, playing their last gig, growling out the melody of the ballad, "How High the Moon."

Rufus closed his eyes and listened. Like a rose in the summer sun, the melody bloomed, the momentum peaked, and the notes dropped like petals in the fading vibrato.

He opened his eyes and glanced over his shoulder. He saw

Claire standing beside a gardenia bush, its elegant flowers resembling clumps of scented snow. She smiled at him for a long moment before she vanished in the shadows of the evening dusk.

Rufus helped Salinas and Rufe into the car. He slid onto the driver's seat, switched on the engine, and drove away.

ABOUT THE AUTHOR

Elsa Cook's background as a jazz aficionado is evident in *The Last Train to Memphis* and her previous book, *Satin Dolls*. Growing up on the banks of the Mississippi, she was enthralled with the stories she heard about the music and the musicians that came up the river, moving from New Orleans to St. Louis, to Chicago. Jazz, blues, and rock 'n roll are major themes in her writing.

Cook has a Bachelor of Journalism degree from the University of Missouri and a Master of Arts from St. Louis University. She has worked as a copywriter, a journalist, and a teacher as well as a fiction writer. She lives in St. Louis with her husband and two daughters.

Excerpt from

MATTERS OF LIFE AND DEATH

BY

LESEGO MALEPE

Release Date: June 2005

THE LEGEND - MAMOGASHWA

A frightening legend lived in Melodi, the black township near Pretoria. Mamogashwa, the snake, hid in the deepest part of the river Moretele where it cut through the Klip Mountain. The mountain bordered Melodi in the North. Sometimes the snake sunned herself on the surface of the water and then she emerged, not in her true form as a snake, but as a white woman on top and her bottom part, still a snake, submerged. Her long, brown, silky hair glistened in the sun, and like some said, diamonds sparkled in her hair. She had a beautiful smile, and her dreamy eyes gave off an angelic glow.

She liked to feast on children's fresh brains, not tough adult brains, which was why all her victims were young. Parents in Melodi always warned their kids, "Don't play in the river. Mamogashwa will take you. Run when you see a beautiful white woman sitting on the water, even from a distance. Once your eyes meet, she will hypnotize you and pull you in. She can also grab you by your shadow."

Mamogashwa drowned at least one child every year. She would drag the victim to the bottom and suck the child's brains out through the nostrils. Usually, she was satisfied with only one brain at a time, so nobody in Melodi forgot the time in 1959 when she took two children, girls, a rare event since it was boys that often were tricked by her. Girls did not go to the river as much.

White police divers from Pretoria fished their bodies out. It was a good thing that there were no black police divers, because Mamogashwa might have drowned them mercilessly. Because she would not harm white people, the white divers were safe in her part of the river.

Once in a while, Mamogashwa glided through the sky to other parts of the river, miles away. To make sure that nobody saw her she unleashed great fury into the sky, roared as thunder, wrapped herself in thick dark clouds, and pounded the earth below her with heavy rain or furious hail. Her eyes threw sparks of lightning in all directions. She rolled the clouds so they made a deep menacing noise like army tanks that invaded the black townships during uprisings. She belched fire like a dragon, leaving scorched houses, cracked electric poles and split trees.

People who dared to look up at the sky and see the light in her eyes were blinded. For most of those who were unfortunate enough to see her, their hearts stopped beating and they died. The few unfortunate souls who saw her but lived could not tell about it, for they lost their minds and their tongues became twisted so they could not talk.

The ignorant and uninformed described Mamogashwa's cover as a natural thunderstorm or tornado, but the wise ones knew the truth. Although there was a lot of disagreement about what Mamogashwa was or when she came to live there, everyone agreed that she first came with white people.

CHAPTER 1

1963

Thunder roared. There was a knock at the back door.

So late at night in the middle of the week? The back door meant it had to be someone familiar or else a stranger who saw that the lights in the front of the house were off. Edward Maru listened closely. It was not a knock, he thought. The wind must have thrown something against the door.

The strange sound almost merged with the thunder, pounding rain and furious winds. It was amazing how rain showers always nourished the earth around Easter, but also very deceiving, because when the weather cleared, cold winter winds settled in. This year though, the rains were unseasonably heavy and rough; it was going to be a tough winter. The cold winds howled outside, but in the kitchen the red coals in the Welcome Dover stove cracked and threw off wild sparks.

Edward continued to grade papers from his Setswana language class at the University of South Africa. His wife, Evelyn, who sat at the round table across from him, also graded papers: hers were Standard Four arithmetic exercises. Her red pen moved fast across the pages. Edward wished she had fewer students in her class.

Evelyn looked up at the window for a moment but did not say anything. Even though cold, the rain was a wonderful blessing. Such a shame she had not been able to work in the garden that afternoon. She continued to grade, but at a slower pace.

They were getting used to the deep quiet and extra space in the house, with all four children at boarding school. The three oldest, sons, had been gone for years now, but this was the first year away for their youngest and only surviving girl, thirteen-year-old Neo. They missed her, but each pretended not to feel it as much as the other did. Her name meant "gift" in Setswana. Evelyn had decided before Neo was born that they wouldn't have more children, but Edward begged for one more. They might get lucky and have another girl. So, when this baby was born, she was Neo, a gift, a precious gift.

All of their children's names meant something related to their birth. Unlike other black children, they did not have Christian or English names. This was Edward's way of showing pride in his own language and culture, both of which Edward cared about deeply. It was, therefore, not surprising that he turned out to be the country's leading expert on Setswana, his language.

Evelyn loved their names. Their first, Pitso, meant a call, it was the beginning. Their second child was Kagiso. Born during the war, his name meant peace, a prayer for peace. Their third, Tiro, meant work. Evelyn had continued to work to the day Tiro was born. And their fourth who had died accidentally four years before, was named Dikeledi, which meant 'tears,' because she was born the day Edward's father died. Then later came their baby, the child they decided would be last, Neo. The final gift of all.

Edward shook his fountain pen. "Neo would get me another from my bag if she were here... The house is awfully quiet without her."

Evelyn wiped her glasses. "She'd be making tea now. Do you miss her?"

"Oh, no, no. She's just been gone two months," Edward said. "I was just making an observation."

Evelyn smiled and looked him in the eye. "You miss her a little, maybe?"

He took off his glasses and rubbed his nose. "There's no doubt about it, sending her to boarding school was the best decision. She's sure to get a good education there."

"She's all right. She's got her brother with her."

A knock drew Evelyn and Edward's attention. The continuous tapping at the back door was clear.

"So late at night," Evelyn said, "in this cold rain."

Edward pushed the chair back and went to open the door.

"*Motlogolo*," he exclaimed in Setswana as he welcomed his sister Mary's only child. "My nephew, Ranoga, come in."

Evelyn noticed that their nephew frowned slightly. She knew he preferred to be called by his English name, Peter, but of course his Uncle Edward would not even acknowledge that name. Edward was fond of saying, "White children don't have Setswana names."

Evelyn did not feel strongly one way or another about these naming matters. Peter preferred "Peter" or his nickname "Snakes," which most young people used.

Edward never ceased to be puzzled by his nephew; whoever heard of anybody wishing to be called a snake? It seemed no coincidence that Peter's surname was Noga. In Setswana, Noga means "snake." There'd been some unkind comments when Edward's sister married a man with that last name. What kind of name was that? It surprised no one then that Peter turned out to be untrustworthy, slithery, slippery and shifty. Setswana-speaking people have a proverb: *leina lebe seromo*. People tend to live up to their names.

Edward offered Peter his own chair, facing the front of the stove. "Sit down and warm yourself. It's cold out tonight. You look like you've seen a ghost."

Peter coughed with a shallow cough, the type used to clear a space before a verbal bomb is dropped. He hit at his chest. "Just irritated."

"Move closer to the fire," Evelyn said. "You could catch a nasty cold in this weather. You know, there's a bad strain of flu coming this year. Hong Kong flu or something."

Peter, who taught at Tiro's school, pressed his throat like a doctor feeling for swollen glands. "Just irritated from talking too much today. Teaching really is a job."

"As you can see, we are also at it, grading," Evelyn said. "How are the children? Are they all right?"

Peter rubbed his hands together. "The children are fine, Auntie."

"They are such a joy at that pre-school age," Evelyn said. "Just feed them, give them a little hug there, and it's all done."

Edward poked the fire through the small horizontal bars on the little stove door. "It is very important to spend time with them. They grow quickly. Is their mother well?"

"She's fine, too, *Malome*," Peter said, using the Setswana

word for uncle. He touched his head. "Oh, sorry, Auntie, I forget I'm wearing a hat." He took off his felt hat, which was an expensive gray Dobbs, and held it between his hands.

"It's this rain," Evelyn said. "They say it's raining in the whole country. I hope it's not flooding in Natal like last year, leaving all those poor people stranded without houses. We are lucky up here."

As she spoke, Peter took off the plastic rain shoes he wore over his shiny black American Florsheims.

As Evelyn watched her nephew, she wondered if he had come to borrow money from them. He had stopped borrowing for quite some time, to every relative's relief. He still acted like a boy, spending a lot of his money on expensive clothes and shoes. It was hard to understand how he maintained such a high life-style.

"You can put your hat on the chair," Edward said.

"No, it's all right, *Malome*." Peter kept his hat in his hands and toyed with it nervously. "I have some bad news."

Evelyn sat upright. "Bad news?" She and Edward looked at each other.

Peter pushed his chair back and sat ramrod stiff as though that would straighten his story. "The police arrested some boys tonight at school in Hebron. Tiro has been picked up, too."

Evelyn sighed. "Arrested?"

"Was there a strike?" Edward asked. Protests, even by students, were referred to as strikes.

Peter tapped his knee. "We are not sure what happened. Maybe they were plotting a strike. You know the authorities don't ignore these strikes anymore. These white principals are like policemen."

"True," Edward said. "These white principals call the police at the slightest provocation."

"They wouldn't do this in white schools," Evelyn said then clucked her tongue.

Thunder grumbled outside. Evelyn felt as if a spark went through her body. Boys usually get into trouble, but at least her family had been lucky.

Edward took his glasses off. "What happened?"

Peter's hands trembled and the hat trembled in them, shaking as though moved by an earth tremor. "Nobody knows."

Evelyn folded her books in a neat pile and rose from her chair. Her forehead was creased and her eyes were narrowed as if she could see better if she squeezed her eyes. She held one hand on her slim waist. "You mean even the teachers don't know anything?"

Peter scratched his forehead. "You know how the Security Police is."

"The Security Police!" Edward leapt forward in his seat.

"What does the Security Police have to do with school children?" Evelyn asked, her voice raised. "Oh my God."

"Since when has the Security Police involved itself in school matters?" Edward asked. "Even during the worst school strikes, the Security Police didn't intervene; the regular police did. Are you sure it was the Security Police?"

Peter nodded and stared at his shiny shoes.

"Tiro's not the type to get into trouble," Evelyn said, more to herself than to the others. She found it hard to believe this news about her third son. "He's always been quiet, and he's never given us any trouble."

"It's probably nothing," Peter said.

Edward stroked the big bald spot on the top of his head. "How many boys were arrested?"

"Four. Some of the students the Security Police were looking for could not be found. Those students must have suspected something."

Peter got up and rested one hand on the back of the chair. "Sorry, I have to go. I have an early morning class tomorrow, and since I'm sleeping at home tonight, it means I have to get up extra early tomorrow." To reduce commuting, Peter rented a room at Hebron and slept there some nights.

"Thank you very much for taking the trouble to drive through this stormy rain to tell us," Evelyn said.

Peter picked up his rain shoes. "Don't have to wear these. I'm going straight home."

Edward and Evelyn walked him to the door. Peter had parked right in front of the kitchen door. They stood at the covered stoop as Peter got into his car and drove away.

Edward shook his head. "Look at him. He told us he was going straight home, but he's going in the opposite direction, God knows where."

"I can't quite put my finger on it, but there's something strange about him tonight with this whole thing."

Edward sighed. "There's something he's not telling us."

They remained standing on the stoop. Evelyn wrapped her arms around her body. "It's so cold. When it clears, we'll find that winter has arrived. It always comes in under the cover of rain."

They went back inside and locked the door.

Edward picked up his glasses from the table. "I think I need new glasses. These are weak now."

Unable to camouflage her anguish, Evelyn pressed her hands together as though to pray and rested her forehead on the thumbs. "Oh God, my son in the hands of Security police."

Edward slumped against the cupboard and wiped his glasses with his handkerchief. He blew onto them and wiped some more. "Boys are always getting into trouble. It's probably something about organizing a strike, maybe..."

She shook her head, tossing out her hands in exasperation. "I can't believe this."

Edward let out a deep sigh. "I hope they don't get expelled. Then, I'll have to go to the Melodi High School principal and put the poor man in a difficult position."

Evelyn understood that he was talking about getting Tiro space at Melodi High School should be expelled from Hebron.

"At least we're lucky he's our friend," Evelyn said. "Besides, we are not the only ones asking for this kind of favor. People do it all the time."

Edward stroked his bald spot and looked down. "The things children will make you do."

He went to the stove, grabbed the poker then turned the coals so the fire crackled with fresh flames and new vigor.

"It's cold," Edward said with a quivering voice.

Evelyn knew Edward was shivering from fear, not the chill in the air, but was pretending for her sake.

"Tiro will be fine," Evelyn said.

Edward retrieved his pipe from the ashtray in the dining room, then sat down in the kitchen and filled his pipe.

"Tiro is strong, and he's his own man. Sometimes he needs to prove it."

Evelyn was in no mood for these psychological explanations. Edward always had neat reasonable justifications for things. Edward's college majors had been psychology and Setswana. Evelyn remembered when Edward taught child psychology at Kilnerton Teacher Training College. But language was always his passion; it was not surprising that he ended up teaching Setswana in the department of African languages at the University of South Africa.

They slowly cleaned the kitchen, turned out the lights throughout the house, then retired to the bedroom. There was nothing they could do to find Tiro at that time of night. Police stations were only open to the public after nine in the morning. In bed, Evelyn and Edward asked each other the same questions. Was it a strike? Was it about the loss of Kilnerton? For hours they talked, unable to sleep. At last, each lay dead quiet, pretending to sleep so that the other could sleep. Outside the wind howled and the rain pounded the gutters. Evelyn prayed silently.

THE LAST TRAIN TO MEMPHIS

2005 Publication Schedule

January

A Heart's Awakening
Veronica Parker
$9.95
1-58571-143-8

Falling
Natalie Dunbar
$9.95
1-58571-121-7

February

Echoes of Yesterday
Beverly Clark
$9.95
1-58571-131-4

A Love of Her Own
Cheris F. Hodges
$9.95
1-58571-136-5

Higher Ground
Leah Latimer
$19.95
1-58571-157-8

March

Misconceptions
Pamela Leigh Starr
$9.95
1-58571-117-9

I'll Paint a Sun
A.J. Garrotto
$9.95
1-58571-165-9

Peace Be Still
Colette Haywood
$12.95
1-58571-129-2

April

Intentional Mistakes
Michele Sudler
$9.95
1-58571-152-7

Conquering Dr. Wexler's Heart
Kimberley White
$9.95
1-58571-126-8

Song in the Park
Martin Brant
$15.95
1-58571-125-X

May

The Color Line
Lizette Carter
$9.95
1-58571-163-2

Unconditional
A.C. Arthur
$9.95
1-58571-142-X

Last Train to Memphis
Elsa Cook
$12.95
1-58571-146-2

June

Angel's Paradise
Janice Angelique
$9.95
1-58571-107-1

Suddenly You
Crystal Hubbard
$9.95
1-58571-158-6

Matters of Life and
Death
Lesego Malepe, Ph.D.
$15.95
1-58571-124-1

320

2005 Publication Schedule (continued)

July

Pleasures All Mine
Belinda O. Steward
$9.95
1-58571-112-8

Wild Ravens
Altonya Washington
$9.95
1-58571-164-0

Class Reunion
Irma Jenkins/John
Brown
$12.95
1-58571-123-3

August

Path of Thorns
Annetta P. Lee
$9.95
1-58571-145-4

Timeless Devotion
Bella McFarland
$9.95
1-58571-148-9

Life Is Never As It Seems
June Michael
$12.95
1-58571-153-5

September

Beyond the Rapture
Beverly Clark
$9.95
1-58571-131-4

Blood Lust
J. M. Jeffries
$9.95
1-58571-138-1

Rough on Rats and
Tough on Cats
Chris Parker
$12.95
1-58571-154-3

October

A Will to Love
Angie Daniels
$9.95
1-58571-141-1

Taken by You
Dorothy Elizabeth Love
$9.95
1-58571-162-4

Soul Eyes
Wayne L. Wilson
$12.95
1-58571-147-0

November

A Drummer's Beat to
Mend
Kay Swanson
$9.95

Sweet Reprecussions
Kimberley White
$9.95
1-58571-159-4

Red Polka Dot in a
Worldof Plaid
Varian Johnson
$12.95
1-58571-140-3

December

Hand in Glove
Andrea Jackson
$9.95
1-58571-166-7

Blaze
Barbara Keaton
$9.95

Across
Carol Payne
$12.95
1-58571-149-7

Other Genesis Press, Inc. Titles

Acquisitions	Kimberley White	$8.95
A Dangerous Deception	J.M. Jeffries	$8.95
A Dangerous Love	J.M. Jeffries	$8.95
A Dangerous Obsession	J.M. Jeffries	$8.95
After the Vows	Leslie Esdaile	$10.95
(Summer Anthology)	T.T. Henderson	
	Jacqueline Thomas	
Again My Love	Kayla Perrin	$10.95
Against the Wind	Gwynne Forster	$8.95
A Lark on the Wing	Phyliss Hamilton	$8.95
A Lighter Shade of Brown	Vicki Andrews	$8.95
All I Ask	Barbara Keaton	$8.95
A Love to Cherish	Beverly Clark	$8.95
Ambrosia	T.T. Henderson	$8.95
And Then Came You	Dorothy Elizabeth Love	$8.95
Angel's Paradise	Janice Angelique	$8.95
A Risk of Rain	Dar Tomlinson	$8.95
At Last	Lisa G. Riley	$8.95
Best of Friends	Natalie Dunbar	$8.95
Bound by Love	Beverly Clark	$8.95
Breeze	Robin Hampton Allen	$10.95
Brown Sugar Diaries &	Delores Bundy &	$10.95
Other Sexy Tales	Cole Riley	
By Design	Barbara Keaton	$8.95
Cajun Heat	Charlene Berry	$8.95
Careless Whispers	Rochelle Alers	$8.95
Caught in a Trap	Andre Michelle	$8.95
Chances	Pamela Leigh Starr	$8.95
Dark Embrace	Crystal Wilson Harris	$8.95
Dark Storm Rising	Chinelu Moore	$10.95
Designer Passion	Dar Tomlinson	$8.95
Ebony Butterfly II	Delilah Dawson	$14.95

Erotic Anthology	Assorted	$8.95
Eve's Prescription	Edwina Martin Arnold	$8.95
Everlastin' Love	Gay G. Gunn	$8.95
Fate	Pamela Leigh Starr	$8.95
Forbidden Quest	Dar Tomlinson	$10.95
Fragment in the Sand	Annetta P. Lee	$8.95
From the Ashes	Kathleen Suzanne	$8.95
	Jeanne Sumerix	
Gentle Yearning	Rochelle Alers	$10.95
Glory of Love	Sinclair LeBeau	$10.95
Hart & Soul	Angie Daniels	$8.95
Heartbeat	Stephanie Bedwell-Grime	$8.95
I'll Be Your Shelter	Giselle Carmichael	$8.95
Illusions	Pamela Leigh Starr	$8.95
Indiscretions	Donna Hill	$8.95
Interlude	Donna Hill	$8.95
Intimate Intentions	Angie Daniels	$8.95
Just an Affair	Eugenia O'Neal	$8.95
Kiss or Keep	Debra Phillips	$8.95
Love Always	Mildred E. Riley	$10.95
Love Unveiled	Gloria Greene	$10.95
Love's Deception	Charlene Berry	$10.95
Mae's Promise	Melody Walcott	$8.95
Meant to Be	Jeanne Sumerix	$8.95
Midnight Clear	Leslie Esdaile	$10.95
(Anthology)	Gwynne Forster	
	Carmen Green	
	Monica Jackson	
Midnight Magic	Gwynne Forster	$8.95
Midnight Peril	Vicki Andrews	$10.95
My Buffalo Soldier	Barbara B. K. Reeves	$8.95
Naked Soul	Gwynne Forster	$8.95
No Regrets	Mildred E. Riley	$8.95
Nowhere to Run	Gay G. Gunn	$10.95

THE LAST TRAIN TO MEMPHIS

Object of His Desire	A. C. Arthur	$8.95
One Day at a Time	Bella McFarland	$8.95
Passion	T.T. Henderson	$10.95
Past Promises	Jahmel West	$8.95
Path of Fire	T.T. Henderson	$8.95
Picture Perfect	Reon Carter	$8.95
Pride & Joi	Gay G. Gunn	$8.95
Quiet Storm	Donna Hill	$8.95
Reckless Surrender	Rochelle Alers	$8.95
Rendezvous with Fate	Jeanne Sumerix	$8.95
Revelations	Cheris F. Hodges	$8.95
Rivers of the Soul	Leslie Esdaile	$8.95
Rooms of the Heart	Donna Hill	$8.95
Shades of Brown	Denise Becker	$8.95
Shades of Desire	Monica White	$8.95
Sin	Crystal Rhodes	$8.95
So Amazing	Sinclair LeBeau	$8.95
Somebody's Someone	Sinclair LeBeau	$8.95
Someone to Love	Alicia Wiggins	$8.95
Soul to Soul	Donna Hill	$8.95
Still Waters Run Deep	Leslie Esdaile	$8.95
Subtle Secrets	Wanda Y. Thomas	$8.95
Sweet Tomorrows	Kimberly White	$8.95
The Color of Trouble	Dyanne Davis	$8.95
The Price of Love	Sinclair LeBeau	$8.95
The Reluctant Captive	Joyce Jackson	$8.95
The Missing Link	Charlyne Dickerson	$8.95
Three Wishes	Seressia Glass	$8.95
Tomorrow's Promise	Leslie Esdaile	$8.95
Truly Inseperable	Wanda Y. Thomas	$8.95
Twist of Fate	Beverly Clark	$8.95
Unbreak My Heart	Dar Tomlinson	$8.95
Unconditional Love	Alicia Wiggins	$8.95
When Dreams A Float	Dorothy Elizabeth Love	$8.95

324

Whispers in the Night	Dorothy Elizabeth Love	$8.95
Whispers in the Sand	LaFlorya Gauthier	$10.95
Yesterday is Gone	Beverly Clark	$8.95
Yesterday's Dreams, Tomorrow's Promises	Reon Laudat	$8.95
Your Precious Love	Sinclair LeBeau	$8.95

Order Form

Mail to: Genesis Press, Inc.

P.O. Box 101
Columbus, MS 39703

Name _____

Address _____

City/State _____ Zip _____

Telephone _____

Ship to (if different from above)

Name _____

Address _____

City/State _____ Zip _____

Telephone _____

Credit Card Information

Credit Card # _____ ☐ Visa ☐ Mastercard

Expiration Date (mm/yy) _____ ☐ AmEx ☐ Discover

Qty.	Author	Title	Price	Total

Use this order

form, or call

1-888-INDIGO-1

Total for books _____

Shipping and handling:
   $5 first two books,
   $1 each additional book _____

Total S & H _____

Total amount enclosed _____

Mississippi residents add 7% sales tax

Visit www.genesis-press.com for latest releases and excerpts.